THIS SIDE
OF HELL

PINNACLE WESTERNS
by BRETT COGBURN

THIS SIDE OF HELL

•A WIDOWMAKER JONES WESTERN•

BRETT COGBURN

P

PINNACLE BOOKS
Kensington Publishing Corp.
www.kensingtonbooks.com

PINNACLE BOOKS are published by

Kensington Publishing Corp.
119 West 40th Street
New York, NY 10018

ISBN-13: 978-0-7860-4170-1
ISBN-10: 0-7860-4170-6

First Pinnacle paperback printing: March 2021

10 9 8 7 6 5 4 3 2 1

Printed in the United States of America

Electronic edition:

ISBN-13: 978-0-7860-4171-8 (e-book)
ISBN-10: 0-7860-4171-4 (e-book)

CHAPTER ONE

The Widowmaker bent over the dead horse's skeleton and snapped the jawbone from its skull. Straightening, he swayed and tottered on his feet while the heat waves in the canyon shimmered around him. He kept hold of the jawbone, but clutched the wound in his side with the other hand. The scars on his face, old scars and newer scars, stood out plainly on the burnt brown of his skin as he squinted up at the molten sky and cursed the desert and everything to do with it under his breath.

It was a burning land he stood upon, where shade was as scarce as water; where the rocks were scorched like cinders and left so lava-hot that they would sear bare flesh at a touch. It was no place for a man, especially for a man on foot without water, and with a ragged hole in his side.

He shifted his gaze back the way he had come, through the chain of rugged mountains and canyons leading up from the desert valley, and to the far side of that valley and the blow sand there. Those dunes were miles and miles behind him, but his memory of them was as clear as if he could see them now. Those shifting, blowing mounds continually reshaped themselves under the hot wind, one grain of sand at a time. The boot prints he had left in those dunes two days before were likely already gone, as if he had never existed in that place at all, a story told and untold. The distance between there and where he now stood was as good a place to die as any he had ever traveled, only he wasn't dead, not yet.

Sixty miles or more he had come, a great deal of that on foot, one staggering step at a time, bleeding until the blood, too, dried up like the rest of him, and then up through the rocky, barren canyons, working himself westward. The hot ground blistered the soles of his feet through his thin boot soles and rocks cut him when he fell. And fall he did, more than once, and each time it took him longer to get back up. Nothing but rage and sheer stubbornness carried him on.

Water—he had thought about it for every one of those miles out of the dune sand and across the valley and suffered for want of it. The pain of the bullet wound in his side was child's play compared to that thirst.

And yet, he kept going, the line of his travel straight and true, even though he knew not the hellish country through which he passed. It wasn't any landmark or some distinctive feature of the treeless, rock-pile mountains to the west that guided him, but rather the occasional hoof print pressed into the earth ahead of him, or here and there where one of those same iron-shod hooves had scored a rock or crushed some brittle desert plant beneath its weight. He wasn't an exceptional tracker, even less so in his current condition, but his bloodshot eyes locked on to the horse tracks, homing in on them like a man reaching for a rope to pull him out of a dark pit. He had become a manhunter, and not for the first time in his life.

He gave one last glance at the desiccated, mummified skeleton of the dead horse lying in the rocks at his feet, the same skeleton that he had jerked the jawbone from. It was hard to tell how long the horse had been dead, a single year or a hundred years. The desert was like that, burning the juices out of you until you were nothing but bits of leather and bone, and then preserving your pitiful remnants to the point that the ancient was new and the new was ancient, everything equally withered and dry.

There was an old, dry-rotted saddle and saddle blanket with the horse's skeleton, and the Widowmaker put a boot against the saddle and gave a shove. The bones scattered and fell apart, and he could feel his own pieces falling away, creaking and popping and crumbling, no matter how hard he tried to keep himself together.

A rattlesnake under the saddle, its shade disturbed, slithered through the horse skeleton's rib bones and then coiled and posed to strike. Its unblinking eyes stared at the man thing that had torn down its kingdom and its tail rattles buzzed as dry and brittle as death.

He ignored the rattlesnake and walked on, the jawbone in his fist swinging at his side. The hoof prints he had been following led up a canyon, so that was the way he went. The only sound in his head was the sound of his worn boot soles scraping and scuffing over the rough ground and the slow, dull throb of his heartbeat pounding in his head.

His stride was uneven and short, especially for a man of his height, but the only way to go left to him was slow. He was so tired that he couldn't tell if the heat waves had grown worse ahead of him or if it was simply that his eyes refused to focus.

As it was, it was nearing sundown when the canyon made a sharp bend to the west around the foot of a rocky mountain point. He rounded that turn and saw a clump of palm trees against a bluff not a hundred yards higher up the canyon. Such trees in the desert likely marked an oasis of some kind, a spring, tank, or some source of water belowground. He blinked once, and then twice, to make sure he was seeing what he was seeing.

There was a trickle of smoke floating up from the campfire someone had built in that grove of palm trees. At the sight of the smoke he forgot about the water and he forgot about his wounds, and he gripped the jawbone in his right fist until the line of ivory teeth in it cut into his fingers.

They would be up there in those palms—seven guns or maybe more, the same men who had left him for dead out on the dunes. The jawbone scraped against the empty pistol holster on his right hip when he shifted his grip on it, and a drop of blood fell onto one of his boot toes from his bleeding hand.

He started toward the palm trees in the evening dusk, making no attempt at stealth, and something hotter than the desert furnace burning in his eyes. "Leave me for dead, will you? Well, I ain't dead yet, but you're going to wish to hell I was."

CHAPTER TWO

Six days earlier, San Bernardino, California

Newt Jones woke with an aching back and a bad attitude. The aching back was a symptom of the sagging mattress on the jailhouse cot he had slept on, and the bad attitude was a result of the month he had spent locked up in a ten-by-ten cell. The morning sunlight shined through the single, barred window at the foot of his cot and struck him full in the face, worsening his mood and causing him to squint and scowl. He was always grouchy when he first got up.

He threw a forearm across his eyes to shield against the sunlight and groaned as he swung his legs off the cot and sat upright. It took him several minutes to decide whether it was worth all the trouble to get up and to come fully awake, but he finally managed to rake back his hair from his brow and settle a crumpled black hat on his head before he stood and went to the window.

Four men were crossing the street going dead away from him, their voices receding as they went. No matter how their voices faded, they were loud enough for Newt to surmise that it had been their conversation that had woken him. Undoubtedly, they had begun their talk under his window and were now moving elsewhere. He scowled again, rubbed a pointer finger absentmindedly along the crooked bridge of his nose, and watched them stop on the other side of the street. The one doing most of the talking had taken a stance on the raised boardwalk in front of Kerr's Emporium, the town's biggest general store, and the other men remained in front of the speaker on the edge of the street.

The man on the boardwalk was tall and thin and dressed in a white shirt, blue denim pants, and high-topped boots. Other than that, Newt couldn't make out much more about him, for the tipped-down brim of the man's hat hid most of his facial features. The distance was too great and the man was talking too quietly for Newt to make out the words, but from the his hand gestures and the way he had the group's attention he was either quite the orator or had something really interesting to say.

The sound of a door opening behind Newt caused him to turn around to watch the city marshal come into the walkway between the row of cells down either side of it. Buck Tillerman was a tidy, stocky fellow with a short-brimmed gray hat as pale as the walrus mustache that draped over his upper lip. The marshal took hold of the Saint Christopher medallion watch fob dangling from the chain across the front of his vest and pulled out a pocket watch which he frowned over, moving the watch farther from his face and to arm's length to properly focus on the time.

"Morning, Marshal," Newt said as he came over to grip the bars of the door to his cell. "When I heard you I figured you were the jailer coming with my breakfast."

"No sense in costing the taxpayers the price of another meal to feed you," the marshal said.

"Well, let me out of here," Newt said when the marshal made no move to open the cell.

Marshal Tillerman continued to monitor the watch face and never bothered to look up at Newt, much less reply to him.

"You're actually counting off my time?" Newt asked.

"Thirty days Judge Kerr gave you, and thirty days is what you'll serve. Not a minute less. Although I'm good and ready to get rid of you, I'll tell you that," the marshal said after he gave a short grunt. "I prefer my prisoners less on the surly side and more repentant."

"This jail cell isn't exactly good for morale and pleasant demeanor."

"You remember that the next time you come to my town." The marshal pocketed the watch and sorted through a ring of keys. "I told you to call off the fight, but still you and that gambling crowd had to try it anyway on the sneak."

"No harm in a little friendly pugilism to pass the time." Newt shrugged.

It was a reoccurring argument between them, almost daily, and one too late to win. Bringing it up again was nothing but sheer stubbornness, but Newt did it anyway. And rankling the marshal had become something of a sport for him to fight the melancholy and boredom, and a sort of minor revenge when he could have no other kind.

"I don't make the laws. Tell that to the reformers in the governor's office or the legislature if you're of a mind to," the marshal said.

"From what I hear, nobody's enforced that prizefighting law out here since they passed it better'n thirty years ago."

"It's still the law, and the Judge is a real stickler for what's right and proper."

"Judge Kerr, I'd as soon never see him again. Once in

front of his bench is enough. That old highbinder wouldn't happen to be the owner of that store out yonder?" Newt jerked a thumb over his shoulder at the window looking out on the mercantile across the street.

"No, that belongs to his brother." The marshal unlocked the cell door and swung it wide open.

Newt followed him to the front office. The marshal went to a cabinet behind his desk, opened it, and pulled out a holstered pistol with its gun belt wrapped around it. The pistol's walnut grips had little turquoise crosses inlaid into them, same as the little blue crosses on Newt's hatband. The marshal laid the weapon on the desk in front of Newt.

"I'm expecting not to see you again. Try and see to it that you don't let me down," the marshal said.

"The thought of disappointing you gives me shivers."

The marshal let the sarcastic remark go by without comment. He went to a rifle rack mounted on the wall and took down a big-bore '76 Winchester with a shotgun butt plate and its octagonal barrel cut down to carbine length. He sat that second weapon on the desk beside the pistol.

"Your horse is waiting at the livery down the street. I had him brought up out of the city pasture yesterday. Go get it and move on," the marshal said.

"I'm a free man same as you, and I'll go or stay where I please," Newt replied.

The marshal shook his head. "Damned if you might not be the hardest-headed fellow I ever locked up. Let me fill you in on something. This is my town. If I say you go, you go. You don't get gone, then I lock you back up. Savvy that?"

"On what excuse?"

"You got a job other than fist fighting for prize money?"

"No, but maybe I aim to find one," Newt said. "Maybe I aim to run for city marshal next election just to spite you."

"No job, huh? That makes you a vagrant. The Judge usually gives three days for that," the marshal replied in a deadpan voice. "See what I'm getting at? This town doesn't want you here. I don't want you here. Your kind is nothing but trouble and we like to keep it real quiet."

"My kind?" Newt took up the pistol, unrolled the belt, and swung the rig around his waist and buckled it.

"Against city ordinance to wear a sidearm on the streets. The Judge'll give you another seven days for that."

Newt gave the marshal a hard look. "Like you said, I'm leaving. I wasn't hunting trouble when I came, and I'll leave the same way."

Newt shucked a Smith & Wesson No. 3 .44 from the holster, broke it open, and found the cylinder chambers empty. He closed the pistol and shoved it back in its holster. When he worked the lever on the Winchester and cracked open the action he found that it was unloaded, as well.

"Plenty of time to load them when you're gone," the marshal said. "I'd rest easier that way."

"Nervous sort, are you?"

"I'm cautious is what I am," the marshal answered. "I wired over to Los Angeles and other places about you when I first locked you up, and then I talked to Virgil Earp down at Colton. Figured a man with a face and attitude like yours was liable to have gotten into trouble elsewhere."

There had been a time when someone mentioning his face would have caused Newt some discomfort, but he had long since grown used to that. It was his face, and there was no changing that, not when it looked back at him every time he stood in front of a mirror. It was a long-jawed, blunt-chinned mug marred by fists and about everything else that could be used to crack a man's face open. Plain to see were the marks of a lifetime of fighting; scars and more scars, from those over his cheekbones and both eyebrows, to his crooked nose that had been broken more than once, and the lumpy gristle of a cauliflower ear.

"Man with a name and attitude like yours, I half expected there to be papers on you," the marshal continued. "But the only one that had anything to say was Earp. Said he'd seen you box a match in the New Mexico Territory a few years back. Said you have quite a reputation as a scrapper out that way, but nothing more than that. Then again, Earp's about half outlaw himself, and I don't know if I'd believe everything that cripple-armed devil says."

"Hate to disappoint you that I ain't the desperado you hoped I'd be," Newt answered.

The marshal was still looking up at Newt's face. "Tarnation, son, maybe you ought to duck once in a while or pick up a new profession."

Newt grinned back at the marshal just to spite him. He had his fill of the proper little lawman's know-it-all attitude.

The marshal eyed the guns he had handed over to Newt. "You go awfully well heeled for a man that makes his living with his fists."

"If it'll make you feel better, I'll rob a train or something on my way out of town." Despite the way Newt sassed the marshal, his release from jail was steadily lifting his spirits and wiping away his surly mood. Maybe the day would get better and better.

The marshal frowned and made as if to say something in reply.

Newt cut him off. "What about O'Bannon?"

"You mean that promoter that was tacking up your fight posters all over town?" the marshal asked, even though he knew good and well whom Newt was talking about. "We've been over this a thousand times. He lit a shuck before I could lay hands to him, him and that fellow you were supposed to fight. Last I heard, they were headed for the coast."

"And you don't have any more idea of where he went than that?"

"Your guess is as good as mine."

"Ed O'Bannon owes me one hundred dollars for showing up for his fight," Newt said. "He guaranteed me."

"You ought to be more careful who you trust."

"That ain't all, and you know it. When you brought me my belongings after you locked me up, there was seventy-five more dollars missing out of my saddlebags," Newt said. "I'm assuming you didn't take it, so that leaves O'Bannon, considering I left my things in his hotel room before the fight."

"Maybe you'll have better luck catching him than I did. Although, I'd say not. That Irishman struck me as a shifty one."

Newt turned and started for the door that led to the street.

"I meant what I said," the marshal called after him. "I expect to see you riding out of town as soon as you get your horse. Maybe I'll even come along to make sure you do."

Newt stood with the door open and the doorknob in one hand. He looked across the street at the group of men still gathered at the boardwalk in front of Kerr's Emporium talking quietly among themselves.

"What's that about?" Newt asked.

The marshal took a few steps forward until he could see out the door, and his white mustache wrinkled in a grimace. "None of your concern."

Newt went out the door with the marshal on his heels. They walked down the opposite side of the street from the gathering in front of the store, but Newt kept glancing at the men across the way. The marshal was doing the same, and the frown stayed on his face as if there was something going on he didn't like.

"Damned fools," the marshal said under his breath like he was thinking aloud without meaning to. "He's got half of them believing him."

"Believing what?" Newt asked.

The marshal picked up his pace and nodded at the barn ahead of them. "There's the livery where I parked your horse. I'm done talking to you, and I'm missing my breakfast. Mrs. Tillerman doesn't like it when I let her food get cold."

Newt listened to his own stomach growling and started to say something about where the marshal could stick his breakfast, but shook off the urge and stepped into the hallway of the barn. There was hay stacked on one side and a line of horse stalls on the other. Only one horse was inside the barn, and it hung its head out over its stall door and with perked ears looked at Newt.

Newt opened the door and stepped out of the way, not even bothering to halter or bridle the horse. A short, stocky brown gelding stepped out of the stall. It trotted down the hallway slinging its head and feeling frisky, but turned back and came to a stop in front of Newt.

"If I didn't know better I'd think you missed me," Newt said to the horse.

The gelding yawned and shook its head, then gave Newt a shove in the chest with its muzzle.

"Wouldn't admit it if you did, would you?" Newt said as he slipped a bit in the gelding's mouth and the bridle behind its ears before bending down to pick up his saddle and saddle blanket off the ground in front of the stall.

He slung the blanket and saddle up on the gelding's back and looped the latigo through the girth ring and cinched the saddle as tight as he could at the moment. The gelding puffed its belly out, an old trick to avoid being cinched tightly, and Newt stood there waiting for the horse to give up. There was a bored look on his face and an equal expression and attitude on the horse's part, as if it was an old game between the two of them.

"That was a fool stunt turning him out of the stall like that," the marshal said from where he stood leaning against a barn post. "He could have ran off and trampled somebody on the street."

Newt led the horse a few steps up the barn hallway and then back again. The gelding finally let out a groan of air, unable to hold its breath any longer, and Newt gave his cinch a last tug at the same instant the horse's belly shrank. He shoved his Winchester down in the saddle boot hanging from the swells.

The liveryman came around the corner at the far end of the barn. He was a short, nattily dressed Mexican fellow with a neatly trimmed mustache and a brown suit. He had a game leg of some sort, like one of his knees was stiff, and he hobbled his way down the barn hallway to Newt.

He took hold of the narrow-brimmed derby hat and cocked it back on his head and gave Newt a look, and then he rubbed a hand over the odd brand on the gelding's hip, a simple circle with a dot in the middle of it.

"This *caballo*, you get him from *los Indios*?" the livery-man asked.

Newt nodded, not sure how the Mexican knew that. "Fellow once told me that brand's supposed to be some kind of Indian medicine wheel."

The Mexican looked thoughtful and acted as if he was about to say more about the matter, but didn't and simply shrugged his shoulders and shook his head somberly. *"¿Quién sabe?"*

"Who knows?" Newt repeated with a shrug of his own.

Newt paid the Mexican two bits for the keep of the horse, and found that expenditure left him with nothing but thirty dollars in his poke, all that remained from his working the docks at San Francisco Bay for the better part of the winter and well into summer. He had been counting on a healthy stake from the prizefight to go with what he'd saved before the marshal put an end to the event just as it was getting started, and before Ed O'Bannon robbed him. But thirty dollars was thirty dollars, and it was more than what he'd started with when he first pulled up stakes and gone west. And he remembered his boyhood when thirty dollars would have seemed like a fortune, or as Mother Jones used to say back in those old Tennessee hills, "a queen's ransom."

Thinking of his mother made him laugh out loud. She had known about as much about a queen as a long-eared mountain mule knew about a Thoroughbred racehorse, but she had a wisdom of her own and a mind as sharp as a skinning knife, she did. He missed her greatly, even after all the years.

Lost in memories, it took him longer than it should have

to notice that the Mexican liveryman seemed to be waiting around for him to leave as much as the marshal was.

"You expecting something?" Newt asked.

The Mexican shrugged again. "I sent my boy down to get him and bring him to the barn. This *caballo* threw him twice and he give up the saddle, no? My boy, he rides good, but he could not ride this one."

"He's a cantankerous cuss at times, but he suits me fine." Newt gathered his bridle reins, stuffed a boot in the stirrup, and swung up on his saddle. The gelding didn't move a hoof under his weight in the saddle, much less buck.

Newt noticed that Marshal Tillerman had left. Apparently, the grouchy old lawman was finally convinced that Newt was actually leaving town and had gone to make sure his wife's biscuits didn't get cold.

Newt rode the gelding to the end of the barn with the Mexican walking behind him but stopped at the edge of the street and looked again at the group of men gathered in front of the store. He was a little shocked to see that the marshal had joined the group, especially given the marshal's earlier disdain for the proceedings. The Mexican came up beside the horse and had a look at the group.

"That must be a hell of a story that fellow over there's telling," Newt said.

"Señor McCluskey, he says he saw the ship. Says he saw it sticking out of the sand," the Mexican replied. "I think they are going to go back with him and find it."

"Ship?"

"Will you go with them?" the Mexican asked after a long moment of silence. "I think maybe I go."

Newt adjusted his hat brim against the sun and glanced down at the Mexican. "Go where?"

The Mexican gave Newt a look that was instantly cagey and filled with suspicion. "You don't want me to go. I see that now. That is the trouble with such a thing. Who can you trust, no?"

"Does everybody in this town talk in circles?"

The Mexican looked up and down the street, as if searching for any eavesdroppers that might overhear him, his expression even more serious than before. Newt started to touch a spur to the Circle Dot horse and move out on the street, but the Mexican took hold of the gelding's bridle.

"You have a good horse. Guns. I have a good horse and guns," the Mexican said in a quiet voice. "Maybe we are partners. Nobody would cheat us that way. *¿Qué piensas?*"

"Partners in what? For the last time, where is it you think I'm going?"

And then a slow, crafty grin spread across the Mexican's mouth, as if they both shared a secret. "After the treasure, what else?"

CHAPTER THREE

The hour had grown late, and the petite woman hovering over the faro bank in a back room of the Arrowhead Springs Hotel shoved a slim cigar into one corner of her mouth. The cigar wasn't in keeping with the fancy New York dress she wore, nor with the mother-of-pearl-and-silver Spanish hair comb tucked at the back of her head above the stylishly curled locks of brown hair draping to her shoulders, but she puffed on it with the steady rhythm of a train engine huffing coal smoke. Her blue eyes twinkled as she played idly with the brooch pinning the lace collar of her dress together. The pointer finger of her other hand tapped at the card box while she stared at the three men seated across from her through the tobacco smoke that wafted in slow-writhing tendrils beneath the lamplight.

"Praise the Lord and place your bets. I'll take your money with no regrets," she said in a playful, teasing tone with a hint of an English accent.

The player farthest to her right scowled at the thirteen-card faro layout on the table before him, shook his head, and stood and gathered what little chips he had left in front of him. "Not me, Alice. I'm done. Your game's too tough for me tonight."

The woman called Alice paid him for his remaining chips and watched him go halfway out of the room before she turned her gaze back to the remaining two players. One was an older man with cowlicked hair and curly white muttonchop sideburns down his jawline. His suit coat was draped across the back of his chair and his shirtsleeves were rolled up to his elbows. Earlier in the day she had observed him hawking some kind of wares to one of the staff in the hotel lobby, and assumed he was some sort of a drummer or traveling salesman. That was only a guess, but he was talkative enough to fit the profession, a real chatterbox with a line of blarney for everything. However, his glib banter had fallen away and he grew more sullen as the evening progressed and his losses mounted. The stack of gambling chips in front of him was even more meager than that of the man that just left the game. And it didn't help that he drank too much whiskey throughout the course of play. The half-empty bottle on the table beside him gave testimony to that. He glared at her and muttered something under his breath that she couldn't quite make out.

Dealing with drunks and sore losers was old hat to her, but the game had gone late into the night and her patience was wearing as thin as the dim light that bathed her faro table. She ignored the complainer and glanced at the cowboy beside him. He was young, hardly more than a kid in her book, but a good-natured kid, at that—big hat, spurs, and a devil-may-care grin no matter how the game was going.

He caught her looking at him and smiled. "Seems like you're about out of punters."

"What about you? You calling it quits, too?" she asked.

He leaned back in his chair, stretched both arms out to his sides, and gave a mock yawn. "Roosters will be crowing before long, and besides, you're dealing too many pairs to suit me and I like a full table of punters and a fast game."

She nodded and began to change out his chips. Despite his complaint about a tough game, she noticed that he had lost little, if anything. He had been a shrewd bettor, no matter how young he was or how much the game had turned in her favor over the last hour.

The old drummer glared across the table at her and slammed a fist down on it for emphasis. "I say you cheat."

The floorboards creaked directly behind her and a big man moved from the shadows to stand protectively at her right shoulder. Even in the dim light, he was a striking man, and not only because he was a giant.

He placed both of his oversized palms on the table's edge, ducked under the lamp overhead, and leaned closer to the drummer. That swath of lamplight revealed a broad, square-jawed face covered almost entirely in dark blue tattoos—chevronlike bars across the breadth of his forehead, and T-shaped designs of dots and lines running down from both cheekbones to intricate swirls on his blunt chin. His long black hair was pulled back tightly and tied behind his head with a leather thong, making the angles of his face seem sharper and more severe. The long-tailed frock coat, vest, and tie he wore would have been at home on the streets of any city, but no one looking at him would have mistaken him for a metropolitan gentleman. The suit was decidedly civilized, but in that moment, his gaze was pure savage. He leaned his weight on the table, staring out of his obsidian eyes at the old man, yet not saying a word.

"Easy, Mr. Smith," she said as she glanced out of the corner of her eyes at the giant Indian beside her. "This gentleman is just having a tough run of luck and didn't mean anything by it."

"Like hell I didn't." There was a quaver in the drummer's voice, and the presence of the big Indian didn't check him at all. "I'd like to have a look at your card box, I would, by damn."

"I would suggest we politely go our separate ways," Alice replied.

"Or what?" the drummer threw back at her. "I'll tell you what I think. I think I'll go let the hotel manager know how you're fleecing his customers and what kind of a woman he's let stay here. What do you think about that? And maybe I'll take a trip down the mountain to San Bernardino and let the sheriff know what's going on up here."

"You do what you see fit." Alice's voice was flat, and she put a hand out in front of the big Indian to keep him in place.

The drummer cast a hateful but cautious glance at the big Indian and then looked back at Alice. "Your beggar Yaqui doesn't scare me. I'm an honest man and within my rights."

Alice could feel the big Indian tense against her arm at those words. "Mr. Smith here is of the Mohave tribe and not a Yaqui. He's a proud man, and I would not imply otherwise, if I were you. Nor would I again slander him. He speaks English as good as you or I, if not better."

The drummer grunted his disdain. "You cheated me."

Alice eyeballed his few remaining chips and slid his payout to him, done with him and ready to put the game at an end. She willed patience and an even tone into her voice, regardless of the fact that all she really wanted to do was to let Mr. Smith tend to the matter. "You play faro quite poorly, and there would be no need to cheat you, even if I were that sort."

"You . . . you smart-aleck bitch!" The drummer started to rise from his chair and a small Colt Clover revolver appeared suddenly in his hand.

Whether the gun was intended for her or Mr. Smith wasn't plain, but the result was the same either way. The big Mohave lunged across the table. One of his hands closed around the pistol the drummer held, and his other hand took hold of the drummer's neck. He yanked the smaller man to him, and gambling chips and cards flew everywhere as the table tipped over under the drummer's kicking legs and flailing body.

The cowboy went sprawling to the floor, and Alice scooted her chair backward so quickly that she almost did the same. Finding her balance, she grabbed up the chip tray that also held her money before it went flying with the table.

Mr. Smith heaved the drummer up into the air, holding him by the throat with one hand as if the drummer weighed no more than a small child. The drummer's pistol slipped from his grasp and clattered on the wooden floor. The Mohave shook him once, and then again. A rasping croak escaped the drummer's throat under the powerful clamp that cut off his wind, and then Mr. Smith backhanded him across the face. The blow cracked like a buggy whip in the confines of the room.

"That's enough, Mr. Smith," Alice said loudly.

Mr. Smith glanced down at Alice and blinked once, as if it took a moment for him to recognize her, while at the same time still holding the drummer up in the air. The drummer's legs kicked vainly for purchase on something, but his shoe soles were four inches shy of the floor.

"I said put him down," Alice said more gently, and reached out to touch Mr. Smith's arm.

The drummer was lowered to the floor, and his sagging legs would have dropped him into a heap if Mr. Smith hadn't switched his hold and taken him by his shirtfront and held him somewhat upright.

"I can take him outside and finish this." Mr. Smith's voice was as matter-of-fact and as stoic as his granite face.

"I'll be happy if you'll simply see him from the room. I believe he has learned his lesson," she said.

Mr. Smith gave the drummer another shaking, as if to see if the man had truly given up the fight, and then he half carried, half dragged the drummer to the door that led out of the room and into the hotel lobby. Mr. Smith remained at the door, even after he had shut it behind the drummer.

The cowboy got up off the floor with a reckless, excited look on his face and let out a low whistle. "Well, that's that."

She frowned at her spilled faro layout and let out an exasperated sigh. "An eventful end to an otherwise mundane night."

"The night's not over, yet." The cowboy's grin was wicked. "I was thinking we might visit the hot mud bath together. The hour is late, and I imagine we would have the room all to our lonesome."

Alice set the table back upright and leveled her gaze on him. "As you have seen, Mr. Smith frowns upon rude behavior where I am concerned."

"I'll never tell if you don't." That wicked grin hadn't left his face.

He wasn't the first man to proposition her with romance during the course of her gambling, but rarely did she see such a display of confidence and audacity on the part of her would-be paramours. He truly believed that she would be unable to resist his charm and would take him up on his offer. Rather than offend her, his youthful, lusty conceit and cockiness suddenly seemed the funniest thing in the world to her. She still felt young herself, despite her thirty-three years, widowhood, and the hard living already behind her. And knowing that men, or a man-child in this case, still found her desirable was flattering, even if she wasn't going to let the cowboy know that. Besides, it was much more fun to humble him a little.

"Shall I call Mr. Smith back over here, or are you content to bathe alone?" She gave a glance at her bodyguard over by the door with his back to them.

"You don't have to sic your mean Indian on me." The cowboy held up both his palms to her to show that he had given up, glancing nervously at Mr. Smith. "Where did you get him? That's got to the be the biggest, meanest fellow I ever did see."

"I did not acquire Mr. Smith, nor did he acquire me," she answered. "You might say there came a situation where both of us found our current business arrangement mutually beneficial."

The cowboy gave her a curious look, but let it go at that. He made as if to leave.

"If I might be so bold?" she asked when he was halfway across the room.

He stopped and looked back at her. "What's that?"

"I suggest you might dispense with the hot mud and find a cold bath instead." She could barely suppress the giggle building in her chest. A smile threatened to crack the deadpan look she fashioned for him, and one corner of her mouth curled up in the hint of the smile she felt inside her.

"I believe I'll pass on that." He laughed. "You know, you really are something, lady."

"Not so much," she replied.

"They call you Poker Alice, don't they?"

"That they do, though I'd as soon they didn't. Plain old Alice suits me fine, or you may call me Mrs. Duffield."

He gave a shrug. "I think Poker Alice suits you better. It's got a little pop to it, you know. Wait till the boys at the ranch hear who I was gambling with tonight."

The fun was over almost as quickly as it had begun, and she suddenly felt tired and realized it must be no more than a couple of hours until daylight. "Pleasant dreams. Maybe I'll see you at lunch or dinner and we can visit again over a good game of poker."

"I don't think I'll call it a night. Not yet. Thought I might take me a ride down to San Bernardino."

"I'd think the hour too late to find any action there."

He gave her a quizzical look. "That ain't what I hear."

"Indulge me, if I'm not being too nosy."

"Nosy? I reckon you're the only one within fifty miles that ain't heard. There's some fellow down the mountain that says he's found the lost ship of the desert."

"Ship?"

"Haven't been in these parts long, have you? Me, myself, I'm from Texas, Bee County to be exact, but I wasn't out here more'n a day before some saloon drunk I ran across was blubbering to me about that ship. You know how it goes. I buy him a drink and he tells me his story. I'm surprised he didn't try and sell me some kind of concocted treasure map or something."

She nodded. She was a woman who had traveled much over the western country, and everywhere she went had its legends. And there was no kind of tall tale that could run neck and neck with stories of lost plunder, whether it be lost mines or buried outlaw loot. People seemed to love to believe those stories.

"I had a man in Leadville try to sell me a map painted out on buckskin that was supposed to lead to Aztec treasure somewhere down in Mexico," she said. "Only problem was that I had seen him trying to sell a map exactly like it to someone else the week before."

"No matter, true or not, there's folks in these parts that set store by this ship thing," he said with a shrug, "though they differ on just where it came from. I've heard it's a Spanish galleon loaded with Incan treasure that got stranded on the sand back in the olden days when the Salton Sink was a little inland sea or some kind of big lake that maybe connected to the Colorado River or the Gulf of California at times, if you can believe that hellhole coming up from Yuma was ever anything but desert. And then there's a version of the story that says it wasn't a galleon but a little boat that had been pearling down the coast."

"You don't sound like you believe any of it."

"No, but I will say you can ride around down there and find watermarks along the bluffs at the foot of the mountains and further down on the desert, and little seashells, too. I'd say there's something to that bit about the basin once being underwater."

"Seashells? That's why you're riding down to San Bernardino in the middle of the night? That's awful thin." She gave a slight shake of her head.

"Doesn't matter what I believe. Like I said, there are folks down there that do, and this fellow that's spreading it around that he's found that ship has got some of them worked up to a point that they're putting an expedition together."

"And you intend to join up?"

"Nah, not me. Reckon there'll be plenty of folks to see them off, and I just want to see a bit of the show, you know. Have a drink and hear a story or two before I ride back to the ranch." He gave her his now-familiar grin.

"Good luck," she said because she could think of nothing better to say.

"Same to you," he replied as he turned toward the door. "Maybe I'll set down at your card table again. Who knows?"

She watched as Mr. Smith let the cowboy out the door. She glanced down at the floor once after he was gone, knowing that she ought to pick up her things, but she remained where she was, thinking about what he had said. After a time she realized that Mr. Smith was standing nearby looking at her, and she didn't have a clue how long he had been there.

She looked a question at him, but he gave no response. Mr. Smith rarely had anything to say, for that matter. In spite of his lack of conversational skills, he was a good listener. But she didn't want to talk, anyway. She was too lost in her own thoughts and coming to a decision.

The door leading to the lobby opened and the hotel manager appeared there. Beside him was the drummer with one cheek already red and swollen and his lip split and bloody where Mr. Smith had backhanded him. The hotel manager looked almost as displeased as the drummer, and it was plain that she was about to be evicted.

"See to our things," she said to Mr. Smith. "We'll be leaving now."

Mr. Smith turned on his heel and strode toward the door, as if leaving a perfectly good resort in the wee hours of the morning was a normal occurrence. The hotel manager seemed about to make an issue of things, but Mr. Smith brushed past the two men as if they weren't even there. Both men decided not to hinder his passing.

The hotel manager regained his composure and a dignified posture and cleared his throat before he spoke. "Mrs. Duffield, a word with you, please."

"No need for that. I'm checking out. If you'll produce my bill we'll settle up," she said. "Quickly, please. I find myself in a bit of a hurry."

The hotel manager had expected an argument, but his confusion quickly changed to pleasure and relief, probably owing to the fact that she wasn't going to make an issue of the matter, especially when he kept glancing behind him where Mr. Smith had gone. The hotel manager gave her a nod and walked briskly from the room.

However, the drummer lingered in the doorway and glared at her. She reached down and picked up his pistol from the floor and tossed it to him across the room. He fumbled the catch, but finally managed to hang on to the weapon.

"If I were you I would count myself ahead for the night, unless you care to take up your complaints with Mr. Smith again when he returns," she said.

It was a foolish thing, giving him back his gun. She knew it before she did it and while she was doing it, yet that had often been her way. Whether it was stubbornness, pride, or simply a tendency to get carried away in the moment, she had long before realized that it was a flaw in her own character—a flaw that could be disastrous for a woman who made her living gambling, rationalizing odds, and guessing other people's weaknesses and tendencies.

She stared back at him and didn't look away, and was somewhat surprised that his gaze broke first. He gave her one last dirty look before he shoved the pistol back in his waistband and followed on the manager's heels.

It was after the drummer was gone that she realized that her knees were trembling. Yet, despite her nerves and the confrontation with the drummer, she was still in a good mood, invigorated, in fact. Invincible. And surprisingly, she wasn't at all put out that she was being kicked out of the resort hotel due to a false accusation of cheating. Not at all.

For some reason, she couldn't get the cowboy's story out of her head, and for some stranger reason that story was the source of her sudden boost of energy and uplifted spirits. It was probably nothing but a wild-goose chase, but she made a living going where the action was. The kind of men who were likely to go in search of a lost ship in the desert were gamblers by nature, and where those kind of men were she might find a treasure of her own.

And if there really was a lost ship loaded with riches? Well, that wouldn't be such a bad thing, either.

She picked up her faro layout, humming an old English milkmaid's tune to herself while she worked. Pausing in the midst of her humming, she tried to remember exactly what the cowboy had said. She didn't know whether she liked the thought of a fortune in pearls or a chest of gold better. Either way, she intended to buy into the game if the play looked right after she rode down to San Bernardino.

For if there was one thing she liked as much as sitting down to a game of poker with some fellow gambling experts, it was money. Money couldn't buy everything, but it could buy her another trip to New York to see the sights and restock her wardrobe. New dresses made her almost as happy as poker and money. Almost.

CHAPTER FOUR

Newt was only a mile out of San Bernardino when he made up his mind that he was leaving California altogether He found his spirits lifted by the thought of moving on to some new country and Montana popped into his head for no good reason other than it was a place he'd never been, although the name of the place was more a vague direction to him than a specific place on a map.

"They say there are mountains up north like none you've ever seen. Water as fine and clear as shining quartz and grass saddle-high," he said out loud like there was someone to hear him other than the Circle Dot horse.

Normally, he was far from a talkative man, but lately he had come to speak to the horse more and more on the long stretches between people and places, whether he realized it or not.

He nodded his head like he had come to a decision and looked down at the horse. "What do you think about going to Montana and having a look?"

The gelding plodded along at a steady, ground-eating walk, not even so much as cocking a single ear at the conversation aimed in his direction.

Newt rode another mile. It would be winter by the time he got there, and he recalled someone saying they had grizzly bears in the North Country as big as wagons.

"I suppose you're right," he said to the horse. "I'd just as soon not freeze to death in a snowdrift, and I imagine you wouldn't appreciate getting chomped on by a bear, either. Huh?"

Ruling out his first choice didn't change Newt's mood, and he continued to think on the matter as he rode. He was still wallowing it around in his mind when he came around a bend and found a man sitting on a rock beside the road.

A single saddle horse stood hipshot and head-down not far from the man, and the sudden arrival of another horse and rider startled it and caused it to skitter sideways down the road, dragging both bridle reins.

The man on the rock didn't seem to notice that his horse was getting away, or Newt's sudden arrival. Newt rode closer, and as he cut the distance between them, he saw that the man on the rock seemed to be crying. The closer he got the more he was sure of that. He brought the Circle Dot horse to a stop and sat it there in the road, but the man on the rock didn't so much as look up at him. After a time of waiting, Newt cleared his throat in an attempt to get the man's attention, which didn't work, either.

"Your horse is about to wander off, mister," Newt said.

Truly, those dragging reins were all that was keeping the man's horse from running off. It kept stepping on one rein or the other, and the bridle bit snatched at its mouth and caused it to jerk its head and stop with every misstep.

The man on the rock looked up at Newt, sniffled once, and made a backhanded swipe at his wet cheeks. His eyes were red and puffy.

Newt wasn't given to crying, and it was especially uncomfortable to watch another grown man do so in his presence. So he trotted up the road and caught the man's horse
and led it back to him for want of a better thing to do at
the moment.

If the man on the rock was thankful, he didn't say it. In
fact, he looked at the animal almost as if he didn't recognize it. It was a good sorrel gelding with a highly tooled
saddle on its back that looked brand-new and from which
hung an equally fancy rifle scabbard with the initials *F.S.R.*
carved into its leather and a rifle stock sticking out of it.
Not an animal or a rig that would be cheap to replace, and
not to mention that it was a long walk in any direction if a
man was to lose his mount.

"You ought to tie him up or hobble him if you intend to
sit there any longer," Newt said, still unsure how to handle
the situation he found himself in.

"Pardon me," the man on the rock muttered, and swiped
at one cheek again.

He was a young man, pale skinned where he wasn't sunburned, and maybe in his midtwenties or so, if Newt didn't
miss his guess. He was a stocky sort with wide shoulders
and hips and a thick neck. A shock of light brown hair
showed beneath the short-brimmed hat he wore. His white
shirt was already sweat-damp and sticking to him, and although without a vest or coat, he did wear a silk cravat
around his neck, an odd thing for a man on the trail. His
brown denim trouser legs ended at a pair of low-topped
lace-up boots. Suede leather gaiters with buckles and straps
on the sides of them reached from his calves down to cover
most of his bootlaces.

"What's that?" Newt asked, unable to understand the
man's mumbling.

"I said, pardon me." The man on the rock got to his feet somewhat unsteadily and dusted off his trousers. He tried to show a stiff upper lip and a set jaw, but his sorrow was still evident, no matter how he tried to hide it. "This is quite embarrassing, you know."

It was only then that Newt noticed the empty pint bottle of whiskey on the ground next to the man's feet. If the fellow had drunk all of that it might explain why he was a little unsteady on his feet and why he might be spending his morning sitting on a rock on the side of the road crying.

"I don't mean to be a know-it-all, but if I was you and I wanted to sit a spell, I'd find someplace out of the sun." Newt offered the reins of the horse he had retrieved, and the man took them.

"I say, this is quite embarrassing, as you might guess." The man's accent was decidedly eastern and a touch on the stuffy side. "I'm afraid the melancholy struck me when I least expected it."

Newt said nothing to that, and the man glanced once at the sky and then got on his horse with the ease of a horseman, easterner or not, half-drunk or not. Wherever he came from, he had been in the saddle before. The Thoroughbred gelding he rode was one of those nervous, high-headed types, but the young man held it in place with a light feel on the bridle reins and an effortless seat in the saddle.

Newt meant to go, but something kept him in place and made him want to see the man off to wherever he was headed, despite the awkward feeling. And he noticed that the man seemed not only upset, but was possibly lost.

"Are you all right now?" Newt asked.

"Oh yes," the man answered, starting up the road to the west, the same way Newt was going. "You only caught me at a bad time."

"Think nothing of it."

The man stopped the horse before it had gone more than a few steps. He looked back at Newt and wrinkled his brow in consternation. "I don't suppose you could be so good as to tell me the way to San Bernardino, could you?"

"It's that way." Newt pointed in the opposite direction to the way the man was pointed.

"Is it now?"

"You'll find it if you stick to the road."

"Thank you for your kindness. I've ridden most of a day and night all the way from Los Angeles in somewhat of a hurry. The lack of sleep must be getting to me, and my travels at night have thrown off my sense of direction."

Newt didn't see anything about the man that spoke of being in a hurry, especially since he had seemed perfectly willing to while his time away slumping on a rock and drinking only moments before.

"You see, I met a gentleman who accidentally shared with me a most interesting story," the man continued. "Said he was some kind of fight promoter or manager or something of that ilk, and I gathered he was on his way back to San Bernardino."

"Fight promoter?" Newt's sudden change of interest was apparent by his tone of voice.

"That's what he said," the man replied, sounding steadier than he had before. "It's what initially sparked our conversation, as I'm somewhat a fan of the pugilistic arts."

"Do you happen to recall his name?" Newt asked. "Wasn't O'Bannon, was it?"

"Might have been, but I'm not sure."

"Short fellow? Wears a derby hat and good clothes and keeps his mustache waxed?"

"That's him."

"And you say he was on his way back to San Bernardino?"

"He didn't say so, but that's the impression I got."

"Did he leave Los Angeles before or after you?"

"Before. I believe he took the train. I recall him saying something about buying a ticket," the man replied. "You sound as if you know him."

Newt nodded. "I know enough that you shouldn't trust him any farther than you can throw a bull by the tail."

"He did seem an oily sort, as you say."

Newt's good mood from earlier in the morning had left him. He thought about O'Bannon and his mood grew worse.

"I'll be going now," the man said. "I'm afraid I'm too late as it is."

"Why are you in such an all-fired hurry to get to San Bernardino? I was just there and it isn't a place I'd recommend for a visit."

"O'Bannon left this on our table in the hotel restaurant. You might say it piqued my curiosity as much as it seemed to pique his." The man reached into one of his saddlebags and produced a newspaper. He unfolded it and handed it to Newt.

It was an issue of the *San Bernardino Guardian*. Newt read the most prominent thing on the front page. It was a short article.

Lost Ship Has Been Found

Zander McCluskey and party will soon attempt to return to what could be the legendary ship upon the desert and its treasure. While there are some in this city who agree that such a lost ship could possibly exist, it seems no two citizens can agree on the origin of such a vessel stranded on the desert. The latest theories being discussed are that the find could be none other than a wreck from King Solomon's navy, a teakwood Indian trading dhow flung astray off the spice routes in a mighty storm in the days of yore, or verily, an even more ancient vessel belonging to none other than the Lost Tribe of Israel. And it is Mr. McCluskey's recent report from his sojourn over the Colorado Desert and the Salton Sink that is the source of all this excitement.

Mr. McCluskey recently crossed the desert from Yuma, and almost met his death there when his horse became lame. It was while traveling on foot that he spied what has our fair city in such a stir, the mast of a sailing ship sticking out of the sand. He was in a poor state at the time, suffering from lack of water and intense heat, but word has it that he is quite sure that what he saw was no desert mirage. However, he was in no condition at the time to further investigate, being terribly busy simply trying to survive.

Whether Mr. McCluskey has found the lost ship and riches to rival Solomon's hoard, or not, several in our fair city believe he has. At their urging, an expedition has been formed to return to the site, along with a contract drawn up to state how the treasure will be divided among the party's members. Rumor has it that none other than our illustrious banker and merchant, George Kerr, has joined the venture and is providing much of its supplies. The party is set to leave two days hence, and is prepared with two good wagons, water barrels, packsaddles, shovels and ropes, and planks to cross the sandy ground. Furthermore, they are all well armed to protect their treasure once found.

From the small number making up the party, it seems the cynics and skeptics, including this editor, outnumber the believers. That is no wonder, for despite all the stories about the ship over the years and supposed sightings of its withered wooden bones protruding from the blow sand or in the rocks of some desolate canyon, no one has yet to produce so much as a single piece of it as evidence of its existence, much less treasure. Many readers and older citizens will recall similar expeditions that have searched in vain for the ship, especially those led by Charlie Fusse that went out almost a decade and a half ago. Mr. Fusse, too, swore that he had seen the ship, yet his expeditions and countless other searches yielded nothing. Regardless, we wish McCluskey's party well, and anxiously await their return when we can see the fruit of their labors.

"Maybe they haven't left yet," the man said. He put the newspaper back in his saddlebags, adjusted his reins as if to depart, but hesitated again and looked skeptically at the road leading to San Bernardino.

"Like I said, just stick to the road," Newt said. "You'll find San Bernardino not two or three miles farther. The road's good and plain all the way."

The man held out his hand for Newt to shake, and close

as he was, Newt could smell the whiskey on him. "Frederic Remington. Glad to have met you."

"Newt Jones."

The easterner had a surprisingly strong grip for a man that was otherwise so out of sorts. Newt gave him another look, considering that he might have missed something.

"Remington, like the guns?" Newt asked.

"A cousin of mine, though I'd say he makes more money with his sewing machines and typewriters than he does his firearms."

Newt wondered if Remington was telling the truth. The young tenderfoot wouldn't be the first wayward rich boy Newt had met, whether they be black sheep American sons sowing their wild oats or titled Englishmen and Scotsmen too far down the royal ladder to have much say in anything and living on stipends from their royal families. Third sons, bastard sons, fourth cousins twice removed of the earl of such-and-such, it was always something like that. Remittance men, some called them. Newt saw most of them as spoiled rich boys with time on their hands and who couldn't make up their mind what to do. Something about the western country drew them like flies.

"I know some that swear by those Remington pistols," Newt said. "Never had much use for one, myself. Grips are too small to fit my hand. But you make a good scatter-gun, I'll give you that."

"I told you, I have nothing to do with E. Remington & Sons. My branch of the family leans more to soldiering, hardware businesses, and newspapers."

"Newspapers, hmm," Newt said.

"What's that you say?"

"Never had much use for newspaper editors, reporters,

and the like. Nosy sorts, most of them, with a penchant for stretching the truth when the truth doesn't suit 'em."

"Don't tell my uncle that. He swears journalists are the last honest men left in the country, although maybe things will get better now that President Cleveland has taken office. I say a good New York man with the know of things ought to straighten out some of the corruption."

"That so?" Newt's disinterested tone told that his thoughts were elsewhere.

"You seem like you don't care for Cleveland. I take it you're a Republican. I am myself, but Cleveland may be what this country needs. And I don't mind saying it. Call me a mugwump, if you will, but I voted for the man. He's not like the rest of the democrats."

Newt squinted at the sun again, at the same time wondering what a *mugwump* was. "I'll have to take your word for it."

"Have I offended you?" Remington asked. "My mother always said a man shouldn't discuss politics or religion with people you've only just met, and here I am doing that."

"No offense taken. Truth is, I'm not much for politics, either way. Politicians are worse than horse thieves."

Young Remington chuckled. "Worse than newspapermen?"

Newt rested an elbow on his saddle horn and continued. "I recall a neighbor back in Tennessee that decided he wanted to run for office. High sheriff it was, and he seemed a pretty good fellow before that. Then he went to making speeches and kissing babies. Got to be sheriff and then he ran for state office. Wasn't long before you couldn't believe a word he said. He'd say one thing to a crowd and then go down to the next town, get up on the stump, and say the opposite, depending on what he thought they wanted to hear. Got caught embezzling state money sometime later. I thought it was probably temptation that got to him and turned him, but Ma said that he was likely already a crook and all the power did was give him the opportunity. Time goes on, I figure more 'n more she was right. Man comes to me and says he's running for office, I ask myself what's wrong with him. I don't know what the exact definition of a politician is, but in my experience you never trust anyone that makes their living convincing other people to believe them. There never was a better job for a liar or someone who has too high of an opinion of their own smarts."

Remington laughed again. "You are a contrarian at heart, Mr. Jones. I tip my hat to you for that, because you say what many of us think but so rarely give voice to. But as my own family is fond of repeating, when good men lose interest in politics this country hasn't long left."

"Maybe so. You mind that horse. A man out here loses his horse and it's liable to be the death of him." Newt could tell from the way young Remington was looking at him that he found the thought overly dramatic, if not downright preposterous. "Country like this, it can be a mighty long ways between water."

Young Remington gave another look at the road. "A few miles, you say? Horse or not, I could do that on shank's mare, and at a good pace at that. My football captain at Yale used to make us run three miles, and that was before practice."

"Your what?"

"You're probably of the opinion that baseball is the new thing, but I tell you, football is the greatest sport this country has ever produced and time will prove it."

"Yale? The college, you mean?"

"First-string rusher and two years with the team. Beat

those bums from Harvard, we did, and tied them my second season. Seven hundred people in the stands cheering us on, and I don't exaggerate in the least." A heady smile spread across Remington's face, and it made him look younger than Newt had first guessed.

Remington must have seen that Newt was perplexed and misread that for something else. "You seem to be less than a fan of my alma mater and its football team. Did you matriculate from a rival college? Don't tell me you went to Princeton."

Newt couldn't tell if Remington was making fun of him or not. He scoffed again and waved a hand about him at the desert. "Only school I've known since the sixth grade is this right here."

"And what school would this be?"

"The school of life, and I tell you, she's a hard teacher."

"I agree, Mr. Jones." The grin disappeared from Remington's face again, but his eyes were no longer wet with tears and he stiffened and straightened his back a little, as if preparing physically to fight off what ailed his soul. "A man can find himself one day happily basking before hundreds of cheering souls, and the next day sitting on a rock in the middle of nowhere contemplating the cause of his doom while the heartless she-devil who put him in such a state goes merrily about her way without a care in the world."

"Something like that, I guess," Newt said to avoid more pointless talk. He started the Circle Dot horse along the road, headed not the way he'd been going earlier, but back toward San Bernardino.

"Ah, I see that newspaper article has caught your fancy, too." Remington put his horse alongside Newt's. "I have my doubts about this treasure story, like any rational man would, but it could turn out to be a grand adventure, don't you think?"

Newt raised his eyebrows at that, but said nothing in reply.

"But if it were true . . ." Remington left whatever else he might say to Newt's imagination.

Newt squinted at the dude vexing him with too much talk. "I get awful leery and go to running backward when somebody starts talking about how easy something is going to be."

"What would life be without dreams and flights of fancy? I have never aspired to fame or fortune. It would take too much work and cut into my leisure time. However, I fancy all kinds of things I could do with a fortune at my fingertips," Remington said. "What would you do with such riches as a treasure ship might provide you? Surely as a boy you dreamed of pirate ships and buried plunder or the like."

"I reckon I dreamt some at that. Mostly while I was picking rocks behind Pa's plow." Newt nudged the Circle Dot horse up to a long trot. "More come of the rock picking than the daydreaming, and that's the lesson that has set with me since."

"I wouldn't have taken you for a farmer." Remington kicked his own horse to keep up with Newt. "In fact, if you won't take offense at my saying it, I first mistook you for some kind of brigand or road agent when you came up to me back there. Thought you were about to ask for my wallet."

"You're lucky I wasn't. You're easy to put the sneak on."

"Goes to show how easily we can misjudge our fellow man. Now here we are traveling together and enjoying each other's company."

Newt was silent, and stayed that way for a time, no matter that Remington occasionally tried to get their conversation going again. He was still searching for a topic that might stimulate Newt's interest when they came in sight of San Bernardino.

"Maybe the newspaper was wrong and the treasure party hasn't left yet," Remington said. "I'd hate to come all this way and miss it."

Newt touched his spurs to the Circle Dot horse's belly and loped down the last bit of road to town.

"Now you're getting into the spirit of it, Mr. Jones." Remington kicked his own horse to a lope to keep up. "Let's run down the pot of gold at the end of the rainbow."

Newt gave him a glance, not irritated this time, but steady and matter-of-fact. "You sure that O'Bannon was coming back here?"

Remington had to grab at his hat to keep a gust of wind from blowing it off his head before he answered. "I think we'll find your friend here if they haven't already left."

"He's no friend of mine, and that's a fact that I intend to remind him of as soon as I catch him."

Remington recognized Newt's tone of voice and the inferences that could be taken from that, and that there was something altogether different in the set of his face and the intensity of his eyes now. It dawned on him that his new traveling companion had no interest in the treasure party.

"Oh, I take it that this O'Bannon has somehow offended you," Remington said.

"You take it right."

"Will there be trouble? Perhaps I should leave you to your own business."

"Suit yourself." Newt reined the Circle Dot horse to

walk, paying close attention to the buildings to either side of them.

"You have given me your views on easy money," Remington said. "Violence, in my opinion, gets us no further."

Newt had all but forgotten that the tenderfoot easterner was nearby. A group of men down the street had caught his attention.

"I guess you're thinking bad things, and I won't be caught up in whatever it is you're planning on doing," Remington continued uneasily. "Perhaps we'll meet again under different circumstances."

Again, Newt didn't answer. He barely noticed when Remington turned his horse off at a street intersection and left him.

Frederic Remington, late of Kansas, and before that New York, watched Newt ride down the street and noted the way the big man's hand rested on the pistol riding on his hip.

Remington shook his head. "Well, Mr. Jones, maybe my first impression of you was closer than I knew. God help that O'Bannon fellow."

CHAPTER FIVE

Newt hunted for O'Bannon throughout the rest of the day with no luck. He half expected to encounter Marshal Tillerman again during his search and didn't relish that event, should it happen. Furthermore, he soon learned that the treasure party had left not long after his own departure earlier that morning, and a boy running deliveries for the local butcher thought that he might have seen a man matching O'Bannon's description leave with the party.

Because of the time he wasted looking around San Bernardino, it was nearing midnight when he rode eastward through San Gorgonio Pass. He was following the old Bradshaw Trail to the north of the Southern Pacific Railroad tracks when he saw a campfire burning to the south along the foot of the mountain there. He crossed the tracks and rode toward the light of that fire, weaving his way across the high valley under a canopy of stars and a sliver of moon.

It was a big fire when he reached it, flames reaching higher than his horse's head, and it was no wonder that he had spotted it from the middle of the pass. He had no clue how they had managed to find so much firewood, and thought them damned fools for making such a blaze that anyone could spot from miles away. He was a cautious traveler and usually built a small fire and chose his campsites carefully where the lay of the land might hide its glow.

"Hello in the camp," he called out when he was almost to the edge of the firelight. He stopped the horse in the darkness, waiting for a reply. He was bone-tired, having come somewhere near thirty miles on nothing more than canteen water and a grudge.

"Come on in," someone shouted back to him.

He came to a line of horses and mules picketed to a rope stretched between two steel stakes driven into the ground. Beyond that there were two wagons on the other side of the flames. Several people were backed up against those wagons, with their flickering shadows dancing against the side planks in a way that made them seem not of this world. He sensed more moving around out of sight beyond the wagons.

He gave those he could see a quick study and then glanced down at the leftovers from their dinner still warming in pots by the fire. The smell of food was a painful reminder of how hungry he was. "Mind if I light and sit?"

"Make yourself at home," someone answered.

"What brings you here?" another asked, and sounded irritated and far from friendly or hospitable.

Newt picked that last one out of the crowd. He was an older man with long white sideburns and a gold watch chain draped across his plaid vest. The way he stood implied he thought he was pretty important, and Newt made a guess as to who he was because of that.

But Newt's gaze shifted to another face he saw dimly by the firelight. O'Bannon was sitting on a blanket with his back against the rear wheel of one of the wagons, and a big man with a short-cropped blond beard sat on his right. That fellow was Darby Cooley, better known as Clubber Cooley among the rough crowd on the San Francisco waterfront, the very same man that Newt was supposed to fight back in San Bernardino before the city marshal busted things up.

O'Bannon always had a shiftiness about him, as if he was continually judging what he could say that would work on you. His round little eyes glistened like wet marbles with the fire reflecting off them, like a rat's eyes peering out of its burrow. Clubber was watching Newt just as intently.

"What do you want? State your business," the old man with the white sideburns asked.

A young woman, very young, came to stand at the old man's side and placed a tentative hand on one of his elbows. She was a beauty and she was proud and vain. That was plain to see even by the firelight. Corn silk hair bound high atop her head and a haughty set to her chin above a long neck, that was her. She stared at Newt like he was something the dogs had dragged in, and wrinkled her pert little nose like she could smell him even from so far away.

Newt thought the old man foolish to have brought her with him, not if there were more men in the party like Clubber, and not with the kind of venture they were starting out on. He wondered if the old man was the one who had built the fire. It was the same kind of thinking, or not thinking.

Newt swung down from his saddle without answering the old man, dropped a rein to ground-tie the Circle Dot horse, and strode toward that preposterous fire. The heat coming off it was too much, and he stopped short of its scorching reach, staring through the flames at O'Bannon and his henchman.

"I said what do you want?" the old man asked more belligerently than was necessary or polite.

Newt's head turned slowly and he looked once more at the man talking to him. "Saw your fire."

"I made it quite clear before we left that we aren't taking on any more men," the old man said, raising his voice a notch higher. He was playing to the others in the party. "If it's a meal you're looking for, we're tight on supplies and can't be feeding every grub line rider that smells free beef and beans."

Many a fire had Newt ridden up to over the years, and rarely was he ever refused hospitality. Men out West, used to hard overland travel and aware of the misfortune that could befall anyone, were usually generous, having had occasions themselves when the shoe was on the other foot and a kind offer to share a camp or a meal was a welcome thing.

O'Bannon moved slightly, and Newt caught that movement out of the corner of his eye.

"Ed O'Bannon," Newt said. "I mean to have my money, or take it out of your hide."

O'Bannon stayed sitting where he was, but Clubber Cooley stood slowly. He was almost as big as Newt, not quite so tall but heavier. What little Newt knew of Cooley was all hearsay, but the man's reputation wasn't based only on his record in the prize ring. There were those in San Francisco who claimed that Clubber was a cutthroat second to none. He had once been a sailor, but found a living more to his liking among the dives and gambling dens along the docks, what had come to be known in the local vernacular

as the Barbary Coast. The story also went that he and the
gangs he ran with, in addition to robbery, arson, and protection rackets, specialized in shanghaiing drunks, which
was nothing more than kidnapping men for work on ships
outbound for points around the world. Men like him
pocketed whatever they could steal from their victims and
then made a tidy fee from whatever ship's captain was
needing crew members.

"I don't owe you anything," O'Bannon said. "I lost
money, same as you."

"You stole from me," Newt replied.

"I never stole a thing from you." O'Bannon had a slick
tongue, and managed to sound almost innocent.

Someone else moved at the end of the same wagon
where O'Bannon and Clubber were. Young Frederic Remington stepped forward into the light and gave Newt a
friendly smile. However, there was a flush on his face and
he was rubbing one palm on the waist of his trousers as if
he was nervous. Newt wondered if he was drunk again.
And it surprised him that the man had somehow managed
to find and catch up to the treasure party, drunk or sober.

And the easterner was wearing a different hat than he
had been that last time they had met. No, it wasn't a hat,
but a helmet instead, and Newt couldn't imagine where he
had come by it. As near as he could tell, it was a pith helmet
like he had seen in magazine illustrations of some of the
Britishers or Spaniards wandering around various jungles.
The entirety of the brim and rounded crown was covered
in white cloth.

"Good to see you again, Mr. Jones," Remington said.

Newt gave him a nod, but kept watch on O'Bannon and
Clubber.

Remington looked from one side of the fire to the other,

from Newt to the glaring Irishman sitting on his blanket and Clubber standing with both thumbs hooked behind the buckle of his gun belt, close to both the handle of the big knife he wore and his pistol. That stance was obviously meant to be both nonchalant and, at the same time, threatening.

"Now, gentleman," Remington said, "we're all friends here."

"Stay out of it," Clubber growled. "He wants some of me, let him come."

"I'm sure whatever is between you men can be worked out peacefully." It said something about what a tenderfoot Remington really was when he thought rationality or the love of peace and honest discourse would have any soothing effect on men like O'Bannon and Clubber.

"I said to shut your trap, fancy boy," Clubber chided.

Remington's back stiffened and his shoulders came back in a futile attempt to salvage some dignity as he brushed past Newt's shoulder. "Most unpleasant men."

Newt called to the Irishman, "So how's it going to be, O'Bannon? Hand it over and admit the thief you are, and I'll try and forget what I've been promising myself I was going to do to you for the last thirty days."

O'Bannon played with the waxed tip on one end of his handlebar mustache and sneered at him. "To the devil with you."

Newt charged around the fire, and Clubber slid his big knife from its sheath at his belt and rushed to meet him while O'Bannon struggled to get up off the blanket. Clubber's blade hissed in a wide, backhand swing aimed at Newt's belly. Newt sucked in his waist with arms outflung. The razor-sharp blade barely missed gutting him, and instead, sliced through nothing but the bunching of his shirt.

Newt stepped inside Clubber's reach, bent his knees and drove his right fist into Clubber's chin. Clubber's head snapped back and he staggered against O'Bannon behind him. The little Irishman almost had his pistol clear of the shoulder holster he wore under his left armpit, but Clubber's weight drove him against the side of the wagon and sent him back to the ground.

Clubber shook his head and made a sound that sounded more animal than man. Blood poured from his mouth down over his blond beard, and he spit teeth and a piece of his tongue to the ground. He made a low, underhanded cut at Newt's guts again with the knife, but he was shaken and his lunge was weak and slow.

Newt closed and caught Clubber's wrist above the knife and grabbed him by the shirtfront with the other hand. He twisted and heaved and slung Clubber into the fire. Coals and firewood scattered as Clubber thrashed and gave that animallike cry again, a mix of rage and pain. Newt watched through a swarm of floating embers as Clubber lunged back to his feet with one side of his beard and a good portion of his hair singed away and one eye blistered and weeping and appearing ruined for good. He was a man on fire, both the flaming clothes on his back and the smoldering hatred in his wild, one-eyed glare.

Behind Newt, O'Bannon came out from under the wagon where he had fallen. He found his pistol on the ground beside him and scooped it up. Newt took hold of one of the cast-iron pots hanging beside the fire and hurled it at O'Bannon as hard as he could.

The pot struck O'Bannon high on the chest, and the force of the blow and the hot bean juice splattering across his face knocked him down again. But Newt didn't get to see the effect of his throw, because Clubber had lost his knife and was going for his pistol on the other side of the fire.

There was no thought to it or time for such. It was simply motor reflex and hair-triggered reaction when Newt's hand dropped for the Smith & Wesson .44 on his own hip. Clubber's pistol was already clear of his holster and coming level when Newt shot him in the chest, once and then a second time.

Clubber staggered in a half circle and then fell to the ground. Newt kept the .44 pointed at him long enough to be sure he was down for good before he swung the revolver toward O'Bannon behind him. The Irishman was back on his feet again, but threw up both hands and started a measured retreat.

"Don't kill me!" O'Bannon cried out.

Newt lunged and struck O'Bannon on the side of the head with the barrel of the Smith & Wesson. The Irishman went down for a third time.

Nobody in the treasure party had interfered with the fight, but when it was over a semicircle of faces lined the far side of the fire between where he stood and where the Circle Dot horse waited for him. Remington stood slightly apart from the others, although he looked no less shocked by what he had seen than the rest of them.

A long silence fell, and the only sound was the crackling of the fire and O'Bannon's dull groans as he writhed on the ground and clutched at his wounded head. Newt's breath came fast and heavy, more from the adrenaline than the exertion, and he inhaled deeply to try and slow the heave of his chest. His vision fluttered at the edges, and he blinked, once, twice. He watched those watching him while he waited for calmness to return to him, and broke open the Smith & Wesson and loaded two fresh cartridges. He shoved the pistol back in his holster with a rasp of leather that seemed louder in the moment than it actually was.

The first one to speak was the man with the white side-burns. "You, sir, are a brute."

The old man's daughter, or whatever she was, stood behind him peering around one of his shoulders. Her eyes were as big as little moons.

Newt grunted at that and put a boot on O'Bannon's chest and pushed hard enough to get the Irishman's atten-tion. "Where's my money? Speak up."

"That man is in my employ," the old man with the side-burns called out.

"This is a private affair," Newt threw back at him.

The metallic clack of a cocking pistol hammer quieted everyone. The tall thin man Newt had seen speaking to the crowd while he was getting out of jail stepped forward, holding the pistol aimed at Newt. Newt assumed he was none other than the Zander McCluskey mentioned in the newspaper article.

"You'd best mind your tongue, mister." McCluskey's voice had a crackly rasp to it, as if his throat were nothing but raw sand and turpentine. "What Mr. Kerr says goes here in this camp, and I don't recall anybody here giving you an invite."

Newt noted the long, thin shadow McCluskey cast across the ground angling away from the fire, and the turkey tail feather stuck in the hatband of the broad-brimmed gray hat he wore. And last but not least, he stud-ied the Colt pistol in the man's hand and the butt of another one like it on his left hip, ivory grips as pale and white as fresh bone turned butt forward for a cross-draw or a back-handed draw. Newt had never known a man packing two pistols that wasn't a killer or didn't want to be one. They stared at each other. There was venom in McCluskey's glassy gaze, calm and cold, but venom for sure.

"Let him up," the man with the sideburns, who Newt assumed was George Kerr, said.

Newt glanced down at O'Bannon under his boot. "He tells me where my money is and then I'll let him up."

"Fellow, you just don't ever learn, do you?" Buck Tillerman, the city marshal from back in San Bernardino, stepped from the darkness to Newt's left. There was a double-barreled shotgun cradled in his left elbow.

"You know the deal, Marshal." Newt pushed his boot a little farther into O'Bannon's chest. "Good old Ed here stole my road stake. Ain't that right, Ed?"

O'Bannon gave a painful grunt at the additional pressure on his chest.

"You killed a man in cold blood right in front of us," Kerr exclaimed.

Remington pointed at Clubber's body. "We all saw it. The one with the beard went for his gun first."

"Only after this one attacked him and threw him in the fire." When Kerr was upset his voice had a whine to it and took on a higher pitch that grated on something inside Newt's head.

Newt realized how tightly wound he was, jittery and still on edge, and took another deep breath. "Search them and search their belongings, and you'll find what I tell you is true."

"Finding money on them doesn't mean it belongs to you," Zander McCluskey said.

"You go ahead and look," Newt said. "I had two silver coins. Never seen their like before, and I bet neither have you. Won them arm wrestling with the crew of a ship bound back to Bombay, India."

McCluskey and Kerr passed a look between them, and
Kerr finally nodded his approval. McCluskey said something Newt couldn't make out, and three men came out of
the darkness behind him. One of those men went to Clubber's body and began searching it, while the other two
came around the fire and went to the saddles and other belongings where O'Bannon had been sitting at the wagon.

Newt noticed that all three were hard-looking, seasoned
men, and that all of them were armed to the teeth, loaded
down with pistol and knife steel on their belts. Not men to
trifle with, unless Newt missed his guess, and more than a
little on the seedy side. He wondered what an old goat of
a businessman like Kerr was doing running with such men
as those and the thin killer, McCluskey.

Finished at the wagon, one of the two behind Newt
walked up to him. Newt took his boot off O'Bannon and
allowed him to get back to his feet. McCluskey's man had
O'Bannon empty all of his pockets and gave him a pat
down.

It didn't take them long to complete their search. The
one that had handled Clubber's body went back to Zander
McCluskey and said something quietly to him. The other
two stayed behind Newt, waiting.

"Cooley didn't have but ten dollars on him, and no coin
like what you said," McCluskey said for all to hear.

"Same here," one of the men beside Newt said. "No
India coins that we could find."

"They're silver rupees, and marked so on one side," Newt
said. "They've got a picture of Queen Victoria on them."

"Nope," the man beside McCluskey said.

"O'Bannon ain't got one, either," came the response
from behind Newt. "He's got about forty dollars on him,
but nothing like that."

"Nothing in the saddlebags or bedrolls, either," the other one behind Newt added.

"Look again." Newt knew the hole he found himself in had suddenly gotten a little deeper.

"They already gave it a good look," McCluskey said. "Nice try, but your story's thin as water gravy, mister. Real thin."

The marshal had made no move to unlimber the scatter-gun he was toting, but he was watching and listening carefully. Newt wondered when he was going to get involved.

"It was a fair fight," Newt said, at a loss for something better to say and feeling things had gotten to a point when words were wasted, anyway.

"You accosted two of my men and gave them no choice other than to fight," Kerr said.

"I'll say it one more time." Newt's voice was low and slightly hoarse like the sound of the wood popping in the fire. "This man here stole from me. I warned him. You heard me. We could have settled it fist and skull, but him and this one pulled on me."

"You hold your horses, Jones," the marshal said, adjusting his grip on the shotgun as if he had suddenly decided he was going to need it. "I see you thinking things that could lead to a whole other kind of bad that you don't want any part of."

"You think?" Newt gave a bitter chuckle.

CHAPTER SIX

A woman shoved her way forward through the men, and it wasn't the one standing behind George Kerr. This woman was older, shorter, and a little more on the rounded side. And she was possibly the best-dressed woman Newt had ever seen.

"Please, Mrs. Duffield," George Kerr said to her, "let us handle this."

"You men, you mean?" She held up something in her hand and slowly pivoted around in the firelight so that all of them might get a look at what she held. It took Newt a moment to make out that it was a coin she had in her grip.

She lowered the coin, moved it to where the light was right to read it, and said, "It's a rupee, exactly like he said. And it's got the queen on the other side, too."

"Let me see that." George Kerr took the coin and frowned at it, whether he didn't like what he deciphered from it, or because he was simply having a hard time reading it in the poor light. "Where'd you get this?"

The woman turned and pointed at Ed O'Bannon. "He lost it to me in a poker game this evening. Lost it and about forty dollars more."

"You never got that coin from me," O'Bannon said, already starting to back away.

An Indian in a suit came to stand beside the woman who had produced the coin. To say he was big was an understatement. Not only was he maybe two inches taller than Newt's six feet and three inches, but he had arms the size of a normal man's legs stretching the sleeves of his coat. His square jaw was as massive as his neck, and the tattoos on his face made his presence all the more looming.

The big Indian said nothing to the Irishman, but the threat in that stare didn't need words.

"Easy, Mr. Smith," the woman said.

"You hear this lady?" Newt asked the marshal.

George Kerr couldn't let it go. "Maybe he did steal from you, but that doesn't change the fact that you gunned a man down in cold blood."

"You just don't quit squawking, do you?" Newt said.

Kerr sucked in a breath and stiffened at the insult. Newt was getting a rough idea of the man, and he had seen the kind before—self-important in his own little world, all because he had more money than most and a say in things because of that. A big frog in a little-bitty pond, that's how Mother Jones would have put it.

The big Indian leaned close to the Duffield woman and said something to her. She nodded agreement.

"Mr. Smith says that Cooley pulled a knife and then his pistol when that didn't work," she said.

"Exactly what I saw," Remington threw in.

Kerr cleared his throat before speaking again. "You, Mrs. Duffield, are not a member of this venture, and I only granted you the courtesy of this camp for the sake of hospitality and not wishing to see a woman have to travel back to San Bernardino at night," Kerr said to her. "Considering that, you should tread lightly here."

"I have every right to be heard," she threw back at him. "You might claim to run this *venture*, as you're calling it, but save your condescending attitude for the mules and wagons you're so fond of reminding us you paid for."

Nobody said anything for a moment while Kerr looked around him for support.

"O'Bannon, you stick where you are," Newt said when he noticed the Irishman sidling away. "I'm not through with you, yet."

It was Marshal Tillerman's turn to clear his throat to get their attention.

"I didn't see the first of it," the marshal said. "But it's plain that O'Bannon took this man's money. Fact is, Jones here made his claim when he was still locked up in my jail, and what Mrs. Duffield has shown us proves it."

"He comes to our camp fresh out of jail and kills a man? Blood in his eyes and pistol in his hand, and that doesn't bother you? I say it didn't have to come to murder. Vigilante justice isn't justice at all, and you know it. The Judge wouldn't let this stand." Kerr gave the word *Judge* special importance and said it rather smugly.

"There's a man dead, and that's not something that sits any better with me than it does with you," the marshal answered. "But I'd say it was a clear case of self-defense, same as I believe most of us here do. And I told you when I first saw O'Bannon and Cooley with you that I would have arrested them for prizefighting like I did Jones if they hadn't been so fast to get out of town. I told you that, but you kept them on anyway."

Kerr rubbed his chin with a thoughtful scowl on his

face like he was swallowing bad medicine, and then he waved a dismissive hand at the marshal. "The Judge . . ."

"Your brother doesn't have any more jurisdiction out here than I do. He's a county judge and not the governor nor Jehovah on high like you let on to everybody that will listen."

"You wouldn't speak so lightly of the Judge if he were here." Kerr blustered a gust of angry air and stuttered momentarily. He pointed at Newt and O'Bannon. "Arrest them both, then. Do your job, Buck. I'd hate to have to bring it before the city council that you're shirking your duty. Might be they would get to thinking they could find a better man to wear the badge."

"Are you threatening me, George?" the marshal asked. "Or are you trying to thin the numbers a little bit and cut me out of the hunt?"

"Don't be ridiculous."

"I won't do it. I paid my hundred dollars to buy in with you."

"You're pushing it too far. Don't think that the Judge will protect you. He and I got you that job and we can . . ."

The marshal cut Kerr off before he could finish. "For better'n five years I've put up with your bellyaching and danced to you and the Judge's whims, but not this time. You hear me? I've still got my doubts about what Mc-Cluskey says he saw, but I'm going with you. And you and your city council can put that in your pipe and smoke it."

"I'll fire you right here and now!" Kerr's voice cracked again, the way some old men's will, like he was choking on phlegm.

They glared at each other. Newt waited, taking the measure of both men and some of the others, and putting the pieces together until they somewhat fit. The marshal, despite his earlier disdain for the treasure party, seemed to have changed his mind, and Kerr was definitely the condescending old goat he had first appeared to be. How the women and the big Indian fit, he couldn't yet say, but he didn't intend to stay and find out. And then there was McCluskey holding his pistol, as well as the other three hardcases who had come out of the dark to do his bidding.

There was a horse waiting for Newt, and all he had to do was get on it and ride—if they would let him. He should have been forty miles on his way to Montana or someplace else by then, and would have been if he wasn't such a hotheaded fool. The bunch around the fire would be lucky if they weren't at one another's throats before they ever reached the desert. A smart man wouldn't come within a stone's throw of them.

He shifted his attention back to McCluskey. "You going to use that?"

"Put it away," Kerr said.

McCluskey held the gun pointed at Newt's belly a little longer, and his eyes were as snaky and unblinking as ever. After he had proven whatever silent point he sought to make, he gave a disdainful shake of his head and holstered his pistol.

"Salty one, ain't ya?" McCluskey said. "Real ring-tailed terror."

"Look out!" someone shouted before any more words could pass between McCluskey and Newt.

There was the sound of running footsteps and Newt turned to see O'Bannon racing for the picket line. Newt made no attempt to go after him, and only watched to see what the rest of them would do.

The marshal stayed where he was, the shotgun an afterthought, even when O'Bannon crashed into the woman who had produced Newt's Indian rupee and all but knocked her down. The big Indian she called Mr. Smith took a swing at O'Bannon, but the Irishman ducked it and kept on running with his coattails flapping like flags.

"Stop that man before he gets to the horses!" Kerr ordered.

McCluskey's Colt was in his fist again and he pivoted to track the flight of the Irishman. There was a deadly grace about McCluskey. His movements were smooth and fluid and unhurried, like hot lead pouring into a mold. The revolver came to level at the end of his arm, and for an instant it looked as if he had a sight on O'Bannon. But he didn't shoot, and O'Bannon disappeared into the darkness. A horse shied and scrambled at the picket line, and then a horse, probably that same horse, could be heard running away.

"He's escaping," Kerr said.

McCluskey shrugged and holstered his weapon. "Afraid I'd hit one of us."

"You know that was likely one of our horses, don't you?"

Again, McCluskey shrugged. "If it is, then that means he left his own. And I'm thinking Clubber won't be needing his anymore. Plenty of stock left to get us where we're going."

"I suppose that goes for you, too, Buck?" Kerr asked.

"Send someone else after O'Bannon if you're of a mind to. I've said my piece."

After the lot of them had their fill of looking into the dark and listening to the fading sound of O'Bannon's escape they turned back to the fire, where Newt still stood. It wasn't lost on Newt that George Kerr, while seemingly deeply offended by Clubber Cooley's death, was angered that McCluskey hadn't shot O'Bannon during his getaway.

That was more than a bit hypocritical of him, but he wasn't the first righteous poser Newt had come across in his travels.

"Reckon I'll be going myself." Newt started toward his horse, not sure how it was going to play out and ready for anything.

"I'm counting on this being the last time I have to lay eyes on you," the marshal said to him as he passed.

"I was in the right, and you know it."

"In the right? Son, I've never seen anything that strikes me as wrong as you do. Best thing you can do is to get out of California. Go back to Arizona or maybe Texas. I hear hardcases are a dime a dozen there. Might be you wouldn't stick out so bad."

Newt was almost to the edge of the firelight when the woman came to him. She held out the rupee.

"You forgot this," she said.

"Thanks. That's my lucky coin."

"You have a strange idea of luck."

He shoved the coin in a vest pocket.

"Mind if we travel with you?" she asked. "Mr. Kerr has made it plain that we're not welcome, and I do not relish returning to San Bernardino in the dark."

Newt glanced at the big Indian standing behind her and started to tell her that there wasn't anything out there in the dark that was liable to bother her with that giant along. But Remington joined them before he could answer her.

"That goes for me, too, Jones," the tenderfoot said. "If you don't mind. I'm afraid I had no better luck convincing Mr. Kerr of my value to his party than Mrs. Duffield did. I'd appreciate some good company back to town."

Newt was about to ask all of them why they thought he was going back to San Bernardino or why they thought he would want to help them, but then he saw Kerr still glaring at him from across the fire. It wasn't the anger in the man's look that bothered him, it was the smugness and the conceit.

"Suit yourselves," Newt said to the three waiting for his answer.

"It will only take us a bit to pack our things," she said.

Newt nodded and went to the Circle Dot horse. He checked his cinch and swung up into the saddle, where he waited in the darkness.

"I warn you," Kerr said to the trio readying to leave from where he stood by the fire. "Don't try and follow us."

None of them replied to that warning, and the woman came out of the dark sitting sidesaddle on a horse so black of hide that it was hard to make out. Saddle leather creaked and the big Indian rode up beside her, and then Remington.

Newt turned the Circle Dot horse around and led them away.

CHAPTER SEVEN

The four horses and riders moved through the night, slipping almost silently across the high valley that formed San Gorgonio Pass, with no sounds other than the occasional creak of saddle leather or the sound of the horses' shod hooves where they clattered over patches of rocky ground. Newt led them across the wide arroyo at the mouth of Whitewater Canyon, and angled closer to the Southern Pacific tracks when a rough finger of hogback foothills and eroded washes coming down from the mountains to the north narrowed the pass ahead of them.

"I don't know how you can find your way in the dark," the woman said when she rode up beside Newt. "Mr. Smith is like that. Eyes like a cat, I guess."

Newt grunted, but that was his only reply to her observation.

"You don't talk much, do you?" she continued. "Mr. Smith doesn't, either."

The last thing Newt wanted was to talk. His mood was dark and forlorn, and he wanted only to be left alone until that feeling went away.

"Thanks for speaking up back there," he finally said. "Wasn't looking to cause trouble."

"Not looking to cause trouble?" she scoffed. "Is that what you call wading into a camp and hitting the first man you see? You have an odd way of making friends."

"Just the same, I put you in a bad spot."

"I'd had my fill of George Kerr, anyway. Pompous windbag is what he is." There was still that English accent of hers, faint and only noticeable with certain words, but there, nonetheless. "I hoped to join his treasure hunt, but he flat turned me down."

"The impression I got is he's already counting treasure he hasn't found and thinking that the fewer splits there are, the better," Newt replied.

"Maybe, but I don't think he liked the idea of a woman going along, either."

"What about the other woman? The blond kid?"

"That's his daughter, Madeline. Now there's a spoiled brat for you. I wasn't in camp five minutes before she was whispering in her daddy's ear about me. I think I somehow offended their sense of moral propriety."

Newt twisted in the saddle to look behind him. The big Indian was right behind the woman, but it took him a moment to catch the bit of movement that marked Remington's position. He was riding considerably behind the rest of them. "You all right back there?"

"Oh, fine." Remington must have kicked his horse to catch up, for Newt could hear its hooves thumping a trot beat. "I'm afraid I got distracted by this all. Quite the nightscape, the way the starlight hits this desert, kind of like it glows."

Newt glanced at the thin sliver of moon overhead and

then at the brushy gravel flat along the railroad tracks. He could see nothing about the terrain that glowed. "I won't come hunting you if you get lost."

"Don't worry about me," Remington answered. "My natural sense of direction has always been unusually strong."

The woman must have been around Remington long enough to catch the irony of his statement, or else she somehow sensed Newt's frustration. "Don't mind him. All artists are a little different."

"Artist?"

"Yes, I gather he's a painter or some kind of illustrator."

Newt gave a surprised grunt. "That so? I guess you meet all kinds."

"You don't remember me, do you?" she asked.

"Can't say as I do. None of my business, but you don't fit in all of this, high-toned woman such as yourself."

"Me, high-toned?" She laughed.

"You talk smart, and you got the way about you. And that dress you're wearing likely cost more than a good saddle horse."

"I'm afraid you overestimate me."

"Not many women go riding after a bunch of treasure hunters."

"You still don't remember me? Well, I remember you. I recognized you right off back there. I never forget a face."

"Is what it is. I never was handsome to begin with."

"Harder around the edges and seasoned some, maybe, since I saw you last, but I never said you were ugly," she said. "Matter of fact, with a shave and a haircut and a new set of clothes you might shine up proper. I'd venture a guess that the ladies look twice at you, even so."

Newt shifted uncomfortably in his saddle, unsure how to respond and wishing she would fall back. He got the sense that she was testing him somehow with her flirtatious and teasing banter. And it was odd that she didn't seem too upset that she had seen him kill a man that very night. Right then, he would have gladly traded her for Remington. The artist, if that's what he was, could be every bit as talkative, but was easier to ignore. He urged the Circle Dot horse to a faster walk, but she kept her own horse alongside him.

"Those scars give you the whole pirate feel, and few women can resist a rogue. It's the danger, you know, like playing with fire. And then we complain when we get burned."

He regretted letting the trio travel with him, especially the woman. That kind of poor decision-making was the very same reason his face looked the way it did.

"Like I was saying, I was dealing faro in Leadville." She didn't sound at all frustrated by his lack of enthusiasm for the conversation, yet her talk wasn't only idle chatter, no matter how she might flit from one subject to another. Again, he sensed something else behind her words, a subtle probing or a purpose that he couldn't fathom.

"You were in Leadville?" he asked.

"Oh yes, and dealing faro. Scandalous, isn't it? Real high-toned." She giggled like a girl half her age. "Want to reevaluate your opinion of me?"

He scowled at her facetiousness. And he didn't like it that he couldn't place her, if they truly had met, even though it had been five or six years since he had been to Leadville.

"You fought a boxing match on the stage at the theater there, the Coliseum Novelty," she continued.

"I did."

"Who was it that you fought? I can't recall his name."

"Bill Wiggins. Some called him Sugarfoot in the fight circles."

"Sugarfoot, that's the one."

"I busted a foot down in the Pittsburgh Mine and lost my job before I could heal up. I was digging graves and doing other odds jobs for my keep until I could find something else, and let me tell you, digging a hole in that rocky ground in the middle of a Colorado winter will make you look for different work. The other man that was supposed to box came down sick, and they asked me if I'd fight Bill so they'd have a show. They offered me fifty dollars, and I jumped at the chance. Sounded better than what I was doing."

"You put up a good fight."

"Bill beat me like a rented mule, and that's the honest truth. I never stood a chance with him, even though I outweighed him twenty or thirty pounds."

"Funny, I remember that you knocked him down to end the fifth."

"Lucky punch. Bill's got the best footwork I ever saw and can slip a punch like nobody's business. That's why they call him Sugarfoot. That lick was about the only thing I landed on him, and he took me out in nine."

"Still, you made an impression on those watching. I was not a fight fan until my husband started taking me around the sporting crowd, but your fight with Sugarfoot Wiggins was one of the best I've ever seen. I was there in the Miners' Arms Saloon when they bought the house a round of drinks in your honor for the fight you put up. I believe we were even introduced when you made your rounds through the crowd," she said. "You still don't remember, do you? I hope all that fighting hasn't left you permanently punchy."

At her mention of a husband, Newt glanced back at the big Indian following her and doubted that he could ever have met such a man and not remember him.

She must have sensed where he was looking, because she laughed again. "Not Mr. Smith, no. He and I are only recent business partners. The husband I mention was a mining engineer. It was an explosion that got him, about a year before I saw you fight that night in Leadville. Gone before his time, and for all his good intentions, he left me with nothing but his last name."

"Sorry for your loss."

"Nothing to be done about it. A fine man he was, and never has another caught my fancy since. Not really. It was him that first showed me poker and faro. I used to go with him and sit behind him and watch."

"That where you learned to gamble?"

"He was on a hard run of luck our first summer, and we had a fight. You know how things get said when you're mad. First thing I knew I popped off something about his gambling, and he said I ought to play myself if I thought I could do better. Well, you know what? I did play and I did a lot better. After he passed on, gambling seemed an easier way to earn my keep. Been at it ever since. I admit it hasn't always been sunshine and roses, but it's never been boring. I despise boring."

It began to dawn on him who she was. He recalled a young woman gambler being the talk of Leadville for a time, and later he heard stories of another such woman playing the circuit in mining camps and towns in Colorado and New Mexico.

"Poker Alice, is that you?"

"I know, it's a silly name. My friends and fellow professionals don't call me anything but Alice."

"Sometimes you get stuck with a name and there's nothing you can do about it," he said.

"Tell me about it. I think people name you so that they can put you in whatever box they've fit for you. No loose ends, you know. Bothers them when things don't fit in those normal cubbyholes. I've had places try to bar me from playing, and I've been called everything from a widow whore to a snake oil act. Usually by somebody like George Kerr."

"Life ain't easy."

"No, it isn't. I thought I had the hard part down when I learned the card games, but that isn't half of what I had to learn. Life's the real gamble and the real game. Just everyday, ordinary life."

"That why you wanted to join up with Kerr? Gambling on a treasure ship buried somewhere out on the desert? I thought you professional sorts stayed away from the long shots. No percentage in it," he said.

"Are you a gambler? Mr. Jones, is it?"

"Newt Jones," he answered. "I've played a few times back in the day, but I found out in a hurry it was a good way to lose my money."

She chuckled. "I grant you, this whole lost-ship story is a bit preposterous, but a thing I've learned is that there's money to be made around the edges."

"I don't follow you."

"The edges, you know? Where there's action, there's usually a profit to be made. The kind of men that will bet their money, their sweat, and maybe their health going after a treasure ship are gamblers at heart. Where there are gamblers there's action, and where there's action I can make money."

"You're pretty sure of yourself."

"That's why I have Mr. Smith. I play cards, and he makes sure I get to keep my winnings."

"Remind me to never play poker with you," he said. "Always thinking around the next corner when the rest of us are looking straight ahead."

"Oh, that's half my secret, but don't tell anyone. You'd be surprised at the number of men that sit down at the table with me only for the novelty of playing a woman. And most of them underestimate me for that same reason."

"Like I said, you're a devious woman."

"That's why I'm the best, only this gamble didn't play out like I thought it might."

"Real modest, aren't you?"

"I tell it like I see it.' Poker Alice stopped her horse. "Now here's a wager for you. Want to bet on who that fire belongs to?"

It was only then that Newt noticed the glow of a fire flickering up in one of the draws leading down from the mountains to the north. It galled him to know that she had seen it first, but that was no wonder with all her talk and distraction. He stopped his own horse, and the others did as well. He watched the fire for a while longer and then turned and looked back the way they had come. The Kerr party's big bonfire was still visible in the distance on the other side of the pass.

"Any guesses?" she asked to break the silence.

"Nope," he replied. "Best we move on and leave whoever that is be. There's a sheep ranch not far ahead that I passed. Maybe they'll put you up for the night, and then you can ride on in to San Bernardino in the morning."

"Sounds like a fine plan, but what say we ride up to that fire first and see if whoever it belongs to has a cup of coffee to spare. I can barely keep my eyes open."

Before he could reply, she started her horse up the draw and left him behind.

"Hold on," he hissed at her. "You don't know who could be up there."

Again came that laugh of hers, like bells ringing. And she didn't sound tired at all. "Sound advice, Jones, but I told you I despise boring."

CHAPTER EIGHT

There was only one man at the fire when they rode up, and it was the Mexican liveryman with the game leg from back in San Bernardino. He didn't look the same, having changed out his business suit for rough clothes more suitable to traveling cross-country, but it was him. He hobbled away to the far edge of the firelight at the sound of the approaching horses. An Evans repeating carbine was clutched in his hands.

And there was a boy with him, maybe in his teens, with an oversized sombrero sagging down around his ears and his scrawny frame covered by a bright red-and-black-striped serape draped over his shoulders. Kid or not, he held a Remington rolling block rifle like he knew how to use it.

Newt knew he didn't have much in the way of a friendly smile, but he gave it his best try. "You're that fellow from back at the livery."

The Mexican nodded at that, but he was on edge almost as much as the boy.

"You're a long ways from your business," Newt said. "Last man I expected to run across out here in the dark."

The horses behind Newt clattered on the rocks, and the Mexican almost brought his carbine up. "*¿Quién está contigo?* Who's with you?"

"This is Mrs. Duffield. The big Indian's with her, and the other fellow there's a pilgrim by the name of Fred Remington. Supposed to be some kind of artist or such. I'm guiding them back to San Bernardino," Newt said.

"*¿De donde vienes?*" The liveryman seemed to revert to Spanish when he was nervous or couldn't find the right words in English, but gathered himself and found his other tongue. "You come from Señor Kerr's camp? I heard shots that way."

"We did."

The liveryman gave Newt a look that said he was waiting for an answer to the rest of his question.

"I had a little disagreement there with some men that stole from me," Newt said. "One of them pulled a pistol."

"Was it that McCluskey? He's a bad one, I think."

"No, it was Clubber Cooley and Ed O'Bannon."

"I don't know O'Bannon, but this Cooley, I have heard of him. You better watch out for Cooley. He won't forget if you have trouble with him," the liveryman said.

"He won't be making trouble. Not anymore." Newt wasn't sure how admitting to killing a man was going to alleviate the liveryman's anxiety, but there it was out in the open.

"Ah," the liveryman said, and his eyes went to the Smith & Wesson revolver on Newt's hip, as if the pistol said it all.

The way the liveryman looked at Newt was the way many others looked at him, seeing nothing but a hardcase and head-thumper, or worse. Newt couldn't blame them, and he also knew it wasn't only his battered face that made them wary of him. He knew he wasn't a good man—maybe not as bad as some, but no good man, certainly. And he knew that he was capable of things that most men were not, the hard things, like pulling a trigger. At times he felt ashamed for some of what he had done. It was a hard, dirty way he lived, and it was as if that life had burned a brand of violence into his skin for the whole world to plainly see.

He met the liveryman's gaze and felt nothing but a sudden impatience. In his opinion, it was a bloody damned world, no matter how you looked at it. Some were ground under it, and others managed to stay on their feet. He'd be damned if he would apologize because he was still standing.

"Didn't mean to startle you," Newt said. "The lady here had the craving for some coffee and rode up on you before I could tell her different. Reckon we'll be riding on and leave you be."

The liveryman gave Newt a last, careful look, and then shifted his gaze to Poker Alice. He bent the brim of his hat to her. "*Perdón, señora.* I didn't mean to be rude. Could have been anyone riding up to my fire. *Quién sabe*, eh?"

Poker Alice gave him a smile that was all diamonds and flash, and the liveryman's hold on the Evans carbine relaxed and he nodded to her, all else seemingly forgotten but the pretty woman before him. For the second time, Newt promised himself he would never play poker with her. One smile from her and the liveryman was thrown off his guard when good sense said he should do otherwise with four strangers showing up unannounced out of the night. A thing like that could get a man killed, but that was what was dangerous about women like Poker Alice. They could get you thinking about one thing when you should be thinking about another.

"No, forgive me. It's been a trying evening, what with Mr. Jones's fight . . . and, you know." She sounded so sincere, even though not a few minutes earlier she hadn't been at all disturbed and had been chattering away at Newt.

"Please, señora, get down and make yourself at home." The liveryman gave a polite, yet dramatic wave of his hand across his camp, as if it were some grand hacienda instead of a little fire on a clear patch of ground on a hump between two brush-choked arroyos. "As my people say, *mi casa es su casa.*"

"That's so nice of you, uh, Mr.?" she said.

"Pablo Lopez. This is my son, Mateo." The liveryman gestured at the boy.

"Glad to meet you," Poker Alice replied.

Pablo, the liveryman, glanced at his son and frowned. The boy took the hint and doffed his sombrero to Poker Alice and mumbled something in Spanish with his head ducked. The kid was a little older than Newt had first thought. There was barely time for such greetings before Alice suddenly acted as if she was so tired that she might fall off her horse.

The liveryman started forward to help her down from her sidesaddle. "You must be exhausted. Come and sit by the fire."

Newt, Mr. Smith, and Remington dismounted, loosened the cinches on their horses, and secured them in a clump of brush at the bottom of the draw. By the time they made it to the fire Poker Alice was sitting on a saddle near it contentedly nursing a mug of coffee. Pablo had covered her shoulders with a blanket. She winked at Newt when the liveryman wasn't looking.

Pablo poured another tin mug of coffee and looked at

the three men across the fire from him. "I only have this one."

Newt waved away the offered mug, although the weariness had settled in his bones and the smell of the coffee was almost too much to resist.

"That's kind of you," Remington said, "but my stomach's been bothering me since this morning."

Whiskey will do that to you, Newt thought, remembering the way he had found the tenderfoot on the side of the road.

Mr. Smith stepped farther into the firelight and took the mug of coffee. It was the first time Pablo had a good look at the big Mohave's tattooed face, and he took an unconscious step backward to put more space between them. He studied the big Indian for a moment longer, looking at him the same way he had looked at Newt. He quickly recovered, but it was plain that he was doing some serious rethinking of his situation.

Pablo went to the far side of the fire where Poker Alice sat and hunkered on his heels between her and his son, who squatted with his Remington rifle between his knees and the barrel resting against one shoulder.

Newt came to the fire across from them and took a similar resting position. Remington joined him, but Mr. Smith remained standing.

Pablo gave Mr. Smith one more look before he turned his attention to Newt. "You didn't join Señor Kerr?"

Newt shook his head, but it was Poker Alice who answered the question. "Tried to, but he turned me down."

Pablo nodded.

"I'd take that as a compliment," Newt threw in while he tried to ignore the smell of the coffee.

Pablo shook his head and squinted at the fire. "Señor Kerr, he said he wouldn't take my money. Said he already has enough men, and that I owe his bank too much for me to invest in his venture. But I know he doesn't like Mexicans. Maybe that is it, or maybe it was that Zander McCluskey whispering his ear."

"Like Kerr or not, it makes sense," Newt said. "He's dead serious about what he's after, and wants to keep as much of it as he can to himself if he finds it."

"*Sí.*" Pablo nodded. "That is a thing I had thought of. Señor Kerr is greedy, and he will think as you say."

"From what I gathered," Poker Alice said, "McCluskey, Kerr, and the marshal are the only partners with a share. The rest of them are hired men working for nothing but wages."

"It's a shame," Remington muttered, and sounded as if he were half-asleep.

"What's a shame?" Newt looked at the easterner and noted the way the man's eyelids drooped.

"Not to find out if the treasure's real," Remington replied. "Even if it isn't, I could have got some ideas for a sketch or two and painted them later if they struck me right."

"Probably nothing to it," Poker Alice added. "But it's something nice to think on."

Newt nodded at the liveryman to show his appreciation for the hospitality, and stood. "Best we be riding."

Pablo gave him a crafty look and Newt knew what was coming before the liveryman even said it. It was taking a great chance, but then again, no matter how commonplace and friendly the liveryman seemed, he had left his business and ridden out into the desert chasing after the treasure party. That very action implied he had courage and faith in his own ability. Newt had been bitten before when he misjudged men.

"We could follow Señor Kerr," Pablo said. "Maybe we could time it right and get ahead of them. Take the treasure before he can."

Poker Alice said nothing to that, but the way she perked up showed that she was listening carefully and weighing the implications.

"I don't claim to be a lawyer," Remington said, "but a sunken ship at sea belongs to whoever finds it. Salvage rights, it's called. I guess this treasure ship on the desert would be the same way. Whoever lost it is long gone. First come, first serve, don't you think?"

Pablo's grin was both sly and happy, and he looked at the boy, who said nothing.

"Me and Mateo, that's not enough," Pablo said, and then paused to look at all of them, one at a time. "But six of us. We might do it."

"That's *if* what McCluskey said about seeing the ship is true, and that's a big *if*," Newt reminded them. "And just because there's a ship doesn't mean there's treasure. It could have been hauling anything or nothing."

None of them had a reply for that. It wasn't what they wanted to hear, and such pessimism flew in the face of the dreams they were dreaming.

"The ship is out there somewhere." Pablo waved his hand across the dark horizon.

"We don't have wagons, tools, or anything of the sort," Newt said. "Kerr will have already been there and back by the time we equip ourselves."

"We can make do," Remington replied. "Like you say, there may be no treasure at all, or maybe only a little treasure. I don't think it will take a wagon to haul a little treasure."

"I say we do it," Poker Alice said. "What have we got to lose?"

"I'm in," Remington said. "I say we give it the old Yale try."

Newt wondered if Remington knew how ridiculous that sounded then and there, especially considering the risks they were talking of taking. What they were about to do was the farthest thing from a college football game with cocky rich boys play wrestling and girls and the students waving pennants and making up silly cheers. No game at all. *Fools,* he thought again, *every one of them, without a clue what they were asking for.*

"Kerr doesn't strike me as a man used to this sort of thing, but McCluskey and those others will be watching their back trail, I guarantee you," Newt said. "And we aren't the only ones liable to have the same idea. Getting whatever it is that's out there doesn't mean you keep it."

"I took you for a bold man," Poker Alice said.

"I didn't live as long as I have taking foolish chances." It was a lie, but Newt said it anyway. Most of his adult life had consisted of taking chances, risking his neck for nothing but wages or some stupid notion that struck him and that he couldn't shake loose from.

Poker Alice knew that for the falsehood it was, same as he did. "I saw different back there at Kerr's camp. What did that get you? A silver coin that might be worth the price of a meal? We're talking about treasure, maybe enough to set us all up for a good long while. Weigh risk versus reward, I say. Nobody gets anywhere not taking chances. If you don't, you wind up . . ."

She didn't finish what she was going to say, but whether

that last remark was aimed at him or not, he took it that
way. And the reason those words hit him harder than they
should have was because he had been thinking differently
lately. He wasn't quite sure when the change had happened,
but it was there, just the same.

He was going on thirty-five years old with nothing to
show for those years. Always working for the other man,
fighting battles that often weren't his own, and nothing to
his name but the shirt on his back, a gun on his hip, and a
crazy Indian horse. Where would he be in ten more years,
twenty? The thought wasn't a pleasant one. And there were
other notions rattling around in his skull—aching thoughts
he kept to himself and could shape no words for, and plans
and dreams that he had once held dear but that could find
no place in the current way he lived.

He gave a shake of his head and glared at the lot of
them. They believed it could be done. Had the fever, they
did, and nothing was going to change their minds. But
what did they know about what was waiting out there for
them, treasure or not? He'd crossed more deserts than he
cared to, seen what men could do to each other over nothing more than the thought of riches or a little loot, and
knew there were nine kinds of Hades between where they
sat and whatever waited for them at the end of that kind
of trail.

He looked up at Mr. Smith standing beside him. The
Mohave stared back at him and simply gave a deep grunt
as if he didn't care one way or the other and would go
where Poker Alice went.

"Count me in," Newt said when he looked back at
Pablo.

"That's the spirit, Mr. Jones," Remington blurted out
louder than was necessary.

You're as much a fool as they are. And Newt knew what caused it. He had the fever the same as they did, and the fever, once it took hold, was a hard thing to shake. The allure and mystery of the lost ship's story and the promise of a treasure had gotten to him. All kinds of things were running through his head. Most of them were so silly he would have been embarrassed to say them out loud.

He was cursing himself while the rest of them chattered about what they would do come daylight, and when he looked across the fire Poker Alice gave him another wink and smiled like she had known all along that he would join them.

Devious woman, that one. Foxy smart and then some. If the treasure hunt didn't get them all killed, she could.

CHAPTER NINE

They slept on blankets around the fire after having stayed up well into the night discussing plans. Newt woke when the first streaks of sunlight were spreading orange runners in the iron-blue sky to the east. He felt far from rested, but the crick in his neck wouldn't let him sleep longer. The fire had burned down to nothing but a smoldering ash pile and the wind was blowing smoke in his face. He rose and frowned at his saddle that had served as his pillow while he rubbed the tender vertebrae at the back of his neck and tried to coax some of the stiffness from the muscles there.

The rest of them were still sleeping, all but young Remington, who was nowhere to be found. Newt went to his saddlebags and prowled among them. He inhaled deeply and frowned again. Even with the woodsmoke lining the inside of his nostrils he could still smell his own stink. He dipped his chin to take another whiff of his shirt and wrinkled his face at the smell. It was somewhere between a stale, musty saddle blanket and a billy goat.

He dabbed a little water from his canteen on a rag and mopped his neck, face, and ears as clean as he could. He swapped his dirty shirt for a clean one from one of his saddlebags and brushed his teeth. Feeling somewhat better after that, he took a sack of coffee and his own mug and strode back to the fire.

Poker Alice was sitting up and watching him. She looked like she wanted to say something, but Newt ignored her and stirred the ashes around until he found a few coals and laid a handful of dead sticks on top of them. Once the fire was going again, he filled Pablo's coffeepot and set it beside the flames to brew.

"How many notches have you got filed on that pistol of yours?" Poker Alice asked him while he waited on the coffee to be made. Several strands of her hair had come undone in the night and hung down across one of her eyes, and she shoved the strands away and stared at him intently.

He scowled at her. "That's the first thing that pops into your head this morning?"

She blinked her eyelashes and shrugged. "Curious, I guess. I've had occasion to know a few shootists during the course of my profession."

"Lady, I mind my manners and I'll ask you to do the same. I don't care if we met in Leadville, or not. You don't know me and I don't know you, and I'm fine if we keep it that way."

"I apologize if I've been overly familiar with you. I was only trying to pass the time and thought maybe I'd get to know you better, considering that we're partners now." There was a hint of anger in her voice, and her lovely eyes flashed at him.

Newt lifted the lid on the coffeepot to check his makings, even though the water hadn't had nearly enough time to boil. He put the lid back, but watched the pot, all the while feeling her eyes on him.

"Filing notches is a tinhorn's trick," he said when the feel of her stare didn't let up. "A man doesn't need notches to keep count."

She spoke more carefully this time, her voice friendly again. "Is keeping count important? I assume it's not something that you're proud of."

He inhaled deeply, as was his habit when he was trying to keep his temper in check. She likely meant nothing by her prying. In his experience, some folks were only interested in the juiciest gossip or the most salacious stories.

"Proud? No," he said, "but killing a man makes an impression, and you never forget a one of them."

"Freddy told me last night . . ."

"Freddy? That's what you call him?"

She wrinkled her nose and restarted. "Freddy told me what they call you. That name. Said he heard the marshal talking about how he had arrested you before you ever rode up to Kerr's camp."

He knew the name she spoke of. It was a stupid name, and not one of his choosing. Just something thrown on him by a drunken Welshman one night in the mining town of Shakespeare after he and a few other guards broke up a mob of miners who had worked themselves up to a riot over how the company was mistreating them. How long ago had that been? Five or six years? It seemed like longer ago than that, and remembering that night was as if he were looking back on the actions of another man that he barely recognized.

It had been a foolish stunt he had pulled, but nothing like some made it out to be. They had come down the street fifty men strong, toting torches and swearing they were going to burn the company office and kill anyone that stood in their way. Every man jack of them was packing lengths of chain, clubs, hammers, knives, and anything else they could lay hand to. The other guards, seeing how outnumbered they were, had hesitated to go out on the street, but he saw what they didn't. Most of that mob was all bluff or simply letting the booze and a few loudmouths lead them to trouble. All he had done was whack a couple of the instigators upside the head with a pick handle to take the starch out of the crowd before they could get started, but it had earned him a name and a reputation. At the time he didn't think the nickname would stick, but somehow it had and, sooner or later, followed him wherever he went.

"Leave it alone, lady."

He left the fire and went to check his horse, and then started up to the top of the little ridge. He had forgotten about Remington and was lost in thought when he walked right to him.

The artist had his sleeves rolled up and sat Indian style with his legs folded and crossed. A sketchbook and sheaf of paper rested on his lap. At that moment, he wasn't drawing, but only staring across the high desert to the mountains that lay before him in the distance. The charcoal pencil he held in one hand was as still as his face, but his eyes were alive, absorbing the moment. The wind blew the tall, scattered grass in the bottom of the pass and a dust devil spun along the railroad tracks a mile away.

"Hell of a view," Newt said after they shared a long moment of silence.

"It is at that," Remington replied quietly. "It's why I came west again. Not the only reason, but a good enough reason."

"You say this isn't your first time out here?" Newt asked.

"First time to California, but my third time *out here*, as

you say. Went to Montana the first time, and the second time Kansas, where I found out I'm not cut out for sheep ranching," Remington said.

Newt almost laughed, unable to imagine the dude as a sheep rancher. "How was Montana? It's cold, I hear."

"That's one way of putting it."

"Are the bears up there as big as they say?"

Remington's face brightened. "Absolutely. I tried to sketch them, but I never could get them right. Fascinating creatures, though more than a bit quarrelsome."

Newt glanced down at what the young artist had drawn on the paper before him. The sketch was only partially complete, but Newt recognized what it was in an instant.

"That isn't really how I look," he said.

Remington glanced down at the paper and shrugged. "I'd say the likeness is very close, although I may have exaggerated a bit to capture the essence of the moment."

The drawing depicted two men brawling by a campfire, and one of them had a fist cocked back and was about to strike the other. Newt's face was the most finished bit of the sketch, and upon it was an expression that was savage. The scene was surprisingly lifelike and depicted the action in a way that told a story without words. The skill it took was impressive, but Newt disliked the drawing on the whole and grunted his disdain.

"It wasn't like that," Newt said. "Clubber wasn't nearly that big, and I wasn't standing in the fire with him when I punched him."

Remington gave a quick look up at him and shrugged again. "It's called artistic license. When I choose this kind of subject I want to be sure that anyone who views the work understands the moment and what I'm trying to convey."

"I thought you artists painted flowers or old ladies sitting in their parlors and such," Newt said.

"Some do," Remington replied. "I like action, movement. You know, capturing the human condition as it happens. Find the proper lighting to give it drama. That's why I like it so out here. So much drama everywhere I look. Don't you agree?"

Newt frowned at him. "I'll do without the drama. All that means to me is that someone's having a really bad day. Usually it's me."

Remington went on. "Some might argue that a man running to catch a streetcar because he is late for work might have a sort of subtle drama, but how can that compare to a cowboy riding a bucking horse or a good Indian fight, or a team of half-wild mustangs hitched to a stagecoach? Hard to capture a compelling story on canvas with the one. Not so hard with the others. People back East are fascinated with the West. They can't get enough of it, and I know why."

"Are you going to put that to paint?" Newt pointed at the sketch on Remington's lap.

Remington shook his head. "No, I'm only practicing my sketching, but now that you mention it, it might make a suitable illustration for the journals or magazines with a little work."

"I'd as soon you didn't. That back there, last night, was between me and Clubber and O'Bannon. Nobody else's business."

"No worries," Remington continued when he saw Newt's concern. "I've attempted to sell my work several times, but I've only managed to sell one single illustration to *Harper's Weekly*, despite my submissions. It seems my efforts at capturing this all . . ." he waved a hand across the panorama before them, ". . . well, my stuff isn't good enough. My art instructor at Yale said my work is too cartoonish. I'm afraid I've yet to prove him wrong."

"I'd say you're pretty good, even if you . . . What did you call it?"

"Artistic license."

"Yeah, that."

"I appreciate the compliment, but *Collier's* and *Harper's Weekly* don't seem to share your opinion."

Newt rubbed the stubble of whiskers on his chin. "My mother always said that sometimes you have to throw a lot of rocks to hit a quail on the fly."

"I don't believe I follow you."

"What she meant was that the really big things we wish for usually don't happen the first try. Maybe you get lucky—some do—but for most, the only way is to stick to it and keep throwing rocks. Keep trying and don't give up."

"That's what Eva said." Remington's voice quieted to a point he almost mumbled it under his breath.

Newt didn't ask who Eva was, sensing the same sadness in the artist that he had when he had found him sitting on a rock in a drunken stupor beside the trail the day before. "Doodling with your pencil on that paper isn't going to get us where we're going. You want to be a treasure hunter, best you get on your feet and let's go saddle our horses."

Remington started to close the sketchbook, and Newt stole one last look at the drawing.

"I don't look like that," he muttered.

Remington chuckled and closed the book and tucked it into a leather satchel, along with his charcoal and a few other odds and ends. "No, you looked meaner. I'll work on it some more and see if I can get you right."

Newt watched the artist sling the satchel's strap over one shoulder and start off down the ridge to their camp. He thought of the way the man had drawn his face, like a scarred mad dog snarling and snapping at the world.

He shook his head and set out behind Remington. Mr. Smith rose up from a clump of grass not far below the crest of the ridge. The big Mohave pointed to the southeast toward Kerr's camp.

"Dust," Mr. Smith said.

Newt searched until he saw what the Indian was pointing out. A cloud of dust wormed along about where Kerr's camp had been located, the kind of dust a couple of wagons and several horsemen would stir up.

Remington stopped and saw the same thing. "George Kerr doesn't waste much time. Barely daylight and he's already on the trail."

Newt nodded at that. "He's got the fever."

"The what?" Remington asked.

"Nothing." Newt moved on to the fire, intending on gulping down a mug of coffee before he saddled his horse, that is, if the woman would leave him in peace long enough to do so.

She had changed into a different dress more suited for overland travel and wore a straw hat. Not so fancy as before, but she was still stunning. Not the prettiest woman he had ever met, not if you picked apart every little detail, but it was hard to get past her flashing blue eyes and her smile. Truly, she put off some kind of force or charm that was mesmerizing at times. He could see it in the way that the other men acted around her, and whether he liked it or not, he knew he wasn't immune to it, either. No man could be.

She was at the fire tending a frying pan full of simmering chorizo while Pablo warmed some corn tortillas on a flat slab of rock next to the coals. Newt poured himself a mug of coffee from the pot and turned his back to her. He could feel her staring at him again, and when he sipped at the coffee it burned his lips.

Pablo brought him a taco. The chorizo was covered in green chili sauce, and the tortilla had a faint coating of ashes on it and was charred in places where the flames had tickled it. But he was hungry, and it was more meal than he had expected on such a morning. He wolfed the taco down in two bites, savoring the hot sausage juice and the spicy bite of the green salsa. The coffee was still too hot, but he slurped his way past the burn of it and finished the mug.

"Here, let me wash that for you," Poker Alice said as she reached for his empty mug.

He ignored the offer and squatted and wiped the grease from his hands on his boots and then rubbed a handful of sand inside the mug until it was scraped dry. She watched him with disapproval written on her face.

"Doing you a favor doesn't mean you owe me anything in return," she said.

"Nothing to do with the favor," he replied. "Don't waste water."

"Mr. Lopez says there's a good creek a little ways over there." She pointed down the mouth of a large arroyo.

"Maybe so, but where we're likely going you'd best get in the habit of minding your water. Might come a time when it'll save you."

"I'm beginning to think that I somehow bother you," she said.

"You got that right."

"Good." The displeased look left her face and a faint smirk bent one corner of her mouth.

Pablo looked from one to another of them. His expression said that he didn't have a clue what was going on between them. "No fighting. We work together, no?"

"If you aim to beat Kerr to wherever he's going, you'd best get your horse saddled," Newt said to her.

Poker Alice chuckled and pointed behind him. He turned and saw Mr. Smith leading their horses to the fire. Mateo, the boy, wasn't far behind with his and Pablo's horses and a little dun mule with a packsaddle on its back.

"We're waiting on you, Mr. Jones," Poker Alice said with a smile, and her little chin and button nose jutted out at him like a dare.

He turned and went to where the Circle Dot horse was tied. The gelding stood three-legged and half-asleep until he walked up to it and slung his blanket and saddle on its back. The horse bent its neck and looked back at him while he tied his saddlebags behind the saddle's cantle.

"What are you looking at?" he asked the horse. "You're as bad as that woman."

By the time he had mounted, the others had packed Pablo's camp gear into the canvas and leather pouches that hung far down on either side of the burro's packsaddle like oversized stuffed socks. *Mochilas*, those were called, the Mexican version of panniers.

Mr. Smith was riding a horse with a stature to match his own. It was a big bay gelding, at least sixteen hands high at the withers, and its heaviness, the shape of its head and neck, and the feathering at its fetlocks above its oversized hooves showed that it had some draft blood.

Pablo led them away from camp, with the boy riding at the rear of the group and the little mule running loose and driven before him.

They hadn't ridden more than a hundred yards when they came to the Whitewater River. It was a river only in name, and more of a creek in truth. A trickle of clear water ran down from the high country on a normal day, and nothing but dust at its worst. At the edge of the desert where they hit its course, a long-legged horse could step across its width in a single stride. The water ran on the surface only a short ways past where they were before it disappeared into the sand and gravel and became nothing more than a dry, wide arroyo snaking its way into the flats of the desert. They let the horses and the burro drink while they stood upstream and filled the canteens and two small wooden water kegs the mule carried.

Newt studied the water kegs and a shovel and pick lashed to the packsaddle, and Pablo saw him looking at the gear. Pablo nodded at him, and Newt nodded back. The Mexican liveryman had obviously given the trip some thought.

The dust cloud they had seen earlier was only faintly visible from the lower elevation at the river, but the pass was open country and the mountains on the far side of it showed the way they needed to go. When they rode away from the river it wasn't Pablo who led them off, but instead, it was Newt in the lead. The Circle Dot horse was a fast walker and it moved along with its little foxlike ears perked up and its head swinging in rhythm with its rapid steps. The others had to trot their horses at times to keep up with the stocky brown gelding with the odd brand on its hip.

The mule brayed loudly and the sound on that still morning was like shattered glass and grated on Newt's nerves. He looked back at them behind him once, and then rode on, shaking his head and mumbling to himself.

CHAPTER TEN

Newt led them across the Southern Pacific tracks and on toward what the old-time Spaniards had called the Colorado Desert when they first explored that part of Southern California. Instead of pointing toward the wide expanse of the valley that opened before them at the eastern end of the pass, he found the stagecoach road and followed it where it hugged the foot of the mountains. He soon came to the remains of the Kerr party's last camp. Not far beyond the still-warm ashes where Kerr's big fire had burned was a grave. Nothing marked the freshly shoveled mound of earth, no headstone, and there was nothing to say what soul's mortal remains lay beneath the ground.

The rest of them pulled their horses up and stared at the grave, but Newt rode on without stopping. After burying Clubber Cooley, Kerr's men had hitched their wagons and moved on. The tracks of wagons and horses were plain in the old stagecoach road and pointed south along the west side of the valley.

Pablo rode up alongside Newt later in the morning and gave a jerk of his head back toward Kerr's campsite and the grave they had passed. *"¿Te preocupan los fantasmas de los hombres que has matado?"*

"¿Qué? You gotta come again with that. I don't savvy what you mean."

"Fantasmas de los muertos. ¿Espíritus que caminan en la noche?"

"Your English is better than my Spanish. Try it that way."

"The ghosts of the men you kill, do you fear them?" Pablo asked.

Newt cocked one eyebrow. And then he looked over his shoulder for a moment, as if he could make out the grave behind him in the distance.

"You don't believe in ghosts?" Pablo asked.

A particularly pronounced scar at the corner of Newt's right eyebrow ticked like a tiny muscle spasm was working there under the skin, and he looked again at Pablo and shook his head. "Are you saying old Clubber's ghost is gonna come rattling chains in the night?"

Pablo crossed himself in the sign of the Cross and the Holy Trinity. "You should not make fun of such things, even if you have no fear."

"Scared? No." Newt shook his head. "Reckon I shot Cooley's ghost, same as I did for him."

"Maybe you are brave, and then maybe again you are crazy," Pablo said. "Sometimes I think maybe you have to be one to be the other. I am not crazy or brave."

"Crazy?" Newt asked. "Reckon you aren't the first to call me that."

Pablo crossed himself again. "I will pray for your soul."

Newt frowned at the liveryman. Why was it that some people thought you could talk your troubles to death? They would work and worry at something, like a hound pup digging up a bone and gnawing on it, as if giving a name to their troubles held some magic that made them troubles no more. To Newt's way of thinking, those things were best left unsaid. On the good days, they stayed buried deep. Talking about them, digging up old bones, brought flavors to life again that you would just as soon not taste.

"How come Kerr didn't load his men and gear on a train and ride the tracks on down close to where McCluskey says he found the ship?" Newt asked.

The Mexican gave that some thought, but finally shrugged. "Señor Kerr . . . how do you say? He is tight with his money. Maybe he wouldn't give his money to the train people."

"You've been over this ground before?" Newt asked.

Pablo gave his peculiar shrug of his shoulders and head. "I know this road we travel as far as the other side of the valley."

"Nothing else?"

"I went with Señor Fusse many years ago."

"What's that mean?"

"Charlie Fusse. He spent many years looking for the ship, but that was long ago."

"And you went with him?"

"Only once. He put together men and wagons, much like what Señor Kerr has done. Even the newspaper gave money for us to hunt the ship. We went out for six weeks, but we found nothing."

"But you still want to look again?"

"The ship is real."

Newt wondered what else the liveryman wasn't saying and what he might be holding back.

"What's out there?" Newt pointed at the desert before

them where the dust lifted in waves and rolled through the scrub in front of the occasional gust of wind.

"*¿Qué?*"

"Not the ship. What's between here and Yuma?"

"There is a little town at Indio and salt diggers at Salton Station." Pablo answered. "Other than that, *nada*. Nothing."

"You know where to find water once we're out there?" Newt asked, and watched Pablo's face to judge how he answered the question.

"Plenty of water here and until we get to Dos Palmas, I think. I don't know this country so well past Dos Palmas." The Mexican shrugged to show his uncertainty.

"Next time we camp, I want you to draw me a map of every waterhole you know of. *Enséñame donde esta el agua. ¿Comprende?*"

"*Sí*, I can do that."

The old stagecoach road did not follow the S.P. train tracks, and instead, aimed toward a point of the mountains directly south of them, cutting along the western edge of the valley. In years gone by, the wagon road had once crossed the desert and led on through the mountains to the east and to the gold diggings across the Colorado River. But the boom camps were long since gone in those parts, and the Southern Pacific had laid its tracks. The stage-coaches no longer ran and the stations were abandoned. All that was left were rutted wagon tracks.

It was one of those old stage stations that lay in the shadow of that mountain point jutting out into the desert. A cluster of palm trees appeared ahead of them, and other such trees were visible in the mouth of a rugged, rocky canyon above it. The trees struck Newt as odd, trees like that with their weird, shaggy trunks and odd green tops in the middle of a desert, although they weren't the first he had seen, having run across their like down in some of the deep barrancas south of the border. But then again, he had seen a lot of unusual things in Mexico; things that reminded him that he had come a long, long way from the hills of Tennessee.

A large pool of water, glass slick and like something out of a dream, showed itself among the palm trees, visible through breaks in the tall grass and tules growing along its banks.

"Agua caliente," Pablo said.

Newt didn't know if Pablo meant that it was the name of the place, or if he was simply pointing out where hot water bubbled up among a clutter of head-sized rocks and drained into the water hole.

On the far side of the water hole, brush huts with grass roofs lay in a cluster, an Indian village. Two mongrel dogs with tails curled over their backs came to the edge of the road and barked at them. Nobody was to be seen in the village as they rode by, and it appeared to have been so recently abandoned that fire pits outside the lodges still smoldered. Whether the village's inhabitants had fled at the sight of Newt and the rest of his party coming along the road, or for other reasons, wasn't clear.

Newt studied the abandoned village carefully, and for an instant, he thought he saw the creased, leathered face of an old Indian woman peering at him out of the grass on the far side of the water hole. That face disappeared as quickly as it had appeared. The Circle Dot horse kicked at one of the dogs and struck it a glancing blow. The dog yelped and fled with its counterpart to a safer distance from the horse.

The stagecoaches may have been a thing of the past, but the station they came to wasn't abandoned. The plaster on the outside of the adobe brick walls was cracked and fallen away in places, but the roof was still semiweatherproof and the door was still on its hinges. Two horses were tied to the crude stave corral, and a sign proclaimed the single-room adobe building as a trading post. Newt nodded at the adobe and gave Pablo a questioning look. The liveryman shrugged as if he didn't know any more than Newt did.

A bald-headed man with a close-cropped beard and a stained apron tied over his shirtfront opened the door and leaned against the doorjamb. He squinted at Newt, and then at the rest of them. The inside of the room behind him was too dark for Newt to make out who else might be in there.

"Welcome," the man in the doorway said to them.

Newt swung down from his horse.

"What are you doing?" Poker Alice asked.

"I'm going to buy me another canteen if they've got one, and ask a few questions about the road ahead," Newt said. "The rest of you sit tight."

"Who died and left you in charge?" she threw at him.

Newt looked at Mr. Smith. "Make sure she stays here."

The abandoned Indian village bothered him, but he was already moving toward the trading post. The man in the doorway went back inside. Footsteps sounded behind Newt, and he looked over his shoulder and saw that Pablo was right on his heels.

A counter that seemed to serve dual purpose as a bar ran the length of the right-hand side of the room. It was made from a fir log split in half and sanded to somewhat of a smooth surface on the flat side. Adze or broadax marks were still visible in the wood. There were two men at the far end, shadowed in the gloom where the sunlight from the open door and the single window in the front wall barely reached the toes of their boots.

Newt ducked under a dried bunch of red chili peppers hanging from the rafter poles and stepped to the bar. The room smelled of damp dirt and tobacco smoke.

"Thirsty?" the man in the apron asked from behind the bar.

"I could use something to cut the dust. Give me a whiskey."

"Ain't got no whiskey," the bartender said.

"A beer then."

"Ain't got no beer, neither. I got tequila, and then I got more tequila. Take your pick."

Newt glanced at a half-full bottle sitting on the bar top beside the man. A ray of sunlight from the window or the open door landed on the bottle, and he could see the worm floating in the amber, oily liquid.

"Believe I'll pass," Newt said. "You wouldn't happen to have a canteen for sale, would you?"

"That's no way to be," one of the men at the end of the bar said. His spur rowels rattled against the dirt floor as he adjusted his position so that he was fully facing Newt.

The one behind him stepped forward so that they stood shoulder to shoulder. The one doing the talking was a skinny little runt with a pinched face and front teeth like a horse. Those teeth wouldn't seem to stay behind his lips, even when he closed his mouth. He wore a red shirt with its long tail worn outside his pants. An army belt with a brass U.S. buckle was cinched down over his shirttail, and a military holster with the flap cut off rested at a cross-draw on his left hip. The gray felt hat on his head was raked over at a precarious angle that Newt assumed was supposed to make him look reckless and tough.

"If you ain't thirsty, you could do us both a favor and buy us a drink," the other one said. He was as fat as his partner was skinny, and the older of the two. He wore no shirt, and the belly of his white long johns was stained brown. A pair of faded uniform pants with yellow stripes down the legs were held up by suspenders and tucked into scuffed cavalry boots. The blue wool forage cap on his head caused the sweat to run down his cheeks. A military holster like the one the skinny one wore rested on his left hip with the flap unbuttoned, and a big sheath knife was shoved behind his waistband kept that belly of his from spilling over his belt buckle.

Both men were drunk. Not drunk enough to be harmless, but the kind of drunk that made some men mean.

"Sorry, fellows, my spending money's running low," Newt said, and looked back at the bartender. "What about that canteen?"

"Pour us all one, Artie," the skinny one said. "This fellow's buying a round for the house."

"Maybe that greaser wants one, too," the fat one in the soldier clothes said. "How about it, greaser?"

Pablo held the fat one's stare, but didn't answer him. He was the only man in the room that wasn't armed, and it couldn't have been a good feeling.

Something rustled in the corner on the other side of the room. Although the sign out front claimed the establishment was a trading post, there wasn't much in the way of goods for sale that Newt could see, and he guessed that the sign was only an excuse to sell liquor to the local Indians. However, there were a few odds and ends hanging on the wall on the opposite side of the room, and others gathering dust on shelves cobbled together out of scrap lumber from old railroad shipping crates. Junk, most of it, but it was among that junk that he had heard someone moving.

His vision was slowly adjusting to the gloom, and he picked out a cot made of peeled poles lashed together with rawhide. A young Indian woman was on that cot, and she stared at him and the other men with frightened eyes and pressed herself against the corner of the room with her knees drawn up to her chest and a deer hide pulled up to cover her nakedness. The deerskin robe was so old or badly tanned that the hair had slipped away from the hide, leaving hand-sized bald patches where bone-white buckskin was revealed. Newt thought he could make out an ugly knot on her cheek, and that her lips were swollen with a crust of dried blood angling down from one corner of her mouth.

"You like what you see, maybe I'll sell you a go at the squaw," the skinny one said.

Newt felt the familiar devil rising up inside of him, and the inside of his mouth was smoky and the clench of his jaw caused his face to start aching.

"Let's have that drink," the fat one said. "She ain't much to look at, but I promise you we ain't rode all the rough off her, yet."

Pablo moved at the bar, restless and on edge with the trouble he saw coming—not ready to run just yet, but his eyes cutting this way and that, as if looking for a way out if it came to that. The skinny fellow stepped out a little where he could see around Newt.

"Where you going?" he said to Pablo. "Now, that ain't mannerly at all. You one of those uppity greasers? Think you're better than us?"

The fat one reached over and grabbed the bottle of tequila. He poured two glasses full where he and the skinny one stood and then slid the bottle down the bar. "Get 'em some glasses, Artie. Hell, I'll buy if they won't."

The bartender took down two more glasses and set them, one at a time, in front of Newt and Pablo. That done, he eased back against the wall behind the bar, putting himself as far away from the trouble at hand as he could. Or maybe he was taking sides. Newt could see no weapon on the man, but the way he kept glancing at something below the bar top was troublesome.

"You go on outside, Pablo," Newt said quietly without looking at the liveryman beside him. "Go on now."

"He ain't going nowhere," the skinny one sneered. "He's going to show some manners and have a drink when it's offered to his sorry ass."

Pablo grabbed the bottle and poured himself a glass. His pouring hand shook ever so slightly and he slopped a jigger's worth of tequila on the bar. He took a drink and grimaced, and then held the glass up for the skinny one to see as a peace offering.

"Well, *buenos días* and bless your brown little heart. Have you another sip, bean-eater, and we'll keep working on them manners of yours," the skinny one said.

"How come you and the rest of them you got with you are all the way out here?" the fat one asked. "Not doing yourself a little treasure hunting, are you? I said to my partner here just last night, whatcha wanta bet that newspaper article will have half the men in three counties out chasing around the desert?"

"Country's filling up right proper all of a sudden," the skinny one chimed in.

The Indian girl in the corner whimpered, and the fat one took a step her way and kicked the end of the cot hard enough to rattle the dust from the walls and the ceiling.

She ducked her face into the deer hide and muffled her pitiful sounds against it.

The skinny one must have seen something in Newt's look, for his hand slipped to the revolver on his hip. "What you looking at?"

Mr. Smith walked through the doorway at that moment. The size of him blocked the light coming through that opening. He gave the two men at the end of the bar a brief, measuring look and then his gaze fell on the girl in the corner.

"Look at the size of this one, would you?" the skinny one exclaimed, trying to hide his sudden nervousness at the sight of the Mohave. "Biggest damned Injun I ever did see."

"Mrs. Duffield said to come check on you," Mr. Smith said to Newt in a flat voice. "She wondered what was taking you so long."

"We were just leaving," Newt answered.

Pablo set down his half-finished glass of tequila.

The fat one moved in an arc across the room, stalking around Mr. Smith while sizing him up and stopping near the door. "You see how this red heathen's dressed up?"

"Regular circus is what it is," the skinny one said.

"Pablo, go get on your horse." Newt's voice was even quieter than before.

"Your ears stopped up? I said you keep your asses right here," the skinny one said. "Maybe we'd like to ask you some questions."

Newt turned his head to the left and then the right, slowly, working away the tension creeping up his spine. He could feel the faint popping and creaking of his neck vertebrae. "Only one not walking out of here is you."

"Watch him, Cleave!" the fat one called out.

The skinny one, Cleave or whatever the fat one had called him, closed his mouth and hid those horse teeth long enough to lick the scraggly whiskers of his mustache. His eyes flicked from his fat friend to Newt.

"Bold talk," he said.

"You're the one talking." Newt's fists were squeezed so tightly that he could feel his pulse throbbing in them. "Talking when you should have pulled that pistol while you had the chance. Now it's too late, and I'm going to hurt you bad."

It wasn't the skinny one who pulled a gun first; it was the fat one off to Newt's side.

CHAPTER ELEVEN

The fat man's army flap holster slowed his draw considerably, and he had to double-grab and yank to get his long-barreled Colt Army clear of his leather, cussing the whole time. As it was, the wooden war clubs appeared as if by magic in Mr. Smith's hands from somewhere inside his suit coat. He brought the left-hand club down on the fat man's gun hand with a crack that shattered bone, and the right-hand club swung in an undercut and smashed him in the face. The pistol dropped to the floor unfired, and the fat man followed it.

Skinny's pistol was halfway out of his holster when Newt moved. He stiffened the fingers of his open hand and jabbed them straight into the sharp knot of the man's Adam's apple. A ragged hiss of air escaped the man's mouth and he let go of his pistol and clutched at his throat with both hands. Newt stepped back as the bucktoothed renegade sagged against him and fell to his knees, choking and gasping.

Newt pulled the pistol from the man's holster. He looked at the bartender, who stood stiffly, but with both hands out of sight behind the bar. "Go ahead and pull whatever you've got back there. Go ahead."

The bartender raised his hands above the bar top, showing plainly that they were empty. "Not my fight, mister. They showed up yesterday evening, and there was nothing I could do about it. Deserters are what they are. I bet you they run off from Fort Mohave or maybe Fort Whipple. Said they had mustered out and come down here after seeing some newspaper article about the lost ship, but I don't believe them. Not the part about mustering out after their time was up."

Newt glanced at Pablo and saw him backed to the other end of the bar and against the front wall. He wore no pistol, but he had drawn a double-edged blade with a wicked needle point. There was a tremor in his knife hand, the same as there had been when he was holding his glass of tequila.

"You can put that sticker away now. It's over," Newt said.

Mr. Smith stood silently over the fat man on the floor. He swept his suit coat back and shoved the clubs underneath it. When he closed his coat again no one could have told that he even carried such weapons.

"Is he dead?" Pablo asked.

The fat man's face was barely recognizable, caved in as it was, and there was no doubt that he was, indeed, dead. Very dead.

Newt ignored the skinny one wheezing for air and thrashing around beneath him and crossed the room to the foot of the cot. The young Indian woman, hardly more than a girl, drew the filthy deer hide closer to her chin and whimpered again. She wouldn't look up at him.

"It's all right now," Newt said, though he knew it wasn't, not for her, not with what she had gone through.

She turned her face away from him and pressed it against the wall.

Pablo tried Spanish on her, but got no response to that, either.

Newt looked at Mr. Smith. "Can you talk to her?"

"She is Cahuilla," Mr. Smith stated, like for some reason talking to her would be beneath him.

"Can you make her understand we mean her no harm?"

Mr. Smith said something to her in what Newt guessed was her native tongue or his own. The big Mohave kept talking to her. She didn't answer him, but after a while, she did turn her face away from the wall and look at him.

"She won't talk," Mr. Smith said when he was finished.

"You think that's her village out there?" Newt asked.

Mr. Smith nodded. "I do."

"Why don't you walk down there and see if her people will come get her. I think they're hiding from these two." Newt tilted his head at the dead fat man and at the skinny one groveling at the foot of the bar.

"You go," Mr. Smith answered. "I am *kwanami*. When they see me they will be afraid."

Newt didn't know what a *kwanami* was any more than he knew what a mugwump was when Remington had said it.

"I will go and try to talk to them," Pablo offered.

Newt swung the pistol he held back toward the bartender. "You're making me awful nervous."

The bartender lifted his hands again. "I told you I'm no part of this. Good grief, man, most of my business is trading with the Cahuilla . . ."

"Selling them liquor?"

"You got it all wrong."

"You saw what they did to the girl, and you didn't do a thing to stop them."

"I never . . ."

"Did you sell her to them, or did you go over to that village with them and help take her?"

"I told you, you got it all wrong."

Newt moved closer to the bar and knelt so that he was closer to eye level with the skinny fellow on the floor. "What about you? You like hurting women? Make you feel big and mean?"

The skinny fellow tried to answer, but whatever he said wasn't understandable. Newt wondered if he had broken something in the man's throat.

"Your partner's dead and you're busted to pieces," Newt said.

He heard the girl get up off the cot and when he looked behind him he saw her standing there staring at the skinny man down on the floor. She had dropped the deer hide and was naked from her bare feet to the top of her head where her black hair was ratted and twisted as wild as a thorn bush. Her eyes were wilder. Hurt and fear and a growing fury all swirled together in those dark pools like something boiling in a cauldron.

Newt could hear the wheeze of air through the skinny man's damaged windpipe every time he tried to breathe. Tears rolled down the man's cheeks.

Newt looked at Mr. Smith, but the Mohave's expression was unreadable. The girl was stilling standing there, swaying on her feet and staring at the skinny man with her jaw trembling.

Newt rose and went to the cot the girl had lain on. She flinched back from him as he passed, but he bent and picked up the deer hide and held it out to her. "We mean you no harm, girl. Take this and cover yourself."

She took the deer hide and clutched it to her chest. The sound of people moving outside drew Newt's attention and he looked out the open door and saw a group of Indians looking inside. They were all adults, women and men. They were a short people. Some wore store-shelf clothing, but most did not. The men were wearing nothing more than buckskin or grass breechclouts and the women bare breasted with no other clothing than knee-length skirts made of woven mesquite bark. The look on their faces, men and women alike, was as stoic as Mr. Smith's, and they seemed unwilling to come inside as though they were waiting for something.

Pablo came through them, moving cautiously. "They came to the village this morning and shot one of the old men and took the girl," he said. "The people, they ran and hid and were afraid to come back."

"Just these two? Nobody else with them?" Newt asked.

Pablo's eyes cut briefly toward the bartender. Newt understood without Pablo saying anything.

He focused his attention back on the skinny little killer who was now sitting at the foot of the bar with his legs sprawled out wide before him and still clutching his throat. "Did George Kerr stop here long enough to pay you to make sure nobody was riding on his back trail?"

The skinny one managed to shake his head.

"You think Señor Kerr would do such a thing?" Pablo asked. "I don't think so."

"He came through here before we did, and you give me

one other good reason why two like these here would pick a fight when they were outnumbered. Their kind doesn't work that way."

"Señor Kerr is many things, but he would have nothing to do with men who would harm a woman," Pablo replied. "I think you are wrong."

Newt moved closer to the bar and held out a hand to the bartender. "Give me whatever you've got hidden back there."

The bartender started to reach under the bar.

"Real easy," Newt said with the pistol once again pointed at the bartender.

A Parker double-barreled shotgun was handed over to Newt. He cracked it open to see the two paper cartridges loaded in the chambers, then snapped it closed again. The bartender flinched at the sound.

Newt offered the pistol he had taken from skinny one to Pablo. It was a fairly new army-issue Colt .45.

Pablo shook his head. "I'm no pistolero."

Newt shoved the revolver in his waistband. "Suit yourself. Comes a time when every man fights or runs, and sometimes we don't get the chance to run."

Newt studied the liveryman, trying to gauge how much mettle the man possessed and wondering if he only then realized what could happen when all the rules and civilized niceties went out the window. And then he went to the fat man's body and picked up the other pistol on the floor there, another single-action Army Colt. He looked at Mr. Smith. Like Pablo, the Mohave carried no sidearm that Newt could tell, but then again, he hadn't noticed those wooden war clubs, either.

"Let's go," Newt said.

The big Mohave and Pablo went out the front door. Newt noticed how the Cahuillas parted and gave Mr. Smith plenty of room. They were as leery of him as if he had been a wildcat, some of them whispering about him.

"Appreciate you understanding how it was," the bartender said to Newt. "I never would have let them do that to the girl if I could have stopped them. They would have killed me for sure."

"You're a liar." Newt started for the door.

The skinny man down at the foot of the bar tried to say something, but the words were too mangled for Newt to make them out.

"What'd you say?" Newt asked.

"Hhh . . . Hileman will kkk . . . kill you for this," the wounded man managed with a hand held to his throat.

"Who's Hileman?"

The downed man gave his best effort at a sneer through his grimace of pain, but choked again and gave a ragged gasp that cut off whatever he was about to say. His boot heels scrambled on the floor and he convulsed wildly as if he couldn't get enough air. When he finally quit jerking and his pain was more at ease, he sat with his back propped against the bar, glaring stubbornly at Newt.

Newt handed the fat man's pistol and the bartender's shotgun to a Cahuilla man closest to him. The Cahuilla was surprised, but quickly recovered and took the firearms.

Newt turned to face the room again and waited until the girl looked his way. When she did, he bent and jerked a knife from the dead fat man's belt. It was an ugly, cheap blade, little better than a butcher knife with its hardwood handles dry-cracked and poorly riveted, and its blade long since turned to a rust brown patina. But its cutting edge was razor-sharp and half as long as Newt's forearm. He flipped the knife and stuck it in the floor between where the girl stood and where the skinny man sat against the foot of the bar.

Her eyes were wilder than ever, and she tracked the flight of the knife and stared at it where it quivered in the floor. But she didn't immediately lunge for the blade, and instead gave Newt one more look. He nodded at her and went out the door.

"What the hell are you doing?" the bartender called after him.

Newt didn't answer him and went for his horse. The band of Cahuillas gathered at the door let him pass, but closed ranks quickly behind him. By the time he had taken no more than a few strides they were crowding into the cantina. Some of the men had clubs similar to the one Mr. Smith carried dangling at the end of their arms. Some had only knives like the one he had left for the girl.

Only one of the Cahuilla remained behind. It was the old man Newt had seen Pablo speaking to. His face was burned to almost a shade of black by years of desert sun, and the wrinkles and creases in his face were as deep and craggy as the mountains.

The old Indian stepped close to Newt, put a hand on his shoulder, and said something in Spanish. And then a few more words passed between them before the old man followed his band into the cantina.

"What was that all about?" Remington asked while Newt swung into the saddle.

Newt noticed that the easterner had a Remington-Lee bolt-action rifle pulled out of his saddle scabbard and resting across his lap. A tenderfoot, maybe, but at least he had shown the good sense to realize something had gone wrong.

"Couple of fellows in there have themselves a little disagreement with the Indians," Newt said.

Remington gave him a puzzled look, and Poker Alice rode closer and was about to ask him another question. But Newt tapped the Circle Dot horse with his spurs and started down the coach road at a trot. The rest of them fell in behind him. They hadn't ridden far when they heard a man scream behind them. Newt thought it sounded like the bartender.

"Keep riding," Newt said.

The sound of another scream from the trading post carried to them, and it caused all of them to look back. All but Newt, who stared straight ahead.

There was a low rise of ground not a quarter of a mile away, and they stopped upon it. By then, the trading post was on fire.

"What's that?" Poker Alice asked as if what she saw wasn't as plain as the smoke rolling through the palm trees.

Mr. Smith said something in Mohave that none of them could understand. Pablo crossed himself.

"Those Indians are burning the trading post," Poker Alice said.

"That they are," Newt answered.

"They're murdering those poor people," she continued.

Newt met Poker Alice's gaze and his voice was flat and harsh when he spoke. "There's a woman back there, not much more than a girl, whose whole world changed this morning in a bad way. You go back and tell her how wrong it is."

He turned his horse to face the desert and led them off

at a walk, knowing as he rode away that she was looking at him. He felt like he had once again moved to the other side of a line that got easier and easier to cross each time he did it—awful decisions made, and decisions he made without flinching, as if there were another man inside him that took over in those moments. He wished he had a bottle of a whiskey and a place to be alone.

The others hung back a few horse lengths behind him, sensing his black mood, but Pablo caught up to him when they had put the Indian village out of sight. "What did the old one say to you?"

Newt thought about the old Cahuilla man who had held back when the others went inside the cantina, and the few words they had shared. He hadn't been able to understand half of what was said to him, but what he understood had stuck.

"He asked what brought us to his country."

"And what did you tell him?" Remington asked.

"Told him the truth."

Pablo must have sensed that Newt was holding something back. *"¿No más?"*

"He said that the ship is real," Newt replied. "He said that it was well known in the time of his grandfather's grandfather."

All of them stopped their horses, looking at Newt as if they weren't sure what they had heard. He kept on riding.

"He said what?" Remington blurted out.

"Did he tell you where it is?" Poker Alice kicked her horse to catch up to Newt.

"His grandfather saw the wreck once," Newt said. "But he said that was too long ago and none of his people that are living remember how to get there, though they tell the story to their children."

"But it's real. That's what matters," Remington said with a smile that reminded Newt what a greenhorn the artist really was, fancy rifle and good horse, or not.

Poker Alice gave Newt another probing look. "You still aren't telling us everything."

"That's what he said."

"Why would he tell you that?"

"He said he had nothing else to give to show his thanks."

"Thanks for what?"

"Por la chica," Pablo said in a quiet voice. *"Por la satisfacción de venganza."*

Newt translated for Poker Alice, assuming that she didn't speak Spanish. "For the girl."

Even translated, she had no idea what he meant. She had not seen the ravaged, beaten Cahuilla girl. Although the tone of Alice's voice, the flare of her nostrils, and the tiny vein he could see pulsing in her pale throat showed that she knew something terrible had transpired. And he could see that it scared her, but the fever was taking hold of her again. What the old Cahuilla had said outweighed all else, and it pushed the fear away to some corner of its own to be addressed another time.

"Why would he tell you at all, this girl you mention, or not? It makes no sense. Why he would tell you instead of getting the treasure himself?"

"He never mentioned any treasure."

She looked back the way they had come. "If they know so much, why wouldn't they get it for themselves?"

Newt barely heard her. The memory of that poor

Cahuilla girl's wild, tormented eyes came back to him, and it was hard to shake away. "Maybe they already have, but he didn't tell me his story so that we could find the ship."

Poker Alice scoffed at that. "Why did he tell you, then?"

"He wanted to warn us to turn back."

"Turn back?" Remington said. "Quit now that we're sure it's there?"

"If you believe him," Newt answered. "Indians like a good story, same as we do. Spend a night around the fire with them and you'll hear some."

"It's real, all right. Pablo said the Indians know, didn't you, Pablo?" Remington replied.

The Mexican said nothing to that, but simply nodded his head at Remington.

"You believed him. I can tell," Poker Alice said to Newt.

"Maybe he told the truth, or maybe he didn't. But I'm going to see if it's out there, one way or the other."

"You know where it is, don't you?" she said to Newt, and then looked to the others. "I knew it. That old Indian told him where to find the ship."

Newt shook his head. "He said that the ship is cursed, and whoever seeks it will die."

Again she scoffed. "Pure superstition. Nothing but medicine man hocus-pocus, like shaking gourd rattles and waving smoke around with an eagle feather to chase off spirits. Oh, I know what some of the Indians believe."

"Maybe." Newt glanced at Mr. Smith to see if he had taken offense, but the Mohave's face was as unreadable as ever.

Newt started the Circle Dot horse down the trail, his last words thrown back to her over his shoulder. "He said those that the curse didn't get, the desert would."

"Did you ever think he might be trying to scare you off?" she called after him.

"It occurred to me."

Nobody said anything to each other for the next hour, each lost in their own visions of the treasure that waited for them somewhere ahead. All of them but Newt had already forgotten the old Cahuilla's warning.

CHAPTER TWELVE

It was an odd country to Newt's eyes, and one of stark contrasts. They encountered more palm tree groves in a few short miles, and other odd clumps of green dotted among the tan desert. He counted two more spring-fed pools of water in less than a mile's travel, and then the coach road passed through a stretch of sand dunes devoid of any kind of vegetation only to come again to another clump of palms and a clear stream running down out of a rocky canyon. A trio of desert bighorn sheep spotted them from a high point on the foot of the mountains to their right and bounded through the rocks in flight. Birds flitted through the trees and brush, and everywhere there were animal tracks. There were the cloven hoof prints of deer, the pad marks left by little foxes, the three-toed tracks of quail and roadrunners, the scurried grooves of lizards and snakes, and even the large, rounded print of a mountain lion, all drawn to the bountiful water.

Twice he saw the remains of Indian villages, small domed huts made of grass laid over pole frames or simple post-and-beam structures with brush roofs. Shallow, rock-lined irrigation ditches, now dry and in disrepair, had once fed water to patches of ground that he could tell had been tilled and planted in crops in the recent past. It was plain that more of the Cahuilla or some other tribe had lived in the area at one time, and it was no wonder, for the north-western edge of the valley looked like a paradise compared to the other desert around it.

They were an hour's ride along the coach road when Newt stopped his horse among a clump of willows lining a dry wash. Ahead of him in the distance was a clump of smoke trees, and he could see the white canvas tops of George Kerr's wagons among them.

Newt dismounted and led the Circle Dot horse under the dappled shade offered by the willows. The others remained on their horses in the road. Pablo and his boy were removed from the others, having a quiet conversation for their ears alone.

"They have stopped at what you white men call Indian Well," Mr. Smith said. "Good water."

"You know this country?" Newt asked, at the same time wondering how the man could go without a hat on his head with the hot July sun beating down. And Mr. Smith was still wearing his suit coat, too, regardless that the temperature must have already been nearing one hundred degrees and it was only late morning.

The Mohave nodded. "Most of my people live not so far north of here and up the Colorado. Once we had a big fight with the Serrano at the well."

Newt studied the tattoos visible on Mr. Smith's face. He'd seen similar marks before on the Mohave and Yuma people he'd met. Both men and women wore them, but none of the tattoos he had seen were as extravagant or numerous as those on Mr. Smith. While the individual meaning of each facial mark was lost on Newt, he understood the overall symbolism without being told. They were warrior marks, and Newt was sure the giant Mohave, fancy white-man's suit or not, had seen many a fight.

"I passed through Yuma last fall, but I cut straight west over the mountains to San Diego. Never came through this country," Newt said. "I'm glad you and Pablo know this desert."

"Pablo doesn't know the desert," Mr. Smith said.

"I got a different impression."

"The boy knows."

Newt looked back at where Pablo and the boy conversed. "His son? That kid is still wet behind the ears."

"He knows. I see the way he looks at the land. I hear some things he says."

Newt hadn't heard the boy, Mateo, say two words since the night before when they had ridden up to Pablo's fire. The kid rarely looked you in the eye and made a point to keep his distance from anyone but his father.

Mr. Smith went to check on Poker Alice. Newt thought him the most unusual manservant he'd ever seen, if that's what he really was. In fact, the whole group was the oddest bunch he had ever thrown in with.

"Do you think they saw us?" Remington asked Newt.

Newt studied Kerr's camp visible in the distance. The half mile of ground between their position and Kerr's was absolutely flat with only scattered desert growth to hide anything, but only the white tops of those wagons were showing, as if they were parked in a depression or a dip in the terrain.

"I don't know. Maybe," Newt answered.

He loosened the cinch on the Circle Dot horse, readjusted his saddle, then tightened the girth once more. That done, he mounted and started through the brush toward the foot of a mountain ridge and a rocky point overlooking the valley.

"Where to now?" Remington asked.

"Up there." Newt pointed at the heights.

"I say, that's a good bit out of our way. What are your intentions?"

"Now there's a hundred-dollar question," Poker Alice said, catching their conversation.

"We watch and wait," Newt said.

"I hate waiting," Poker Alice replied.

"Reminds me of an old preacher we had back home," Newt said. "His horse threw him, and one of the church deacons comes along on his way to Sunday service. He sees the preacher down on his knees in the middle of the road beside the horse praying and asks if the preacher was praying for a gentler horse. The preacher says no, he was praying that he could ride the one that threw him."

"I take this is you reminding me to be patient again," Remington said wryly.

"Just a story, that's all."

"Another of your dear Mother Jones's tales?" Remington asked.

"She had plenty of them, but no," Newt replied. "You can credit that one to old man Porter. Him and his boys made more whiskey than they grew crops or meat, but they were the best storytellers in the hills. I've heard old Davy Crockett used to tell it that he could grin a bear out of a tree, but I bet he couldn't hold a candle to those Porter boys. They had a charm, they did. Make you laugh when you needed to. The oldest boy could play a fiddle. Really make it ring so that even the shyest folks would dance, or at least pat their foot and clap their hands."

"By *hills*, where do you mean?" Remington asked.

"East Tennessee."

"I take it that's home."

"Was."

Remington sighed. "Ah, so many of us so far from home."

"That we are, pilgrim. That we are." Newt was already off his horse again and leading it on a winding course up the slope and through the rocks.

George Kerr, president of one bank in San Bernardino and a board member of another in Colton, and the owner/operator of a successful general merchandising and expansive freight business that covered the southern third of California, stood beside Zander McCluskey, looking back to the north along the stagecoach road.

"You see something?" McCluskey finished rolling a cigarette and licked the paper to seal it while he looked across the desert.

"Thought I did. Out in those willows. I don't know. Too far to tell," Kerr answered. "That smoke we saw worries me."

"Probably just some Indians burning off brush," McCluskey said, but there was a faint frown on his face as if he, too, was thinking about the smoke they had seen an hour after leaving Agua Caliente.

"I still say we should have taken the train," Kerr muttered.

"And I tell you I need to go slow and look things over to backtrack myself." McCluskey struck a match against the grip frame of his right-hand pistol and lit the cigarette. He squinted through the tobacco smoke at Kerr while he drew the cigarette to life. "How many people you think would have got on that train with us? Huh? Want to lead them right to the ship? This way we can mind our back trail and see if anybody follows us. Wait them out or wander around a bit and throw them off if we have to."

"You said you could find it again."

McCluskey shook the match out and flicked it to the sand. He took his hat off and wiped the sweat from his brow and from the hat's sweatband, the cigarette dangling lazily in one corner of his wide mouth. "Another day and we'll be close."

"I've got a lot invested in this."

"So you keep telling me. Don't you forget I cut you in on this when I didn't have to."

"You came to me first," Kerr huffed.

"And you didn't waste any time digging your spurs in, either. Did you?" There was no passion to McCluskey's voice, only calmness.

Kerr gave McCluskey a look like he was about to say something more, but in turning to face him he saw something beyond the man that drew his attention to other matters.

His daughter was standing by the rear wagon. Most of the men were pulling water from a well at the edge of the road and topping off the barrels lashed to the side of the lead wagon, but one of them was talking to her. Whatever he said made Madeline mad, and she slapped him. She started toward where he and Zander McCluskey stood, her steps quick and angry. The man she had left behind laughed loudly at her.

McCluskey was a man who, to all impressions, never spent any energy that he didn't have to. He was slow and languid in his movements, almost lazy at times, as if the heat of desert made him sluggish or reluctant to spend his reserves. His life pace seemed, like the careful cadence of his speech and his gestures, nothing more than a long, slow siesta spent rocking in a hammock in the shade on a hot afternoon. But in contrast to the rest of him, his eyes always were alive and bright, sharp and questioning. He turned to see what Kerr was looking at and took in the situation at a glance. His eyebrows lowered slightly, and the faint frown formed.

"I've had enough of this," Kerr said. "I'm going to give that man a piece of my mind and then I'm going to fire him."

"I wouldn't do that if I were you," McCluskey said. "Bull's touchy and he might take it wrong."

"Take it wrong?" Kerr almost choked on the words and his voice cracked. A faint bubble of froth appeared at one corner of his mouth, sticking to both lips and stretching and contracting like a web with each movement of his mouth.

It didn't take Madeline long to cover the distance to them, her yellow dress swishing over the sand with every stride. She stormed up and stopped in front of them. Her face was flushed red. The cloth sunbonnet she wore had fallen off her head and hung by its tie strings. Her blond hair where it was braided and pinned high in a coil had come undone in places, and strands of it lay sweat-damp against her brow and neck.

"What did he do?" her father asked.

"That man . . ." She drew a deep breath and pointed behind her. "That man . . . he . . . he . . ."

"I told you to leave the girl at home," McCluskey said.

"I'll put an end to this." Her father started back to the wagons.

McCluskey took hold of Kerr by an upper arm and stopped him. "Let me handle it."

"Unhand me," Kerr snapped. "I'll have him horse-whipped is what I'll do."

McCluskey let go of Kerr and looked to Madeline. The slump in his shoulders shaped him like a long, thin hook. "What did he do to you?"

Even with him standing stooped over like he was, the top of her head came barely to his chin. When she looked up at him her blue eyes were open wider than normal and beads of sweat dotted her trembling upper lip. "The audacity of that filthy man! Like I would have anything to do with the likes of him."

"He insulted you? How?" McCluskey asked.

"That's the second time he's followed me and tried to catch me alone. Father, do something."

"Did he lay a hand to you?" McCluskey asked.

She waved a hand to pass the cigarette smoke away from her face and gave a disgusted scoff. "No, but he said things."

"What did he say?"

"He asked me to take a walk with him tonight after we make camp. And he said other things that I won't repeat." She put both hands on her hips and glared from one to the other of them as if she was daring either of them to take issue with her accusation.

"Hmm." McCluskey stared at her.

"Do you hear that, McCluskey?" her father asked.

"Miss Madeline, why don't you go back to the wagons and sit with Marshal Tillerman?" McCluskey said. "I'll have a talk with Bull."

Madeline looked back to her father. "That man scares

me. Every time I look up, he's watching me. And he's not the only one."

"Bull may not have the best manners in the world, but I assure you he's harmless," McCluskey said. "It's nothing but a misunderstanding."

"There was no misunderstanding," she spat at McCluskey. "He propositioned me like I'm some common . . . some common trollop."

Marshal Tillerman could be seen at the end of the rear wagon, shading his eyes with one hand and looking at them.

McCluskey cleared his throat. "Go over there with the marshal, and I'll have a talk with Bull."

"I think he should be horsewhipped like Papa says." Madeline glared at him, and then at her father. She gave a huff and spun on her heels and stalked away.

"I hired those men on your say-so," Kerr said when his daughter was away from them.

"They're a little rough around the edges, but you can't find anybody with angel wings to skin mules and bust their backs for day wages," McCluskey said. "Besides that, they're all good men."

"They're a foul-mouthed bunch of ruffians."

"I told you not to bring her. What did you expect? This here's no Sunday picnic. No place at all for schoolgirls." McCluskey gave Kerr a level look.

Kerr sighed. "We never expected to have another child so late in life. I guess I've spoiled Maddy since her mother died, but what do I know about raising a girl?"

The merchant banker, hair already gone white and with his skin beginning to show liver spots and the papery texture of the elderly, truly looked far too old to have sired such a young girl. And where he had been angry before, he now seemed suddenly tired.

"She'd have stayed behind if you put your foot down," McCluskey said.

"You don't know my Maddy."

"I'll talk to Bull and the rest of them. Everything will be all right."

"I'm paying their wages, and you tell them I won't tolerate any more of their antics."

"It would help if you told her to stick close to you or the marshal," McCluskey said. "Her prancing and prissing around the camp is only going to cause more trouble."

"How dare you blame her."

"I'm not blaming her. I'm just trying to make you understand. We need those men."

"So you keep telling me, although I think we could have done this ourselves."

"That why you let the marshal come along?"

Kerr scowled at him. "Marshal Tillerman's married to my niece."

"His cut's coming out of your share, you remember that."

Kerr's lips formed a straight, tight line, like he didn't like to be reminded of that, but he nodded. "Fifty-fifty, you and me."

"I think it was a damned fool thing, letting him come," McCluskey said.

"I only offered him a pittance. Let him hand over his hundred dollars like he was really something. He's a proud old fool. Never has had any sense when it came to making money or keeping it," Kerr said. "Only reason he got his marshal job is because of me and the Judge. I guess I'm in a habit of trying to keep a roof over his head."

"Your loss, not mine."

"We don't know what we'll find. Somebody could have already found the ship years ago and carried away anything worth the trouble."

"I never promised you anything except that I saw the ship, plain as day."

"I wish you had given it a closer look."

"Easy for you to say. I'll remind you, I was in a pretty poor shape at the time. And besides, the ship's half-buried."

"We'll dig it up," Kerr said with some passion returning to his voice. "Whatever it takes."

Among the supplies and equipment in the wagons were picks, shovels, buckets, wheelbarrows, and all manner of rope, pulleys and sheaves and other lifting gear. Both men had discussed in detail what might be needed to expose the ancient bowels of the sailing vessel, and Kerr's warehouses and store in San Bernardino had supplied the equipment and tools, the same as his freight yards had supplied the wagons and mules.

"I saw you reading again last night," McCluskey said. "I told you those papers won't help you. Charlie Fusse was wrong. I've seen the ship, and he wasn't close, not even after all the years he looked."

"Still . . ." Kerr hesitated and seemed to consider his words carefully.

McCluskey continued, taking advantage of the pause, "You never said how you got hold of Fusse's papers."

"I helped outfit his third expedition. Grubstaked him another time before he gave up looking," Kerr said almost reluctantly, as if it was something he didn't want to admit.

"And what did you get out of it?"

Kerr shrugged. "I took his journal and all of his notes when he got back the third time."

McCluskey slapped Kerr on the shoulder. "We're going to get it this time. Forget about what Fusse said. He was nothing but a con man. If what I hear is true, he never went the same way out on the desert twice and acted like he was lost half the time. Just an old prospector working anyone he could for a grubstake."

"Don't know why I brought them with me," Kerr said. "I guess I figured I might learn something. Get a feel for what we're doing and what we might find."

"I took my landmarks real good. I know how to get back to the ship." McCluskey slapped him again on the shoulder.

Kerr looked down at his shoulder where McCluskey had touched him and frowned. He did not like hands to be laid on him. "Now that we're out here, I'd feel better if you told me where you found the ship. Better that both of us know in case something were to happen to one of us."

McCluskey gave a grim chuckle. "No, like I told you before, that ship's my insurance. And I'm going to be the only one that can find it right up to the point we get there."

"You'll talk with the men?" Kerr asked. "It can't happen again."

"They'll behave themselves. Now you go find yourself some shade. Have a cool sip of water while we load out the barrels," McCluskey said as he squinted up at the sun now almost directly overhead. "Going to be a hot one today."

"One more day and we'll be there?"

"Depends. Maybe two."

Kerr headed back, while McCluskey remained where he was for a time, thinking. His shadow was as long and thin as ever, warped where it lay along the sand.

CHAPTER THIRTEEN

The McCluskey-Kerr expedition laid over at the well to wait out the hottest part of the day, the men and livestock taking advantage of whatever shade they could find while George Kerr, his daughter, and Marshal Tillerman rested under a canvas fly stretched from the side of one of the wagons. But Zander McCluskey wasn't resting. He found the man called Bull farthest from the wagons and sitting on a rock beneath the shade of a gnarled and twisted smoke tree.

Bull was only a nickname, but few knew the Swede's real name, or anything much else about him, other than McCluskey. What McCluskey knew made him cautious. Bull was a slow thinker and a slow mover, but that didn't mean he wasn't dangerous.

He was coarse of features, broad nosed with fleshy cheeks, and the heavy ledges of his eyebrows almost folded over and covered his eyes, giving him a piggish look. He was a man who frowned more than he smiled, and took offense easily. Not a fastidious sort by any means, but he liked to keep what little hair he had left shaved down to the skin, a daily ritual he rarely missed. Right then, he was running the razor edge of his skinning knife over his sweaty head. His face was bowed to the ground, his mind seemingly lost in the methodical, rhythmic scraping of the blade passing over his stubbly scalp.

"I told you to leave the girl alone," McCluskey said.

Bull stopped with the knife and rested it on one thigh, finally looking up. McCluskey could see him lightly thumbing the blade near its guard, as if testing the sharpness of the edge, and that testing hinted at other things the Swede might be thinking.

"I don't like how you're talking to me," Bull said.

"I don't give a damn what you like."

A drop of sweat hung for an impossibly long moment off the tip of Bull's sunburned, pox-scarred nose. He was still fondling his knife. A thin red line of blood appeared on his thumb where the edge of the blade had cut it.

"That girl would spit on both of us if she thought she could get away with it," Bull said.

"Stay away from her."

"She knows what she's doing. You've seen it. Give me a little time with her and she won't act so high-and-mighty."

"You thinking on trying that knife?" McCluskey's right hand was already on one of his pistols. "You go ahead and I'll kill your sorry ass right here."

Only four feet separated the two men, not much more than the length of Bull's arm and the knife. The drop of sweat fell from Bull's nose, and he licked at it where it struck his lips. McCluskey remained standing over him for several breaths, his hand still on the gun. A weak gust of wind passed through the smoke tree and the turkey feather in his hat fluttered.

"I'll leave her alone," Bull said.

"You do that. George Kerr asks you to jump, you ask how high and when you can come down," McCluskey said. "That girl comes sashaying by you and batting her eyes, you tip your hat and go the other way. You do your work and keep your mouth shut, and don't you give Kerr any reason to think you're not as happy as a pig in shit to be working for him. You aren't messing this up."

"I hear you."

"Good." McCluskey backed away a few steps. He was well out of reach of the knife before he turned his back on Bull.

"Can I have the girl when it's time?" Bull called after him, but quiet enough that no one at the wagons could hear.

McCluskey kept walking and didn't answer Bull, but the question did get him to thinking. He hadn't planned on the girl coming along.

Madeline Kerr held a small silver-framed mirror in one hand and was brushing her hair with her other hand when he returned. She paused often to turn her face this way or that, pursing her lips occasionally and changing her facial expressions as she studied her reflection.

Her father fanned himself with his hat. The heat seemed to be getting to him, even in the shade, and his mouth sagged open slightly and his skin seemed more papery and lifeless than ever, as if the juices were slowly being sucked out of him. Something about the old man right then reminded McCluskey of a lizard panting on a hot rock.

"I saw you over there talking with that Swede, the one you call Bull," Kerr said.

McCluskey glanced back at Bull and then his gaze turned on Madeline. "Don't you worry, Miss Kerr. I laid the law down to him. He'll mind his manners from here on out. It was all just a misunderstanding like I said it was."

Madeline glanced at where Bull sat with a disgusted look on her face. "Just keep him away from me."

"Man ought to mind the way he acts around women, but he understands now," McCluskey said. "Never could stand a scoundrel. Shames me that it came to this. A young lady such as yourself shouldn't have to deal with the likes of that."

Madeline nodded primly, but said nothing else and returned her attention to the mirror she held.

"I appreciate it." The old man was still fanning himself with his hat. "There are certain standards for men in my employ, and I will brook no misbehavior, especially where my daughter is concerned."

"Think nothing of it. You believed me when a lot of people didn't. Now you rest easy for a while longer. Come evening we'll move on."

"You get us to the ship and you've more than held up your end of the bargain," Kerr said.

McCluskey put a lot of effort into the smile he gave both father and daughter. "Oh, I'll take you. I start a thing and I'm going to see it all the way to the end. You can't imagine how much thought I've given this."

"Just the same, I'll be glad when we get there. I've thought about this myself for fifteen years or more, and I admit to being more than a little anxious." Kerr tugged his hat back on his head.

It was a nice black dress hat with a wide silk band and a pencil-rolled brim, and made of real beaver and not a cheap blend fur felt. It was the kind of hat a wealthy banker would wear, and had looked new and straight out of the box the day before. But already the old man had sweated through the crown and the band, and the dust was sticking to the damp felt and discoloring it. The hat had lost some of its luster, the same as the pompous edge falling away from its owner, as if both man and hat were slowly disintegrating bit by bit.

McCluskey thought how ridiculous the man was, wearing a hat like that on such a journey. Not enough brim on the hat to block the sun, as fake and pretentious and arrogant as the man himself. McCluskey liked seeing the desert cut the banker down to size.

McCluskey smiled again and nodded. "Won't be long now. Before you know it you'll be safe and sound back home."

"And hopefully a bit richer, eh?" Kerr chuckled.

"That's the plan," McCluskey said. "That's the plan."

CHAPTER FOURTEEN

Newt was hunkered down behind a boulder, using it to rest his elbows while he scanned the desert before him with his G. & S. Merz binoculars. They were good 4x German optics, yet the shimmering heat out on the valley floor messed with the focus and fatigued his eyes so that he could use the glass for only brief moments.

"How long have they been moving?" The Mexican boy, Mateo, came up and sat down beside him. It was the first time the boy had spoken to him or approached him alone.

Newt glanced at the sun, then studied the moving line of the treasure party in the distance without using the binoculars. The wagons were at least two or three miles beyond Indian Well, and that distance pushed beyond the magnification limits of his binoculars. Through the lenses, the wagons appeared as blurry white blotches among the drab tans and browns of the desert. It was easier to make out the dust cloud churned by the rolling wagon wheels and hooves than it was to make out the wagons.

"They broke camp less than an hour ago," Newt said, and offered the boy his binoculars.

Mateo shook his head, refusing the loan of the optics.

"I figured you were sleeping like the rest of them." Newt looked lower down the ridge to the small copse among the rocks and an almost-level pad of ground where his gelding and the rest of their horses stood unsaddled and resting hipshot and three-legged. Mr. Smith was the only person visible, the rest of them probably among the rocks where shade could be found.

"Their wagons are heavy." Unlike his father, Mateo's English had little to no Spanish accent, but there was a hint of something else.

Newt gave Mateo a careful look.

Mateo must have interpreted the questioning look for what it was. "They will go slower now. Big wagons, loaded heavy. Did you see how their wheel tracks bit deep into the road this morning? And now they hit the sand. Mules will grow tired. Hard pull."

As the boy said, a stretch of blow sand and low dunes stretched across the stage road before the wagons. Each of those two wagons was pulled by a four-up team of good mules, but even four stout mules would find it hard pulling on such sandy ground. Six-up hitches would have been better for that country, and Newt was surprised that George Kerr, who they said owned a freighting company, would not have planned accordingly.

"They ought to find a way around those dunes and then work their way back to the road," Newt said.

Mateo nodded again. "The sand moves with the wind. One time the dunes are there, and when you come back they in another place."

At first Newt assumed Mateo to be in his teens, but he was reconsidering that. It was hard to tell. Mateo's sombrero brim shaded half his face. His wore an oversized white shirt and a red-and-black-striped wool serape rolled up and worn over one shoulder and across his body with the ends belted at the waist of his baggy pants. That loose clothing hid as much detail as the hat. In fact, everything about him was nondescript and shapeless, the kind of kid that never drew a second look, half-hidden without effort, and at the periphery of everything. But Newt waited until the boy looked his way again and noticed the measuring dark eyes under the shadow of the hat, the sharp angles and determined set to his face, and the square, level jaw-line and skin the color of oiled mahogany. He wore his hair long and bobbed off bluntly at his shoulders. His facial features reminded Newt of an Indian more than anything. He guessed the boy's mother was Indian, for his father had none of those looks.

"They move at night," Mateo said.

"Cooler that way," Newt replied. "Or maybe they wanted to wait awhile and see if anyone was following them."

Mateo shrugged.

"Where will they stop next?" Newt asked.

Mateo thought for a moment before answering. "Depends on whether or not they stay on the stage road."

"And if they don't stick to the trail?"

"There's a cutoff once they get through those dunes," Mateo said. "The Southern Pacific built a big depot and hotel. It's where they load their engines with water."

Newt put his binoculars in their case and scooted back from his vantage point. The sun was low atop the Santa Rosa Mountains by the time he walked into their camp. Mateo left him and went to the horses.

Fred Remington sat on his saddle, rubbing some oil on his rifle. He gave Newt a mischievous grin. "Our sentinel returns."

Mr. Smith was sitting cross-legged with his heels under

142   *Brett Cogburn*

him on a flat patch of ground inspecting his war clubs. The tattooed warrior had removed his suit coat and carefully folded it and set it aside. His shirtsleeves were rolled up to his elbows revealing that his massive forearms were also covered in an intricate web of tattoos. No doubt the Mohave was aware of Newt's presence, but he didn't look up, intent on his work. Newt leaned against a big rock and watched.

The two war clubs were different in style and shape. One was a short weapon with a straight, thick handle and an enlarged, four-inch-diameter cylinder or knot on its end. It was all carved from a single piece of wood, and looked like nothing so much as an overgrown potato smasher. The end of the club's knot had been burned out or carved out to make it concave, and the edge around that cupped depression sharpened. It was painted or dyed a dark red, and the handle black. The other club was a simple, straight stick about two inches thick and about two-and-a-half-feet long, all painted black, and with the same wrist loop built into it.

At that moment, Mr. Smith spied something on the potato masher that he didn't like and rubbed at the spot with a handful of sand. It dawned on Newt that the Mohave was cleaning bits of gore from the knotted end of the club.

Mr. Smith looked up and saw Newt watching him. He hefted the potato masher before him. *"Halyawhai,"* he said, and then he reached and picked up the straight club beside him and held it up for Newt to see, as well. *"Tokyeta."*

Both clubs looked to be made from some dense hardwood, and without handling them, Newt guessed that the wood was mesquite. "Nasty bits of business you've got there."

"Some carry only the *halyawhai* when we go to war,

and some only the *tokyeta*. I carry both," Mr. Smith said
with something like a hint of pride.

"Mohave warriors, you mean?"

"*Kwanamis*, what my people call brave men. It is the
old way. The way it was when we were strong."

Newt looked away and located Mr. Smith's saddle lying
on the ground near the horses. The stock of some kind of
rifle stuck out of a scabbard on that saddle. He tilted his
head toward the rifle.

"Old ways are good, but I see you've also got a rifle,"
Newt said.

Mr. Smith's eyes gleamed and a grin almost formed on
his mouth. "Yes, I have a gun, but it is much better to be
close to your enemies. The *kwanamis* know the warrior's
way, to look our enemy in the eyes and to strike true."

Mr. Smith took a club in each hand. First, he mocked a
quick, stabbing, uppercut stroke with the potato masher.
It was plain to Newt that the Mohave was pantomiming
driving the club up into the chin or face of an enemy. Next,
the he raised the straight club above his head and made a
downward slashing strike.

"Each requires a different way of fighting," Mr. Smith
added.

Newt thought of the kind of power a man the size of the
Mohave could put behind those clubs. And he remembered
the sickening crunch of the potato smasher caving in the
man's face in the trading post. Simple weapons, yes, a con-
cept old as mankind. Little boys and little girls know it
from the time they are born. Pick up a stick and whack
something with it. Simple but deadly.

Mr. Smith stood and Newt saw that what he thought
had been some kind of leather suspenders to hold up the
man's pants were actually a shoulder harness. Mr. Smith

tucked the clubs away, one low under each armpit with the handles hanging just below his beltline. At a glance, it appeared that some kind of spring steel retention clips held each club in place, the weapons snapping into those keepers, and the whole rig working similar to shoulder holsters for pistols. Newt tried to spot any sign of the clubs when Mr. Smith had rolled his sleeves back down and once more donned his suit coat, but the bulk of the man and the length and the cut of the coat concealed any hint of their presence, almost as if the garment had been specifically tailored for such.

"Like you say, Mr. Jones, those are interesting weapons. Quite deadly in the right hands, and almost beautiful in a way," Remington said, and then patted the stock of his rifle. "But I'll stick to the modern. I can't hide it under a coat, but I'll take a good, accurate rifle every time."

Newt paid closer attention to the rifle on the artist's lap. "Heard of those Remington-Lees, but I haven't seen one before. Bolt action, isn't it?"

Remington smiled proudly and propped the rifle butt up on one thigh. He cammed the bolt open and slid it back to reveal the inside of the action. "It's a new preproduction prototype, an improvement on their 1882 model. As a favor to me, they trimmed down the forearm and shortened the barrel to twenty-four inches. More of a sporting model flavor, you know, and not quite so heavy as the military ones. I was hoping to get a chance to take a deer or maybe a bear with it."

Remington saw Newt's interest in the firearm and handed it to him. Newt worked the bolt open and closed a few times, and then shouldered the rifle and sighted on several targets.

"How does it load?" Newt asked.

Remington pitched a small, blued steel box to Newt, who caught it on the fly.

"Removable magazine," Remington said. "You snap it in the bottom of the gun."

Newt could see the top cartridge in the magazine, a fat .45-70 round. "How many does it hold?"

"Five."

"A full-length Winchester holds more than that."

"But I can load mine ten times faster. As soon as I fire my last shot, I press that release there and drop the empty magazine and snap a new one in as quick as that." Remington held up a canvas bandolier with pouches along a portion of its length that looked shaped to hold more magazines. "I have several spares."

It was a novel design, far different from the lever-action rifles with fixed tube magazines that Newt favored. "How does it shoot?"

"Marvelous."

Newt hid his skepticism of the tenderfoot's marksmanship abilities. "I thought you said you didn't have anything to do with E. Remington & Sons."

"I said that it is owned by a cousin, but I never said we weren't on good terms," the artist said. "As soon as I wrote him and told him I was going west again, he sent me the rifle and requested that I field-test it and write back to him. And he also sent me a fine, nickel-plated pistol. Would you care to see it as well? I have it in one of my saddlebags. I don't know why I'm not wearing it. I've already seen a very large rattlesnake over there in those rocks, and that leads me to believe a sidearm would be most handy as long as we are in a country so rife with poisonous snakes."

"No, that's all right," Newt said.

He didn't say it, but he would rather Remington keep the pistol where it was. A pistol was much easier to accidentally point at your body than a rifle was, due to its shorter length, and the last thing they needed was for the tenderfoot to shoot his foot off or maim someone else playing with his pistol.

Newt scolded himself. Maybe he was too harsh. Greenhorn or not, Remington was bearing up well and seemed comfortable roughing it up to that point, as if he might have truly spent some time in wild country or in a camp setting or two. A hot wait in the rocks with little shade and nothing to drink but lukewarm canteen water put most people in a foul mood, but Remington seemed as jovial as ever.

"The more I think about it, the more I think I'll retrieve my new revolver and dispatch that snake," Remington said right when Newt was just starting to think he might be more competent than he seemed.

"Don't go popping your pistol," Newt said. "You might consider that those we're following would hear your shot."

"Oh?" Remington said sheepishly. "I hadn't thought of that."

"Ah, boys and their toy guns," Poker Alice said as she came out of the ring of rocks to join them. She was brushing sand from her skirt and carrying her bedroll blanket over one arm, likely having used it to lie down on or as a sunshade while she napped.

"Not so," Newt said. "Mr. Smith here was just telling us how he favors playing with sticks. Keeps a pair of them tucked up inside his coat."

"Yes, Mr. Smith can be most abrupt when it comes to use of his *sticks*, as you call them," she said. "I've known a few bartenders and bouncers who were good with a bung or a slapjack, but Mr. Smith seems to consider striking men over the head an art. I'd say you two should get along quite well."

Newt handed the rifle back to Remington. "Best we saddle up."

"Is it time?" Poker Alice asked.

"No hurry," Newt answered. "We can move down to the well and water the stock. By the time we finish it'll be dark, and let Kerr and his bunch get a little farther on their way."

Mr. Smith began to saddle her horse and his own without her telling him to. Newt did the same for the Circle Dot horse, and then helped Mateo put the packsaddle and mochilas on the burro and load Pablo's gear. By the time they were finished the rest of them were saddled and mounted.

They wound their way single file down the mountain ridge in the growing dusk, and it was almost true dark by the time they rode up to the well. It was a good well, and someone in the past had gone through a lot of trouble to dig it and to line the edge of it with mortared stones. A single, broken adobe wall was the only remains of another stage station, and it was barely visible a little upslope of the well in the last of the fading light.

There was a rope and a bucket, and a hollowed-out half of a cottonwood log for a trough. Newt and Mr. Smith took turns pulling water and pouring it into the trough while the horses drank. Remington and Poker Alice filled the canteens, while Pablo and Mateo stood a short distance away looking down the stage road to the south where Kerr's party had gone.

Newt bathed his face with a damp cloth and noted the

sliver of moon overhead. There wasn't going to be much moonlight, and that was a good thing.

"I'm hungry," Remington said.

Newt retrieved a small sack of venison jerky from his saddlebags and offered it to Remington, who took a piece and handed the sack back. The jerky was dry and hard, made in thin slabs that resembled nothing so much as pieces of tree bark. The texture was much the same. The deer meat the jerky was made from had a rank, gamy flavor, not at all masked by an extraordinarily heavy dose of red pepper seasoning.

Newt stuffed one end of a piece in his mouth and began to chew gingerly, waiting for his saliva to make the jerky soft enough to chew. He could hear Remington's jaws popping as he worked to chew his piece. The sack of jerky soon went to the others, and they stood for a time, not talking and everyone gnawing at the tough meat and washing it down with well water.

"Thanks, but please don't take this wrong," Remington said after he had finished his piece of jerky. "Next time I won't ask you to do the cooking. That was positively awful."

Newt chuckled. "Bought it from a pair of Basque sheepherders I met on my way to San Bernardino. I thought they were being friendly, but now I know why they sold it to me."

"I think I broke a tooth," Remington said.

Mr. Smith's square-cut jaws worked methodically at his third piece, and when he was finished he took a slug from his canteen. He found that there was no more jerky left and handed the empty sack back to Newt.

"Here, you can have the rest of mine," Poker Alice said.

"Mr. Smith doesn't seem to mind the jerky," Remington said.

"You don't like?" Mr. Smith asked.

Though they couldn't see Mr. Smith very well in the growing darkness, they could hear him clench the last piece in his teeth and rip off the end of it.

"That stuff's horrible,' Remington replied. "You actually like it?"

Mr. Smith grunted and shrugged. "Good meat, but it needs more pepper."

A half hour later they rode on, moving the horses at a walk, wary lest they travel too fast and come upon Kerr's treasure party. Newt was fifty yards ahead and nearing the stretch of sand dunes when he thought he heard something off to his left. And when he jerked his head that way he thought for the briefest instant that he saw a moving shadow flickering through the brush where the sound came from. But if it was really anything at all, it was gone now. He had his horse stopped and was still looking in that direction when the rest of them caught up to him.

"What is it?" Remington asked.

"I don't know. Something moved out there. Coyote, maybe, or some other critter."

After a time of searching the dark and listening, he led them on into the sand dunes. None of the ridges of sand were very tall, most of them no bigger than knee-high, and the tallest of them head-high. But the sand was powdery fine and the horse's hooves sank deep. Even at a walk, Newt could feel the Circle Dot horse beneath him having to work a little harder than normal.

"They had to dig here and then they laid down boards for the wheels," Mr. Smith said.

Newt didn't know how the Mohave could read sign in the dark. The next dune was the tallest and widest yet, more of a sand hill with scattered grass and brush growing on it and the sand much more firmly packed. Mr. Smith stopped in front of it.

Newt dismounted and the two of them scrambled to the top of the low hill. Later, the others joined them, not dismounting but spurring and lashing their mounts up the slope.

It was the last of the blow sand, and before them, under the faintest of moonlight, the desert stretched flatly on to the east for what seemed like forever. They could see lights not far ahead.

"That's Indio," Pablo said in a hushed voice. "Those are the lights of the depot and the hotel."

"Hotel?" Poker Alice said. "Now you're talking."

"No," Newt said.

"What?" she asked.

"We don't know if Kerr stuck to the stage road or if he decided to spend the night yonder. He sees us riding in and he's going to know we're after the same thing he is."

She sighed. "I suppose you want me to sit out here in the dark all night."

"We wait."

She clucked her tongue. "And just when we were starting to get along so well."

"I'll go have a look," Mr. Smith said, and then he was gone in the night.

They watched the lights of Indio, none of them talking. After a time Mr. Smith returned.

"They are not far ahead of us. I could hear them," Mr. Smith said.

"That close?" Newt said very quietly, knowing how far

a voice could carry on a still night. "It must have taken them longer than I thought to get through this little patch of sand."

Remington struck a match, the flash of the flame was bright in the instant before he cupped it in his hand and started it toward the bowl of the pipe he clenched between his jaw teeth.

"Put that out!" Newt hissed.

The artist shook out the match. "You don't really believe somebody could see that little flame, do you? I think you are being a bit overly cautious."

Newt started to tell him how far you could see such a flash of fire in open country, but he decided not to. It was a foolish thing to have done, but maybe he was worrying too much. Someone would have had to have been looking in their direction in the exact instant the match was struck and before Remington put it out. Still, it bothered him.

"There was a soldier I saw down in Mexico who used to think like you do," Newt said. "Lit him a cigarette while he was on sentry duty and an Apache shot off three fingers on his right hand."

"You've been around Apaches?" Remington asked. "I read in the newspapers last week that Geronimo is off the reservation again and that the army is preparing to go after him. I have written letters requesting an assignment as a correspondent to cover the campaign."

"Old Gok is off the reservation again, is he?" Newt said. "Well, if he is, the army will have a hard time catching him. That's for sure."

"You know of Geronimo?"

"I met the old devil once."

"You've actually met him?"

"Go back down behind the dune if you want to smoke your pipe."

"Were you in the army when they caught him the last time?"

"No, I went to Mexico after some lost boys. By the time I left I didn't know why I was down there."

"You're full of surprises, Mr. Jones. We should talk more," Remington said. "What did he look like? Geronimo, I mean."

Instead of answering him, Newt led the Circle Dot horse back down the dune the way they had come.

Remington turned to Mr. Smith beside him. "Is he mad at me? He seems mad."

Mr. Smith shook his head. "When I was younger, if we were on a raid I would have beaten you for what you did."

The Mohave went the way Newt had, followed by the two Mexicans and the pack mule. Remington and Poker Alice were left atop the dune.

"Your man was joking, wasn't he?" Remington asked her.

"Mr. Smith has never shown much of a sense of humor," she said.

The artist was the last one to leave the dune. The shadowy shape of his tall pith helmet skylined in the faint moonlight made his head seem overly tall and awkward, and he was mumbling to himself.

CHAPTER FIFTEEN

Less than a mile on the other side of the dunes Zander McCluskey sat his horse watching his back trail. If the night hadn't been so dark a stranger would have been able to tell that his searching was as much a habit as it was a result of a cautious nature, and that it wasn't the first time he had felt pursued over the course of his life. He was both a man who knew how to hunt, and a man that had been hunted.

The tiny flash of light didn't last but for the briefest instant, but still, he saw it. He thought about that light, questioned whether he had really seen it, and then speculated on its source.

Bull was driving the hind wagon and he stopped beside McCluskey. "You see something?"

They spoke in hushed voices.

"I think somebody out there struck a match," McCluskey said.

"A match?"

"You don't believe me?"

"I didn't say that."

"You remember when those two Polacks were waiting for me in the storeroom to put a shank in me?"

"I remember. You're lucky they didn't kill you. Bloodied you good before you did for the both of them."

"You know why they didn't kill me?"

"*Ja*, because they were dumb Polacks."

"No, because they left the storeroom door cracked open so they could see me coming, and when I saw that I knew they were waiting for me."

"It didn't hurt that you bribed the guards and had a chunk of water pipe buried in the yard. A bit of pipe is handy, *ja*, when you're outnumbered like that."

"What matters is that I pay attention to the details, and I know a damned match fire when I see one."

"Who do you think is out there? Somebody following us?"

"Could be. You drive on into Indio and get us settled in for the night."

"What are you going to do?"

"I'm going to wait here and see if anybody comes along. If somebody's following us, I aim to know it." McCluskey's saddle creaked as his horse shifted its stance.

"I could wait with you. We could kill them if there aren't too many."

"You want to do your killing with that station right there?"

"I was only offering to help."

"Let me do the worrying." McCluskey shifted his weight to one stirrup to ease the ache in his joints. "If you see any of the boys you tell them I want to talk to them."

"They'll all be at Bitter Spring."

"You don't know that. Do like I said."

Bull gathered his ribbons in one hand and took hold of

the wheel brake with the other. "Let me have the girl when it's time. You can have my cut."

"You'd trade your cut for the girl?" McCluskey didn't need to ask that. He knew his old cellmate's weaknesses. Bull was a sick man when it came to women, and those twisted tendencies were going to get him hung one day. A rope around his neck was what he deserved, if any man deserved anything. But it would be a bloody world, indeed, if everyone got what they deserved the moment they deserved it. They all had it coming, one way or the other.

"Think on it." Bull disengaged the wheel brake and chucked softly to the mule team to get the wagon rolling, leaving McCluskey in the trail behind him.

McCluskey watched the point in the distance where he thought he had seen the match flare. He wanted a cigarette badly, but he wouldn't make the same mistake that whoever was out there had. It was the little things that you couldn't overlook. The tedious minutiae that sometimes didn't seem so important at first could train-wreck the best-laid plans. Something new could pop up when you least expected it or when you weren't paying attention. Most men had no discipline, following their impulses without thinking. They weren't careful and were the kind that ended up raped or stabbed to death in a prison storeroom or caught by some posse. He had made his own mistakes, and paid for every one of them. He wasn't going to make any this time. He was due for a payday and nothing was going to stop him from getting it. He needed only a few more days, that was all.

He ran over the plan again in his mind, savoring it and looking for weaknesses. He had laid the trap so carefully.

A coyote yipped somewhere out on the desert. Another answered it from afar. He listened attentively and relaxed.

It was not quite peace he felt, but something as close to it as he ever got.

Some people despised coyotes, but he had always admired them in a way. They could live almost anywhere. He had been a lot of places, but never one where there weren't coyotes. Woodlands, plains, mountains, deserts, cold country or hot, they thrived, living off nothing but their own wits. Hunters always, and scavengers when they needed to be. You had to admire that kind of flexibility. A wolf or a bear might starve to death in hard times, but not a coyote.

Not the biggest or the strongest or the meanest, but they were the best survivors he knew. They were smart. That was their trick. You could see that intelligence in their eyes and by the posture of their slinking walk, as if they saw everything and measured what they saw against some scale or yardstick of their own devising. They could work alone or in packs, knowing that you sometimes needed help for bigger prey. Always hungry and always looking for a way to feed that hunger. Cunning. Dumb ones didn't live to breed.

Coyotes. He thought of the few times his father had taken him along for companionship on his various *trips*. The man had been inconsistent in his desire to spend time with his children, most likely due to his tendency to disappear for weeks at a time to play cards with the soldiers in some hog ranch saloon or half out of his mind on the poppy and laid up with some lice-infested, diseased whore. His father wasn't a dependable or steady man, a thing that had worried his mother to an early grave and resulted in the trips coming to an end and he and his two younger siblings often being left alone on a Kansas homestead where they were expected to fend for themselves until their father returned. Zander was only ten years old at that time, the youngest child, the baby sister, was three.

To a young mind, the trips with his father, while they lasted, were desirable but also usually confusing, and not solely due to their random and infrequent nature. Reflecting on those excursions, he still didn't know what to make of some of them.

On one such trip they had traveled cross-country in a sleet storm for two days toward Fort Scott near the Missouri border, only to arrive at a farm in the middle of nowhere long after sundown. The younger version of himself had been shocked at the gathering of saddle horses, buggies, and wagons outside a large barn. It was not a place that should have drawn such a crowd, especially in bad weather and so late at night.

Lanterns had been lit inside the barn, and that lighting revealed a low-sided ring with rough-sawn lumber bleachers on one side of it. Thirty or more men stood gathered round or sat in the bleachers. Tobacco and corn liquor were in abundant supply, and the banter between the men was ribald but friendly. No women were present.

During the course of the night, he was to learn that the ring was referred to as *the pit*, and various animals were brought to it. In the first two hours game roosters fought against each other. The men managing the pit called out the rules of engagement prior to each fight, including how the roosters would be armed for combat. The birds' natural leg spurs above each foot did not provide suitable bloodshed or death to suit the bettors. There were curved spikes of different lengths that he learned were called gaffs, and knives that could be secured to the roosters' legs, all made of sharp steel. Growing up on a farm, he had occasionally been flogged by a foul-tempered barnyard rooster, but never would have guessed until then that weapons would be provided to fighting fowl. He would have been no less shocked if chickens bearing guns came marching into the pit.

Money exchanged hands as bets were made and then the handlers went through various rituals to make sure the birds were "on the fight." This done, the roosters were cast together. Sometimes they danced a circle around each other before engaging, their slender necks raised up high with the steel-sheened neck feathers standing straight out like ruffed manes, beady eyes brooking no mercy. And sometimes they went immediately at each other. The end result was always the same. They pecked at each other's heads as quick as the jab of any boxer, and they would flap their wings to get the elevation to put their feet in play. In a blur of motions and a tiny cloud of dust, one or both roosters stabbed away, sometimes puncturing each other multiple times in a single pass before returning to the ground. Feathers flew and little specks of blood freckled the spectators leaning close over the pit. Once the loser had succumbed to a mortal blow, the victor often pounced upon its body and continued to maim it until its handler pulled it away. Sometimes both birds died in the pit, and many of the victors were in poor shape and on the verge of death themselves. The handlers were careful, lest their bird wound them. Many of the roosters knew no loyalty when it came to their masters, no matter how much they might be praised after success on the battlefield.

And then came the dogs. No two were alike. There were curs and feists and terriers and hounds, and all manner of crossbreeds, some picked for their aggression and some bred up over many generations specifically for it. Once in the pit, they snarled and growled at the end of their chains, jerking their handlers forward as they strained to get at each other. When released they were savage in their struggle. Roosters bled, but nothing like dogs.

Sometimes the fight ended when one of the dogs turned tail and tried to escape or was obviously beaten and putting up little defense, and sometimes a dog's handler surrendered the match to save his animal. The handlers used thick sticks of wood to pry the dogs' mouths open when a fight was at a stalemate or the winner wouldn't let go of its victim. One handler used a different technique and shoved his finger inside his dog's rectum to get it to let go. He learned all kinds of things that night, things he would consider for many days afterward.

Occasionally the fight was to the death. Several crippled dogs were taken outside the barn and shot to end their suffering. A squat, scarred bulldog missing one eye was invincible on that night, winning two fights. The men in the crowd bragged on his prowess and debated the finer points of his anatomy and spirit that allowed him to be so successful: strength, strong jaws, loose hide that kept his opponents' teeth from his muscles and bone, a willingness to fight on a moment's notice, the instinct to go for the throat, and all manner of things both subtle and easily apparent. Zander understood from their tone that many of the things they admired in the bulldog were the same things they admired in men.

Somewhere into the night Zander noticed another boy about his age staring at him from the far side of the pit. He was the only other boy there, and his gaze was intent and mysterious. For a moment, Zander wondered if he and the boy had been purposefully brought to the barn and would be made to fight.

And then they brought in the coyote in a wire cage. She

was a small female who looked not to have eaten or drunk since her confinement. Her thick winter pelt was matted with feces and one front foot was bandaged where she had been caught in a steel trap. She could not be trusted to stay within the confines of the pit, so a long length of grass rope was left trailing from her collar with the other end tied to the pit wall when she was freed from the cage. A large, leopard cur male with two blue eyes and weighing about fifty pounds was first set against her. The bitch coyote would have weighed no more than twenty or twenty-five pounds. She backed against the wall with her ears flattened against her head, and her eyes darted all around her and at the men above her.

The cur tried her immediately, coming head-on and misinterpreting her stance against the pit wall as cowering. She bared her teeth and snapped him twice on the side of his face, sending him back across the pit. He would not try her again, and only stood there barking at her. Men laughed at both the cowardly dog and its owner.

The leopard cur was removed and another dog was brought into the pit. This time it was a black-and-tan that was at least half hound. It had no better luck than the cur, but it did bark louder after the coyote bitch had ripped half of one of its ears off. Its bawling bark reverberated in the confines of the barn.

Some of the men who had brought dogs briefly conversed about the matter. After their talk, two large dogs with grizzled, brindle coats like wolfhounds were brought to the pit. They looked like littermates, and their eyes were a deep gold and intense with calm fury.

More money changed hands. Most bet on how long the coyote would last set against two such dogs, and nobody considered that it could win. They were right.

Outnumbered, the coyote bitch didn't stand a chance, no matter how hard she tried. She fought with her tail and rump tucked to protect her blindside and cover her guts, head on a swivel and teeth snapping. She could bend and contort her spine in any direction to bring her teeth to bear.

The dogs had obviously fought together before, and they came at her from different directions, timing their attacks. She wounded them, but her jaws lacked the strength to stop them. They growled continuously as they tore at her and shook her. Strangely, they even wagged their tails while they killed her. The coyote fought and suffered silently, and she died quietly, too. Not a sound.

After a time, the dogs were pulled off her and led away. There were no more fights, and the men began to gather at the door of the barn. Coats were buttoned, and mufflers wrapped around necks in preparation to go out and load up the fighting animals and hitch the wagons or saddle horses. The barn was eerily silent after the buzz of so many voices and the sounds of maddened animals.

He stayed at the pit for a while watching the coyote lying inside it. For some reason, he climbed over the low wall and went closer to her, glancing once around him to see if anyone noticed.

He had guessed her dead, but was surprised to find the bitch's ribs still heaving weakly, despite her many wounds. He put a hand to her side, fingers splayed, and pushed through her fur to feel the rise and fall of her rib bones to see if it was true. She was hanging on to some last thread of life that she refused to let go of, no matter that her eyes were already growing dim. He watched her carefully and kept his hand on her side. He did not notice one of the men come into the pit beside him until that man shoved him aside and then stomped a boot into her ribs, once and then a second time to collapse her lungs or perhaps to stop her stubborn heart. She wheezed the first time her rib bones popped, and was truly dead under the second blow.

"You want her hide?" the man asked him. "You can skin her if you want."

Zander shook his head that he didn't want the hide, then he left her there and went to find his father. He wanted to ask several things as they rode back toward home, but it was bitter cold and his father was drunk. He didn't think his father had the answers he sought, anyway.

He had come to know things on his own, learned that night or at other times, both before and since, both free and locked away in prison, a place more like the pit in that Kansas barn than anyplace he had ever been. You had to be smart and you had to be cunning, and you had to learn how to fight. Because there came a time when everyone ended up in the pit, one way or the other. Some never got out, and winning and losing weren't always so different. Sometimes all that mattered was how long you lasted.

The coyotes yipped again on the desert, answering one another with their odd, high-pitched songs. That sound brought him back into the moment. He inhaled deeply, sucking in the cool, dry desert air.

"Quiet, brothers," he whispered to them. "I've got thinking to do."

Indio wasn't a town; it was really more of a settlement. The Southern Pacific had built a two-story building that served as a combination train depot and hotel. It was an impressive structure. Long front porches stretched across both levels on the front and faced the tracks. A water tower stood beside those same tracks so that the train engines could pull alongside it and top off their reservoirs.

The water tower made sense, but why the railroad had decided to build a fancy depot and hotel in such an out-of-the-way spot on the desert was anybody's guess. The place's only distinction other than water and a stand of big shade trees was that it was the halfway point between Yuma and Los Angeles. Other than those attributes, it had nothing in its features to recommend it to anyone. The tracks ran into Indio and they ran out, desert all around. Some said the railroad built the structure because the station was so forlorn and far from anywhere that the employees manning the station wouldn't have lasted a day otherwise before they ran off and found themselves another job.

Besides the hotel and depot, there were only a few other buildings. There was a small, frame lumber store that served dual duty as a post office on the same side of the tracks as the depot and hotel, and across the tracks were a saloon, a few homes, sheds, and barns.

McCluskey rode into Indio at a little past midnight, having stood watch in the desert for an hour. He stabled his horse and met Bull and his other two men at the hotel. The Kerrs and Marshal Tillerman had already retired to rented rooms for the night, and the four men stood and talked on the hotel porch bathed in the dim lamplight spilling through the front windows.

The other two men on the porch besides McCluskey and Bull, were a long-jawed older man and a twitchy Mexican who paced while he listened to what McCluskey told them.

"Henry, I want you to ride on to Bitter Spring and tell the boys to move on to Dos Palmas. They can expect us there tomorrow evening or so," McCluskey said to the older one. "I'll tell Kerr you quit and run off on us. Bull and Jorge can handle the wagons without you."

"No need for that." Henry's left eardrum had been shattered by a shotgun fired too close to his ear, and his voice was always louder than he thought it was, far from the whisper the rest of them used. "Bendigo is already waiting for you across the tracks. It's the house with the green door past the livery barn."

"Who's he staying with?"

"Some woman who does laundry for the railroad crews," Henry said.

"I told him to stay at Bitter Spring."

"You know Bendigo, he likes him a woman nearly as much as Bull does. He said he'd leave a lantern burning low on the back porch."

"All right then, get some sleep. Let's have the wagons hitched and ready to pull out of here at first light."

The trio of men left the porch and crossed the tracks and headed to the big barn where their wagons and horses were being kept. None of them liked not being able to take a hotel room, but it wouldn't have looked right for mule skinners and day workers to throw away hard-earned money on luxuries like hotel rooms. Bedrolls spread on a bit of hay would have to serve as their night's beds. But they didn't complain to McCluskey.

After they were gone, McCluskey took a seat in a rocking chair on the porch, giving him a chance to finally smoke a cigarette. His lean face was faintly lit each time he drew on the burning tobacco, his eyes squinted against the smoke. The rocking chair grated back and forth slowly on the gritty porch boards like the strokes of a saw.

He made sure there was no one stirring outside before

he stood and ground out the cigarette butt beneath his boot heel. He left the porch and crossed the tracks, passing in front of the big barn that kept the wagons. His pace was leisurely and slow, like a man out for a stroll when he couldn't sleep. He thought he was alone, but he didn't see Buck Tillerman step out from the door of the barn after he passed.

The marshal truly couldn't sleep, and he had gotten up and gone to the barn to have a nip from the pint bottle of tonic he kept in his saddlebags. Not even his wife knew he imbibed now and then, nor did his priest or his father-in-law, the Judge. He was a man of few secrets, but found solace in that one, private vice, mostly because it was his and his alone.

He paused with the whiskey bottle to his lips and watched McCluskey going down the tracks. He waited long enough to give McCluskey a lead and then set the bottle inside the barn wall on a siding stringer and followed him, walking as quietly as he could, stopping often. Later, he thought he had lost McCluskey in the dark, but then he saw the man's thin shadow lit in the faint flow of a lantern on the back porch of little shanty seventy yards back from the track bed.

There was a fenced garden on the near side of the shanty, kept by the railroad men. The marshal stepped behind a mesquite corner post at the garden fence and watched and waited through the stalks of a scraggly row of okra plants. The lantern went out, and he heard the back door open and close. The door hinges creaked with rust or misalignment.

McCluskey was inside for only a few minutes and then he reappeared on the porch. The marshal couldn't see well, but he thought there was another man with McCluskey.

There was a brief discussion between them, too hushed for the marshal to make out any of the words.

McCluskey headed back for the hotel, and Marshal Tillerman squatted behind the fence post and let him pass. He hadn't moved yet when the other man came out of the shanty and went to a small corral and saddled a horse. He, too, passed close by the marshal, his horse already at a trot. It was too dark for the marshal to get a look at the rider, but he caught a strong whiff of woodsmoke off the man as he went by.

The marshal went back to the big barn. McCluskey must have already gone inside the hotel. There was only a little whiskey left in the bottle, but the marshal took his time finishing it off while he tried to piece together what he had seen and how it fit together. Coming to no conclusions that didn't bother him, he put the bottle away and went back to the hotel.

Behind him, McCluskey stepped from the dark depths of the barn. He had a feeling he was being followed the whole way back from the shanty, and ducked into the barn and waited. It wasn't long until the marshal appeared.

He had watched the marshal drink his whiskey and then climb the hotel steps, and he considered how to handle another unexpected detail. A number of ideas passed through his mind. All of them involved violence, but that was to be expected. Despite the pride he took in his planning, like all such men of his leanings, violence was truly his stock and trade. You had to be smart in the pit if you wanted to live, but no matter what, it was always a fight.

CHAPTER SIXTEEN

In the gray light that comes before true dawn, Poker Alice stood from where she had sat upon the ground and hugged herself with both arms and shivered away the chill that had settled on her for the last few hours. The thin jacket she wore and the blanket draped over her shoulders did little to warm her, and the men had been dead set against building a fire, even if there had been something to fuel a blaze nearby, which there wasn't. Nothing but sand.

"How can a desert be so cold at night? Burning hot one minute and then freezing cold the next," she said.

Newt lay on his belly on the top of the dune that blocked them from being seen by anyone in the direction of Indio. He set aside his binoculars and looked down at her. "Not enough moisture in the air to hold the heat."

"Oh, I know that. It's not really that cold, but I can't shake the chill."

"How long do we wait?" Remington asked. For some reason he was especially chipper and smiling, considering that none of them had slept, unless you counted fitful dozing while reclined against their saddles on the ground.

"Hard to say," Newt replied.

Poker Alice wanted to chastise Newt, although she couldn't say why. Maybe it was because his calmness irritated her as much as his reticence. It made him seem smug, given the circumstances, especially when she felt so uncomfortable and on edge. If he wasn't the most over-confident man she had ever met, he was certainly in the running. He didn't brag and he didn't talk much, but she could see it in him. He was big, true, but was he so foolish as to think that he could beat down every challenge in his path? Such men never listened. Every time she spoke to him his face was like stone, and she was one to know a good poker face when she saw one. And she admitted to herself that she had been purposely goading him almost since they set out, partially to vent her frustrations, but mainly to get some kind of reaction out of him and to bust through his thick shell.

"So, we're going to stay out here all day? Is that it? First you freeze me, and now you're going to roast me as soon as the sun comes up," she threw at him.

"The more I think about this, the more I think it won't work," Remington said. "If all we do is follow them they're going to get to the ship first. I don't see how we beat them to it."

Pablo came over to Remington and squatted on his heels. "I agree with Señor Jones."

"What's that mean?" Poker Alice asked.

The rest of them moved closer, seeing that the livery-man had something to say.

"We wait. When we think they are close and we are sure of the direction they go, we ride fast and have a look before they get there," Pablo said. "If Señor McCluskey saw the ship, then we can see it, too, if we know where to look. That is the secret."

"How are we going to follow them long enough to get in the general vicinity of the ship without them knowing it?" Remington asked. "You can see for miles in this country, especially the farther we go out into this valley."

"Are you ready to quit?" she asked Remington. *Now they were getting somewhere and finally talking things through. Men and their silly posturing.*

"Oh no." Remington grinned. "Success or failure, I wouldn't miss this for the world. I only think we need a better way of going about this."

"What about you?" she asked Newt.

"Pablo, I wish you would quit calling me Mr. Jones," Newt said. "Plain old Newt is good enough."

"You didn't answer my question," Alice said a little testily.

"I'll see how it plays out," Newt answered. "The rest of you can do what you want."

Her eyes narrowed as she kept her gaze on him. There it was again, that attitude that he didn't give a damn. Or was it only an act? "You can deny it all you want, but that old Indian told you something. That's why you're so cocksure. You have an idea where the ship is, don't you?"

He gave her a patronizing look that annoyed her greatly. It was somewhere between a weary smile and an exasperated smirk, as if she were a child and he the all-knowing adult. "Lady, I don't know where it is any more than the rest of you, and I'm not sure about anything. Two days ago I had my mind on going somewhere cool and green. Swore off ever setting foot on another desert, but here I am."

She gritted her teeth. She swore she was going to slap him if he called her *lady* again.

"What about you, Mr. Smith? You haven't said what you think," Remington asked.

Mr. Smith sat on his saddle. He had his shoes off and was polishing them with a rag and a tin can of black polish. He finally looked up at them. "I go where Mrs. Duffield goes, but you are right. McCluskey must be taking them toward the salt flats. It will be hard to follow them there without them knowing it."

Pablo nodded. "*Sí*, that could be where they go. *La playa*, that was heart of the old sea. How do you say? The . . . shoreline . . . is that right? . . . in places you can see where the old shoreline was. There are marks, seashells, and the fish traps of the old ones. Maybe that is where he goes. He will ride to Dos Palmas for water, and then maybe onto the playa."

Alice bit her lower lip, her gaze moving from one man to another and then back to Newt. She hated being indecisive, and she hated the feeling that she knew less than any of them. In a world of men, it was too easy for a woman to be pushed aside. Not speaking up often meant you were run over, but she didn't have the information necessary to make decisions or even to suggest them. She had been widowed and on her own too long to take any kind of orders well, and did not like feeling at the mercy of others, especially arrogant men.

She questioned her decision to pursue Kerr's treasure party, and not for the first time. What had possessed her to go along with four strangers, strangers that she did not or could not trust? Mr. Smith had been loyal since they had come together to form whatever odd partnership they had formed, but she didn't truly know him, not even after two years of each other's company. And even he seemed changed since they had started out after the ship. It was if he was growing wilder with every mile as they went deeper into the desert. He was still as polite and attentive to her as

ever—no failing of his strangely impeccable manners—
but the things he said and the way he carried himself were
noticeably different.

And then there was whatever had happened back at the
trading post at Agua Caliente. None of the men would say
what that was, not even Pablo, who was obviously shaken
by what had occurred. When she had cornered Mr. Smith
about it he had only hinted that it was best she didn't know.
That had only made her think about it more, and her imagination ran to the worst possibilities. For certain, those
Indians had killed someone in that trading post and burned
it to the ground, yet nobody with her spoke of it again.

Freddy Remington seemed harmless and exactly what
he was supposed to be, although she thought he might be
running from something and out on the desert not only to
draw pictures of horses and mountains. She wondered if
she was the only one that had noticed the pale strip of flesh
around the ring finger on his left hand where a wedding
band had likely been not too long ago.

Pablo was friendly and polite with his old-world manners, and had a kind smile and an easygoing disposition.
He lacked the hard edge of Mr. Smith or Newt Jones, but
she also sensed in the little liveryman something that she
couldn't quite frame. You could hide all manner of things
behind a ready smile and good manners. It said something
that he had agreed to partner with a giant Mohave with
tattoos on his face or a scar-faced brawler like Jones so
quickly. He was either a fool, like her, to mix his fate with
strangers, or he thought he could handle whatever might
happen . . . or knew something he thought none of the rest
of them did. Her best guess was that he was no fool.

And then there was Pablo's son, Mateo. He was definitely odd, to say the least. She had tried to get a good look

at him several times, but he kept his hat pulled low and his head down when she tried to meet him eye to eye, and usually he rode at the rear of their procession. He did not give off the impression that he was timid, but instead, that he was very cautious. Often when she would look back she would find that he had stopped in the trail. In those times she might find him facing back the way they had come or staring at something in the distance, as if he was continually afraid he might become lost or that they were somewhere they shouldn't be. Or as if waiting for something or someone.

What she had first thought was a bold move on her part, now was beginning to seem like pure recklessness. It was that same recklessness that had caused her to hand back that drummer's pistol at the resort. It was the same rush she felt when she called or raised a bet and pushed her chips or her money into the middle of a poker table. She should have turned back the moment George Kerr had turned her down.

She knew nothing about deserts, nor did she enjoy "a bit of roughing it" as Freddy called it. Smoky gambling dens and saloons were her world, with a good hotel and room service when she could get it, with a deep tub with hot water and perfumed soap after a long night at the table. There should have been enough adrenaline and challenge in gambling over cards to satisfy even her rebellious spirit.

She frowned at her dirty clothes, and brushed at her skirt where the sweat and grime on her horse's shoulder had soiled the fabric. Only a day on the trail, and already the garment was likely past saving. It was her plainest outfit, a simple brown split riding skirt and a red-and-white-checkered blouse with a high collar and the sleeve ends trimmed in lace and real mother-of-pearl buttons, but

she had paid a St. Louis dressmaker twenty-five dollars to
tailor and sew it for her. She had left her luggage back in
San Bernardino when she and Mr. Smith outfitted themselves for what she had thought at the time would be a
quick jaunt out into the desert, and she had only one other
dress in the valise she carried tied with her bedroll on the
back of her saddle. And she had been careless and forgotten to take her straw hat off before she fell asleep. The
brim of it now had a crease where the woven fibers were
broken past repair and where it would no longer keep
the dashing shape that had caused her to buy it. She knew
she was sometimes frivolous and vain when it came to her
sense of style, but still, it bothered her. Her clothes were
as much a part of her image and her arsenal as the wits she
had been born with. At the rate she was going she would be
dressed in rags by the time she returned to San Bernardino.

Such sacrifice required a payoff, and the farther she
went on this journey, the more she doubted there was any
chance of success. Right at that moment, she could be playing cards and making money, instead of chasing around the
wild country and ruining good clothes.

She sat down on the ground and began to unlace one of
her high-topped shoes. The sand had gotten inside it and
was chaffing her foot. She frowned at Newt while she
worked at the shoe, thinking again on what the old Cahuilla
might have told him. There was that, the main reason she
didn't have Mr. Smith saddle her horse and the two of them
leave right then.

Gamblers won when they played smart and stuck to
what they knew. Get the other fellow to play your game.
That was the ticket that always put you at an advantage.
Either know you have the winning hand and play the cinch
bet, or play with the odds in your favor. Now she found

herself in a game that was new to her, whose rules she was not even sure of.

She thought of the Southern Pacific depot not far beyond the dunes. She could likely get on a train and be in San Bernardino by sundown. Come tomorrow, she could be in Los Angeles or San Francisco—a sea breeze, good food, clean sheets, a little chat over lunch with a handsome man, and a good sporting crowd with lots of action and fast play.

But the rest of them were going on, and she had a hunch none of them were saying everything they knew or thought, especially Newt.

Maybe she didn't know the desert, but that wasn't all there was to it. What she needed to do was think of the ship and the treasure it might hold as stakes in the game. Everyone after the ship was a player, and if there was one thing she was really good at, it was reading people, given enough time and study. And if she could read them she could outsmart them, or at least stand a chance. For if there was one thing she knew for certain, it was that nobody could be trusted if they found the treasure. For all their talk about working together to find the ship, none of them had ever gotten around to discussing how they would split up the treasure. Looking for it and going after it were two vastly different things, and the game would change at that point, if the ship was found. She needed to be prepared for that, as well.

Her brazen, sassy act before the men was wearing on her, the hiding of her doubts and concerns, but she felt her confidence returning to her bit by bit the more she thought about her situation, despite the rapidly changing mix of emotions that often washed over her. She checked off the knowns and the unknowns, the likelihoods and long-shot possibilities, one by one, and thought of how she could play her hand.

Having the best hand wasn't the only way to win if you could read the players well enough. Sometimes all it took was patience and time enough at the table to pick the right moment. Many a time she had come out of a bad night winners on nothing more than a good bluff. Truth be told, her life was one big bluff, like playing the part of Poker Alice when she often felt like only plain Alice. She had been bluffing herself as much as the men she played against ever since she had come back from her husband's funeral and counted the little money she had left and decided where she was going next in her life. Had been since that moment when she wiped away her tears and decided she wasn't going to be a schoolteacher or spend the rest of her years doing laundry or waiting tables, or any of the other nine million mundane ways that would slowly and methodically leach away the spark of life she craved; that moment when she told herself she could do it. She could survive her own way. No, not only survive, but live. Really live. And she could take whatever cards life threw at her and win in spite of that hand.

Newt half walked and half slid down the face of the dune. He did not stop when he came to her, but went toward his horse.

"Where are you going?" she called after him.

"I'm pretty sure I saw Kerr's wagons leaving," he said as he picked up his saddle.

"And you weren't going to say anything? Just get on your horse, that's all?"

He swung his blanket and saddle up on his horse's back and ducked under its neck to make sure the girth was hanging right. He looked at her over the saddle while his hands worked, and there was that irritating hint of a smirk playing at one corner of his mouth again. Pablo was already saddling horses, while the boy packed the little dun mule.

"Mr. Smith," she said in a voice too strident, "would you be so kind as to saddle our horses?"

By the time Mr. Smith had saddled her good black mare and his own mount, Newt was already aboard his brown gelding and parked at the foot of the dune looking back at her. She put a foot in Mr. Smith's cradled hands and let him boost her up on her sidesaddle. After rearranging her skirt around the saddle's leg post, she adjusted the sagging brim of her straw hat until it felt better, and then she tossed back her head and met Newt's gaze.

"I'm ready now." Again, she knew her voice gave away too much, the dare in her words so plain that even a dense sort like Newt Jones could sense it.

He did it again, that smirk that in a better mood she would have taken for a faint smile. "Figured you would be."

He was already riding up the dune and didn't give her a chance to reply. She lashed the black mare across one hip with her riding quirt and chased Newt up and over the dune. The crushed brim of her hat flopped down over one eye, and by the time she had shoved it back up he was too far ahead to hear her. She urged the mare to more speed, all the while thinking of how she was finally going to give him a piece of her mind.

CHAPTER SEVENTEEN

Ed O'Bannon, sometime fight promoter and boxing manager, and always a crook, was late getting to Bitter Spring, where he knew the rest of McCluskey's men were waiting, and where he hoped to join up with them. In fact, he hadn't made it to Bitter Spring at all and had reached Indio by only noon of the next day after a miserable, all-night ride where his only rest was to lie down in the middle of the stage road and catch three hours of fitful sleep with his horse's bridle reins wrapped around one wrist. He was a city man and afraid to leave the road, not entirely sure he wasn't lost. He knew nothing about Indians, but greatly feared one possibly stealing his horse, for he had heard tales of their prowess in that regard.

He knew there were Indians nearby, for he was given to understand that he was near or within some kind of reservation for them, and also because he had passed through two of their villages on his way, first at Agua Caliente, then another farther south when he went the wrong way at a fork in the road. His first idea had been to camp at the second village if they would let him, but the Indians there were in a foul mood and shouted at him. He was too slow in interpreting their clamor for the warning it was, and by then one of them shot at him in the dark.

He did not suffer more wounds, but by the time he started out on the road again he was in no good mood himself. He was saddle sore and tired, and those were his minor issues. The skin on one side of his face was red and blistered in places where the bean juice from the cook pot Newt had hurled at him had burned him, and his headache from the pistol-whipping he had taken had gotten no better.

He caught up to a drilling crew on the road. They were bound for Indio to drill water wells for some farmer, though he couldn't fathom who would want to try farming in a desert. His own boyhood home in Ireland was quite lush and green, a place where it sometimes seemed to rain every day, yet even so, famine had either starved or scattered a large part of his fellow countrymen all over the world.

The well drillers did have a bucket of axle grease suspended under one of their wagons, which they were willing to share with him. He dabbed some of the grease on his burns, but it did little to soothe them. He took directions from the well drilling crew, felt less lost, counted that as an improvement, and moved on. His headache went with him.

In such a state, he arrived at Indio, intent on paying a visit to an apothecary if there was one to be found. Perhaps he could buy some medicine, but if not, he would settle for a bottle of whiskey at the local tavern.

There was no druggist in Indio, but he was able to find a saloon. Accordingly, he was heavily engaged in doctoring himself in that fashion well into the next night when he went to the saloon door and was surprised to see George Kerr's wagons rolling into the light cast by the hotel.

Zander McCluskey was not going to like him being in Indio, especially if he was seen.

His horse was tied alongside the tavern and somehow went unnoticed by the treasure party. He ducked out the back door and mounted. He did so in a surprisingly quick and athletic fashion for a middle-aged man with short legs and who was also quite inebriated. Even more impressive, at least in his own opinion, was that he had been level-headed enough to bring his whiskey bottle with him. It was not good Irish whiskey, nor was it good whiskey in any sense, but it did pack the necessary punch to somewhat mitigate the discomfort of his wounds, both those to his body and those to his ego.

Bitter Spring lay somewhere not far down the tracks, according to what he had heard McCluskey say before they had left San Bernardino, yet he did not pay much attention to his course of travel in the rush and panic of his flight out of Indio. By the time he had slowed his horse he found himself well out on the desert.

His fear of being lost returned until he noticed the lights of the Southern Pacific Hotel behind him. Being off clearly defined byways still bothered him, and for many reasons. It was hard to judge distance on the desert. What looked liked a matter of a mile or two often turned out to be several hours' ride. The local men did not give directions as a matter of so many city blocks, or by streets as he was used to, nor did they state distances in miles. When asked how far it was between one place and another they phrased their answer in how long it took to get there. For instance, it was not thirty miles from one place to the next, but a day's travel. It was disconcerting.

He glanced carefully around him, for he knew the desert to be home to all manner of creatures that would gladly bite or sting. Not the least of which were serpents. He had seen several of them the day before, odd reptiles as thick in body as his wrist, with rattles on their tails and fanged heads the size and shape of a spade. They slithered in a sideways manner even more decidedly evil than your normal rattlesnake whose movement was usually straight ahead. He envisioned one of those rattlesnakes using such sideways locomotion to come up and bite his horse. He had no doubt that one of them, given their size, could deliver enough venom to kill a horse, as well as a man. That was one thing he missed about the old country. Saint Patrick had run all the serpents there into the sea long before, and a man didn't have to worry about where he trod in order to avoid being bitten.

No, he didn't relish trying to find Bitter Spring at night when he couldn't see properly, both to find the road south and to be able to avoid those vipers. Nor could he return to Indio without risk of being seen.

He began considering his options and the merits of different tactics. Maybe he could find the railroad tracks and follow them. However, his mind soon flitted aimlessly from one thing to another until he was depressed again and felt like crying. Or maybe that was the whiskey. Whiskey often made him sad or angry.

He was forty-two years old, and he hadn't been so broke since he was a dirty-faced boy fresh off the boat from County Mayo with nothing to his name but the ragged clothes and a set of fresh whip scars on his back where he had gotten caught stealing from the captain's cabin boy while coming across the Atlantic. Years ago, but the memories were so vivid it seemed like only yesterday; ducking and dodging among New York City's Five Points and trying to steal food from the vendors and grocers, or ghosting along the Bowery picking the pockets of the swells in their fancy clothes coming and going from the theater at night. It would never leave him, the smell of the butcher shops and tanneries, sewers and the heaps of rotting garbage lining the inside of your nose like an oily film; the sound of running footsteps coming behind you in a dark alley or the shrill shriek of a copper's whistle. The gray skies and smoke, the soot-stained faces of the men shoveling coal, the maze of streets and alleys and hiding places, busted windows and rotten wood, crazy crooked stairways that led up to nowhere, the way a knife felt when you pushed it into flesh and the way it felt when steel pierced your own. Images and memories piled and warped together in his mind like melted candle wax, the mold and the mildew on the granite walls and steel bars of the Tombs and how it slid like grease under your hand, the grate of a plate of slop pushed along the floor and through your cell door; the echo of his mother's dry cough against the tenement walls and the spots of blood from her lungs dotting her handkerchief, graveyards in a drizzle of rain, children crying in the orphanage.

He had scrapped and clawed his way all the way from the old country to New York, and then when he had enough of that and learned the way of things he had climbed on a train bound west, looking for opportunities, but mostly as a way to avoid being conscripted to fight in the war and to keep ahead of the Dead Rabbits and the Kerryonians, who had marked him for death. The rush may have been all over by the time he made it into California as a young man, but there were still gold nuggets to be had, although of a different sort, ones you didn't have to pan or dig for. And he had done quite well for a time, especially among the sporting crowd and the dives and brothels of the Barbary Coast, or the red-light district stretching along Pacific Street to the docks. Yes, he had done well, with only a couple of bad moments in the scheme of things, until now. He should have never left there.

It came to him that the railroads were partially to blame for such restlessness and radical behavior. Compared to other, slower means of travel, a train journey took no time at all. A single train station might have many trains per day going in all directions. A man could hop on one and go practically anywhere to suit his latest whim, no matter that the notion might not be in his best interest, like his going to San Bernardino in the first place, a backwater town that in no way compared to San Francisco, or even Los Angeles. Had there not been a railroad so handy he would have had the time to think the matter through more carefully. Had the trip taken a greater investment in time and effort he might have elected to stay where he was.

Bad luck, and then more bad luck. First, that city marshal had busted up the prizefight in San Bernardino, one that had promised to be lucrative. Most of the early betting had been on Clubber, and that was a good thing. He had made sure to spread around an embellished version of Clubber's reputation as a brawler and his boxing record to the locals. Accordingly, with most of the bets placed on Clubber, he had instructed him to put on a good show, but at the right moment to take a little chip on the jaw and go down. That had been no easy thing, getting Clubber to agree to take a fall. However, it had all been set up nicely, until the marshal stepped in the middle of the ring waving his pistol around and the suckers scattered in all directions like foxes fleeing from the hounds.

He and Clubber had gotten out of San Bernardino by the skin of their teeth and after a long and wild footrace through that town. Escape, yes, but in the process he had hidden the money box holding the stakes in a woodpile in someone's backyard in fear of being caught and the money confiscated. Hot pursuit on the marshal's part did not allow him to immediately get back to the woodpile the next day as he had planned, and ended up with him and Clubber fleeing south to Colton, where they caught a train to Los Angeles to let things cool off for a while.

He had returned to San Bernardino on an evening train almost a month later, and went to retrieve the money box. It was a worrisome thing, not only worrying if the money would still be there, but because there were undoubtedly a lot of angry men looking for him to get their bets back, men who might not be very understanding if they found him in their city once more. And there was the marshal to think about.

He searched for the woodpile for an entire night before he found it, and when he finally did, the money box wasn't there. At first he thought it was the wrong woodpile. It had been dark the night they ran from the marshal, and there had been little time to get his bearings. He checked and double-checked and walked over what he thought was his route that night, but in the end he was sure it was the wood-pile where he had hidden the box. Plainly, and to his cha-grin, somebody had found it before he could return—a gain of more than a thousand dollars on their part, and a devastating loss on his. But at least he had avoided jail.

And there was Zander McCluskey. He hadn't recog-nized the name in the newspaper article about the treasure hunt, but he had recognized the man when he stumbled across him in a San Bernardino saloon. The new name might have thrown some off, but you never forgot one like him. The last time he had seen him was on the Yuma prison yard three years earlier. The yard, now, there was a place. O'Bannon didn't like to think of his year in prison. McCluskey had run the yard, while he had only barely survived it. Another bit of bad luck, that. Another bump in the road.

McCluskey had always given him the shivers, but the man had a plan. And he needed a few more men to help him. It was not O'Bannon's preferred or usual sort of outlawry, but it did promise to be a quick way to recoup his losses. With the money he would make with McCluskey he would get his gold pocket watch and diamond ring out of hock from the pawnshop, buy a new suit of clothes, get his shoes polished, and catch a train bound back to San Francisco. Everything would be fine—should have been fine.

How was he to know that gristle-headed Jones would reappear and wreck everything? Jones had been the last man he expected to show up at that campfire. And all for what? A few measly dollars taken from him? What kind of man hunted you down and went through so much trouble for that? The man was as bad as the damned Italians he had known back in New York. Steal from them or cross them, and they would buy a straight razor especially for you and pack it around for years waiting for a chance to cut your throat with it. There was no sense of equal retaliation with them, no tit for tat. Their sense of revenge was out of proportion to the insult you gave them. Steal an apple and they broke your feet with a hammer. Kill one of their family and they killed everyone in your family and maybe your dog.

He greatly regretted ever recruiting Jones for the fight, no matter how good of an idea it had seemed at the time. He had been at the Olympic Club in San Francisco one morning when in walked this big fellow off the street with a face like a bad mile of County Mayo road and shoulders as wide as a boxcar door. Said his name was Jones and claimed he wanted to exercise a little with the mitts on, but didn't even have so much as a towel to wipe the sweat off him.

The club was the place to be for the fight crowd in San Francisco, and it was packed. A dozen boxers and their coaches, a handful of swells and players of every kind, and even a couple of city coppers were there that morning. All of them had heard the newcomer's backwoods accent and had seen his less-than-stylish attire, and they stared at him like he was some country farm boy straight out of the potato patch. The only reason they hadn't turned him away was because they all thought they were playing along with some kind of joke and couldn't wait to see him make a fool of himself or have some fun at his expense.

Jones didn't seem to notice any of them and had simply stripped off his shirt, changed his boots for a pair of Indian moccasins, donned a pair of work gloves, and went over and proceeded to beat on a body bag that hung near one wall. The sound of his fists hitting that bag reverberated throughout the club, and soon everyone was staring at him for a different reason. They all watched him hammer that bag with a power and ferocity that was something like a steam engine about to overheat its boiler. None of them laughed after that. O'Bannon had immediately sauntered over after Jones was finished and introduced himself.

Jones claimed to have a little experience boxing in the mining camps away to the east, but nobody in San Francisco seemed to know him. Oh, when he had asked around, the word on the docks was that Jones had knocked a few heads in the usual rough-and-tumble shenanigans that went on down there, but nobody knew more than that.

Not satisfied, he had sent a telegraph to his cousin who worked the mines in Colorado. That cousin had asked around Denver and learned a little more, the best news of which was that Jones had a fight name that was a promoter's dream.

Widowmaker Jones, now, there was a name you could print up on an advertising poster and get some attention.

Even better, Jones hadn't seemed too smart, kind of the sullen, brutal sort that you could bend to your will with the right words placed here and there. Touring him around some of the small towns and backwater settlements and pitting him against Clubber should have been easy money. Only it all went wrong.

And to top it off, Jones had killed Clubber, regardless that Clubber was unusually deadly with both a blade and a gun, or any kind of weapon, for that matter. He had never seen Jones wear a pistol, much less use one, and until that point he had assumed Jones was nothing but a tramp boxer and vagabond. And yet he had drawn that gun like some kind of shootist and shot Clubber full of holes as easy as you please.

O'Bannon hadn't particularly liked Clubber, never had, but the two of them had made a good bit of money over the years since their first foray together firebombing businesses so that the owners could collect the money on the insurance policies they had taken out. Clubber's demise was going to put a damper on any immediate plans where muscle was needed, and he would have to start looking for a new henchman, that was for certain.

He thought about his misfortune so long that he finished off the last of the bottle, and he was in no shape to ride when he started his horse again toward what he thought was the south and the direction of Bitter Spring.

He was dwelling on his growing hatred of Newt Jones and what vengeful actions he might take should he ever run across him again when he fell off his horse for the first time.

Luckily, the horse did not wander far off, and allowed itself to be caught again. He fell off the horse for a second time and decided to stay where he was. It did dawn on him that he was making himself particularly susceptible to snakes lying on the ground like he was, but he was too drunk to get back up. It also dawned on him, after a time, that his horse was standing directly over him, greatly increasing the possibility that he might be trampled. His last vision of that night was not of the stars overhead in the sky, but of his horse's belly. The whiskey bottle lodged under the small of his back was not comfortable, nor was the hard ground beneath his head.

He slept well past daylight. The thin suit coat he wore left him chilled through most of the night, and the steadily warming sun and the alcohol in his system made him lethargic and reluctant to rise. However, the train whistle was very loud, and along with that sound, the skin on his ankles and shins was suddenly stinging very badly.

He came off the ground in a lunge and staggered several steps before he found his balance, all the while slapping at his legs. It was if they were on fire. The steam whistle sounded again from the depot while he dropped his pants and struggled to get free of them. His shoes hung up in his pants legs, and he fell down. He rolled and scrambled, and grunted and strained, and finally got his pants removed.

There were red ants all over his legs, all biting and stinging him repeatedly. He brushed them away where he could, and pinned others down and crushed them with his thumb. Each time he thought he had them all, another would hurt him. Little red bumps appeared where each ant had marred his tender flesh.

Once he had gotten the last of them he noticed the large mound he had disturbed during his sleep. Shin-high, it was crawling with more of their kind, little red demons who attacked in droves and who were so vicious they would willingly give their lives to inflict pain on him. He kicked the mound, scattering it before he put his pants back on. The pain of the bites and stings grew worse over time and itched terribly.

He felt like he had traveled a good ways from Indio, but was surprised to find that the depot building was only a few hundred yards away and in plain sight from where he stood. He rubbed at his eyes and scratched at an ant sting on one knee. His horse had left him during the night, and he feared the animal had been stolen or run away until he turned and saw the horse standing not a few yards behind him. He brushed off his clothes as best he could, twisted the ends of his handlebar mustache into shape, and then caught the horse and mounted.

The added elevation from his saddle allowed him to see over the low desert scrub and over a slight upswell of ground between himself and the road out of Indio. What he saw were Kerr's wagons already on the trail and headed southward. And for a moment, he again panicked. He should have already been at Bitter Spring or he ran the risk of being cut out of the action.

He tried to calculate how long it would take the wagons to travel that far. Two hours or three, maybe twice that much if they stopped or had to navigate any rough patches they might come across. There was plenty of time for him to get ahead of them, although that meant leaving the trail. It also meant a hard ride when that was the last thing he wanted to do. Along with his burns and his ant bites, he also had a terrible hangover. Not only that, but he was thirsty and hungry. His canteen was empty and there was nothing in his saddlebags that resembled food, and he couldn't remember the last time his horse had been allowed to water. In fact, the horse was looking rather poorly.

He considered McCluskey's plan and the parts of it he did not like. And he thought about how he was the odd man in the gang without a shared history or alliances of his own, and the possibility that they would cut him out of things, even if the plan worked. McCluskey was a treacherous bastard in prison, and undoubtedly men he would recruit would be no better. And nothing so far had gone right, not even such a seemingly simple thing as a short trip to a meeting point. At the rate he was going, there would be only pieces of him left by the time he reached Bitter Spring. There came a time to cut your losses.

It did not improve his mood to be quitting what could be a good thing, but with his mind suddenly made up, he started back to the depot. If he could sell his horse and saddle he could more than pay for a meal and a night in a good bed. It would also leave him with enough funds to buy a train ticket back to San Francisco, where, in his opinion, criminal enterprises could be undertaken in a much more civilized and predictable fashion.

He struck the railroad tracks and turned along them toward the little settlement. Within the hour he had sold the horse and saddle, had purchased a train ticket for that evening, and was checked into the hotel intending to sleep through the day.

He was standing at his second-story hotel window overlooking the train tracks when the Widowmaker rode into sight, followed by the English gambling woman, her big

Indian, two Mexicans, and the dude in the funny helmet.
O'Bannon stepped away from the window and pulled the
curtains closed.

He had no doubts that the Widowmaker and the others
were following McCluskey, thinking he would lead them
to the lost ship. The sight of the Widowmaker made him
look at his pistol lying on the bedside table. He briefly
debated taking it up and thrusting it out the window
and taking a shot at the Widowmaker. But he was outnumbered, and should he miss, he wasn't likely to escape
the hotel. And he was almost too tired to care anymore.
All he wanted was some sleep and a train ride back to San
Francisco. *Was that too much to ask?*

The thought of fleeing did cross his mind, but he decided his best course of action was to simply remain in his
room. Maybe they would be gone by the time the train ran
again.

He made a crack in the curtains and looked down at
them one more time, right below him, and then he lay
down on his bed. *Let the snakes and the ants and the
Indians take them all. And if the desert didn't get them,
McCluskey would.*

CHAPTER EIGHTEEN

County Judge Elias Nostradamus Kerr, otherwise known in San Bernardino as *the Judge*, came out of his big house exactly at nine o'clock in the morning as he said he would. The men he had requested were already sitting their horses waiting for him, even though they had come on short notice. The Judge was known to be a stickler for anything to do with time and a staunch advocate for every minute detail of the law or any instructions he might give. All of them had made sure to be prompt in their arrival so as not to displease him. The Judge was sometimes hard to get along with, but his request for their presence might make them some money and he wasn't above doing a man a favor in his court that had served him loyally in the past.

The Judge always wore a black suit. In fact, he owned two of them exactly alike, one to wear while the other one was being laundered and pressed for duty the next day by his Mexican housekeeper, a very young and pretty woman whose presence in the Judge's household had led to all kinds of rumors about romantic dalliances. The Judge was a widower, and that added greater fuel to speculation about scandalous responsibilities the housekeeper might have other than his laundry and sweeping his floors. But as pertained to his clothing, none of them knew which suit he wore, for they, like the rest of San Bernardino, thought he wore the same suit every day.

As usual the Judge's silky, long white hair was parted at the back of his neck and equal halves of it were draped over each shoulder and hanging down over the black cloth alongside his coat lapels in the front. Not many men wore their hair long like that, especially not successful and conservative men like the Judge, but he was more than a bit on the eccentric side.

The only thing different about him when he came out onto his front porch was that he was wearing his suit pants tucked into the tall tops of a pair of new boots with high riding heels, and there was a broad-brimmed straw hat with a flat, low stovepipe crown on his head. He stamped his boots on the porch boards to settle his feet in them, as if the boots weren't properly broken in yet. The boots were as black as his suit and the polish on them as immaculate as the starched and ironed white shirt beneath his coat. He wore no spurs, but a fancy braided rawhide quirt was looped over his right wrist. He tapped the quirt lightly against his thigh as he studied the men before him.

While he studied them, some of the men caught a glimpse of something else that was also new under the Judge's suit coat. He was wearing a pistol and a belt full of brass-hulled cartridges at his waist. If the Judge had carried a sidearm in the past, he had kept it better concealed. It was unusual, but so was the entire morning. Every one of them had been at work and had to throw down whatever they were doing to make it to the Judge's hacienda in time.

He continued to stare at them, gathering his words the

way he did when he was about to pass sentence from his bench in the courthouse, or when some unruly and testy lawyer bedeviled him. He was older than his brother, George, and shorter by an inch, although the citizens of San Bernardino thought him the taller of the two. But that was no surprise. He was a man who gave off the impression of greater stature than he actually possessed, as much by his demeanor and bearing as by the ramrod stiff way he stood. Truly, he was an average-sized man who acted like a tall man.

The quirt popped against his leg one more time, and the men paid attention as if it was a cue, like the whacking of his gavel. They knew he was about to bring court to order, and they all wondered why he had sent for them. The marshal usually put a posse together if it was city business, and the sheriff when it was a county matter. But the marshal was gone chasing after treasure with the Judge's brother and the sheriff was gone off to the capital in Sacramento on some piece of business or the other.

"Men," the Judge said in a deep voice, "you are probably wondering why I have brought you here."

That was exactly what they were all wondering, but none of them said so, nor did they even nod their heads. The Judge didn't brook interruptions when he was speaking formally. His years in the court where it was perfectly acceptable for him to be a tyrant had spoiled him in that way.

"As many of you may know," the Judge continued, "my brother left us two days ago to go chasing around the desert after the lost ship."

They all knew that, and they knew that George Kerr wasn't the only one of the Judge's kin to have gone off treasure hunting. His son-in-law was the city marshal, Buck Tillerman. Good old Buck might act stiff as a board to try and mimic the Judge since they had pinned that badge on him, but everyone knew he was a sucker for any kind of treasure story. When he was younger and long before he married the Judge's ugly spinster daughter and got the marshal job, Buck had gone out with Charlie Fusse's expedition and had to be brought back on a litter after a Gila monster bit him on the hand while he was digging around in the rocks looking for pieces of Spanish armor Fusse had insisted were there.

"I do not share my brother's optimism when it comes to finding lost treasure, and would not usually get myself involved," the Judge said, and then cleared his throat. "However, I have received a telegraph from Marshal Tillerman this morning that gives me grave concern."

"They haven't found the ship, have they?" one of the men asked.

The Judge scowled at him, which was his way of warning them not to interrupt him again. "No, it is a more serious matter than that. I had my suspicions about that McCluskey fellow from the moment he came here. I told my brother of those concerns, but he did not listen. Now Marshal Tillerman has wired me with similar worries."

"What's the matter?" another of the men asked, one of the local blacksmiths.

The red under the Judge's pale, smooth-shaven face rose to the surface, and his bushy eyebrows lowered at the man who had interrupted him. "Max, that horse of yours looks lame."

"No, he's fine," the blacksmith replied.

"I was watching out the window when you rode up. I'm sure I saw him limping," the Judge said. "Why don't you go on back to your shop. We'll handle this without you."

The blacksmith looked shamed, but he didn't argue with the Judge. He turned his horse and rode away.

"As soon as I received the telegraph I had Deputy Lester send some more telegraphs," the Judge said after the blacksmith was out of earshot. "One of the places he wired was Yuma. Many of you will remember that there was a prison break there about six months ago. Biggest one they've ever had."

A few of them gave careful nods. News of the prison break had been in all the papers for a while and the talk of Southern California and Arizona Territory. The warden at the territorial prison at Yuma ran a tight operation, and men didn't escape from there very often. The few that did were usually caught quickly. The desert gave a man only so many places to run to, and there would be lawmen and trackers there waiting on him.

"There were three men who escaped, and they have yet to be caught," the Judge said. "Among those three was a man named Zander Hileman. His description from the prison records seems to match the man who talked my brother into going after the lost ship."

The men waited to see if the Judge was through talking, and one of them finally asked, "What did this McCluskey do to get himself locked up?"

"Two counts of train robbery, one count of murder, and one count of kidnapping. He was charged with more, but that's what he pled to. He was supposed to serve a thirty-year sentence," the Judge answered. "With him when he broke out were one Bendigo Lynch and another man, Lars Bergerson, who goes by the name of the Bull Swede. Bendigo was sentenced to seven years for trying to steal an army payroll, and the Swede was sentenced to life for raping an elderly woman and her daughter in San Diego."

"You're sure Zander McCluskey is the same man as the Zander that escaped from Yuma?" one of the men asked when the Judge hadn't said anything else for a safe enough period of time to make sure it wasn't taken as cutting in on his speech to them.

"No, but I think it likely. Marshal Tillerman and the treasure party were at Indio early this morning, and he has begun to suspect that McCluskey is not as he portrays himself. Although, he is not aware of who this McCluskey might really be and has not replied to my return message."

"You're sending us after them?" the same man asked.

"I'm going with you."

It took a while for that to soak in on them. The Judge was going in person.

"Hard to believe that a man fresh from a prison break at Yuma would show up here with a treasure story," another man said. "You'd think he would be long gone and as far away from Yuma as a man could get."

"A lot of smart people think everybody else is dumb," the man beside him observed.

At that moment one of the county sheriff's deputies rode into the yard leading two loaded packhorses and a spare saddle horse. The Mexican housekeeper came out on the porch carrying the Judge's rifle. It was an 1881 Marlin with an engraved receiver, checkered wood stocks, double-set triggers, target sights, and a long octagonal barrel. The Judge was proud of his marksmanship and set store by that rifle. He had won three hams at the annual city shooting contest the last time it was held.

The Judge's prowess with a rifle was attributed by many as a result of his having served in the late War Between the States. However, past newspaper articles, primarily intended to flatter the Judge, relayed that he had indeed served in the war but not in a capacity where he would be called on to shoot men. Those articles claimed he served in New Orleans as a personal assistant to Major General Benjamin Butler while that city was held under martial law and military rule. Butler was the general who ordered anyone who cheered for Confederate president, Jeff Davis, to be sentenced to three months' hard labor, and who also ordered any woman who showed contempt for the Union soldiers to be treated as a common prostitute. The portion of the local citizens who had sided with the Confederacy during that conflict were not happy to learn of the Judge's connection to Butler, yet there weren't enough of them to cause him problems. And the Judge was careful to never mention the war, perhaps for that reason.

The Judge came down off the porch and shoved the rifle in a scabbard hanging from his saddle on the horse the deputy had brought him. That horse was a big gray gelding as nice and expensive as the rifle. The Judge mounted and looked at them again. Riding such a big horse made him seem even more commanding.

"That's an awful long ride, and they have a two-day head start on us. I should have had my wife pack my bedroll more carefully," one of the men said. He was the night guard at George Kerr's bank.

The Judge's voice was firm, but there was some nervousness or impatience in it that had never been there before. "We're going to ride to Colton, and then we're going to get on the train and take it down to Salton Station."

"And what then?" the same man asked. "That's an awful lot of country to go over, and we don't know exactly where your brother and this McCluskey fellow were going."

"We'll find them," the Judge snapped.

"Are we working for you or for the county?"

"Maybe you want to go home, too, Sam?" the Judge said in a more level voice, and he looked in the direction where the blacksmith had gone to give emphasis to his hint.

Sam, the night guard, didn't ask any more questions. He did not want to fall out of favor with either of the Kerr brothers and possibly lose his job. Either way, working for the county, or working for the Judge, he wasn't going to get paid much. The Judge was as tight with his money as was his banker brother.

"You'll be working for the county," the Judge said to settle the matter. "Two dollars a day and found for you and your horses. Raise your right hands and repeat after me."

He quickly deputized all five men, then he led them toward the road to Colton. He cut quite a figure on his pale horse and in his fine clothes. Many people who they passed along the way took the time to wave or doff their hats to him.

The men making up the posse were all good steady men, but they were also men who knew how to use a gun and how to get around in wild country. One of them had recently retired from the army after years of chasing Apaches in the Arizona and New Mexico territories. Another had a chest full of war medals back home he was given for shooting reb soldiers from great distances with his Sharps breechloader during the war, though he was now one of San Bernardino's grocers. Another had briefly worked as a Wells Fargo detective before marrying and settling down and opening a funeral parlor. The last of them, Charlie Two Horses, was a Paiute half-breed who at one time or another had tracked for most of the lawmen in the state. It was a formidable posse by anyone's standards, and it went without saying that the Judge had picked his men carefully. But the Judge was like that. When he set his mind on a thing, he would not settle for anything less than it going exactly the way he wanted it to.

The county deputy leading the packhorses dropped back to ride alongside some of the men, giving the Judge ample space. The deputy pointed at the Judge's back. "I haven't seen him stirred up like this in a long time, maybe never."

None of them had an answer for that. The Judge did seem perturbed. Maybe he was simply worried about his brother and his son-in-law.

"You know," the deputy added after they had gone a little farther down the road, "I think he was going after his brother even before he got that telegraph. He had me make sure the packhorses were reshod and gather supplies for a trip yesterday."

The men exchanged glances, but none of them was really shocked by that news. While the Judge might be worried about his family, everyone knew how much he liked money. And he could say what he wanted to about his brother being a fool for treasure stories, but he, too, had gone out with Charlie Fusse that time all those years ago looking for the ship, the same as Buck Tillerman had. It seemed possible that the Judge might intend to have one more look for the lost ship if his concerns about his brother and son-in-law turned out to be false.

Everyone in the area considered George Kerr a wealthy man, but the Judge was likely the richer of the two, though exactly how he got his money was anyone's guess. His house was the biggest in San Bernardino, a monstrous white thing with a columned porch big enough to park two wagons on. The Judge had built that house on a large chunk of land, thousands of acres that were a part of an old Spanish land grant that he acquired many years earlier when he first showed up in San Bernardino.

"How did he even get to be a judge?" the mortician asked. "In all my years I've never seen a judge like him."

"He's a politician, that's all," the deputy said. "That's how you get those kinds of jobs."

"I heard he's from Boston," another of them offered. "Old family whaling money, and I heard he first showed up in San Diego on a sailing ship."

"I recall hearing something of the sort. Fellow that told said me it was the Judge's money that George started his bank with," the county deputy said.

Charlie Two Horses didn't talk much, but he jutted his chin at the Judge. "I wouldn't cross him. Not even over a nickel."

"You won't cross him because he pays you more than anybody else," one of the others said.

It was widely known that Charlie Two Horses was hired for nearly every county posse that went out, and that he was paid a premium for his tracking skills. And it rankled them to know that he was likely making higher wages than they were.

"What's he paying you this time, Charlie?" one of the men asked.

"Three dollars a day," Charlie said.

"Shit."

"Like I said, I wouldn't cross the Judge, whether he's paying me or not," Charlie said. "That's a hard man there."

None of the others disagreed with the half-breed's assessment. The Judge could buy about anything he wanted done, but there was also the sense that he could handle things himself if it came to that. They rode along in silence, thinking of other things they either guessed about the Judge or rumors they had heard about him. There were lots of stories.

"You ever hear that he wasn't really with General Butler in New Orleans?" the county deputy asked after he looked to make sure the Judge hadn't slowed his pace and couldn't overhear them. "There's a version that claims he was a captain in the Union navy commanding a frigate during the blockade. And how he came to the first of his riches by selling off some of what he confiscated from the Confederate blockade runners."

None of them had ever heard that, and they thought carefully about it and how it fit with what they knew.

"Wouldn't surprise me at all," the deputy said. "A damned old pirate is what he is. Blood and plunder, one or the other, that's what he's after. He'll catch him a few bad men if that's what it takes, but maybe he'll have him a treasure, too."

CHAPTER NINETEEN

Newt Jones sat at a table in the hotel dining room with the men long after they had finished their breakfast. All but Mateo. The kid had said he wasn't hungry and had gone off somewhere on his own.

Newt's hands rested on the wood tabletop and one thumb tapped impatiently on it while he looked out the front windows at the long line of train cars parked on the tracks. Coal smoke wafted intermittently down the side of the train when the wind shifted.

"I would have liked a bath myself," Remington said.

Newt frowned. They should have long since been on the trail of the treasure party and not sitting and waiting on Alice to finish her bath. He appreciated being clean as much as anyone, but considered it frivolous and a waste of money to pay the full price for a hotel room to have it only long enough to take a bath. Especially when there were other more pressing matters to deal with.

But Poker Alice had insisted that she wash some of the road grime off her and had marched right up to the hotel clerk and rented a room and put in a request for her tub to be filled with hot water. She had left them while they were all still working at their food, promising to return in the matter of an hour. That had been two hours ago.

Pablo was saying something to Mr. Smith about their horses, but Newt was too distracted to catch it all.

"What's taking her so long?" Newt asked.

Remington chuckled, and so did Pablo.

"You must never have been married," Pablo said. "A woman, she moves at her own pace when she wants to."

"That's so true. My Eva, she could spend hours primping and prepping when we were about to go out. She . . ." Remington stopped himself and did not finish. He seemed suddenly embarrassed.

They waited another fifteen minutes. Newt glanced repeatedly at the clock near the door to the lobby.

He looked out the window again and was startled by the sight of Poker Alice on the outside of it. Instead of arriving from her hotel room she was coming around the train engine at the water tank and from the far side of the tracks. She was walking fast and she was carrying something.

"Now where's she been?" he asked.

She disappeared from sight for a moment, but she soon walked through the doorway into the dining room. She was wearing the same riding skirt and checkered blouse as before, but her face was so clean it was glowing and she had somehow managed to repair the broken, flopping brim of her hat. She came into the room at a brusque pace, and despite the ruddy glow of her freshly scrubbed cheeks, her expression was not a happy one. She seemed quite serious, if not angry.

She stopped and pitched a long tube made of some kind of oiled leather onto the table. "Mind telling me exactly what this is?"

She aimed her words at Pablo, and Newt was surprised

to see that the normally good-natured liveryman was glaring at her.

"You had no right," Pablo threw at her.

"Maybe not, but you've been holding out on us," she said.

Pablo scooted away from the table and stood so fast that he almost overturned his chair. His hand darted for the tube of leather, but she reached for it at the same time. They ended up with a hand on each end.

"*Dámelo*," Pablo growled.

"No." She tugged hard at the tube, but could not break it from his grasp.

"What is that?" Newt asked.

"Why don't you tell him, Pablo?" she asked. "Why don't you tell us all?"

Newt studied the tube on the table. All of them were looking at it. The leather of it appeared very old and darkened and cracked in places. One end of it had a removable leather cap and was tied closed with a braided strand that looked to be made of some kind of hair.

Poker Alice looked down at Newt. "I didn't expect any of you to still be here after I had my bath, so I went to where we left the horses, looking for you. You weren't there, either, but I saw Pablo's saddlebags lying on top of his gear."

"So you thought it was a good time to pilfer through his belongings?" Newt asked.

"Say what you want, but I've had a feeling about him. And this proves it." She gave the tube a tug, but Pablo wouldn't let go of his end of it.

There were only two other people in the dining room, a pair of railroad workers hurrying to finish their breakfast before they had to run out and relieve the crew at the train outside. Both men were looking at the strangers arguing at the table across the room from them.

"I think we might have this discussion elsewhere," Newt said.

"No, we're going to have it here and now," she said.

Newt glanced again at the train men, but they were getting up from their table and doing a poor job of trying to act like they weren't eavesdropping. Nothing else was said until the train men were gone and they had the dining room to themselves. Both Pablo and Alice kept hold of the leather tube, neither willing to let go of it and glaring at each other intensely.

Newt looked over the leather tube again, and then looked at Alice. "He's right. You shouldn't dig through a man's belongings."

"He's got a map," she said.

"A map?" Newt said. "That's what this is over?"

"An old map. And there's other stuff. Papers. Maybe letters or a journal, I don't know. They're written in Spanish. Just take a look and you'll see what I mean," she said.

"It is nothing," Pablo said.

"Take a look," she said to Newt. "Those papers are dated over three hundred years ago."

Pablo gave the tube a hard jerk and the violence of it almost pulled Alice onto the tabletop. She gave a grunt as her body struck the edge of the table. Mr. Smith grabbed Pablo's forearm. The Mohave's other hand reached inside his coat. At the same instant, Mateo appeared in the doorway. He had his rolling block rifle in his hands, and cocked it.

Newt stood, placing himself directly between Mateo and the table. "Kid, you let the hammer down on that rifle. And Mr. Smith, get your hand out of your coat. There isn't anything here worth a killing."

Pablo sighed. "Mateo, put away your gun."

"That goes for you, too, Mr. Smith," Newt said. "Mrs. Duffield is fine. Nothing hurt but feelings here."

Mr. Smith's hand came out from behind his coat lapel without a club in it, and Mateo uncocked his rifle. Poker Alice got her feet back under her, but did not relinquish her hold on the leather tube. She was flustered, and it made her face redder than it had been.

"Let it go," Newt said.

She gave him a mad glance like she was going to refuse, but finally let go of the tube. Pablo pulled it to him.

"I'm sure Mrs. Duffield is sorry for taking that," Newt said. "Aren't you, Mrs. Duffield?"

"I am not."

"This does not belong to you," Pablo said.

"I don't care whose it is," Newt said. "Why don't you tell us what's in that tube."

Pablo's shoulders sagged ever so slightly and a look of resignation settled on his face during the space of one exhaled breath. "It is a long story. I'll tell you and I'll show you, but not here."

"Open it," Alice said. "Open it now."

Pablo placed the tube under one arm, pinning it tightly to his side. "What's inside is a treasure in itself. A rare treasure. A gift from my brother and a gift from Mateo's people."

Newt looked at Mateo. "I'm a little late to the party, but I take it he's not your son."

"No. I have a son, but it is not him. I am sorry that I lied to you, but I thought it necessary at the time."

"You say it's a treasure. Does that map she saw show how to find the lost ship?" Until that moment, Remington had been quiet. Yet he said what they all were thinking.

"You will see," Pablo answered. "This I promise. You will see and you will believe as I do."

Alice dabbed at a strand of damp hair that had come loose from under her hat and gave Pablo a slight nod of her head meant as a tentative peace offering. "We can use my room."

CHAPTER TWENTY

They all followed her out of the dining room. Mateo stepped aside, intending to go up last, but Newt stopped beside him and gestured that Mateo should go ahead. Mateo did not argue the point, and Newt followed a few steps behind him, giving the kid and the rifle a little extra room. It was obvious that Mateo didn't like to feel cramped for space.

Poker Alice's hotel room was on the second floor. By the time Newt was inside it, Pablo had already opened the tube and was carefully removing its contents. The paper was as yellow as an old bruise and cracked and broken in places where the fibers it was made from showed like frayed threads.

First, Pablo gently unrolled some of those papers tied together with a leather thong. When he laid them out on the bed Remington immediately began sifting through them.

"Careful, amigo," Pablo said. "*Ellos muy antiguos*. Very old."

Poker Alice shut the door and came to the bed and began to look at the papers herself, with Remington handing

them to her one by one after he had given them a careful
glance. Newt and Mr. Smith looked over their shoulders
to get a look of their own. Mateo went to the window and
stood with his back to them looking out at the desert.

The words upon the papers were carefully and beauti-
fully written in a flowing hand. On other pages, toward the
bottom of the stack, the penmanship was less neat, less
artistic, as if the writer did not care any longer, or as if he
was in a hurry or distracted. Some of the words were faded
and some were blotched by an unsteady hand or a smear
or smudge of ink.

The writing was all in Spanish, and though Newt could
read only a word here and there, he could plainly decipher
the dates given. The papers were obviously some kind of
journal or log, for the writings were chronologically
arranged. At first there was an entry for every day, but as
Remington and Alice sorted through the stack, Newt saw
that the writer soon began to skip days. Or perhaps the ac-
count of those days had been lost, for there were three
months with no entries all. Some entries were short, with
only a couple of sentences, others took up a third of a page.

And Newt noticed that the last two pages were not made
of paper, but rather some kind of animal skin scraped so
thin that the light shone through them. And the faded and
sooty writing on that skin parchment was not done in ink,
but appeared to have been written with charcoal. And then
there was one last piece of parchment, only this time the
marks on it were not written in charcoal, but some other
kind of ink. The lines were thicker and stiffer on the
parchment and stood up so that you could see them in
three dimensions and feel them when you brushed your
fingers over them. It was like they were written in some
kind of plant juice or tar, and as if whoever had put down

those words was out of regular ink and experimenting with whatever he could find.

But it was the dates that caught his attention most. The entries were scattered over parts of two years, 1539 and 1540.

Remington took back the first page from Poker Alice. "I don't speak Spanish at all, but I can read it a little."

He began to read aloud, haltingly at times while he struggled over the translation and pronunciation, purposefully keeping his voice down.

"July 8, 1539—I, Capitán Francisco de Ulloa, set forth on this day from the port of Acapulco in New Spain with the three ships, the Santa Agueda, *the* Trinidad, *and the* Santo Tomás, *granted to me by Don Hernando Cortés de Monroy y Pizarro Altamarino, Marquis of the Valley of Oaxaca, and under the beneficent blessing of His Majesty and Holy Roman Emperor, King Carlos, and Antonio de Mendoza y Pacheco, Viceroy of New Spain. It is my duty to survey the coastline northward and to explore the passage east of the island of California . . ."*

"They thought California or the Baja was an island," Poker Alice said, interrupting him.

"I'm having enough trouble with this as it is. I don't know if I'm getting half of this right." Remington frowned at her and then gave an apologetic shrug to Pablo. "Please forgive my pronunciation of the parts I have to say in Spanish."

Remington continued, *". . . and to determine the quantity and quality of the oyster beds that are rumored to be found there like those Don Hernando discovered near the Bahía de La Paz. Furthermore, my orders are to assess any other resources or riches identified during the course*

of my journey, to survey the lands near the shoreline for
potential new settlement sites, and to establish trade rela-
tions with any Indians I might encounter and to impress
upon them the magnificence and power of His Majesty.
May God grant me fair weather and may his breath fill my
sails. And may the goodness and mercy of his light forever
shine on me and the valiant men who go with me."

Remington stopped reading and raised his head from
the paper and looked at all of them. Poker Alice cleared
her throat.

"It's real," she said in a voice that was slightly shaken.

"I assure you that these documents are . . . *¿Cómo se*
dice? . . . How do you say? These documents are genuine,"
Pablo said. "My brother is a priest in the village of San
Felipe. One day he found an Indio boy on the desert who
was sick and all but dying. He brought the boy back to his
church and tended to him. The boy left when he could walk
again, but returned again the next year. When he came
back he brought with him these things. They were a gift
for my brother for saving his life."

Newt nodded at Mateo's back. "I'm guessing that Indian
boy was Mateo there."

"That is so," Pablo said. "Mateo is of the Cochimi tribe.
Once there were many of them south of here along the sea,
but now they are few."

"Mateo, where did you get these papers?" Newt asked.

Mateo kept his back to them, but answered. "My grandfather found them many years ago in a cave in the mountains far to the south in the lands of the Guaycura and
Pericú. He passed them down to my father, and it was he
who said I should give them to the priest. My people
thought they were things of power, but my father thought

that it was a power not for our people and that the priest would know what to do with them."

Alice looked to Pablo. "Do you think that one of the three ships Freddy read about is the lost ship of the desert?"

"I am certain," Pablo answered. "And it is not any of the three, but most certainly *La Trinidad*."

"Read more," Alice said to Remington.

"The next entry is hard to make out, and I'm not even sure I've translated correctly what I've read so far," Remington said.

"There is no need," Pablo said. "I know the story so well I can almost tell it word for word. My brother is an educated man, such as yourself, Señor Remington. I had him read to me every night for a month what the *capitán* wrote on these papers. I know his story almost as if it is my own."

Remington and Alice sat on the bed, while Newt and Mr. Smith leaned against the wall. Mateo remained where he was at the window, but he did turn to face them, his attention focused on Pablo and what the liveryman was about to say.

"Two of the three ships were caravels, what my brother says were small ships with round bottoms and two masts. Square sails would be used for crossing oceans, and lateen sails, little triangles, would be used for coasting. These caravels could move upon very shallow water, and had oars for rowing. The third ship, the *Santo Tomás*, was smaller still, little more than what the English call a long ship. It was the wrong time of the year to sail and the weather was bad from the beginning. All of the ships were poorly made and were damaged. The *Santo Tomás* was lost in a storm almost before their journey had even begun and was never found.

"More storms came and the remaining ships had to stop

twice for repairs. The crews became angry because of the hardship and began to think that the *capitán* was cursed so he had trouble getting them to take orders. The *capitán* of the *Santa Agueda* wanted to take over command of the expedition, but could not. He threatened to take the *Santa Agueda* back to Acapulco.

"It took over two months for them to enter the Sea of Cortés, what some now call the Gulf of California. The sailors' mood was better, for they discovered an Indio village when they landed in search of freshwater. It was in the sailors' minds that they might discover black pearls as Don Hernando Cortés and others had a few years before, or perhaps gold. And if they could not find such riches they would make the Indios tell them where they could be found. But the Indios saw that the Spaniards had bad hearts and fought them and put them back to sea. Three of the sailors were killed, and one musket and a small cannon, a falconet, were lost in the battle. Capitán Francisco de Ulloa was wounded.

"Again a storm came, a terrible storm, and the two ships became separated. When the skies cleared and the wind calmed the *capitán* and the *Trinidad* sailed northward once more until he came to a wide marshland and floodplain and he could go no farther. The *capitán* was almost sure he had found where a mighty river emptied into the sea and thought about searching for the main channel, but the water was shallow and he feared risking his last ship."

"The Colorado River," Newt said. "At least it sounds like that's where he was."

Pablo nodded. "Yes, the Rio Colorado. The *capitán* turned back to the south and followed the coast on the west side of the sea all the way back to the tip of the Baja. He rounded the cape and sailed for a few days up the Pacific coast, but decided to turn back, for his ship was taking on water. On the cape at La Paz there was a tiny settlement and two villages of many Indios that Don Cortés had visited in the years before, and where he had discovered his black pearls. And the *capitán* and his men were made glad when they saw that the *Santa Aqueda* was not lost as they had believed, but was instead anchored in the bay and waiting for them. There was much celebration.

"The sailors were all but starved and had suffered much by this time, but the Indios at La Paz fed them what they could and helped load the ships' casks with freshwater. And then they showed the men the oyster beds where pearls could be gotten. The sailors spent a week working the oyster bed, but were much disappointed to find very few jewels, and all tiny and of poor quality. Some of the sailors held a meeting on their own and it was decided they would go back home while they still had their lives."

Poker Alice shook her head and interrupted Pablo. "How can the ship we're looking for be one of Captain Gulloa's if he went back home?"

"Patience, señora," Pablo said. "You see, not all of the men wanted to go back, nor did Capitán Francisco de Gulloa when those that held the meeting confronted him. There was a fight, and a few more of the sailors died before it was decided that the other *capitán* would take the *Santa Aqueda* and all that wished to go back to Acapulco. The rest would remain and explore farther."

"So now we've got only the *Trinidad*?" Remington asked.

"It gets better, much better," Pablo said with a sly smile. "The *capitán* and some of the others knew something that those that left did not, or at least they believed they did. You see, while some of the men were working the oyster beds the *capitán* spent his days sitting with the Indio chiefs in the village. He gave them gifts and asked if they knew of cities of gold and rich silver mines, or where more black pearls could be found. And when he had earned their trust, they told him of a land far to the north up the great river he had seen that emptied into the sea. Or perhaps they lied to him in order to get him and his men to leave. Either way, there they said he could find riches as in dreams, so much gold and silver that he could not fit it in his ship. The *capitán*, well pleased with this news, shared the knowledge with certain of his men and told them to keep it a secret.

"Restocked with freshwater and dried fish and other supplies, the *capitán* and his remaining men sailed northward once again toward the great river. On their way, they came upon another oyster bed. There they anchored for a week while the men cracked shells and searched for pearls. Unlike the oyster bed at La Paz, this time they filled a small chest with black pearls, some of them very big and of great luster. And while they worked the oyster bed an Indio came down from the mountains and traded them a small figurine of a lizard made of gold.

"The pearls had made the sailors greedy for riches, and the sight of the golden lizard made them even more determined to go up the river and find the legendary city the chiefs at La Paz had told about. They set sail again, but found the river was in flood. The capitán put his men to the oars, but the current fought them. He decided to wait for the water to calm before he again attempted to go upriver. While he waited, the men fished and shot and netted birds for their food.

"The river eventually slowed a little, but they had a difficult time finding the main channel, for the mouth of the river was spread very wide. They were surprised when they found that they were not going upriver, but had come onto a large lake or another inland sea. It was very shallow in the beginning, but the farther north they went the deeper it became. They thought they might have found the straits that some believed would lead them around the island of California, or perhaps the rich cities and the gold and silver that the Indios at La Paz had mentioned being to the north might be found on this new water instead of on the river itself."

Pablo's voice had grown somewhat louder and quavered slightly as he lost himself in the story he told. His dark eyes glistened with passion. "They sailed for two days on this new sea they had found, but there was nothing to see like golden cities. It was determined that they would return to La Paz, restock their provisions there, and then sail home. This did not happen. The water had dropped until the floodplain was no longer passable and no channel leading to the river or the sea could be found."

"They were stranded," Poker Alice said.

"*Sí*, very much so," Pablo said. "The *Trinidad*'s hull struck bottom and could not be moved. Within a day what had been water was now sand beneath their feet. The men were very brave and knew they were fighting for their lives, but there was nothing that could be done. Twenty-eight men, stranded on the desert.

"It was decided that they would walk south and they hoped they could make it back to La Paz, where ships might come and rescue them. They took up what little food they had and their weapons. There was no way to carry the chest of pearls or other things so far. The *capitán* considered carrying the pearls himself in a purse or perhaps dividing them among his men, but he did not trust them and feared that the strong men would kill him or each other if the chance arose. For even though those with him had sworn loyalty to him when the other *capitán* and the *Santa Agueda* had left him, there were still those who were difficult to control and who whispered behind his back. The *capitán* was not a kind man, and he had driven them hard all those days until then. The worse their situation became, the worse his men behaved.

"So the chest of pearls was buried beneath the ship with all of the cannon in order that the Indios or other men did not come along and take those treasures while they were gone. The *capitán* marked the location of the ship well so that it could be found again if he or any of his men should survive and be able to return to it."

"A chest of black pearls," Poker Alice said. "How big of a chest do you think it was?"

Pablo smiled at her. "Oh, that is not the only treasure they buried. I have not said this until now, but among the crew were two Jesuit priests who were journeying with the *capitán* in hopes of starting a mission somewhere in the new country. But the Indians were not friendly to them and the land was very harsh, so the priests decided they would go back to Acapulco with the *capitán* and relay such difficulties to their superiors and see if they still wanted to build a mission in that country.

"Among the priests' belongings were ceremonial, holy things for the new church they were to build, rich things of gold and jewels. Crosses, candleholders, vestments embroidered with golden thread, and silver plates and chalices. My brother has written letters to search the archives in Rome, and has an inventory of the things the priests brought on the ship."

"And they buried those church things with the pearls?" Newt asked.

"The *capitán* did not write this, but I think they did,"

Pablo answered. "Once they left the mouth of the river, food began to be very hard to find. They came across some Indios returning from a fishing trip and tried to trade with them, but the Indios attacked them. Perhaps those Indios were Serranos or the Cochimi people that Mateo was born to. Who knows? What is certain is that two Spaniards died with arrows in their bodies, one of the priests among them. While still strong in number, they were in no condition to fight after months of too little food, and had among them only two matchlock rifles, two crossbows, and their swords and knives.

"It was a long walk to La Paz, perhaps seven hundred miles or more. They knew not the way except to follow the coast. At times they followed trails made by the Indios, and at others they clawed their way over broken desert. The fish they sometimes caught was not enough to feed them all, and they lived on lizards and bugs and other vile things they hunted among the rocks and cactus. Their clothing became rags and their shoes and boots wore away until they had nothing but blistered, bare feet. Four more men died. Two others refused to go farther and were left behind to die on their own, including the second priest.

"Almost from the beginning of their walk, they began to throw away things that were too troublesome to carry. Helmets, weapons, and other things that weighed on them were left scattered behind them. More men fell during their long journey, from hunger and from thirst, and some simply because they did not want to suffer so anymore. With each month they became fewer. Their hair and beards grew long and they were so dirty and almost naked that they did not look like men at all. Exactly five months from the day they set out on foot they arrived in La Paz. There were three of them left, counting the *capitán*.

"The Indios at La Paz fed them, and soon their bodies began to heal while they waited for a ship to come. In their hearts, in the *capitán*'s heart, I guess there was little hope, for they all knew that it could be years before a ship came, if at all. But a ship did come that year. As soon as they saw its sails in the distance the two of the *capitán*'s men left to him attacked him and stabbed him to death with their knives. I do not know why, but I think they had come to hate the *capitán* and to blame him for all their troubles. And I think they wished to kill him before the ship arrived so that they would be the only ones who knew where the treasure rested, perhaps intending to come back some other time. *¿Quién sabe?*"

None of them said anything when Pablo finished, until Newt straightened from the wall and said, "How do you know that they stabbed him to death? He couldn't have written that in his journal or his log, or whatever you call it."

"No, he did not," Pablo replied. "But my brother went to La Paz many years ago, and he spoke with the people there. There is an old story handed down among them that a Spanish *capitán* was murdered there after his ship had been lost and after he had come a long way over the desert."

"So you don't know that Captain Gulloa was killed," Newt said. "For all we know he may have gone back to Acapulco or wherever. He may have come back with another ship and retrieved his pearls and the church treasure, or anything else he wanted."

"I do not think so. I think the *capitán* knew or feared he was going to die. I think that is why he hid his papers in the cave before he reached La Paz."

"You don't know that he was the one to put the papers in the cave. You don't know that the men who killed him didn't return for the treasure. In fact, there's a lot about this that's guesswork," Newt said.

"Mr. Jones, how can you stand there and talk like that?" Poker Alice said. "Of course it's guesswork! Maybe we don't know all the details, but we can be sure now that there was a ship left on the desert somewhere not far away from here. And it's a ship that might have a chest of pearls and who knows what buried beneath it."

"Maybe you're right, but we still don't know where it is," he said.

"Not exactly, but we know where to look," Pablo said, pointing at the last unrolled paper left on the bed.

When he unrolled that paper they all saw that it was a hand-drawn map. It was twice the size of the paper that the log had been written on, as if it was made to lay on a table. Newt imagined the captain bending over it in the swaying confines of his cabin while at sea, jotting down notes and carefully drawing in the outlines of the coast as he saw it and the distances and bearings as he calculated them.

Numerous notations and other marks and symbols were written onto the map, and toward the northernmost, top of the map was a tiny drawing of a ship with two masts and square sails. That ship was drawn on dry land between the Gulf of California and what had once been the inland lake the captain had mentioned in his log.

"What are these numbers?" Poker Alice pointed at the map at a point near the drawing of the ship.

"I believe those are meant to be latitude and longitude, degrees and bearing and so forth," Remington said.

Pablo shook his head. "That is the difficulty. The ship is marked on the map, but that is a big country."

"If it's still there," Newt said. "After all the years I don't know how much there will be to find."

"True, but the desert has a way of preserving what it keeps," Pablo said.

"You've searched for it before, using this map, haven't you?" Newt asked.

Pablo looked at Mateo and then nodded his head almost reluctantly. "We searched once two years ago, and twice more last winter. Neither time did we find the ship."

"Even with this map?"

"Yes, even with the map."

"So what's going to be different this time?"

Pablo shrugged. "If Señor McCluskey heads in the direction where this map shows the ship to be, then I will know that he may have seen where it rests. That is why I told you that we could follow him and then go ahead when we thought he was close."

"And if he doesn't go in the right direction?"

"Then we will have a choice. A simple choice, *más o menos*. We can either follow him and believe these papers and this map mean nothing, or go search for the ship on our own where the map says it rests."

"I won't quit, not now," Poker Alice said.

Remington sat down on the edge of the bed, sifting through the papers with a delicate touch and mumbling to himself. "Can you believe it? The ship's real. I wish my Eva was here."

"And you, Señor Jones, what will you do if McCluskey does not go in the direction that this map shows?" Pablo asked.

Newt pointed at the map. "Show me where Dos Palmas is."

Pablo pointed at a spot to the north of where the captain

had drawn the ship. The place he indicated was near the eastern shore of the lake marked on the map and toward its north end.

"How long of a ride from there to here?" Newt put his finger on the map right on top of the drawing of the little ship.

Again, Pablo looked at Mateo.

"A day and a part of another riding slow to take care of our horses," Mateo answered.

Newt kept his finger where it was. "And what kind of country is here?"

"What do you mean?" Pablo asked.

"What's it look like?"

"It is bad blow sand and dunes almost all the way from the end of the old lake bed to Yuma," Mateo said. "Big dunes. It is not a place where one would go without good reason."

Newt's jaw muscles flexed and his eyes took on a hard gleam. He nodded his head.

"You are thinking about what that old Cahuilla told you, aren't you?" Poker Alice asked. "What else did he say about the ship?"

Newt's eyes met hers, then his gaze moved around the room from one to another of them, eventually coming back to her again. "He said the ship was to be found amongst the dunes south of Dos Palmas."

"Ha!" Her fingered stabbed down on the map beside his own finger where he held it over the drawing of the ship. "Just like right here."

"Just like right there," Newt repeated.

"Well, what are we waiting for?" Remington stood from the bed. His almost ever-present smile was stretched wide across his square, handsome face.

One side of Newt's mouth cracked in what was his own version of a grin. For once, the tenderfoot was right.

He led Mr. Smith, Mateo, and Remington down the stairs to the hotel lobby intent on saddling their horses while Pablo and Poker Alice gathered Captain Gulloa's papers. They were almost out of the hotel when they heard a crash upstairs, and then Alice shouted frantically for help.

Newt shucked his Smith & Wesson and headed back up the stairs at a run. Mr. Smith had drawn his war clubs every bit as quickly and was right on his heels.

CHAPTER TWENTY-ONE

Ed O'Bannon was tired, but he was also a very light sleeper. What's more, no matter how fancy and well built the Southern Pacific's hotel and depot was on the outside, its interior walls were paper-thin. Sound carried through them almost as if they weren't there at all.

It was the sound of people talking that woke him. He tried to go back to sleep, but couldn't. He was sitting up on the bed when he heard the words *ship* and *treasure*. He pressed one ear against the wall and recognized some of the voices. It was the Widowmaker and his friends. And then he heard them talking about the map, in fact he over-heard almost everything they said. Suddenly very awake and excited, he slipped out of his bed and dressed quietly. When he walked across the room to his door he did so with care to keep the floorboards from creaking.

He pressed one ear against the door, the same as he had done at the wall. He did not have to do so, for the sound of the men passing down the hallway outside his door was very loud and plain. When he cracked the door open he could hear that the woman and the Mexican man were still in the room.

He glanced once down the hallway toward the stairs to make sure that the rest of them were gone. For a moment he debated what he was about to do. It was chancy, no doubt, but what he had overheard was worth taking a chance for. He took a deep breath and hoped his luck had finally changed to the good, and drew the cartridge-conversion Colt Pocket Police out of his shoulder holster. And then he moved down the hallway toward the sound of the woman's voice.

She almost ran into him at her door, and he shoved the barrel of his little revolver into her belly so hard that she grunted. The Mexican behind her stopped where he was, surprised and indecisive. That was to O'Bannon's advantage, and he shoved the woman back in the room and nodded his head at the leather tube the Mexican held in his hands.

"I'll be taking that," O'Bannon said.

The Mexican didn't seem to understand him, so he pointed the pistol at the man's forehead. That did the trick and the Mexican handed him the tube.

The Mexican appeared unarmed, but O'Bannon backed slowly toward the door, keeping a careful watch on them both. He took a quick glance down the hallway to make sure he had it to himself.

He tapped the tube against his hat brim, mocking a salute or a tip of the hat to the lady. "Don't be sticking your head out this door too quickly, not if you know what's good for you."

With that he ducked out the door and slammed it behind him. He started for the stairs but the woman shouted for help and there followed the sound of running footsteps in the lobby below. He looked down the hallway in the other direction, but there was nothing there but a window at the dead end of it.

The Widowmaker's hat was the first thing to show above the stairway landing, and O'Bannon raised his pistol and fired. The Widowmaker fell back and O'Bannon turned and sprinted for the window. He didn't slow at all as he approached the glass.

Damn, this is going to hurt.

A pistol roared and a bullet clipped Newt's hat brim just as he was reaching the top of the stairs. He fell back two steps and gathered himself after Mr. Smith ran into his back. The Mohave helped right him, and then reared back and hurled one of his clubs over the landing and down the hallway in hopes of distracting whoever was shooting at them. Newt lunged upward and followed the flight of the club with his .44 pointing ahead.

The first thing he saw was a man running down the hallway away from him, and the next thing was Poker Alice coming out of her room. She held a Colt Lightning revolver and she aimed at the fleeing gunman's back. Her .38 barked just as the man dove through the window in a shower of busted glass.

Newt held his fire with Alice in his way, and he charged past her. He made it to the window in time to see the man who had gone through it picking himself up off the ground below. The man threw a wild glance up at Newt in the window, and then took off in a hobbling run. Newt recognized O'Bannon instantly and took aim at him as he rounded the front corner of the hotel, but the train was still there and he held his fire for fear of striking it or someone with it.

Newt turned and started back to the stairs.

"He's got the captain's papers!" Poker Alice said as he passed her.

Newt and Mr. Smith went down the stairs and out the door. Newt went around the front of the train's engine while the Mohave climbed between two of the cars. Neither of them caught sight of O'Bannon once they were on the other side of the tracks.

They split up, moving fast. They hadn't gone very far when a horseman barreled out of the back of the big barn ahead of them. He was ducked low in the saddle and going all out, he veered his horse and put the barn between himself and Newt, all the while whipping and flogging his horse with the tail of his bridle reins.

A man came out the other end of the barn, waving his arms and shouting. "He stole my horse!"

Newt holstered his pistol.

"I'll go after him," Mr. Smith said.

"By the time you saddle he'll already be long gone," Newt said.

"I can find him."

"Might take days," Newt answered, having little doubt that Mr. Smith could do as he said and noting the calm almost bored way he had said it. "And we don't have days to spare."

People had gathered at the depot porch, railroad workers and train passengers, by the time Newt and the Mohave came back around the train. They ignored the gawkers and went back into the hotel. Nobody stopped them to ask questions.

Remington stood at the top of the stairs. "What was that all about? Mrs. Duffield says that somebody stole the map."

Newt ignored him and went past him. Poker Alice was standing at the busted window at the end of the hallway, and Pablo was with her. Newt noticed the splintered window frame where her bullet had struck. Ed O'Bannon was lucky to have survived his fall, but twice as lucky that she hadn't killed him first. Her bullet had come very close to him, even though it was a snap shot at better than thirty feet.

Newt gave her a careful look. He had never noticed that she carried a gun.

"Where have you been carrying that?" He pointed at her pistol as he said it.

Her face was flushed again with excitement, but she willed that away and gave him her usual saucy smile. "A gentleman doesn't ask a lady a question like that."

"Did he get away?" Pablo asked.

"He did." Newt pointed at Pablo's waist. "You want to rethink that pistol I offered you? I've still got it in my saddlebags."

"I told you I'm no pistolero."

"You could have gotten her killed."

"Perhaps, but maybe she lives because I didn't have a gun."

"Maybe, but if the bad guys are wearing guns I intend to have one myself. I guess even old Daniel in the lion's den might have appreciated a good Colt pistol if somebody had pitched him one while he was in the thick of things."

"You should not make light of God's word," Pablo said. "He is always listening."

"I'm not making light of anything," Newt said. "You and the lady are all right. It could be worse, a lot worse. I'd say we got lucky."

"How did he know we had the map?" Poker Alice asked.

"Maybe he saw us in the restaurant, or maybe he's been following us," Remington said.

"Doesn't matter," Newt said.

"What do you mean it doesn't matter?" she asked. "He's got the map and everything else."

"We know where we're going. Let's go get our horses," Newt answered. "I don't know if we're too late, but I'd like to beat Kerr and McCluskey to Dos Palmas if we can."

"He got a three-hour head start on us," Remington said.

"Best we hurry then," Newt said. "That Thoroughbred you ride looks like he's fast, but is he a stayer?"

"He'll still be going when the stubby little brown gelding of yours falls over dead," Remington said.

"That'll be the day."

"If we're in such a hurry, I'd say we quit talking about horses and get out of here," Poker Alice said.

"What about you, lady?" Newt asked.

"Are you asking if I'm a Thoroughbred or a nag?"

"I'm asking if you know what you're getting into. You've just been robbed at gunpoint, and I can't guarantee you that worse won't happen. I'd feel better if you stayed here."

"Are you trying to cut me out? Is that it?" She whirled around to face him.

"No, I'm trying to look after you."

"What makes you think I need looking after?"

"I was thinking . . ."

"You were thinking what?"

"I was thinking that I'd hate to see something happen to a lady."

"Oh, *really*?"

"Really. That's bad desert out there. Do you know what that means? It'll take guts. We're going to have to ride hard and fast. There won't be any time to stop and take baths or comb our hair or rest just because we're sleepy. No turning back because we're thirsty or hungry or too worn out to go on. There are other folks after the ship, maybe some that we don't know about, and men can do bad things when they get greedy. If we're going to find it first and keep it, we're going to have to get tough. Mad-dog mean if it comes to that. It's been easy so far, but from here on out it's likely to hurt."

"Mr. Jones, there are a lot of things I would like to say to you right now, but all I'll say is that you are a condescending, arrogant pig. Other than that, you can rest assured that there is no need to look after me or wait for me. Not this lady. I'll be right behind you all the way, and there's not a thing you can do to stop me. And if you don't go fast enough to suit me I'll pass you by and leave you behind."

Newt stared at her for a moment, his face expressionless and unreadable. He could have been mad, he could have been frustrated, or he could have been about to hit her. It was hard for any of them to tell. And then he shocked them all and gave her a crooked smile. "Good, that's what I wanted to hear. You do me a favor and keep that pistol handy. Might be we all get thrown in the lion's den before too long. Pablo can pray for us, but I might need some help with the shooting while he's getting his message through."

Pablo crossed himself and shook his head somberly. *"Que Dios te perdone."*

"I think Pablo feels you're being sacrilegious again," Alice said.

"Sorry, Pablo. I reckon I respect a righteous and God-fearing man as much or more than anyone, but Mother Jones always said my own faith was smaller than a mustard seed. But isn't it in the Good Book that the Lord helps those who help themselves?" Newt said.

"No, I think it was Benjamin Franklin that said that,

and one of my professors at Yale claimed he copied it from some Englishman who got it from the old Greeks," Remington offered.

"Well, whoever said it, they were my kind of fellow. What say we go help ourselves?" Newt started down the hallway.

The rest of them waited a moment after he had gone down the stairs.

"I would not want Señor Jones mad at me, although I think he is a better man than he seems," Pablo said.

"He's a likable rascal, I admit, but you know what they call him, don't you?" Remington said. "The Widowmaker, that's what that marshal back at Kerr's camp said. Widowmaker Jones. Makes you wonder what he did to get a name like that."

"He's a rough, distasteful man, but that's an awful name for anyone," Poker Alice said. "And I wouldn't advise calling him that. I don't think he would like it."

Mr. Smith, who until that time had said nothing, laughed deep and loud. That sound coming from him shocked them so much that none of them could speak and they stood only looking at him.

"You white people are funny sometimes, especially for the things you don't understand. A warrior should have a name. Strong name," Mr. Smith said. "Sometimes he may have more than one name, that which he comes to by himself or amongst his people, and that which his enemies give him. The strongest warriors are always named by their enemies. To be feared by those who would come against you is an honor and not a bad thing."

Mr. Smith went after Newt, his big shoulders seeming to fill the hallway as he passed along it. For so big a man, he moved with the grace of a slinking panther.

"He's even scarier than the Widowmaker sometimes," Remington said.

"Just be glad they're on our side, Freddy," Alice said.

When they went downstairs and out of the hotel they found that Mateo had saddled the horses and led them over. Newt was already mounted.

The Southern Pacific Hotel manager came out onto the porch and wanted to talk with them. He was clearly displeased with the destruction of a perfectly good window, and wanted an explanation for what had happened and perhaps compensation for the damage.

"Why don't you explain it to him?" Newt said to Alice in a quiet voice when he saw the hotel manager appear. "Use that charm of yours and smooth things over."

She arched one eyebrow at Newt. "Oh no, Mr. Jones, I wouldn't think of interfering with your manly duties, a poor little helpless woman like me. And I'm really quite terrible with hotel managers lately. I'm afraid they find me difficult."

"You, difficult? Never would have thought that."

The rest of them got into the saddle and then they rode away from Indio. And they did not ride slow.

CHAPTER TWENTY-TWO

Zander McCluskey led George Kerr's wagons alongside the train tracks southward for eight or nine miles and struck the old Bradshaw Trail where it crossed the tracks at exactly high noon. The trail ran southeast from there, aiming straight for Dos Palmas and the notch between the Orocopia and Chocolate mountains behind it at the eastern edge of the valley.

He pushed hard, and the mules and the saddle stock were tired and thirsty. Men and beasts alike were covered in a pale coating of dust, and the mules and horses drank two full water barrels empty when he finally called a midday stop six miles from Dos Palmas. It had been relatively easy travel, as deserts went, so far, but the farther they went the worse it was getting.

That didn't worry McCluskey, for he had no intention of going any farther than Dos Palmas. That was far enough.

The men had set the fly up again on the side of the wagon for George and Madeline Kerr. Father and daughter sat on camp stools underneath the shade of the canvas roof. When he walked over to them, the old man pointed at the horse he was leading.

"You ought to unsaddle your horse and let him rest," Kerr said.

"Thought I'd scout ahead a bit. Check the trail," McCluskey replied. "Big wash ahead and I thought I'd see how hard it's going to be to cross with the wagons. We'll lay up at Dos Palmas for the night. Good water there."

"And how close will we be then?"

"Close."

"It's out on the sink, isn't it? That's where you found the ship."

"Isn't there a salt company there, Papa?" Madeline asked. "I remember you saying something about buying them out. I would think they would have found a ship if there was one on the old lake bed."

Kerr patted his daughter on the arm. "That old lake bed is very big, and they've only worked a part of it."

"I never said the ship was on the playa," McCluskey said.

"No, you never did. This close, and you're still keeping it to yourself, eh?" Kerr asked.

"I'll be back in an hour or so."

"I don't know how you do it," Kerr said. "It's almost unbearably hot, and I don't think I could have ridden another mile if you hadn't called a stop."

"Well, you didn't see the ship," McCluskey said. "I did. That's pretty strong motivation."

"Still I appreciate your dedication. I'm no desert rat, and I'm afraid I'm having a harder time at this than I expected. Oh, there was a day when I could skin a mule as good as any man. Go all day and all night, mile after mile. Started my first freight business with nothing but one wagon and me driving it. Bad trails, bad weather, nothing stopped me. Built up the business with my back and two good hands, but I'm afraid I've spent too many years behind my desk since then," Kerr said. "Ah, to have the energy of a young man again, such as yourself. You wouldn't understand that, would you? I suppose not. What man in his prime would? But I promise you, sir, the years take their toll. Truly they do."

McCluskey started to get on his horse.

Madeline Kerr lifted a hand to get his attention. "Mr. McCluskey, would you be so kind as to go over there and get me a dipper of water?"

He paused for a heartbeat, staring at her before he smiled and said, "I'd be glad to."

He went to the rear of the wagon to the water bag hanging there not eight feet from where she sat. He took up the tin dipper, filled it, and carried it to her. She took a little sip from the dipper and then tossed the rest of the water on the ground.

"Thank you. I feel so much better. Perhaps you could ask the men when they will have lunch ready," she said.

"I'll ask them."

He did not ask them; he did not say anything to them when he rode away. *That spoiled little rich brat, talking to him like he was the hired help, like some kind of damned butler or her maid.*

He rode three miles along the trail toward the rocky foot of the Orocopia Mountains, and when he came to Bitter Spring he was surprised to find his men still there. A wide man in a leather sombrero and with a red beard hanging down to his chest was the first to rise from where he and two other men sat on the blankets spread on the ground around their campsite. He shaded his eyes with the flat of one hand held to his brow and waited until McCluskey rode up to him.

Bitter Spring wasn't a good camping place, there being little to offer comfort other than a few low and scrubby trees and brush to give shade. And the water flow out of the spring was weak and unreliable, and tasted bad unless you were very thirsty. His men had been camped there for two days and more, and from the look on their faces, they had enough of waiting.

"'Bout time you got here," the man with the red beard said.

McCluskey gave Bendigo a scornful look. Bendigo was a middle-sized man, height-wise, but thickly made, with wide wrists and big hands and a torso like a barrel. He was so overly broad that it made his arms and legs look short and out of proportion to the rest of him. Low and squat, and as hard to move as he was hard to get along with, that was Bendigo.

Bendigo hooked both of his thick thumbs behind the wide leather cartridge belt he wore around his waist. A row of brass shotgun shells gleamed in the loops built into the belt to hold them, and a Webley British Bulldog revolver with yellowed ivory grips rode in a holster high on his right hip. His whiskered jaws worked methodically at the wad of tobacco in his mouth. When he spat it was a black stream that splattered like tar on the sand in front of his big, booted feet.

"I told you to go on to Dos Palmas," McCluskey said.

"We're a little slow getting around today, but we were just about to ride over there," Bendigo answered.

Bendigo was from Alabama, but the mush-mouthed and slow way he talked didn't hide his contempt or the sly, cruel undertone in everything he said. McCluskey never had liked Bendigo any more than he did Bull. Bendigo was a sour man that couldn't let things lie, always picking at matters and bringing them up at the wrong moment. Three years locked up with him, and McCluskey couldn't get the stink out of his nose. It was the same stink as the inside of a prison cell.

McCluskey rode past Bendigo and saw the two empty whiskey bottles tossed beside the ashes of their last campfire, and knew why they hadn't gone on to Dos Palmas like they were supposed to. The men with Bendigo, both Mexicans, looked like they had just woken up, and neither of them looked in any shape to ride.

"Your little treasure hunt about over?" Bendigo asked.

"This little treasure hunt, as you call it, is going to make you a fair profit."

"It's chancy. I say we stick to the original plan."

"Plans change."

Bendigo scratched at his beard and grimaced. "Mighty chancy."

"It'll work. Trust me."

"Trust you? Remember how you said you had it all figured out back in the calaboose? You said we were getting out of there slicker than owl shit," Bendigo said. "Only it wasn't easy, was it? I was the one that had to kill that guard, me and Bull. If they catch me again they'll sentence me to life if they don't hang me, and here we are not two days' ride from the prison we broke out of."

"You'd rather still be locked up?" McCluskey asked.

"No, but I'll be happier when we're back in Mexico. This one worries me."

"Down there robbing peons for pesos? That ain't living."

"Mexico suits my style just fine. Trying for the big score will bring too much thunder down on us. You wait and see."

"It's worth the chance we're taking."

"Smart's the reason I threw in with you, but you're too smart sometimes. You got a big fat brain all full of things, but that brain'll be the end of you if you ain't careful. If I want to steal something I walk over and take it. If I want to kill a man I do it. You, you'll spend forever scheming and convincing yourself that you can do something that nobody else can. Always looking for the big job with the highest stakes. You never think that if a thing's that complicated maybe you shouldn't do it at all."

"You're going to lecture me after that botched job you pulled off on that payroll? How'd that go for you?"

Bendigo spat again and worked his chaw to his other cheek. "Yeah, maybe I botched that one. What of it? I was drunk for three days and still drunk when I saw them army boys come by with their wagons. Never had even thought of taking that payroll until then; never even knew about it. I saw it and thought to myself, *Now, Bendigo, there's a sight of greenbacks waiting for the taking.* So quick as that, me and the boys went and made our try. No planning, no thinking, just going with my guts and seeing what happens. You've got your ways and I've got mine. You might be smarter than me, but for all your smarts, they caught you, too. Caught you and locked you up in Yuma same as they did me. In the end it's all the same. Something gets stole or somebody gets killed. It's all nothing but bad notions and guts."

"Where are the rest of the men?"

"We've got enough help. It'll either work or it won't."

"I asked where are the other two, those two army deserters that were with you before I left you in Hermosillo?"

"I don't know. I sent them up the trail to watch for you, and to come back when they spotted you headed this way."

"That figures. The idiots didn't even have enough sense to get rid of their uniforms. You should have picked better men."

"I'll run an ad in the newspaper next time. Dependable killers and thieves wanted."

McCluskey was mad and growing madder the more Bendigo jerked his chain. Some men he could cower down, but not Bendigo. The man had no fear, as if he were born without that feeling among all the other missing pieces of him, like a thing that looked like a man but wasn't. McCluskey was better with a gun, maybe, but the redhead would take a lot of killing before he went down for good. A man that tangled with him was going to bleed and bleed a lot, even if he won.

McCluskey nodded at the Mexicans with Bendigo. "Either of those two speak English?"

"They savvy enough," Bendigo answered. "I've worked with both of them before. Juan's steady if things don't get too hot. Carlos is the best man with rifle I've ever seen, and he don't mind pulling a trigger."

"If this goes right, we won't have to fight," McCluskey said. "We simply get the money and fade away."

"Hope you're right."

"If you don't believe me, why'd you even come?"

Bendigo shrugged. "Same as you. That's a lot of dinero. I've been stomped on, shit on, and shot at. I wouldn't mind getting paid off for all my trouble for once."

"I'll have the wagons at Dos Palmas a little after dark," McCluskey said.

"We'll be there. What are you going to do with the old man and the woman when this is over?"

"I don't know. She gives us more leverage, but if we get caught . . . I don't know. We'll have all the law putting on war paint and coming after us as soon as it's known there's a woman involved, especially a young girl with her family name."

"They'll hang us if this goes bad, no matter what. No witnesses, no bodies, that's what I say."

"I never killed a woman."

"No different than a man. Some squeal and some don't."

McCluskey rode his horse to the spring and the gelding buried its muzzle in the tepid, stained water and slurped noisily. McCluskey thought about a lot of things while the horse drank. When it had its fill he rode back to Bendigo.

McCluskey reached into his vest pocket and took out an envelope and handed it down to him. "You have one of those fellows ride to Salton Station and mail this."

Bendigo tapped the letter against an open palm. "You're kind of jumping the gun, ain't you? I thought we weren't going to send this until we were back in Mexico."

"The quicker the Judge gets that note, the quicker we get paid."

"You're getting nervous, ain't you?"

"I just want my payday, same as you."

CHAPTER TWENTY-THREE

"They beat us here," Poker Alice made sure to keep her voice down when she said it.

All of them sat their horses side by side staring at the firelight flickering and casting the two palm trees in the distance in shadowed silhouettes. Occasionally they could see someone pass before the fire.

"That's not them," Newt said. "There's no way those wagons could get here first."

"Who is it then?" she asked.

"Might be anybody."

They had ridden as fast as they could without burning out their horses, and had come cross-country from Indio instead of following the trail. They had been confident that they would get to the springs at Dos Palmas first.

Remington's Thoroughbred didn't like to stand still. It chomped at the bit and fidgeted and stamped. It was always a nervous and poorly broke animal, but Newt wondered if it somehow sensed the other horses at the water hole ahead. The wind was to their faces, so he didn't believe the Thoroughbred smelled them, but sometimes animals, and even people, sensed things in a way that couldn't be explained. It was the same as when you felt like somebody was watching you or pointing a finger at you without actually seeing them, that moment when the hair on the back of your neck stood up and tingled, or that funny feeling in the pit of your stomach that something was wrong.

"Keep that horse quiet," Newt said.

"We need that water," Pablo said. "Many a night I have shared a campsite with strangers. It is how I met you, is it not?"

Newt had traveled deserts often himself and understood how such water holes funneled traffic to one point, both wildlife and men. But something made him hold back. Maybe it was the feeling in the pit of his stomach that riding the last mile into Dos Palmas meant danger, like he was standing on the crumbling edge of something.

"Where's the next water?" he asked.

"There is another spring close by, and then another farther south," Mateo said.

"It is true," Mr. Smith said. "My people once traded there with the Cahuillas when I was a young man. There are scattered springs most of the way to Yuma. Some good water, some bad. Some are always water, and some are sometimes water."

"I do not know these springs, but I have heard it is so," Pablo said. "There is a fault line that runs on this side of the sink. This, I think, must be what lets the water come to the surface."

"Fault?" Newt asked. "You sound like a prospector or one of those . . ."

"Geologists," Remington said.

"Yeah, that's it."

"It is simply a thing I have heard said. Men who cross deserts speak much of water," Pablo said. "It is good if Señor Smith and Mateo know the places we can find it."

They moved over the desert, keeping the horses to a walk and maintaining their distance from Dos Palmas. The terrain was all but flat except for humps of sand and thinly scattered, low-growing vegetation. Though the moonlight was dim, they did not want to risk being seen.

A mile away they came to a long, low dune of blow sand, crossed it, and a little farther on found another oasis with a lone palm tree and several springs seeping water into shallow pools. Mesquite brush grew around the edges of the oasis, and by the springs and beneath the palm the tules and grass were so thick that it was hard to find the water. Newt found it when his horse bogged up to its knees, and they dismounted and hacked the growth away with their knives and the blade of the shovel on the pack mule.

They had purchased a feedbag for each horse at Indio and filled those bags with corn bought there, as well. The corn cost four times what it should have, but they thought it a good investment. Their plan was to ration the corn for each horse out over several feedings. Though their travel had been relatively easy until then, the horses were already looking gaunt and losing their spark. There was little forage to be found on the desert, and not enough to graze stock at night and get by solely on that. So a little corn might not totally solve that problem, but it might help. There could come a time when it would be highly important to have some bottom left in their mounts, and as Newt had told Remington, there were places out there where a man on foot was as good as dead.

After the horses were watered, they tied their feedbags on them and let them have a feeding of corn. Newt gathered some of the cut grass and mounded it in front of the Circle Dot horse after he removed the gelding's feedbag.

"You think highly of that horse, don't you?" Remington had begun to gather some of the rank, tough grass for his Thoroughbred.

"He's pulled me out of a pinch a time or two. Never quit me, even when I made it tough on him," Newt said. "There are men I can't say that much about."

"Where did you get him?"

"Comanche give him to me back in Texas. They thought he was cursed or had a bad spirit in him or something."

"Apache and now Comanche. I thought you a pugilist and not an Indian fighter or some kind of scout."

"I've known an Indian or two, that's all. Fought 'em when I had to, camped with them from time to time when things were good. They're people, same as us. Some good, some bad. Different ways than us. Some that we don't cotton to, but they don't like our ways any better."

"What do you think of Mr. Smith?" Remington kept trying to get the Thoroughbred to eat some of the grass, but the sorrel gelding was a picky eater and refused the offering.

"I don't know what to think about him. He's kind of peculiar."

Remington gave up trying to get his horse to eat the grass. "Did you notice that a couple of those tattoos on his arms aren't like the rest of his marks? Look like tattoos I've seen on some sailors that have been out on the Pacific or to the Polynesian islands."

"No, I didn't notice that."

"Makes you wonder, doesn't it?"

"You go ask him if you want to know where he got them."

"You're not at all curious?"

"I figure if he wants me to know he'll tell me."

The Circle Dot horse finished the grass given him and pushed at Newt to get to the pile Remington had made for the Thoroughbred. The night was growing cool, and Newt untied a light canvas jacket from behind his saddle and put it on. The others came from the spring and were doing the same. There would be no campfire, nor were they going to stay long, for they soon heard Kerr's wagons rattling and bouncing on the trail to the north.

"I told you there was no way Kerr beat us to Dos Palmas," Newt said.

"They don't seem to mind the company," Poker Alice said. "They're going right on in."

It was at that moment that Remington's Thoroughbred nickered. The horse did it again before the easterner could get to it and distract it. A horse, and then another, answered the Thoroughbred from somewhere to the north, either from Kerr's party or from whoever had made camp at Dos Palmas. A wagon mule's loud braying came next, and it caused Pablo's little red dune mule to start its own racket.

"Now that we've advertised we're here, it's probably a good idea to get moving." Newt was already bridling the Circle Dot horse.

"Just where is it that we're going?" Remington asked.

"Far enough that they don't wake up in the morning and find us camped next door," Newt replied.

"Salton is not a few miles from here," Pablo said. "There is a bunkhouse that the salt diggers use. Maybe they will let us sleep there for the night."

"Lead the way."

"We will reach the dune country tomorrow," Pablo said.

"And what then?" Poker Alice asked.

No one had an answer for her until Mateo spoke up.

"We can find a place at the foot of the mountains and watch and see if the wagons come."

"And if they don't?" Alice asked.

"One day at a time," Newt said. "Let's go to Salton."

"I must admit a real bed sounds good. Any kind of a bed," Alice said. "I swear I haven't slept more than an hour without waking up since we started this."

Remington pointed back in the direction of Dos Palmas. The nearby sand dune blocked their sight of the campfire, but they all knew what he was pointing at. "They'll be bedded down before long, and with any luck we'll have this Salton place all to ourselves."

Some of the posse's horses didn't want to get on the train, and it took a half hour of coaxing and cussing and dragging and shoving them up the loading ramp to get them loaded in the stockcar. That delay, and the Southern Pacific men informing them that the train wouldn't get to Salton until the next morning due to its usual stops to off-load freight and to take on and let off passengers put the Judge in a foul mood. It was half past seven in the evening when the train finally rolled out of Colton.

Charlie Two Horses and the county deputy stood in the open doorway watching the countryside fly by and enjoying the cooler air. Most of the men rode in the stockcar, leaving the Judge to brood alone in one of the Pullmans hitched farther up the train.

"The Judge thought he could pull some strings and get them to run a through train for him," the deputy said. "I guess he found out he doesn't run the railroad like he runs the county."

"Maybe it'll give him an excuse to buy the railroad," Charlie Two Horses answered.

"I don't know why he's fretting so," the deputy said. "We'll get to Salton by daybreak. Nothing we could do in the dark, anyway. I don't even understand why he's putting us off there, of all places."

"He didn't say. I just track for the man," Charlie said. "But I'd wager he thinks that his brother and that Mc-Cluskey he's with are moving south and he wants to get ahead of them."

"You ever been down there on those flats? Worst place I've ever seen. Nothing but hot and more hot. Flat as a pancake with a whole lot of nothing as far as you can see. Sometimes I regret taking this job. I sure do."

"You took it because you're getting paid."

"Some of us don't make three dollars like you, Charlie. Some of us ain't treated special only because we ride out ahead sometimes and find a track or two."

"The Judge pays me more 'cause I don't talk so much and I don't ask questions."

The deputy scuffed one boot against the swaying floor of the stockcar and sent a little cloud of dust floating out the open door. "There won't be anybody at Salton but those salt diggers. I'd bet you anything. You see what you can find down there to track besides pissants and lizards. Won't be no three dollars' worth, I promise you."

CHAPTER TWENTY-FOUR

Bendigo rose from the campfire at the sound of the wagons coming his way. The Mexican with him took his rifle and faded back into the darkness. Bendigo picked up a shotgun, a double-barreled Lefever 10-gauge, and held it rested in the crook of one elbow while he waited with his back to the adobe walls of the old stagecoach station.

McCluskey came riding into the firelight alone, a ways ahead of the wagons. He looked like he was about to say something, but a horse nickered somewhere out on the desert.

"That didn't come from the wagons," McCluskey said.

They listened as the nickering horse caused the horses and mules with the wagons to answer with more nickering and braying.

"Whoever it is, they ain't far off," Bendigo said. "You got somebody on your back trail?"

"I've had that feeling."

"We'd best get it done now. I'll sleep better if we get out of this country."

The lead mules of the first wagon came into the fire-light, followed by George Kerr on his saddle horse. Madeline Kerr and Marshal Tillerman were behind him on their own mounts.

"Good evening," George Kerr said to Bendigo. "I hope you don't mind us barging in on you, but I guess there's plenty of room for us to camp and not be in your way."

Bendigo worked his chaw of tobacco between his jaw teeth, trying to squeeze the last of the juice out of it. "No trouble at all. Ain't that right, Zander?"

"You two know each other?" Kerr asked McCluskey.

It was Bendigo that answered. "Why, me and Zander are real good friends. Ain't that right, amigo?"

"George," the marshal called out. The concern and warning in his voice was plain.

There was the faint beginning of uneasiness in Kerr's voice and in his expression, as if he was only then coming to realize that things weren't as they should be. "I appreciate the hospitality. We've had a long ride."

"Oh, I understand, banker man. Believe me, I do. You see, we've been waiting for you," Bendigo said.

The Mexican with Bendigo came into the light. Kerr saw that and backed his horse away from them a couple of steps.

"What do you mean you've been waiting on us?" Kerr asked. "I don't believe I know you."

"George, come over here with me," the marshal said.

Kerr glanced at his daughter and then at Marshal Tillerman before he looked at McCluskey. "What's this all about? I asked you when we saw the firelight, and you said you didn't know who was here."

McCluskey stepped down from his horse, and for a moment he was out of sight behind it. When he came around the front of the horse there was a pistol in his right hand. He pointed the Colt revolver at Kerr. "You go ahead and get down."

Marshal Tillerman's horse moved at the edge of the firelight, and at the same instant Bendigo shouldered his shotgun and fired twice, two booming blasts spaced only a split second apart. The first charge of buckshot struck the marshal's horse in the head, staggering it. The second shot, fired on the rising recoil of the scattergun, hit the marshal. The marshal toppled from his saddle and his wounded horse ran off into the dark.

The gunshots were so close to Kerr's horse that it scrambled backward. It reared high and almost fell over, toppling the banker from the saddle in the process. Kerr hit the ground hard, and then McCluskey's horse, shying almost as violently from the report of the shotgun, went over the top of Kerr and stepped on his arm.

Madeline screamed and reined her horse away and lashed it across the hip with her riding bat.

"Get the girl!" McCluskey shouted.

The Bull Swede was driving the last wagon with the Mexican, Jorge, on the seat beside him. Bull dropped the driving lines in Jorge's lap and launched himself through the air at Madeline as she ran her horse past him. His flying tackle caught her around the waist and the weight of him dragged her from her sidesaddle. He kept hold of her from behind with his big arms wrapped around her as they got to their feet.

He leaned over her while she kicked and screamed, and pressed his cheek against her ear. "You go ahead and squirm, little *kvinna*. I like it when you fight."

"Papa!" she cried out.

George Kerr lay on his side with his wounded arm

clutched against his chest while the outlaws hustled to catch and calm the frightened horses. Through the dust and shadows and dancing horse's legs, he saw the marshal lying lifeless and on the ground.

"Buck?" Kerr called out in a ragged voice. "Buck?"

Bendigo walked over to the marshal, thumbing two fresh cartridges down the pipes of his shotgun as he went. The marshal's body lay facedown, and Bendigo used his shotgun to prod and roll the marshal over to look at his face.

"Damn you, Bendigo," McCluskey said. "What the hell did you shoot him for?"

Bendigo kept his back to McCluskey and acted as if he hadn't heard. "Buckshot tore him up good."

"I didn't tell you to start anything," McCluskey said.

"He reached for his pistol. What did you want me to do?"

"I didn't see him reaching for his pistol."

Bendigo turned around to look at McCluskey and saw that the slim gunman was still holding his own pistol hanging at the end of his arm alongside his leg. "You bring a lawman with you and wonder why I shot the bastard?"

"That marshal was the Judge's son-in-law. Why don't you go ahead and shoot the old man and the girl? Right now! Make sure we don't get paid!"

"We'll get paid," Bendigo said.

"You don't listen."

"You going to shoot me, Zander?" Bendigo's shotgun was pointed at the ground in front of McCluskey's feet, but ready in his hands.

McCluskey met the red-bearded bandit's stare for a long moment before he holstered his pistol. He glanced at George Kerr lying wounded on the ground nearby, and then over by the wagons where Bull held the struggling girl.

"Bring her over here," McCluskey called out.

Bull brought the girl and slung her to the ground. He gave a vicious grin. "I think she likes me."

Madeline crawled on hands and knees toward her father. She tried to hug him, or perhaps to help him to his feet, but he groaned and pulled away from her when she bumped against his wounded arm.

"Get over by the fire and stay put," McCluskey said to them.

Madeline rose first and took her father by his good arm and helped him up. They leaned against each other as they went. When Kerr sat down beside her at the fire he momentarily lost his hold on his injured arm and it flopped loosely and he moaned and clutched the arm back to his chest.

"Let me see that arm," McCluskey said.

Kerr wouldn't let go of it. "Get away from me."

"Can't you see it's broken?" Madeline sobbed.

"Flopping like a little old chicken wing," Bendigo said.

"Leave him alone!" Madeline shouted as she stood and stepped between her father and the outlaws.

Bull slung her back to the ground and drew back one arm as if to hit her.

"Leave her be," McCluskey said. "Go help unhook the wagons and get those mules strung together. And find a hole to stick that marshal in."

"We're leaving the wagons?" Bull asked.

"Too slow."

"They'd bring a good price."

"Not a drop in the bucket against what we're after."

Bull gave Madeline a last, leering glance and headed to the wagons. The other men were already starting to unhook the teams. The mules were haltered and the lead rope from one mule's halter tied to the neck of the one in front of it, until there were two strings of mules.

"Get anything you want out of those wagons, but you better be able to carry it," Bendigo said. "Weigh yourself down too much and you'll get left behind."

"You lied about seeing the lost ship just to steal my mules?" Kerr asked McCluskey. The banker's voice was ragged with pain and filled with the shock of both his injury and what was happening. "You . . . you killed Buck."

Bendigo prodded Kerr with the shotgun. "You carrying a gun, old man?" He checked Kerr for weapons, but found nothing.

"I said leave him alone! Can't you see he's hurt bad?" Madeline said. "Take the mules and leave us be. Take it all, I don't care."

"Oh, we're going to take it all," Bendigo said.

McCluskey motioned Bendigo away from the campfire, and the two of them went off and held a hushed conversation. The Kerrs were left alone.

"Papa, I'm afraid." Madeline sat pressed against her father and hugged him. Her hair had come loose from its gathering and tear streaks lined her dirt-smeared face.

"I was a fool, Maddy," her father said as he watched some of the outlaws dragging the marshal's body into the brush. "A pure, unadulterated fool. All I could think of was that ship. Been thinking about it for years and I wanted it so badly. I . . ."

"Take me back home," she said. "I want to go home."

He patted her forearm and tried to straighten his face. "Keep close to me and do like I say. We'll get out of this yet, you wait and see."

"They killed Uncle Buck."

He swallowed, trying to choke down the hard, dry knot in his throat. "We need to keep our wits about us, that's what we need to do. Maybe they'll take what they want and leave us be."

McCluskey came back to them and squatted on his heels across the fire from them. He studied them for a long time, his face as still as his posture. The mesquite wood popped and crackled and the flames danced over his face. He looked like some kind of demon lit in red.

"I need you to listen, and listen real close," McCluskey said to them. "You do like I say when I say it. Hear me? We're going to move fast. You don't make trouble and maybe you get out of this in one piece."

"I trusted you," Kerr said.

"That was your first mistake."

"All that talking you did when you first showed up, the hints dropped in the saloons when you were drunk, the story you told the newspaper, the same story you told me trying to use it as collateral for a loan to outfit you to go back out on the desert . . . you were only planting seeds, weren't you? Nothing but a way to get someone out here to rob?"

McCluskey's thin lips spread thinner. "That's right, at least at first. Never figured a big fish like you to take hold of the bait, and I changed things up because of you."

"You sir, are a scoundrel, a despicable human being."

McCluskey didn't flinch at that, nor did he seem angered by the insult. "Do you know what it's like to be locked in an eight-by-ten cell with three other men, day after day? Badmen, the kind of men you can't even imagine? Breathing the same air with those animals and feeling the walls pressing down on you tighter and tighter? The roaches crawling over you in the dark and lungers coughing and hacking their sickness until you couldn't sleep if you wanted to? Making sure to keep your fingers out of the door grating when the guards come so you don't give them a chance to bust your fingers? Knowing how bad the privy bucket is going to smell as soon as the sun gets good and up and it goes to getting hot? Real hot. Nothing to do but sweat and think.

"Well, believe me, I did some thinking. Had this cellmate, died from a sunstroke busting rocks for the warden, but not before he told me all about old Charlie Fusse's treasure hunts. Said he'd gone with Fusse a time or two. Talked for hours about that lost ship, no matter that most of what he said didn't make any sense. Couldn't shut him up about it. But finally it came to me. People are blind when they want to believe in something. Get them to dream, and then they'll jump off whatever cliff you want them to."

"So you came to San Bernardino with your treasure story . . . your confidence game." Kerr sounded as tired as he was hurt.

"Figured we'd get a party together and take them out on the desert. Get whatever they had that was worth taking— horses, mules, wagons, guns, gear, petty cash."

"Will you at least leave us our horses so that we can get back home?" Kerr asked. "There is nothing that my daughter or I can do to hinder you. I assume you will be long gone before we could get anywhere to tell of your crime."

"You're going with me. Both of you."

"We will not," Madeline threw at him.

McCluskey pointed a finger at her. "Listen . . ."

"I won't listen to you, not another word," she said. "The law will catch you and you will be punished. Uncle Elias will see to it that you hang."

Bull came back to the fire and heard what she said. "I can shut her up if you don't want to."

"You hear him?" McCluskey asked. "Bull likes hurting girls."

Madeline slumped slightly and pressed close again to her father. She shook with rage, but the Swede looming over her kept her quiet.

McCluskey stood and his gaze locked on the girl. "Right now there's a letter on its way to the Judge letting him know we have you and that he's to have thirty thousand dollars delivered to Campo two days from now if he ever wants to see you alive again. I don't particularly like hurting women, but the fact is, for that much money I'll let Bull here do about anything he wants to you if it makes sure I get paid. So you're going to get on your horses and come along nice and easy, or bad things are going to happen. *¿Comprende?*"

"Kidnapping and ransom, so that's what this is all about?" Kerr said.

"Now you're listening."

"That's preposterous. I couldn't put together thirty thousand dollars if I had to."

"You're a poor liar, Mr. Kerr."

"Certainly not on such short notice."

McCluskey gave him a careful look. "Between you and your brother, I think you can. You don't know how much thought I've given that number and trying to gauge what kind of money your people can scrape up quick. Ask too much and it would take you too long to get it to me, or maybe your brother doesn't pay at all. Ask too little and I'm taking chances on the cheap. No, I think that number is about right."

"You're a fool. Nobody keeps that much money on hand."

"Call me a fool again and I'll break your other arm." McCluskey turned his head and looked at Bull. "Hurt him until he gets up and on his horse."

Kerr held out his good arm to try and fend the Swede off, but it didn't work. Bull grabbed him by his shirt and yanked him brutally off the ground. Kerr began to bawl with agony.

Bull slapped him across the face. "Quit your crying."

Madeline got up and steadied her father, begging, "Please don't hurt him anymore."

The outlaws let her help Kerr button up his broken arm inside the front of his suit coat to serve as a sling. She walked side by side with him as they went to the horses.

"Help me get him up on his horse," she said to McCluskey.

One of the Mexican outlaws and Bull took hold of Kerr and got him in the saddle. They did not do it gently. The banker reeled in the saddle, once aboard, and seemed on the edge of passing out and falling to the ground.

"Tie him in the saddle if that's what it takes," Bendigo said.

Kerr straightened and sucked in a deep breath. "I can ride."

"Leave the old man alone, but tie the girl. I won't have her trying to run again," McCluskey said.

"Get your hands off me," Madeline said as she was put up on her sidesaddle.

Bull shoved through the outlaws in his way. He took a manila grass lariat rope and bound her wrists together and then ran the tail end of the rope through her bridle bit shank. He coiled what was left of the rope and laid the coils over his saddle horn. "I make sure you don't run, girlie. *Ja*, I'm going to keep you real close."

"Put out that fire," McCluskey said as he got on his horse.

McCluskey rode over to Bull and took the rope that secured Madeline. Bull glared at him but didn't argue.

Everyone was mounted except for one of the Mexicans, and he led his horse over to the fire and began to scatter what was left of the burning wood and coals with his boots. He was about to kick sand over it when the sound of a trotting horse stopped him. All in one motion, the outlaws shucked rifles out of saddle scabbards or pistols from their holsters as they turned to face the night and whoever was coming for them.

The Mexican outlaw Bendigo had sent to Salton with the letter rode into the dim coal glow of the dying fire. Ed O'Bannon followed him. O'Bannon's horse looked half-dead, as if it had run all day, and it shuddered and slung its head and shook froth and sweat from its body when the Irishman quit kicking it and pulled it to a stop.

"I find him on the road and bring him," the Mexican said in bad English.

McCluskey put his pistol away. "That's a good way to get yourself killed."

The Irishman looked around him to get a handle on the

current situation. There was caution in his voice when he spoke. "I didn't think I was ever going to find you."

"Who the hell is he?" Bendigo asked.

McCluskey ignored Bendigo and stayed focused on O'Bannon "What do you think you're doing?"

"You said you had men waiting at Bitter Spring," O'Bannon said. "After Clubber got killed I decided to head this way to lend a hand."

"You're late."

"What do we need this runt Irishman for?" Bendigo asked.

"Oh, I think you need me," O'Bannon said.

"What's that supposed to mean?" Bendigo threw back at him.

O'Bannon turned in the saddle and looked at the Mexican that had ridden into camp with him. "Tell them."

"What's he talking about, Carlos?" Bendigo asked.

"I take the letter to Salton like you say. But a man there, he tell me that there are many policeman coming on the train. He say something about a judge with them," the Mexican said.

"He said the Judge is coming?" McCluskey asked.

The Mexican shrugged. "That's what he say."

"When is the Judge's train supposed to make Salton?" McCluskey asked.

"Mañana."

"That isn't all," O'Bannon said.

Again, the Mexican shrugged. "On our way here, we see others. We find a place and we watch. Six riders. They don't see us."

"It was Jones, and that gambling woman. Her big Indian and two others were with him," O'Bannon added.

"Jones?" McCluskey asked.

"The one that killed Clubber. Him and those with him have been following you."

"You're sure?"

"I saw them in Indio this morning and overheard them talking, then we saw them again not an hour ago. They were coming into Salton as we were leaving."

"Who's this Jones, and why's he following us?" Bendigo asked. "And why in the hell is the Judge already almost here? I told you that you were biting off too big of a chunk."

Bendigo went to his horse and swung into the saddle, and then he rode over to one of the string of mules and took hold of it from one of the other outlaws.

"What are you doing?" McCluskey asked.

"I'm getting out of here. These mules ain't much, but they're better than nothing."

"We've still got these two." McCluskey nodded at the Kerrs.

"Do what you want with them, I don't care. Me myself, I'm getting across the border, and I ain't wasting any time doing it."

"The Judge won't risk something happening to the old man and the girl," McCluskey said.

"And what are we going to do if he corners us? I don't doubt he's already wired to Yuma calling in help, and who knows where else. Too thin, I say. Too thin."

"The Judge will back off and pay up as long as we've got him by the short hairs."

"The Judge coming down from the north, and maybe a posse from Yuma or who knows where else waiting for us at the border? I say we're more likely to get our necks stretched."

They glared at each other, saying nothing else, while the rest of the gang kept well out of the way.

"Gentlemen," O'Bannon said. "Before we fight amongst ourselves, I think you should hear me out."

"Nobody asked for your two cents, Irishman," Bendigo said.

"Oh, it's more than a few cents I'm talking about." O'Bannon grinned, though it was too dark for the others to see that. "What I'm about to tell you is what me dear mother would call the icing on the cake."

CHAPTER TWENTY-FIVE

Newt and his party spent the night in the bunkhouse belonging to the New Liverpool Salt Company on the eastern side of the Salton Sink. The Cahuilla Indians working for the company gave them one end of the long, narrow shack to themselves and the loan of a single kerosene lantern. Too tired to discuss the events of the day, they spread their blankets over the thin tick mattresses and hard bed slats and lay down. The only sound was the wind hissing through the cracks between the lumber siding and the Cahuillas whispering about them from the other end of the room. The lantern was barely extinguished before all of the travelers were asleep.

Newt arose before daylight when the stars could still be seen in the gray sky overhead and the first thing he saw when he went outside was a crudely painted sign set atop a short post alongside the railroad tracks that proclaimed, SALTON, ELEVATION—262 FT." The only buildings were the bunkhouse, a few shacks and equipment sheds, and the processing plant rising three stories high over the expanse of the dry lake bed spread out before him. As far as he could see to the south and west, there was nothing but miles and miles of flat, cracked earth. It was as lifeless and desolate as anything he had ever seen.

As the sun began to rise he could see the white glare of salt and the outlines of the two steam engines the company used to power the dragline pulling the salt plows. Already, the Indians were at work in the sink, seeking to get most of their work done before the afternoon heat made it impossible. They moved along the furrows cut by the dragline and made curious coned mounds of pure, white salt with their shovels, while others pushed handcarts loaded with the stuff along a set of narrow-gauge rails leading from the salt works back to the processing plant alongside the Southern Pacific train tracks.

The wind was picking up as the sun rose higher, and a gust of it cast a wave of sand and fine gravel through the saltworks. Through that haze of rolling dust Newt saw Mateo and Mr. Smith moving toward the horse corral. The wind had picked up more by the time he joined them. He slid the silk bandanna tied around his neck up over his nose to protect the lower half of his face and to filter the dust. Mateo wore his striped serape over his head like a hood, one hand holding it closed about his face while he led the horses to water with his other hand. Mr. Smith seemed unbothered by the dust storm.

The salt company pumped in water from some source to the east, and an overhead tank served as storage. The tank had a branch of piping plumbed to a water trough, and Newt filled the trough and helped water the horses. All of their mounts were acting spooky, snorting or shying due to the windy conditions or frightened of Mateo's blanketed appearance.

"Windy," Newt said.

Mateo did not bother to open his blanket long enough

to speak, but Mr. Smith squinted against the gritty bite of the wind and nodded. "It would be a good thing if we could stay here today and wait this out."

"How long do you think it will last?"

Mr. Smith's black suit was already covered in dust, as was his face. "It could last for hours, or it could last for days. But I think it will get worse before it gets better."

Pablo came out to help them, and by the time the horses were saddled and the mule packed Remington motioned them over to the mess hall. All six of them sat down at a long table to cracked and chipped graniteware plates heaped with fried eggs, bacon, and buttered biscuits. Newt looked around for the company cook to thank him while he waited for his turn at the coffeepot, but there was no cook to be seen.

"You can thank Mrs. Duffield for the food. She's really quite the cook, even under such rustic conditions," Remington said, and then shoved a bite of biscuit in his mouth.

"Don't look so surprised, Mr. Jones," Alice said from a place at the far end of the table. "What, you don't think a woman like myself capable of whipping up a breakfast?"

Newt shoveled a forkful of eggs into his mouth to avoid having to answer her. She looked different that morning, and it wasn't only the dab of flour on her nose or the sweat-damp hair framing her forehead and the healthy glow of her cheeks from hovering over the cookstove. The hint of a smile she gave all of them reminded Newt of the way his mother and other women he had known had looked upon friends and family at the dinner table, taking pleasure in the sight of others enjoying good cooking. She was right, he hadn't expected that.

"Were the culinary arts something they trained you in at the ladies' academy?" Remington asked with a mischievous grin.

"Oh no," Alice said, laughing. "Etiquette, yes, but nothing so practical as how to cook your own food. Did you know a lady should only sit on the outer one third of her chair, and that she should never hold her teacup handle with more than three fingers?"

They all watched as she mimed a proper, stiff-backed pose at the table and held up a hand with a pinky finger snootily elevated as if sipping at a tiny teacup.

Remington laughed the loudest. "Ah, it's such a pleasure to be around a refined lady again."

Alice reached out and put a hand on top of Remington's on the table, as if she detected something else in the artist's laughter. She kept her hand on top of his for a moment, giving him a soft, searching look.

"You should go to her when this is over," she said to him. "Win her back."

Remington pulled his hand away and seemed embarrassed when he noticed they were all watching him. He ducked his head and busied himself with his food.

Newt wondered if Alice referred to the woman named Eva that Remington had mentioned a couple of times, and he also wondered how the artist had known that Alice attended college or some type of boarding school. The more he considered that, the more he thought it should have come as no surprise, for the longer their journey went the more he saw the two of them talking. Often, he heard them behind him laughing and chiding each other over one thing or another as if they were old friends and not recent acquaintances.

It seemed to have gotten harder for Newt to get to know new people over the years, and not simply because of the way he lived. Keeping his thoughts to himself had become a habit, and he realized now more than ever that he had become a clan of one.

Mr. Smith finished his plate and shoved back from the table, a reminder to all of them that it was time to leave. Newt was the next to rise.

"I don't relish riding in this," Remington said, expressing what they all were thinking when an especially strong gust of wind rattled the plank siding.

"Think of it this way," Newt said. "Kerr and McCluskey will most likely stay at Dos Palmas until this blows over. We'll have a good head start on him if we ride now."

"What about those gunshots we heard last night?" Remington asked.

Newt shrugged. They had all heard the gunshots that sounded like they came from Dos Palmas as they were riding into Salton, but there was nothing to be said about them. Still, the thought of those blasts in the night made him uneasy and restless.

Newt, Mr. Smith, and Mateo went outside to get their mounts while Remington and Pablo remained with Alice to clean up their dishes. In another half hour they were riding out of Salton.

Newt pulled his hat down tighter on his head and hunkered his chin down against his chest as they moved into the wind. Beside him, Remington, now sporting a pair of driving goggles and a long linen duster to go with his pith helmet, was having a hard time getting his horse to go the way he wanted it to. The unruly and skittish Thoroughbred

did not like going head-on into the wind and blowing dust
and it repeatedly tried to double back on him.

"How are you liking your adventure now?" Newt asked
the artist.

"What's that?" Remington wiped dust from his goggles
as if he was having trouble seeing Newt.

The salt works was almost invisible behind them by the
time they had ridden two hundred yards, lost in a cloud of
dust, but the sound of the train coming down the tracks
was plain. Newt looked back when he heard the train, and
could barely make out the dim glow of the engine's lamp.

And then he tucked his chin again and let the Circle Dot
horse carry him southward toward the dune country north
of Yuma. While behind him and around him, unknown to
him or the rest of them, other men moved upon the desert,
all with similarly risky intentions and all riding toward the
same point. All riding toward a treasure and a reckoning.

CHAPTER TWENTY-SIX

The storm was weakening, but the dust-coated outlaws had spent the last two hours hunkered on the lee side of a rocky hill at the foot of the Chocolate Mountains on the eastern side of the valley, waiting for the storm to pass. The dust had boiled up so thick that it found every crevasse and gap in their clothing. It got in ears and it got in eyes, and in every fold and crease on their bodies. It chafed and galled and stung like needles pricking them, and it choked them and made their voices raw and hoarse. The horses stood humped and as miserable as their masters, with their tails to the wind and heads low to the ground.

For the first hour there had been nothing said among the outlaws while the wind howled and they suffered through the worst of it, each of them lost in their own thoughts. But now that the wind was dying off they came out from under their blankets and hacked up muddy wads of phlegm and wetted their burning throats with water from their canteens. And when they finally talked again their conversation drifted back to what O'Bannon had been talking about the night before.

"It's easy pickings," O'Bannon said.

"With the lawdogs already hot on our heels? That's a hell of a way to run a holdup," Bendigo answered. "Has the sun fried your brain pan?"

"I guarantee you they're headed for the dunes," O'Bannon said carefully, wary of angering Bendigo further. The red-bearded outlaw scared him almost as much as McCluskey did, but he needed to sell them on his plan but still keep what he held in his possession a secret.

He regretted running to join the gang. It had been only fear of Jones chasing him that had made him do so. Mc-Cluskey was the nearest protection he could think of, but now he found himself in another kind of jam. If he had gone his own way it was likely that no one would ever have associated him with the kidnapping of the Kerrs. What was inside the antique leather tube tied behind his saddle was more than enough to get him back on his feet, but there he was. If the law caught them his neck would be in the same noose—more bad decisions and bad luck.

He looked over to where George Kerr and his daughter huddled together in a crack between two boulder slabs with a blanket pulled up to their chins. Not for the first time, he thought the old banker looked like he was about to die. The girl had managed to make a sling for her father's arm out of a strip of canvas she had begged from one of the outlaws, but not before O'Bannon saw the bloody bone poking through the skin right below the old man's elbow. If Kerr didn't get to a doctor quickly he was going to lose that arm, if not his life.

George Kerr's eyes were closed right then as he leaned his head on his daughter's shoulder. Maybe he was sleeping, but O'Bannon wasn't sure that he wasn't already dead. On the other hand, the girl's eyes were wide open. She kept watch on them all, and every time one of the outlaws moved in the slightest she flinched and tried to draw herself and her father back farther into the niche in the rocks.

O'Bannon thought McCluskey stupid not to have taken better care of his captives. Not only were they worth a lot of money, they were the only bargaining pieces he had if the law managed to run him down. But that was the problem with pistol work and muscle jobs. The kind of men who were good at it didn't know the meaning of finesse.

Now that O'Bannon had more time to think about it, he was desperate to get away from them without getting himself further involved in their bloody game. However, there seemed no way out short of the wild plan that had begun to formulate in his mind. It was risky, but maybe he could pull it off and then break off on his own once they were across the border. The idea he had come up with provided a chance to buy him more than enough time to decide what to do with the map and journal, if he could only convince McCluskey to help him.

He had purposely not told McCluskey's gang about what was inside the leather tube. He told them only that he had overheard Jones and the others with him talking about their intentions to look around the dunes for the lost ship. There was no way he would tell such men what he had stolen from Jones and his friends. That would be like playing with raw meat while locked in a cage with a pack of starved wolves. No, he was keeping that particular information to himself because it was as good as money in the bank. There were lots of things a man could do with what he had. At the very least, the papers would fetch a pretty penny from the right sucker.

McCluskey came back from where he had been lying on his belly atop the rocks scanning the dust-blown basin for any signs of pursuit from the north. He put his back to the gravel bank they were using as a windbreak and lowered his neckerchief from his mouth so that he could be heard more plainly. His eyes were red-rimmed and his eyelashes were white with powder. He must have overheard the bickering between O'Bannon and Bendigo.

"Are you still talking about that gambling woman?" McCluskey asked O'Bannon.

"Have you got something against making a little extra profit on our way to the border?" O'Bannon asked.

Bendigo gave a hiss of disgust. "There's likely a posse after us. You want to fiddle around and get yourself caught, have at it. Maybe you'll slow down that judge long enough to buy me some time."

"Do you know who that gambling woman is?" O'Bannon asked. "That's the one and only Poker Alice. Ever heard of her? Card Queen of the Rockies, that's what they say."

"I've heard of her," McCluskey said. "You sure?"

"I'm sure. Took me a while to put it together, but it's her." O'Bannon gave a cunning smirk, suddenly more confident now that McCluskey was listening again. "What kind of gambling roll do you think a high-stakes player like her carries around with her? Huh?"

"How much do you think?" McCluskey asked.

"Who knows?" O'Bannon shrugged. "Couple of thousand, maybe more."

"You're as crazy as he is," Bendigo said to McCluskey, and then got up and headed for his horse.

O'Bannon ignored Bendigo, knowing the window to sell McCluskey on his idea was narrowing by the second. "I told you right where she's going to be. She and the rest of them will be looking around those dunes for that ship. We hit them quick and we hit them hard."

"You mean you want *us* to hit them hard." Bendigo swung his saddle on his horse's back and settled it there. "You don't strike me as a gunhand. What you strike me as is the kind of little snake that gets other men killed."

O'Bannon said nothing to that, noticing that McCluskey seemed to be giving more than a little consideration to what he had told him.

Bendigo jerked the latigo tight on his saddle cinch and pointed a finger at O'Bannon. "I'd leave your sorry ass right here if it was me."

McCluskey stood and removed his hat and slapped it against one leg to knock the dust from it. Then he looked at Bendigo. "How long you think before the Judge's posse is on our trail?"

"I imagine he'll go to Dos Palmas first thing," Bendigo answered. "He'll find our handiwork there and be bawling on our trail like a bluetick hound as quick as that," Bendigo said.

"Then he'd be at Dos Palmas right now at the earliest." McCluskey looked to the north as if calculating how far he had come from Dos Palmas before the dust storm forced them to stop and take shelter.

"That'd be about right if he didn't wait out the storm at Salton," Bendigo said. "Say he did. That means he'll just now be riding for Dos Palmas."

"Three hours' head start on him? Maybe four?"

"You aren't seriously considering this, are you?"

"Like you said, this ransom business might not play out like I want," McCluskey said. "If that gambling woman is carrying a hefty road stake with her it's too good of an opportunity to pass up."

"You're getting too greedy."

"How good's Carlos with a rifle?"

Bendigo's bushy eyebrows narrowed to a contemplative squint. "I told you he's good. Real good."

"You leave Carlos with me and take everyone else with you. Go on to Alamo Mocho and lay up there and wait for me," McCluskey said.

"What if Carlos doesn't want to go with you?"

"Ask him."

"And what if you don't make it?"

"Whether or not I make it, you and the men can have my cut of the mules."

"You're buttering me up for something. How long do you expect us to wait for you?"

"Do what you want if I'm not in camp by tomorrow morning. Try for the ransom or ride for Ensenada, whatever you think best. There will be a ship waiting there. It'll take you up the coast to San Francisco."

The Bull Swede had been quiet until then. He rose and unwrapped himself from the saddle blanket he had used to ward off the dust. "Bendigo and the rest of them can have the mules. I want the girl."

"You're coming with me," McCluskey said.

"I'll go with Bendigo."

"I'm not leaving you with the girl. She's worth too much." McCluskey's right hand rested casually on the pistol on that side of him, as if it landed there by accident, even though it didn't.

Bull licked his thick, cracked lips. "You're pushing awfully hard."

McCluskey looked at Bendigo. "Take care of the Kerrs. I'll be at the wells by morning."

The other outlaws, giving McCluskey and Bull plenty

of room, were already moving to their horses, including O'Bannon.

"O'Bannon, you're coming with me, too," McCluskey said.

Bull remained faced off against McCluskey, his round eyes blinking slowly beneath the sagging hood of his brow.

"Try him, Bull, or go get on your horse," Bendigo said. "I'm tired of watching you stand there and quiver."

"The girl is mine when this is over." Bull licked his lips one more time before he turned his back to McCluskey and went to saddle his horse.

Bendigo led his horse close to McCluskey and gave a jerk of his head toward Bull. "I wouldn't sleep too soundly around him. You've made an enemy there."

"Bull doesn't worry me," McCluskey said. "You ever beat a dog, Bendigo? No matter how mean he is, once you beat him he doesn't forget. He'll tuck his tail and flinch from you every time you raise a hand or talk loud."

"Maybe, but that same dog will still snap your fingers off if you corner. Bite you out of pure reflex, no matter what kind of bluff you hold."

In a matter of minutes the outlaws were all saddled and the two strings of mules were readied for travel. George Kerr had to be all but physically carried to his horse and set in the saddle. Once mounted, he slumped as if he had no strength left.

"He can't ride. You're killing him, can't you see?" Madeline looked frantically from one outlaw to another, searching for an ounce of mercy where there was none.

"All he's got to do is make it a little farther," McCluskey said. "Now you get up on your horse. Bendigo here will send for a doctor as soon as you get to the wells, won't you, Bendigo? Have that arm set and splinted up proper."

"Sure thing," Bendigo said.

The look on Bendigo's and the rest of the outlaw's faces was the same. Every one of them knew that there was no doctor within forty miles of Alamo Mocho. And even if there was, nobody was going for one.

"How many did you say were with that gambling woman?" McCluskey asked O'Bannon.

"Five of them, the big Indian, Jones, that tenderfoot wearing the funny helmet, and two Mexicans," O'Bannon said. "Take out Jones and the Indian, and I think the tenderfoot and the Mexicans will run."

Carlos, one of the two Mexican outlaws who had come to Bitter Spring with Bendigo, laid his Winchester across the big flat saddle horn of his charro saddle and gave O'Bannon a cold look. "Not all Mexicans run, *pendejo*."

McCluskey gave a dry, throaty chuckle. "I think you offended our Mexican friend, O'Bannon."

McCluskey studied Carlos more carefully than he had up to that point, a whipcord lean man dressed like a vaquero, from his preposterously-sized sugarloaf sombrero and clanking spurs to the leather charro leggings with silver dollars set up the sides of them. His thick black mustache set off the wolfish angles of his brown face, and he sat a horse like he was made to it, languid and relaxed. He was young, but McCluskey sensed the deadliness in him.

And then he looked at the bandit's Winchester again. Despite Bendigo's assurance that the Mexican was an exceptional marksman, the Winchester was nothing special— nothing but a '73 saddle ring carbine. No fancy sights, no long heavy barrel, no set triggers like a target rifle, but simply an ordinary gun with the stocks nicked and scarred and the bluing rubbed away in places from where it had been carried in a leather scabbard.

"I take it you're coming with us?" McCluskey asked.

Carlos nodded. "*Sí*. You say this woman you speak of has money. I like money and I like women."

"Are you as good with a long gun as Bendigo says you are?"

"I don't know how good he say I am."

"Not much of a rifle you've got there."

Carlos patted the stock of his Winchester and smiled. "The gun is not so important as the man who pulls the trigger, no?"

O'Bannon was up on his horse by then. McCluskey took note of the poor condition of the Irishman's mount. It looked worse than it had when he rode it into Dos Palmas the night before, and in no shape for a run if it came to that.

Bull swung heavily onto his own horse and rode close to Madeline Kerr and stopped. He leaned out in the saddle close to her. "You have yourself all washed up and pretty when I get back, little *kvinna*."

Madeline spit in Bull's face. He reared back a fist to strike her, but McCluskey's voice stopped him.

"Leave her be," McCluskey said.

Bull never even looked at McCluskey, but he lowered his fist and didn't hit her. He wiped the spit from his face and leaned close to her once again. "Zander's being nice until he gets your papa's money. When he's through with you it's going to be my turn."

Before Madeline could reply, Bull reined his horse away. Bendigo took the rope tied to her and her horse and led off, headed west across the valley. Behind him came the three other outlaws going with him, one on each side of George Kerr to make sure he stayed in the saddle, and another leading the mules.

McCluskey waited and watched until Bendigo and

those going to Alamo Mocho were well away, and then he set off to the south toward the Algodones Dunes at a trot. O'Bannon followed him. Next came Carlos, with Bull riding last and well behind. O'Bannon could hear the Swede grumbling and talking to himself.

"Come on, Irishman," McCluskey said when O'Bannon's horse began to lag off the pace. "Time to go scavenging."

O'Bannon kicked his tired horse after McCluskey. "I don't think I've ever heard it put that way."

"What else is it? You think you're a badman, O'Bannon? A hard-assed, cold-eyed killer like Bendigo or that vaquero behind you? Think you're a curly wolf at the top of the pecking order because you can hold a pistol on a man or trick him and take what's his?" McCluskey asked. "Doesn't matter how hard you are or how mean. Some pretend they've got rules and some don't. Some die quick and some take longer, but we're all the same where it matters. All we are is scavengers, waiting for a chance to dart in and snatch a bite of the scraps or picking at bones. Take what we can sink our teeth in and what we think we're strong enough to keep, for as long as we can keep it."

O'Bannon didn't know what to say to that. He never had understood half of the strange, dark things McCluskey had said back in prison, and that was part of the reason the man scared him so. Maybe some of that talk was a head game meant to give him an edge on his adversaries, but that wasn't all of it. On the outside, McCluskey wasn't the animal Bendigo or the Bull Swede were, but the inside of him was as black as the bottom of a twisted, turning hole dug straight to perdition.

O'Bannon glanced behind him at Carlos. The Mexican stared back at him, still holding the Winchester across his saddle swells.

"I don't like how that Mexican is looking at me," O'Bannon said in a quiet voice intended for only McCluskey to hear.

McCluskey threw a quick look at Carlos and then turned his attention back to the desert ahead of him. "Yep, I don't think he likes you."

"Him riding behind us with that rifle doesn't bother you?"

"There's never been a minute of my life I didn't feel like there was a gun pointing straight at my head, except for when I'm pointing a gun at somebody else. That's the trick to it all. Be the one with the gun or the most guns."

CHAPTER TWENTY-SEVEN

The Algodones Dunes stretched for forty-five miles north to south, and in a swath five to six miles wide at their widest point. Ridge after ridge of pure, loose sand, mounded and shaped like waves by the prevailing winds. Some of the dunes reached as high as three hundred feet above the desert floor. The Southern Pacific tracks passed through a strip of tight ground between the eastern edge of the dunes and the foothills and bare brown slopes of the Chocolate Mountains on their way south to Yuma.

Newt led them south following the old Indian trading trail and wagon road paralleling the train tracks, and by the time the dust storm was over they came into sight of the northern tip of the dunes. The sand was only a mile wide before them at that point, and relatively flat. But not too far in the distance they could see the beginning of the real dunes.

Newt moved them along the edge of the sand. Two miles farther on, and with the evening sun burning low in the west, he stopped the Circle Dot horse and gazed at the vast labyrinth of dunes before him. There was still enough wind to whip sprays of sand from their knife-edged crests and to stir dust devils to life on the flats, and he knew he was witnessing the slow and infinitesimal changing of the landscape right before his eyes. He wondered how a man could ever hope to find a ship stranded three hundred years earlier among all that shifting sand. The impossibility and immensity of what they had set out to do struck him hard.

The others must have been having the same thoughts, for they grew quiet. Even Remington's youthful exuberance was gone for once. Poker Alice simply looked mad and frustrated, showing what they all felt. They moved on, and the farther south they went, the more expansive the dunes became.

"How much sand would you have to move to find a ship in all of that?" Remington finally asked.

"Maybe that's how McCluskey found the ship," Alice said hesitantly. "Maybe the wind uncovered it."

"If that's the case, how do we know it isn't covered again?" Remington asked. "I never thought it would be like this. We could look for a lifetime and never find it. I wouldn't even know where to start."

"Then we stick to the plan," Newt said. "Let's wait and see if Kerr and McCluskey come this way. Take us a high place where we can use my binoculars."

With that in mind, Newt led them out onto the sand toward a group of larger dunes, and then into a narrow pass between two of them. The sand grew heavier and looser the farther they went and the horses were already struggling. The way he chose eventually led them behind a high, peaked dune and dead-ended there. They dismounted and hobbled their horses.

In single file, they followed him on foot up the slope of the big dune. It was a hard climb. In the steepest places, the sand cascaded down the dune face and caved in around their boots and buried them to their ankles. They were scrambling on hands and knees by the time they neared the crest, all of them with quivering leg muscles and gasping for air.

Newt sat at a place where he could peer over the top of the dune but not skyline himself. The others began to take similar positions.

He took his binoculars from the case slung around his neck and glassed the desert, panning slowly in a wide arc.

"See anything?" Remington asked.

"Not a thing."

Alice arranged her dress skirt about her legs and sat on the sand next to Newt. "How long do you intend to stay here? I wouldn't call this a good place to make camp."

"I guess it's a half hour till sundown. Come dark, we'll move across the tracks to those mountains. Find us a place to watch from tomorrow morning," he answered.

"What then? What if they don't show?" she asked.

"Then we have our own look around, or we quit."

"It's impossible if McCluskey doesn't guide us to it, isn't it?"

"Think about something else," he said. "That always makes the waiting easier."

He looked beyond her and saw that Remington had brought his bedroll blanket with him. He watched as the tenderfoot unrolled it and laid it over his head and shoulders, and then used his rifle butt grounded in the sand to form a sort of a tent pole for the shade he was improvising.

"Where'd you learn that?" Newt asked.

"The Bedouin and Tuareg people of the Sahara Desert use this technique, either using a blanket or unwinding the cloth from the turbans they wrap around their heads," Remington said.

"You've been to Africa?" Alice asked.

"Unfortunately, no, but when I was a boy I read Captain Riley's memoir of his shipwreck and troubles upon that desert," Remington said. "Quite a fascinating book, really. You should read it if you ever get a chance."

Mr. Smith chuckled and all heads turned to him in surprise at the sound coming from him.

The Mohave looked back at them and gave them a superior lift of his chin. "I do not know these tribes you speak of, but my people have known that trick for as long as there have been men upon the desert. Our women and children know that without being told or reading it in one of your books."

Remington nodded his head at Mr. Smith to acknowledge the statement and then gestured at Mateo sitting beyond the Mohave and at the broad-brimmed sombrero sagging down on the young man's head. "I think Mateo has it over us all. His hat is big enough to shade two men."

Even Mateo laughed at that. The depression that they all seemed to have been feeling lifted some with the laughter.

"What about you, tenderfoot?" Newt asked. "That chamber pot you're wearing on your head doesn't give you enough shade?"

Remington grinned at him. "Go ahead, make fun of my headgear if you will. But I assure you it's light as a feather and keeps my cranium much cooler than that felt lid of yours. You should consider purchasing one yourself."

"That'll be the day." Newt handed his binoculars to Alice. "Keep a lookout. I forgot my canteen and I'm going down to get it."

He was halfway upright when the bullet struck him and knocked him backward down the slope. The blow was followed almost immediately by the report of a rifle. Stunned, it took the others a moment to react as they watched Newt's body slide and roll down the dune.

Poker Alice's mouth opened, and it was unclear whether she intended to scream in shock or to call out some warning to the others, for another bullet struck the sand in front of Mr. Smith. Before she could utter a sound, the Mohave took hold of her arm and jerked her with him when he dove headlong down the dune. She was faintly aware of more guns booming, but by then he had lost his grip on her and she flew into an uncontrolled somersault and landed head-first in the sand.

CHAPTER TWENTY-EIGHT

A narrow strip of tight ground and a dry wash choked with desert brush reached out like a finger into the blow sand east from where Newt and his party waited on the dune. On the far bank of that arroyo, McCluskey watched as Carlos sat with one knee upraised and rested his battered .44-40 carbine's forearm on his left hand braced atop that knee. The Mexican had folded the front of the brim of his sombrero up to keep it out of his sight picture, and he nestled his cheek to the walnut buttstock and took careful aim.

McCluskey tried to estimate the distance between their position and where Newt Jones and those with him perched atop the dune. It was at least two hundred and fifty yards if it was an inch. However, the Mexican didn't seem fazed by the challenge at all.

"That's a hell of a long shot," McCluskey whispered to Carlos.

"Shoot the Indian as soon as I pull the trigger, if you can," Carlos said without lifting his head from his Winchester.

McCluskey's own rifle rested in the fork of a scrub

mesquite and he struggled to find a good sight picture on
the Indian. The buckhorn sights on his '76 Winchester felt
too coarse at that range, and he worried over how much
elevation to take. The big fat .50-95 cartridge the gun was
chambered for carried well and hit hard at distance, but
McCluskey knew the limits of his own marksmanship with
a rifle. He preferred a pistol in his hand and his opponents
at close range.

He took a quick look at O'Bannon a little ways down
the gully from him. The Irish flimflam man didn't have a
long gun, but he held his little Colt Pocket Police, regardless of whether or not he could do something with it.

Beyond the Irishman, Bull lay on his belly with his own
big-bore Winchester stretched out before him. He was still
mad at McCluskey, and hadn't said more than a few reluctant words to him since they had split off from the rest of
the gang. But mad or not, the Swede gave a slight nod to
him when he saw him looking his way.

McCluskey focused his attention back on his rifle sights
and the faint shape of the Indian wavering before them.
The sun was so low on the horizon that it cast the portion
of the Indian he could see in a clear, dark silhouette. His
finger found the trigger, kissing it softly, ready to squeeze
it as soon as Carlos fired.

The bellow of Carlos's carbine surprised McCluskey,
even though he was expecting it. He had a brief glimpse
of Jones tumbling down the dune, before he steadied his
aim as best he could and fired his own shot at the Indian.

He knew he had missed even as his rifle recoiled against
his shoulder, and he worked the lever on the Winchester
frantically to jack another round in the chamber. By the
time he was ready again the Indian was gone, so he swung

his aim toward a big Mexican hat he could make out and fired again. Beside him, Carlos fired a second shot, a split second behind his own, and Bull was shooting, too. McCluskey worked the lever on his own rifle as fast as he could, firing two more shots, none of them aimed at anything more than flashes of movement and indistinct shapes as their victims disappeared from sight.

Carlos raised his head from his carbine stock and looked McCluskey's way when they stopped shooting.

"Did you get him?" McCluskey asked as he thumbed fresh cartridges in the loading gate of his rifle.

"I hit him," Carlos said.

"I missed the Indian, but I might have got one of the others."

"I think I hit the Indian, too," Carlos said.

McCluskey didn't know how that could be possible. By the time Carlos had been able to get off a second shot the Indian was already diving down the dune. Yet, the Mexican seemed confident that he had made not one, but two difficult shots, one of them a snap shot at a rapidly moving man at over two hundred yards away.

No return fire from the dunes came their way, and that surprised McCluskey.

"Think what's left of them are running?" he asked.

"Maybe," Carlos replied. "Or maybe so they get ready to fight."

"What now?" O'Bannon's voice was higher and tighter than usual.

"Now we go get our hands dirty." McCluskey looked to Carlos. "You stay here in case one of them shows and tries to take a potshot at us."

McCluskey rose and moved down into the gully and

followed it around a bend to where their horses waited. Bull and O'Bannon came behind him, but the Irishman hesitated instead of getting on his horse.

"I don't like the thought of riding into those dunes if they're laying for us," O'Bannon said.

"Get on your horse," McCluskey said.

O'Bannon mounted and the three of them rode slowly in a wide arc that would put them on the sand somewhat south of the cluster of big dunes. McCluskey gradually drifted away from the Irishman, and Bull did the same. They rode fifty yards apart, putting space between them so as not to make it easy for anyone who might be waiting to take a shot at them. McCluskey rode with his rifle butt propped on his thigh and stopped his horse often, searching the dunes for signs of life and trying to determine a course through them that would be to his advantage.

The sun was right on top of the mountains to the west by the time they worked their way behind where they had last seen their victims. When they topped over a sand ridge McCluskey saw the woman kneeling over Jones's body halfway up the side of the big dune. Below her in the V between two dunes, two other men were taking the hobbles off their horses.

McCluskey barely had time to take that in before a Mexican boy stepped out of the horses and fired a rifle at him. The bullet somehow missed him, and he charged down the dune straight at the kid with his horse lunging and stumbling in the deep sand.

The Mexican kid held his ground and tried to reload his single-shot rifle, but McCluskey held his Winchester out one-handed like a pistol and fired it into the kid's chest at almost point-blank range. The kid's rifle flew from his hands and he went down.

Behind the kid, the tenderfoot wearing the helmet appeared out of the milling, frightened horses, and McCluskey spurred his mount straight at him. His horse's chest struck the tenderfoot solidly and knocked him flying. He had barely come to a stop when he saw the other Mexican, the older one, swing up on a horse and whip it to a run.

McCluskey threw his rifle to his shoulder and swung the weapon's front sight toward the Mexican, but a pistol cracked from somewhere nearby and his horse staggered sideways and then went down as a bullet struck it high in the neck. He kicked free of his stirrups barely in time to avoid the horse rolling over him, and had his rifle knocked from his hands by the dying animal's thrashing hooves.

McCluskey tripped and fell to his hands and knees but came up again clawing for one of his pistols. Some of the horses were running away, frightened by the gunfire, but several still had their front legs hobbled and could only mill and lunge about. On the ground in the midst of that confusion, he could not see who it was that had shot his horse from under him. Bull charged past him, firing his pistol at the fleeing Mexican.

McCluskey caught a flash of movement out of the corner of his eye and spun in that direction and saw O'Bannon still sitting his horse atop the dune with his pistol uselessly pointing at the sky.

The Irishman seemed frozen in place and stunned by the commotion he saw. Whatever he intended to do, if anything, he thought about it too long. The big Indian rose up out of the sand behind him like a ghost and swung some kind of club in an overhand blow that struck O'Bannon in the side. The Indian grabbed O'Bannon's bridle and fought with the horse until he bent its neck and jerked it down. O'Bannon was pinned underneath the horse as it fought to get back up, and the Indian moved over him and reared back with the club to strike again.

McCluskey thumbed the hammer on his Colt and fired a shot at the Indian. The revolver bucked in his fist and he saw the Indian take a step backward as if struck.

O'Bannon's horse surged upright with the Irishman reeling in the saddle, and temporarily blocked McCluskey's view of the Indian. The horse fled down the dune with O'Bannon clutching weakly at his saddle horn. The Indian was nowhere in sight once O'Bannon was out of the way.

A bullet whipped by McCluskey's head. A horse in front of him broke the rawhide hobbles tying its front legs together, and when it ran away he found himself face-to-face with the woman. She held a pistol leveled on him, the end of the barrel inches from his nose.

He should have been dead, but she didn't pull the trigger quickly enough. He slapped the pistol aside with his free hand, felt the hot lash of her bullet pass his side and the sting of unburned powder, and then slapped her in the side of the head with the barrel of his Colt. She staggered, and he struck her again.

The woman wilted at his feet, and McCluskey kicked her in the chest and put her on her back. He put a boot on her to pin her down and pointed his pistol at her forehead. She glared up him with blood trickling down one side of her face.

He looked away from her long enough to ascertain he wasn't about to be attacked from elsewhere. When O'Bannon rode up to him he was clutching his side and humped over his saddle. His face was pale and sickly in the gray evening light.

"Where's that damned Indian?" McCluskey snarled.

"I don't know," O'Bannon groaned.

"Well, look for him!"

"I'm hurt bad."

McCluskey glanced up the dune at Jones's body. The man lay with his back to him, but even from fifty yards away he could see the blood soaking through Jones's shirt, dead to all appearances.

But then the body moved. Jones rose slowly, one hand braced against the sand while he got a leg under him. McCluskey watched as Jones got to his feet, swaying and reeling weakly and staggering a step down the dune toward him. There was as much blood on the front of him as there was on the back.

McCluskey raised his pistol and aimed. The wounded man almost fell, and then came on another step. McCluskey fired and Jones fell down the slope and skidded to a stop facedown on the sand.

"Ride up there and make sure that son of a bitch is dead this time," McCluskey said to O'Bannon. "You can do that much, can't you?"

O'Bannon rode a ways up the face of the dune. He grimaced when he looked down at the body. "He's done for. You put one through his head."

"Well, keep a lookout for that Indian and the rest of them," McCluskey said.

And then McCluskey looked to where he had run over the tenderfoot in the helmet, but couldn't see any sign of him. O'Bannon had said there was six of them, counting the woman. Jones and one of the Mexicans were down, and Bull was chasing the other Mexican. That left the tenderfoot and the Indian.

He looked down at the woman and saw her staring at her pistol not far from her on the sand where she had dropped it.

"You just don't quit, do you?" he asked her.

She glared at him, but said nothing.

He bent and snatched up her pistol. It was a Smith & Wesson .44 with walnut grips inset with little blue turquoise crosses.

"Now that's a big pistol for a little woman," he said.

She struggled underneath his boot, and he pressed down harder with it until she quit. He tucked the pistol behind his belt and took his boot off her. She rose to a sitting position, but did not get to her feet.

His attention was jerked away from her by the sight of Bull coming back with his horse at a run.

"Riders!" Bull said when he reined in, his blowing horse showering Newt with sand.

"Where?" McCluskey asked.

"To the north," Bull answered.

"Is it the Judge?"

"I don't know. All I saw was their dust. Maybe two miles out, maybe less."

"Did you get that Mexican?"

Bull shook his head. "He got away."

Carlos appeared and rode to them.

"Catch me a horse," McCluskey said to him.

All but two of the horses were gone, a big, lanky sorrel and a brown. The sorrel was so scared it was trembling, and it shied wildly when the outlaw vaquero rode to it and caught it by the bridle. Carlos waited until the sorrel quit fighting him, and then dismounted and untied the hobbles from its legs.

McCluskey looked down his pistol barrel at the woman. "Where's your money?"

Again, she didn't answer him.

He kicked her in the side. She folded over, gasping from the pain.

"Lady, do you realize how bad this can get?" he said when she finally looked back up at him.

"I don't have any money," she said.

He could see her formulating which lie she thought he might believe. "Where's your gambling stakes? I won't ask you again."

"I put it in the bank in San Bernardino," she said.

He made as if to kick her again, and she held up a hand in a futile attempt to ward the blow off. He took a slow breath trying to decide whether she was telling the truth or not.

Carlos was going through the saddlebags on the sorrel's saddle. He found nothing, and went and caught the brown and searched the gear on its back the same way.

"No money," Carlos called out. *"Nada."*

"Which horse was yours?" McCluskey asked her.

"Mine ran off with the others," she said.

Carlos handed O'Bannon the reins of the sorrel and the brown and rode up to the top of one of the higher dunes and looked to the north.

"What did you do with it?" McCluskey snarled at the woman. He fought down the rage he felt coming over him and the urge to pull the trigger and splatter her brains all over the sand. "You've got the money on you, don't you?"

"I told you, I left my stakes and my luggage in San Bernardino."

"We need to go," Carlos called out to him.

"They're coming this way?" McCluskey called back to him.

"They come," Carlos said. "They getting close. Must hear our guns."

McCluskey calculated how much light there was left—maybe ten minutes, maybe less. There was a good chance that the dust Carlos had seen was the Judge's posse. They might not find him in the dark if he stayed put, but they would track him down in short order come sunup. It was time to run.

"Get up," he said to the woman.

When she didn't get up quickly enough to suit him he grabbed her by the hair and jerked her to her feet. She cried out and swung at him, but he shook her once and then took hold of the red-checkered blouse she wore and ripped it halfway off one shoulder, revealing the flesh at the top of one breast and the black bodice she wore.

"You hand over the money or I'll search every inch of you," he said to her.

She pulled the torn fabric and clutched it to her chest to cover her nakedness. "I told you, I don't have it with me!"

He snatched at her blouse again, took hold, and ripped it more when she tried to pull away from him. It was then that he saw the pistol. He yanked it from its hidden holster built into the ribbing of her bodice beneath her breasts. It was a snub-nosed Colt Lightning .38.

He threw the pistol in the direction he had thrown the first one. "Sneak gun, huh? What else have you got hidden on you?"

"That posse is going to be all but breathing down our necks if you don't hurry," O'Bannon said.

Bull licked his lips before forcing himself to look away from the woman. "Much as I enjoy this, the Irishman's right. Quit fooling around. We need to ride."

"Watch her," McCluskey said.

McCluskey went and found his rifle where it had been kicked from his hands, and then he went to his downed horse and stripped off a few items of gear. When he returned to them he took the brown gelding by the reins and led it to her.

"What are you doing?" O'Bannon asked.

"She's coming with us."

"Forget her," O'Bannon said.

"I said she's coming with us," McCluskey snapped.

"I like the way you think," Bull said.

Carlos rode back to them.

"You didn't see any of the horses, did you?" McCluskey asked him. "Her money must be with her horse."

"I see them running a long ways off, but if we go after them we will have to fight."

McCluskey cursed and jerked the Winchester free that was in the boot on the brown gelding's saddle. He pitched the rifle to Carlos. "Man that can shoot like you needs a better rifle."

Carlos caught the rifle. He stuffed the weapon in his own saddle scabbard and kept his familiar carbine to hand.

"Get on the horse," McCluskey said to the woman.

She tried to ignore him, but he took hold of her, slapped her hard when she resisted, and all but physically lifted her onto the horse's back. She kicked at him, but he knocked her foot away and took hold of one of her arms and squeezed hard.

"You fight me one more time and I'll take my knife and cut you seven ways from Sunday," he said. "Hear me? I'll peel you all the way down to the quick."

Her chin quivered and her eyes were shining with tears, but she nodded at him.

He kept her bridle reins and led her horse over to the sorrel Carlos O'Bannon held for him. He mounted and pulled her horse close to his.

"I need another horse," O'Bannon said. Truly, his mount looked worn out, but there was no other horse to be had.

"You should have thought of that quicker," McCluskey said.

He spurred his horse off, leading the woman's horse behind him. The other three outlaws followed him. Instead of heading eastward toward the railroad tracks where the escaped horses had fled and where he would have gotten out of the sand more quickly, he pointed them westward. The sand limited the speed of their flight, but he pushed as hard as he could, knowing they had to put as much distance as they could between themselves and whoever was coming from the north. With any luck they could lose them in the dark.

Theirs was a wild ride out of the blow sand, trying to avoid the worst of the dunes and fighting the pull of the sand the whole way. Twice McCluskey thought the big sorrel Carlos had caught for him was going down, but each time it got its legs back under it.

They eventually struck tight ground again at the edge of the dunes and pointed southwest toward the border, spurring and lashing their tired horses to a run. McCluskey was pleased to discover that the big lanky sorrel could really run. A fast horse was ever a welcome thing to a man on the wrong side of the law.

O'Bannon's horse stumbled and went to its knees when they crossed a wide dry wash. The others stopped and turned back to see what had happened.

O'Bannon's horse was back up, but O'Bannon had been thrown from the saddle and was on his hands and knees at the bottom of the wash.

"Don't leave me," O'Bannon begged. "Catch my horse for me."

McCluskey knew it didn't matter. O'Bannon's horse was done, and O'Bannon looked too injured himself for the ride ahead of them. McCluskey turned his horse and rode away. Bull laughed and did the same, but Carlos hesitated for a moment, his horse dancing in place.

"Can't you see? I'm all busted up," O'Bannon said. "That red savage caved in my rib bones."

Carlos reached up and took hold of the brim of his sombrero and gave a mock tip of it to O'Bannon, followed by a malicious grin. *"Adios, pinche cabrón."*

Carlos let his horse go and it tore after McCluskey and the woman, leaving O'Bannon in the bottom of the arroyo alone.

CHAPTER TWENTY-NINE

At the sound of the gunshots, Charlie Two Horses pulled up his mount a hundred yards in front of the posse. It wasn't long before the Judge and the rest of them caught up to him.

"Is it them?" the Judge asked.

Charlie pointed to the loose horses running across the desert in the distance. "Some kind of fight going on out there."

The Judge took up his telescope from where it hung from his saddle horn and extended it out to its full length. It was a spyglass of brass and wood, like the kind used on sailing ships. He stood in his stirrups and put the optic to his right eye and scanned the desert before them.

"What do you make of that?" the Judge asked when he put the spyglass down and sat back in his saddle.

"Their trail splits back there in those rocks you left a mile back. Half of them went west with the mules, but the other half went south.

"Why would they split up?" the Judge asked, not liking what he heard.

"I don't know, but not long after they split up six more

riders came along going right behind those three headed south."

"How do you know they didn't all come through at the same time?" the county deputy asked.

Charlie gave him a smug look for an answer. The Judge scowled and tucked a strand of his long white hair behind one ear. Charlie knew that the Judge was thinking about having to split his posse and weighing what that implied.

"Could you tell which bunch took George and Madeline?" the Judge asked.

Charlie nodded. "The ones with the mules. The water diggings at Monument Station went dry years ago, so I guess they're heading for Sackett's Wells and then Jacumba Pass. Or maybe they aim to cut south for the border before then and water at Gardener's Wells or Alamo Mocho."

The Judge glanced at the loose horses running across the desert not far in the distance where the gunshots had come from, then he looked to the west across the valley the way his brother's captors had gone.

"We've got some of them right here. We'll tend to them and then go after the rest," the Judge said, "Charlie, you take half the men and go down this side of the dunes. I'll take the rest of the men and go down the west side."

Charlie nodded at the Judge. He knew it wasn't easy for the old man to delay going after his family in order to tend to those of the outlaws that had split off from the rest of the gang. First the Judge had been handed the ransom letter the instant they got off the train at Salton, and then not an hour later they had found the abandoned wagons and Buck Tillerman's corpse. He hadn't said more than a few words since they had left Dos Palmas, but Charlie could tell he was furious. Not the loud kind of mad, but the deep-down, cold, methodical kind of fury that comes over a man when he has been wronged but knows there is no quick way to take his revenge.

The posse wasn't as calm as the Judge, by any means. At first, the outlaws' trail away from the springs had been so plain that they didn't even need a tracker to follow it, and they had all wanted to rush off at full speed. But the Judge made them take the time to bury Buck and then kept their pace to a walk or an easy trot the rest of the day while he sent Charlie ahead to track. The Judge aimed to catch the men who had killed his son-in-law and taken off with his brother and niece, but he was smart enough to know that it might be a long chase and he needed to take care of his horseflesh. And he had also spent the time back in Salton to send telegraphs to Yuma and other places before they had even set out for Dos Palmas. The Judge might act like a city man most times, but he understood such things. Hauling his posse down on the train had been his first smart move, and then taking it easy on his horses until they slowly caught up with their prey was his next piece of strategy.

The Judge stepped down from his gray gelding and checked his cinch before he climbed back up on the horse and shucked his rifle from his saddle boot. He pointed out the half of the men that he wanted and pulled his straw hat tighter down on his head.

"What if Charlie's wrong and they've got your brother or niece?" one of the posse members asked. "Be hard to know where to shoot without hitting your family, Judge. That's all I'm saying."

"Be careful," the Judge replied.

"I don't think they'll surrender easy."

"I'm not interested in prisoners," the Judge snapped.

"I figured . . ."

"You saw what they did to poor Buck. Buck was a good man, a friend to you all. I shudder to think . . . I verily quake with rage and worry over what they may have done, or might do, to my poor niece and brother." The Judge paused, his hard eyes scanning over them, one by one, to drive his message home. When he spoke again, his voice was louder and deeper. "Hear me now. Sometimes, extraordinary circumstances require extraordinary measures. These men we seek are the most heinous, vile animals on God's green earth. And I remind you that justice is not always simply just, but it is wrath and righteous fury meant to not only protect the weak, but to avenge them. Whether we hang them by the necks or you gun them down like the dogs they are, it will be equally just. Here and now, on this day, at this moment, you men are the embodiment of the law and I am the court, and I pronounce a sentence of death on all of them, so help me God."

"Judge?" one of the men asked.

The Judge cut him off. "I'll personally pay fifty dollars for every one of those outlaws you men put down."

The Judge did not wait to gauge the posse's reaction to his words, and lashed his horse across the hip with his riding quirt and put it to a run. The half of the men going with him spurred away after him.

Charlie Two Horses did not lead his half of the men off immediately. He sat his horse and watched the Judge ride away, the look on his face one of contemplation. The other men with him had the same look, and they remained where they were, even after Charlie finally set out.

The county deputy looked at the man beside him. "Did you hear what I just heard? Ole Law and Order himself just turned us into a lynch mob."

"The Judge is right," the man beside him answered.

"Buck was a good man. Considered him a friend of mine. Killing those that killed him might not bring him back, but they damned sure won't do the same to anybody else."

"The Judge ain't himself right now. It's not . . ." The deputy didn't finish what he was about to say.

The rest of the men were already spurring off after their tracker.

"Come on, Deputy," the man said. "That damned Charlie won't wait for anybody, and I aim to get my licks in for what they did to Buck."

CHAPTER THIRTY

Ed O'Bannon caught his horse and got back on it, but it took him far too long. By the time he rode out of the wash the other outlaws were out of sight. He tried to make his horse go in the direction they had fled, but despite his urging and cursing, it would not break out of a walk.

He stopped and looked back at the dunes. McCluskey had said that all of the other horses were gone, but he wondered if they might not have gone too far. If he could catch one, he might be able to escape the posse and get out of the desert alive.

He looked in both directions for a while, debating his options. After a time, he turned his worn-out horse back toward the dunes. He could plainly see where they had disturbed the sand in their passing, but his horse was making hard work of it. He was barely out on the sand before his horse gave a groan and went to its knees. He slid out of the saddle and kicked it in the belly until it got up again. Getting off and on the horse and kicking it made the pain in his ribs almost unbearable and caused him to have a fit of coughing.

Every time he moved wrong he could feel his rib bones

grating and grinding together, and it hurt simply to breath, much less to cough. And he was coughing more and more. He was shocked when he dabbed at something wet at the corner of his mouth and saw a smear of blood on his hand. The Indian's war club seemed to have broken something inside him, and that scared him more than anything else.

He tried to recall how far it was back to the ambush site, but wasn't sure of anything. His thoughts were cloudy and unsteady and he began to doubt he would make it at all. His horse stopped and was about to go down again, but he couldn't find the energy to fight with the animal anymore. The horse slowly buckled under him, and he let out a sad sigh. For some reason, he thought not of the desert around him, or even San Francisco or New York City. No, in that moment his mind floated to visions of the damp green fields and stone fences of County Mayo and the smell of peat smoke wafting from a chimney and lamplight glowing softly in the window of a sod-roofed cottage at the end of the road on a rainy night. *So far from home. Life could take a man places he could never imagine.*

Something struck him in the chest, and the next thing he knew he was on his back on the sand and staring up at the darkening sky. He hadn't noticed until then that it had grown so late and that the moon and the evening star were already visible.

He started to get back up, but didn't. Couldn't. No matter, it felt fine lying where he was. He glanced down at his shirtfront and saw the dark blotch of his own blood expanding across the fabric with every slow beat of his heart, and he saw the busted bits of bone and shredded meat explode out of the exit hole below his chest. It dawned on him then that he had been shot, though he couldn't fathom how it had happened. He hadn't even heard a gunshot.

He tried to get back up, but his body wouldn't work at all. The only thing he could seem to move were the fingers on one hand. He clenched those fingers into the sand, feeling the grit grinding into his palm. He took one more ragged breath, and that hand clenched more tightly and stayed that way. Both of his eyes were wide open, and the reflection of a star twinkled in one of them until the gray haze of death wiped it away.

The Judge rode his big gray gelding close to O'Bannon's body. He shifted his Marlin rifle to his other hand and leaned down from the saddle to have a closer look.

The posse came up behind the Judge, and one of them got down and struck several matches in a bunch and held them over the body so that the Judge could see better. "Hell of a shot, Judge. I'd say a hundred and fifty yards, and offhand from the back of a horse at that."

The Judge straightened in the saddle and pointed at the downed man. "Any of you recognize him?"

None of them did.

The Judge shook his head in displeasure. "That's not Hilcman or the other two that broke from prison with him. Not from the descriptions the warden gave me."

One of the men rode over to the dead man's horse. The poor beast had lain down on its side. The man dismounted and spent some time over the horse. When he was mounted again he rode back to the Judge.

"Found this," he said to the Judge.

The Judge took the leather tube handed to him.

"Strike another match so I can see," the Judge said.

Instead of matches, one of the men lit a kerosene lantern and held it over the Judge. The rest of them pushed their horses as close as they could to the Judge, curious as to what he held.

"Give me space," the Judge said.

They backed their horses a few steps away, but still peered at what the Judge held. The Judge stuffed his rifle in his saddle boot and opened the tube. He pulled out the roll of papers inside it and gave the first few a quick scan.

"What is it, Judge?" one of his men asked.

"Nothing, just some papers," the Judge said as he stuffed the papers back inside the tube.

"Was that one I saw some kind of a map?" the same man asked.

"No. Cut that light and go back over there and put that poor horse out of its misery."

All of them went to tend to the horse. It was plain that the Judge didn't want to talk and wanted to be left alone. With the lantern put out, none of them could see the look on the Judge's face. As such, they didn't see the frown on the Judge's face lift and the slight look of pleasure come over him.

The Judge had tied the leather tube behind his saddle with his bedroll by the time the pistol shot cracked and one of the men put a bullet in O'Bannon's horse's skull. That sound carried far over the desert, and it wasn't long before the sound of running horses could be heard not far away, guided to them by the gunshot.

"Somebody's coming, Judge," one of the men said.

The men spread out and readied their weapons, but it was Charlie Two Horses and the rest of the posse that rode in out of the night.

"Damn, Charlie. I like to have shot you," one of the men with the Judge said.

The Paiute tracker ignored the man and rode straight to

the Judge. His horse almost stepped on O'Bannon's body and shied wildly away from it.

"We found where those loose horses we saw came from," Charlie said when he got his horse back under control. "Back there in the dunes."

"Did you get any more of them?" the Judge asked.

"No. They were already gone. Looks like the four that split off from the rest of the gang ambushed those six riders I told you were following after them. Lucky they rode into the trap and not us."

"And where are the ones that got ambushed?" the Judge asked.

"Found a Mexican kid and a white man killed. Dead horse and not much else," Charlie said. "I'd say the rest of them got away, but it was too dark to tell. I barely had a chance to look at the sign before we heard your shot and thought they might have jumped you."

"We got one of them, but the rest got away," the Judge said.

"No way to track them in the dark," the county deputy said. "Not even Charlie is that good."

"I don't have to track them," Charlie said. "They aim to join back up with the rest of their gang. Headed for the border, like I said before. If we ride hard that way it shouldn't take us too long to pick up their sign again come morning."

"What'll it be, Judge? What do you want to do?" the deputy asked.

The Judge tapped his quirt on his thigh, once, then twice. "The sheriff at Yuma answered my telegraph and promised he'll have a posse riding west along the border with the intent to cut off any flight in that direction."

"If that's the case, I say we push hard for Sackett's Wells," Charlie said. "If we beat them there we'll have them cornered."

"That how you want it, Judge?" the deputy asked.

The Judge tapped his thigh again with the quirt. "We ride all night if that's what it takes. Their horses are bound to be about used up, so we'll push 'em hard. Ride them down or run them into that Yuma posse."

The Judge rode off to the west before any more questions could be asked of him. Charlie Two Horses took the time to take a swig from his canteen, and the rest of them waited with him.

"Well, what are you waiting for?" Charlie said to them when he put the stopper back on his canteen and hung it on his saddle horn.

Charlie put his horse to a trot going after the Judge, and soon all but the sound of his horse's hooves were lost to them in the night.

"You reckon the Judge will keep after them even if they get over into Mexico?" one of the men asked.

"The mood he's in, he'll chase them plumb to hell if that's what it takes," another answered.

"Come on, boys," the deputy said. "It is what it is. Time to earn our money and help the Judge set things right."

CHAPTER THIRTY-ONE

As bad as it was, it was the pain that let Newt know he was still alive, and it was the pain that brought him back to his senses. The throbbing of his skull was so intense that it felt as if his head were slowly being pried open and the intensity of that drowned out any cohesive thought. He groaned and pushed his face up from the sand, fighting against the dizziness. He fell the first time he tried to get up, and then fell again a second time. When he finally managed to get to his knees a sudden bout of nausea struck him and he leaned over and vomited until there was nothing left for his stomach to give up. Each heave of his abdomen made his head hurt worse.

He stayed there on his knees, gritting his teeth against each pulse of pain that came in time with every beat of his heart. He closed his eyes and waited, trying to find his balance and willing himself not to give in and lie back down. When he opened his eyes again his vision returned somewhat. Slowly, the blurry world before him cleared, and under the faint bit of moonlight, he saw the shadow of Mateo's body lying downhill from him. Not far away was what looked to be a dead horse.

A wave of dizziness overcame him again, and he sat on the sand and put his head between both hands. When the worst of it eased, he tenderly probed the wound on the right side of his head above his ear. He could feel the raw groove where the bullet had grazed him, skidding along his skull until he could feel bare bone.

And then he pulled up his blood-crusted shirt and checked the other bullet wound low down on his left side barely below the bottom of his ribs. The bullet had barely caught him there and punched clean through him just below the skin and through the meat above his hipbone. He couldn't see the exit hole, but he could feel it. The wound was still slowly seeping blood, so he tore two pieces from the tail of his shirt and stuffed them in the holes in him, front and back.

He wanted to sit for a while, but he knew that if he didn't get up then, he might not ever get up again. He picked up his hat and set it gently on his head, then surged to his feet and staggered the rest of the way down the dune to the dead horse. A thirst had come over him greater than any he had ever felt, and he guessed it was due in part to the blood he had lost as much as it was the length of time since he had last had a drink.

The dead horse was still wearing a saddle, but there was no canteen to be found on it. He sat on the horse and tried to clear his head. He knew his life hung as precariously as it ever had before.

He tried to remember how far it was back to Salton, and how long it would take him to get there on foot. And he considered whether or not he might make it before the sun came back up, or how far on to Yuma it might be if he headed south.

There was no way he could make it to either place

before sunup, but Pablo had said there were springs scattered up and down the fault line running along the east side
of the Salton Sink. If he could find one of them he might
make it, but many a man had died of thirst or succumbed
to the heat looking for water in a desert he didn't know.

The thought of the Mexican liveryman reminded him
of the others. He went to the body on the sand and kneeled
beside it. The moonlight was too faint to tell who it was,
but when he felt the rough weave of the wool serape with
his hand he knew that it was Mateo lying there.

Where had the rest of them gone? Were they all dead,
or had some of them gotten away?

As if recalling a bad dream, he remembered then the
sight of McCluskey standing over Poker Alice with his gun
drawn. And he remembered Ed O'Bannon on a horse. The
events of the ambush were all jumbled together, impressions and visions mixed and matched in a confusing blend.

His hand dropped to his pistol holster and found it
empty. He couldn't remember where or when he had lost
his .44. He checked for his knife and found it was still in
its sheath.

One of his boots bumped against something when he
got to his feet again, and when he reached down for whatever it was he took hold of Mateo's single-shot, rolling
block rifle. The action was already open and there was no
cartridge chambered. He knelt again over Mateo's body,
but could find no other ammunition for the gun.

Using the long rifle for a walking stick to help support
him, he moved along the V between the two dunes. He had
a vague plan to get out of the sand and move north along
the foot of the Chocolate Mountains until he might find
one of the oases said to be along the fault line, but he

hadn't taken very many steps before he heard a gunshot to the west.

He stopped and listened, but no other shots came. That shot could have been Alice or the others still fighting for their lives.

He thought again about McCluskey pointing the gun at him and felt the ache of his wounds. Amidst the pain, a rage slowly took over. He had no clue whether water could be found to the west. No matter, the men who had shot him and left him for dead had gone that way, and so could he, for however long he could last.

His plan was a simple one, and might have been impossibly daunting to a man in a better state of mind and body. He would walk until he could find a horse, and then he would run them down. He said a small prayer, not that he would live through his ordeal, but simply that he would live long enough to have revenge. What he wished for wasn't a miracle; what he wanted was one last fight. And he set out across the burning sand, moving slowly, but determined, as if the muscle and gristle and bone that tied him together could not fail him.

CHAPTER THIRTY-TWO

Bendigo stopped his horse, and the rest of them behind him did the same. He scanned the dark desert to the south. The border was only a mile away, and the wells at Alamo Mocho only a couple of miles into Mexico.

"What do you see?" Henry, the oldest of the outlaws, asked, his voice far too loud because of his bad ear.

"Look there to the south. Somebody's fire," Bendigo said.

After some searching, most of the outlaws spotted the tiny flickering flame of a campfire in the direction Bendigo was looking.

"I don't like that," Henry stated, saying what all of them were thinking, making an effort to keep his voice down.

"I'll bet you anything that fire belongs to the Yuma law. If that judge is after us, then he likely wired south for help," Bendigo said. "We can push on to Sackett's Wells."

"If they're at Alamo Mocho, they'll be there, too," Henry said. "I say we run for it."

"We might get past them in the dark, and there are plenty of places to water in those marshes and diggings along the bed of the Alamo. Might work, but our horses ain't in any shape for a run if they got wind of us."

"Take us close to that campfire and let us go," Madeline Kerr said. "Let us go and it will go easier on you if the law catches you."

Bendigo couldn't see anything of her but a faint black shadow in the night. They were the first words she'd spoken since they had left the dunes other than once asking for them to stop and let her father rest.

"Little girl," Bendigo said, "you're worth too much to let you go, and if we get caught nobody's going to go easy on us. This here is root-hog-or-die."

"They're hemming you in, and you know it," she said. "You're a fool if you think you're going to get paid a ransom now."

"You're right about one thing," Bendigo said. "Zander's plan has gone out the window with the wash water."

"Let us go," she pleaded. "Can't you see how bad Papa is?"

Truly, the old banker was in a bad way. In fact, Bendigo had expected the man to fall out of the saddle hours ago.

"Pinto Canyon," Bendigo muttered.

"What's that you say?" Henry asked with his good ear cocked in Bendigo's direction to hear better.

"I know a place where we could lay up and wait for those lawdogs to get tired and go home. Give our horses a rest and make a run south when things cool down," Bendigo said. "Plenty of water there but not much feed for our stock. An old mountain man showed it to me when I first came west. Him and Pegleg Smith and some others used to run horses back and forth across the border. Reckon I could find it again."

"How far?" Henry asked.

"Three, four hours' ride southwest of Sackett's Wells. We could be there by late morning."

Bendigo took a plug of chewing tobacco from his vest pocket and clenched it between his jaw teeth and tore a chunk off, thinking about the string of wells and springs scattered along the old Butterfield stagecoach road and the southern emigrant trail stretching across his front along the border and then angling northwest into the mountains. If there were lawmen stationed at each of those waterings, then slipping between them and riding for Pinto Canyon might be their best chance. Pinto Canyon spilled into Davies Valley, which offered an easy way into Mexico.

"Please let us go." Madeline sounded like she was crying.

"Maybe Zander's ransom scheme is shot all to hell, but we could still sell her to Cut Face," Bendigo said to Henry.

"Is that old renegade Yaqui still alive?" Henry asked.

"He's still alive," Bendigo said. "His bunch is hard to find, but he always has plenty of Mexican gold. He'd pay a fair price for a yellow-haired white girl."

"He'd be just as likely to stick a gut knife between our rib bones or feed us to his camp dogs," Henry said.

"No, me and him have traded before."

Bendigo could hear Madeline's breathing, and waited for some kind of reaction from her. When none came he said, "Don't take it so hard, girl. Maybe if you treat Cut Face real nice and keep him happy you'll make it."

"You don't think Zander and Bull are coming back?" Henry asked.

"They ain't going to make it, you mark my words."

"If he catches up to us, you'll have to kill him if you want to sell this girl to Cut Face. Zander's dead set on getting that ransom money."

"You let me deal with Zander if it comes to that."

"From what I hear, you ain't seen the day when you can handle Zander with a pistol. They say he's pure poison with those Colts of his."

Bendigo spit a stream of tobacco juice into the dark. "Zander might be salty with a hogleg, but he's like you, old man. Talks too much when he ought to shut up and shoot."

CHAPTER THIRTY-THREE

It was almost sunrise before Newt found another dead horse and Ed O'Bannon's body, and by then he was so spent that he didn't even notice the horse until he was all but right on top of it.

He gave O'Bannon's body only the slightest attention before he went to the horse. When he found the canteen on the dead horse's saddle he pounced on it, half out of his mind with thirst. He unscrewed the cap and turned the canteen up and let the tepid water pour down his parched throat. For a moment he glugged the water greedily, but got control of himself and set the canteen aside. Already he was feeling nauseous again as the water settled in his stomach, and it wouldn't do to drink too much, too fast, and vomit the precious liquid back up.

He searched the rest of the gear on the horse, and then O'Bannon's body as the morning sky grew lighter and lighter. Whoever had shot O'Bannon had taken the leather map tube from the Irishman, as well as the pistol from his shoulder holster. But a firearm or a treasure map was the least of Newt's concerns right then.

He found nothing that might do him any good other

than a paper box of Tiger matches and a tinned can of peaches. He took a short sip from the canteen, then shook it to determine how much water was left in it. It was less than half-full.

There was a spare shirt in one of O'Bannon's saddlebag pouches, but it was far too small to fit Newt. After bathing the wound in his side with little dabs of water from the canteen, he used the shirt as a bandage and wrapped it around his torso above his waist and tied it in place. He put the matches in his vest pocket and cut open the peach can with his knife. He drank the sweet syrup first, then speared the peach slices one by one and ate them. Whether it was the sugar, or simply moisture he badly needed, he began to feel steadier. The bleeding of the wound in his side seemed almost to have stopped.

That wound and the one on his head needed tending, but there was little else he could do for the moment besides deal with the pain. But it could have been worse, and now he found himself not totally unarmed to face the desert. A man with water, a knife, and the means to make fire had a fighting chance to survive. And if he could survive long enough he had a chance to set things right.

The urge to lie down and sleep was almost over-whelming, but he eyed the climbing sun and knew to sleep was to die. He had to move.

His bleary eyes studied the confusion of horse tracks around him on the sand. He could make little of that sign, but was sure that the tracks were from many horsemen. Some had come out of the dunes the same way he had, and the others had come from the north. All of the tracks headed off to the southwest together.

He got to his feet again, took up the rolling block rifle again as his walking stick, then set out following those horse tracks. Before him lay fifty miles or more of flat, sunburned desert. There was no color on that brown expanse other than the dull, gray-green dotting of sagebrush and a few scattered clumps of creosote. It was going to be a long walk.

He walked as far as he could before he rested. The temperature was one hundred degrees or better, and it wasn't even noon yet. The empty rifle became too hot to hold and too cumbersome, so he pitched it away.

More than once, the futility of a wounded man on foot trying to chase down well-mounted adversaries struck him. Regardless, he pushed away such thoughts almost as quickly as they formed, stomping on them and grinding them out as he would burning embers scattered from a fire.

After a while, he stopped for a moment and looked behind him. He could still see the dunes where he had left them, and he hadn't come as far as he had hoped. It came to him that he should take a break again, only a short one to let his weary legs recover and perhaps catch a quick nap. He fought off that urge, but it came again and again. Before he had covered the next mile he had drunk his canteen empty.

There was the momentary temptation to throw away the empty vessel to lighten his load, but he slung it back over his neck. If he did find water ahead he would need something to carry it.

He adjusted his hat on his head, tilting the brim of it to a better angle to block the sun, and the hat's sweatband tore away the crusted scab that was beginning to form over his head wound. He felt a slow trickle of blood sliding down his temple.

How much blood did a man have inside him to give? How much had he lost and how much had it diminished him? His skin felt as dry as the inside of his mouth, as if the outside of him were becoming nothing but a withering husk. The only sound in the world was the hot wind that sucked the sweat from his body and the scuff of his boot soles on the ground, step by step.

He was little more than five miles from the dunes where he had been shot when he came to the lip of a narrow, but steep-sided arroyo cutting through the flat. The horse tracks detoured down the wash, no doubt because the horsemen he followed were looking for a place to cross where the far bank wasn't so steep or straight. Instead of following the horse tracks, he cut straight across the wash, taking the shortest course and intending to pick the trail back up on the other side.

He half skidded and half fell down the bank to the bottom of the wash. On the far side, the bank was even higher where the wash cut into the side of a low swell of ground. He used both his hands and his feet climbing that bank, digging and clawing for purchase as the loose, eroded sand gave way underneath him. A clump of sagebrush growing at the lip of the bank offered a handhold, and he took hold of it and pulled. It was a young plant with its taproot yet to grow sufficiently deep, and in the moment when his full weight was supported by the bush it pulled free. He fell and landed back in the bottom of the wash.

The impact brought on more agony, but he got up and climbed again. When he bellied over the top of the cutbank he lay there on the ground with his chest heaving for air. He closed his eyes for a moment, and when he opened them again he saw the hole in the earth made where the clump sagebrush had ripped free.

He blinked, then blinked again to make sure that what he saw was really there. In the bottom of the little hole where the plant's root ball had been there showed a patch of rusted metal. He reached out to touch it, thinking it was some old belt buckle or other cast-off bit of metal left by other travelers. He was surprised to find that it was bigger than he thought when he reached for it, and that it seemed as solid as a stone.

He rose to his knees and began to dig the hole deeper. It didn't take very long for him to expose enough of the metal to be able to determine what he was looking at, although he could hardly believe his own eyes. There before him was the muzzle end of a cannon sticking out of the sand.

He slid back into the wash and looked more closely at the cutbank. He walked fifty yards to the north along its eroded course and found another cannon barrel almost fully exposed in a notch where the top of the bank had caved in and been washed away in some desert cloudburst.

There was also something else exposed in the side of the arroyo. A few inches of one corner of it was revealed, and when he took hold of it, splinters of dry wood tore free.

And then he heard a mule bray somewhere not far away. All mules held in common that bawling, annoying call, ending in a high-pitched whine. However that might be, he recognized the sound and the particular mule that made it, for the little braying devil had been annoying him for almost three days. When he climbed out of the arroyo again he saw Pablo's little red dun pack mule standing not fifty yards away. The mule looked at him, shook its head, and flopped its long ears, then opened its mouth and stretched its neck and brayed again.

CHAPTER THIRTY-FOUR

The morning sky was growing lighter when young Frederick Remington heard horses coming up through the rocks to him. He had barely risen from the spot of ground where he had slept when Mr. Smith came through the boulder field leading two saddled horses. One of them was Mr. Smith's own big horse, and the other was the one that belonged to Mateo.

"Where did you find them?" Remington asked.

Mr. Smith did not answer him, but simply handed him both horses, took his traveling bag off his saddle, and went and sat down on a rock.

Remington stared at the Mohave for a moment, amazed that a man on foot could chase down horses. There was no telling how far he had to walk to find them, yet Mr. Smith didn't seem exhausted.

Remington examined the horses and found that both of them seemed sound. It pained him to lose his sorrel. In a fit of anguish, he had traded his half of a saloon in Kansas for that horse and five hundred dollars. He had grown fond of the high-strung Thoroughbred, but he had also been fond of that saloon. It had been a great place to while away a day or an evening drinking and sketching, or swapping stories with the patrons. The saloon was much better than the hardware business he had tried before it, and a whole lot better than sheep ranching. Of all the things he had tried, the saloon business was best and hardly felt like real work at all.

His wife had never liked the saloon or the time he spent there, insisting that he had squandered his inheritance on nothing more than an excuse to get drunk and hang out with the rowdies. Trading part of the saloon for the horse had been meant both as a peace offering to her and a means for him to make another trip out West to clear his mind. But his wife had left him and gone back to New York, swearing she was gone for good, and he had neither horse nor saloon nor wedded bliss. His heartache was as immense as his sense of loss.

He heard something behind him and turned to see what Mr. Smith was doing. He was shocked to find that the Indian had removed almost every stitch of clothing and stood before him mostly naked. Instead of the stark and conservative black suit, he was dressed in nothing but the skin he was born in and some kind of loincloth belted at his waist and dangling down front and back to barely cover his more embarrassing parts.

Mr. Smith was even more heavily muscled than he appeared when fully dressed. Never had Remington seen a man who appeared so strong, not even his teammates at Yale who had all been unusually husky, burly lads. The Mohave was simply massive. And like his arms and face, his entire torso was covered in tattoos, his body decorated and dyed in abstract symbols like the wall of some cave.

Mr. Smith reached inside his open valise and took out a pair of leather sandals and strapped them on his bare feet.

Then he put in place a leather headband to keep the part in his shoulder-length black hair in place and out of the way of his eyes. He used a length of grass rope for a belt, and he threaded it through the scabbard of a large, antler-handled knife and buckled it around his waist. Next he tucked his war clubs behind the belt.

Once he had neatly folded and put his white-man's clothes inside the bag, he buckled it closed and rose and went to his horse. He hung the bag there on his saddle before turning to look at Remington.

"Why, Mr. Smith, you are a savage," Remington exclaimed.

Mr. Smith stared at him, those dark eyes unusually intense, even for him.

"I . . . I mean that in the best way," Remington hastily added. "No offense."

"None taken," Mr. Smith said in his reserved and formal English, just as he always spoke.

Hearing that voice and pronunciation, and at the same time seeing the Mohave in his aboriginal glory, struck Remington as even more strange. He could have closed his eyes and imagined the voice belonged to many men, civilized men, but never such as the one who stood before him then.

"I see your hand has quit bleeding," Remington said.

Mr. Smith glanced at his bandaged hand. Remington had used his own handkerchief to wrap the wound. The Mohave's left ring finger had been shot off at the middle joint during the fight. It had to be a painful injury.

Mr. Smith grunted as if it was no big deal.

"Go to Salton," Mr. Smith said. "It is not hard to find. Stay to this side of the playa and you will see it. You will not make it there before it gets too hot, so find shade along the foot of these mountains and move on again when evening comes."

"And where are you going?" Remington asked.

"I go to make war on our enemies, and to get Mrs. Duffield back if it can be done."

Remington still wasn't over what had happened to them the evening before. While on a rational level it was easy to understand that outlaws had set upon them, but the violence of it was shocking. Even more shocking was realizing that he had almost been killed. And it had all happened so fast. The promise of adventure had excited him, but the reality of his thrill-seeking was settling on him in a most unpleasant fashion.

All men have an image of themselves, no doubt flattering in most ways. He considered himself no coward, a manly man, whose ancestors were soldiers and mountain men, and who had fought in wars upon wars before his time. Yet, he had been utterly ineffective in the fight. It seemed he had hardly been able to come to grips with the Widowmaker getting shot out of nowhere before Zander McCluskey was riding him down, like it all happened in the same instant and too fast for him to be brave. Not only did his poor showing bother him, but he would have certainly died afterward had it not been for Mr. Smith finding him.

After being struck by McCluskey's horse he was knocked almost senseless. Being unarmed, there was little to do but flee. While scrambling through the dunes he had come across the wounded Mohave. Before they could make their way out of the blow sand they had spied horsemen coming their way in the evening dusk. Being unarmed other than Mr. Smith's clubs—little use against so many men with guns—they had remained hidden until the strangers were gone, wary of more of the outlaws looking for them to finish what they had begun.

It was Mr. Smith who had told him that Mrs. Duffield was still alive and that she had been taken away by those that attacked them. The Mohave had gone back and briefly spied upon the site of the ambush before finding him. He also told him that Mateo had been killed, along with the Widowmaker, and that Pablo wasn't to be found.

Pablo had likely met the same fate. All dead but him and Mr. Smith, and with Mrs. Duffield kidnapped and taken who knows where. The thought that he had abandoned her in her hour of need shamed him greatly. There was little chance to get to know her, but she was generally enjoyable to be around except when her sharp tongue and her wit got the best of her. In some ways she reminded him of his Eva, vexing but lovely.

"I will not go to Salton," he said.

"You will go. It is farther to Yuma and I do not think you could find your way there. I've never seen a man get lost so easily as you," Mr. Smith replied.

"No, I'm going with you," Remington replied. "I could never look at myself in a mirror again knowing I left Mrs. Duffield in the hands of those men without at least trying to rescue her. I may have failed her once, but I hope I can make up for that."

"You are no warrior."

"I may not be *kwanami*, as you say, but I am acquainted with the use of several models of firearms and have spent a goodly amount of time with the mitts on my fists under the tutelage of some very fine pugilists."

"You have no weapons." Mr. Smith's expression was unreadable.

"Then I will pick up a stick or a rock. You may think

me a coward, but I will fight, sir. Have no doubt of that. On my family name, I will not run again."

"You will slow me down." Mr. Smith got on his horse without even using a stirrup and with only one effortless swing of his leg and a leap.

"I will go after her whether you let me ride with you or not," Remington said.

Mr. Smith frowned at him, but reached down and slid his rifle from his saddle scabbard and pitched it to him. It was a new Whitney-Kennedy lever-action.

Mr. Smith's thoughtful frown slowly changed into a wolfish grin, matched by a slight twinkle in his eyes. "Come ride with me on the warrior's trail, white man. We will see if your power is as strong as your words."

Remington readied his horse and mounted, determined but nervous at the prospect before him. They rode west.

After a time, Mr. Smith said, "It's a shame we have no *axwe satumac* with us as it should be."

"I don't understand that word," Remington said.

"Among my people it is one born with the power to take the scalps of the enemies we kill," Mr. Smith said in a friendly, almost jovial tone, as if the prospect of crossing a desert to face a fight where they were greatly outnumbered was the best of news to him.

"Scalps?"

"Yes, scalps. To take captives and to hear the wailing of the enemy women is good, but scalps are much better. It reminds us that our blood is still strong. The *axwe satumac* would purify the scalps and then take them back to the *kwaxo*, who would tan the skin and clean and comb the hair before presenting our trophies of war for all the people to see."

"You speak as if your people are no more."

"Many of us still live, but it is not the same." Mr. Smith's tone turned somber. "The Pima and the Maricopa defeated us, and then your soldiers came against us and burned our farms."

"I'm sorry to hear that."

"Do not feel sorry for my people. They live and they die as it should be, and as it has always been. It only saddens me that the old ways are fading until they will be no more."

"You don't fear death?"

"Why should I fear what is sure to happen one day?" Mr. Smith asked. "I only fear that there will be no one to sing for me and dance the story of my last battle."

It was hard for Remington to listen to such fatalistic talk when his nerves were so jittery. "I envy such bravery, Mr. Smith, truly I do, but I'm afraid your affinity for scalps is a touch too barbaric for my tastes. I would simply settle for the return of Mrs. Duffield and to see her to safety."

"Barbaric?" Mr. Smith asked. "Wasn't it the English poet and playwright, Jonson, who bragged that he had killed an enemy in single combat and took the man's weapons as trophies of war?"

"You've read Ben Jonson?"

Mr. Smith gave one of his deep grunts that he often used in place of words. In this case, Remington assumed the particular grunt was meant to be one of irony.

"What?" Mr. Smith asked. "Are you shocked that I can read, or that I have read English literature?"

"Why, both, I guess."

"I can read, though it is something I was not born to and learned later in life," Mr. Smith said. "And I have read much of your writings. I do not to claim to understand all that I have read, though. I have known many tribes and many strange people in my travels, but you white men are the strangest of them all."

"Who taught you to read?"

"A New Englander such as yourself. He was my captain."

"Your captain?" Remington thought about some of the Mohave's tattoos, and how they resembled those he had seen on sailors who had been to the Polynesian islands and farther east.

"It was after the army defeated us that I walked to the west, all the way to the great ocean you call the Pacific. At the time I did not know why I did it or what it was that I sought. But he took me on his ship and I sailed with him for ten years," Mr. Smith said. "In time, he tried to teach me many things and explain to me the meaning of what I saw in the far lands where we sailed. I thought that if I listened to him I could come to understand your power and some-day go back to my people and show them how to make use of it."

"And did you go back to your people?"

"I did, but they would not listen. The things I told them I saw and what I had learned seemed only stories to them. I was shamed among them and thought to be tainted and poisoned by the white man. None would say so, but I saw the way they looked at me and heard them whispering."

Remington tried to envision a man such as Mr. Smith going back to a primitive people and trying to explain to them the modern world. To them, his stories would be only fantastical lies. For a proud man of a warrior caste such as Mr. Smith, that must have been devastating. And he wondered what point it was in the Mohave's story where he came to associate himself with Mrs. Duffield. Was he a tribal outcast, a man outlawed among his own people and cast adrift astraddle of two worlds, white and red? And how would she acquire the loyalty of such a man?

Mr. Smith must have noticed that he was lost in his thoughts and misinterpreted that brooding as something else.

The Mohave laughed loudly and deeply, his mood suddenly lifted again. "Don't worry, white man. We will have our fight, I promise you. Last night I dreamed of a great battle. I feel it was a true dream. A power dream."

Remington wondered how Mr. Smith had found time to sleep and dream. "Did we survive in this vision of yours?"

"It was my dream and you were not there."

"But did you die?"

"Yes, but not before I killed many enemies," Mr. Smith said. "Hurry your horse and let's go see if my dream was true."

CHAPTER THIRTY-FIVE

George Kerr died two hours after sunrise. Maybe it was the loss of blood or the trauma from his shattered arm, or maybe his heart simply quit him. He fell from the saddle in a heap, and the outlaws stopped and sat their horses over him while Madeline dismounted and hugged his body and sobbed. The loss of her father seemed to extinguish whatever last bit of defiance and hope that she had sheltered within her, and she went limp with grief and had to be picked up and put back in her saddle.

"At least have the decency to bury him," she cried as they were about to ride away.

But they did not turn back and tend to George Kerr's body, for they were tainted men barren of remorse, and who dug no graves except for their own.

The desert was as flat as a tabletop and they feared someone would spot them if they passed too close to Sackett's Wells, so they kept well to the south. The jumbled, rock-pile slopes of the Jacumba and In-Ko-Pah Mountains visible not far to the southwest of them gave them hope, for all of them felt that they stood a chance of getting away clean once they were within that maze of tumbled boulders and tight, twisting canyons.

They stopped at the first of the brown foothills they came to in order to rest their horses. Madeline Kerr looked back the way they had come and saw the buzzards gliding and circling high in the air over where they had left her father, and she began to cry again.

Bendigo gave the buzzards only the briefest of glances, for something else drew his attention. Somebody was trailing them.

"Lawmen?" Henry asked when he saw the dust on their back trail.

Bendigo didn't answer him and kept his watch on the dust cloud worming its way closer and closer to their position. They could make a run for it, but their horses weren't in any shape for a race. They had used the last of the water in their canteens and their horses and mules hadn't drunk since midday when they had chanced upon a clump of old, stunted mesquite trees in the bottom of a wash whose leaves seemed a brighter green than normal. They had to dig six feet down, but enough water had seeped into the hole to provide the stock with a scanty but much-needed drink.

And there was no more water within miles of where they now were. It was a poor place to take a stand and fight because of that. All a posse would have to do was to pin them down and wait them out. Let the desert do the dirty work for them.

He looked to the girl. She might give them some leverage and make a posse hesitant to fire on the gang, but there was always some nervous fool who would pull a trigger when good sense said he shouldn't. Either way, run or fight, Bendigo was worried.

"I say if they keep coming we shoot for their horses. Test their mettle and put a few of them on foot," Bendigo said. "Then we make a run for it."

The rest of the gang must have agreed with his tactics, for some of them were already getting off their horses and readying weapons. However, old Henry still sat in the saddle with one hand held up to shade his eyes.

"I don't believe that's a posse," Henry said. "I think that's Zander and Bull and that Mexican of yours."

"Are you sure?" Bendigo asked.

"Hell, I ain't sure about nothing, but I think that's them. Something keeps flashing in the sun and I bet you that's those silver peso conchos on the side of that vaquero's leggings."

Bendigo gave the old outlaw an irritated look.

"Got somebody else with them," Henry added.

"The Irishman," Bendigo said.

"No, I don't think so."

"Make sure the Kerr girl is out where she can be seen in case Henry's wrong," Bendigo called out to the other outlaws in the rocks at the foot of the slope behind him.

But Henry wasn't wrong. He might be half-deaf, but apparently his eyesight was more than serviceable. Five minutes later McCluskey reached them on a lathered sorrel gelding that he hadn't been riding when they last saw him. And he was leading another horse with a woman in the saddle.

"Are you going to steal every woman in the whole damned country?" Bendigo asked.

McCluskey glared back at him, but gave him no answer.

"She didn't have any money, did she?" Bendigo asked.

"The whole thing went to hell. That judge's posse came on us before we could finish," McCluskey said.

"You shake free from that posse, or are they still after you?" Henry asked.

"I saw dust earlier this morning, but not since then," McCluskey said.

"There's somebody at Alamo Mocho," Bendigo said.

McCluskey nodded. "Men at Gardener's Wells, too. Come across your trail after we headed west."

"Where's the Irishman?"

"Gone under," McCluskey replied. "Where you headed?"

"Pinto Canyon."

McCluskey took a bit to consider that, as if he knew of the place and hadn't considered it until then. "That might not be bad, not bad at all. Give us time to deal with the Judge. We could ride on to Hacienda Tecate tomorrow. That'd put us close enough to Campo to send runners back and forth until we get the ransom money."

Bendigo spit a stream of tobacco juice to show his disgust, then wiped at his chin whiskers with the back of one forearm. "Are you hearing yourself? The whole border is crawling with law, and it's going to get worse. You stick around and play with that judge if you want to. I'm getting gone."

"Suit yourself. Maybe some of the others don't think the same as you do." McCluskey raised his voice slightly to be sure that the others in the gang heard him.

"I got a better idea," Bendigo said. "What say we take these women and sell them to Cut Face?"

"Who's Cut Face?"

"Yaqui. Him and some others deserted from the Mexican army years ago. Been running from the Mexicans and raising hell since then. Rawhide, beggarly-looking bastards, but they've stolen everything that wasn't nailed down in their country. And there ain't but two things they'll spend their loot on, and that's women and guns."

"Madeline Kerr is worth thirty thousand dollars and you want to sell her to some renegade Indian for a rawhide bag of pesos? Take this one and sell her if that's what you're of a mind to do." McCluskey gestured at Poker Alice.

"Cut Face won't pay much for her."

"You've got the mules and this one. Leave it at that, or you can stick with me and see this through like we planned it." McCluskey's voice had a growing edge to it.

Bendigo walked closer to where Poker Alice sat on her horse. She was in a sorry state, filthy with grime and bruised and battered, and with her clothing torn to rags. But even in her current condition she didn't duck her head or fail to meet his eyes. In fact, she stared back at him defiantly and with pure hatred. She was prettier than he had first thought her to be.

"You roughed her up a little, didn't you? I don't know if Cut Face would take her at all," Bendigo said.

"Clean her up and she'll shine enough for an Indian."

"Maybe."

"The rest of us have got a say in this." Bull had been listening to their conversation, and his face had grown redder with anger with every mention of the women.

McCluskey looked at the other outlaws, pausing to make eye contact with every one of them. "You do what you want. Go with Bendigo, but the Kerr girl stays with me. Hear that? She stays with me. Before too long, that judge that has you all so worried is going to bring a big bag of money to Campo whether he likes it or not, and he's going to hand it over to me. All I need is a little time to sweat him."

Again, McCluskey's eyes moved over them before he

continued. "Your choice, but I aim to get it all. And then I'm going to get on a ship at Ensenada. While you're hiding out in some hellhole with a bunch of beggar Indians and drinking rotgut mescal I'm going to be sailing away counting a lot of money. You want in on the take, you reach down and find your cojones."

None of them said anything, but their expressions were thoughtful.

"We'll work out who's going with who after we get to Pinto Canyon," Bendigo said.

"Suits me," McCluskey replied. "Where's the banker?"

"He didn't make it."

"I needed him."

"You want him, you ride back about two miles and get him. Only ones that will argue with you are the buzzards and the worms."

In a matter of minutes the gang was on the move. They traveled in single file into the mountains, and by late afternoon they rode through a boulder-strewn pass and found Davies Valley before them. The bottom of the valley was relatively flat, offering an easy way through such rugged terrain. Furthermore, its narrow course ran straight as an arrow south for less than five miles before its mouth opened into Mexico. The entrance to the side canyon they sought ducked off to the northwest within an easy gunshot of the border, although that imaginary line that divided the States from Mexico was too vague for the outlaws to place any reliance on it. The country looked the same to either side of it and no such line was going to stop a bullet or shield them from an overzealous posse simply because some surveyor or treaty said a certain landmark was in one country or the other.

By sundown they had ridden into Pinto Canyon. They

followed its narrow, winding course until they came to a brushy junction where two other smaller canyons ran down to meet. Beyond that junction and around the point of a mountain jutting out into the canyon, they spied a clump of palm trees at the foot of a bluff. Amidst those palms and well under the shade of the rock canyon wall was a trickle of water a hand wide that ended in a shallow pool barely as big as a washtub. But that water was cool and clear, and the first good water they had seen since leaving the springs at Dos Palmas. Men and horses fought to be the first to get a drink. And then they rested and argued over what they should do next.

Not so far away from them, three buzzards rode a thermal updraft high in the clear blue sky, hardly flapping their wings at all and turning in wide, lazy circles like water slowly swirling in a draining tub. Second only to their sense of smell, their keen, searching eyes missed nothing. Not the men who had gone into Pinto Canyon, nor the other men moving on the desert far below them.

Twenty-five miles to the north of Pinto Canyon the Judge's posse was camped at Sackett's Wells. Other lawmen waited at the water holes along the border along the old Butterfield road. Even farther away, a strange Mohave and a New York artist were slowly making their way west. And among all those travelers was a lone man, a tiny speck upon the great expanse of solitude. He moved slowly, but steadily.

The buzzards feared humans, but regardless, they kept circling instead of flying away. For even a buzzard with its little brain had learned that where men went, death often followed. To a patient scavenger, the next meal was sometimes only a matter of knowing such things and waiting.

CHAPTER THIRTY-SIX

The Judge sat in a wicker-backed chair under the roof eave of the dilapidated station house at Sackett's Wells with his Marlin rifle leaned against the wall beside him within easy reach. He was smoking a thin cigar and had one foot propped up on his other knee with his hat hanging from the toe of that boot. Occasionally, he ran an absent-minded hand through his long locks of white hair or fondled the braided rawhide quirt he held. But he kept his thoughts to himself, whatever they were.

He had sat like that for much of the day, either pouring over the old papers from the leather tube they had found on O'Bannon's horse or staring at the surrounding countryside while he waited for the scouts he had sent out to return. The hand-dug wells that gave the place its name, three of them, were to be found in the bottom of Coyote Wash, but other than that wide scar cutting a groove through the earth, the desert around him was as flat as a tabletop. To the south-west, a craggy range of mountains rose up suddenly as the only thing that drew the eye.

The men remaining with the Judge had chosen to sit with the horses in the bottom of the wash where they could make use of the stunted mesquites growing there for shade. Two of them sat where they had a good view of the Judge.

"Did you know the Judge could read Spanish?" one of those men asked the other.

"You say those papers are written in Spanish?" the other asked.

"Yeah. Kind of funny that the Judge seems more interested in those old papers than he does that ransom note in his pocket."

"You think he'll pay the ransom if Charlie comes back and says he couldn't find their trail?"

"I don't think he'll pay. I heard him tell Charlie that paying them didn't mean he would get George and the girl back, like he believes they're as good as dead whether he pays or not."

As if by the mere mentioning of his name, the Paiute tracker and the other posse member sent to the south with him along the old stage road appeared out of the dusty haze in the distance, growing larger and clearer as they neared, like men walking out of a shimmering veil.

The Judge had also sent the county deputy and another man in the opposite direction along the road as far as the next water seventeen miles away at Carrizo Creek. Those two had come back to the wells an hour earlier to report they had found no sign of the outlaw gang's passing.

"Charlie's got something across the back of his saddle," one of the men said when the Paiute rode closer.

They came up out of the wash and went to stand with the Judge, timing their move to coincide with the tracker's arrival. It was plain what Charlie Two Horses was packing with him even before he reined his mount up in front of the Judge and dismounted. It was a body wrapped in blankets.

The Judge put his hat back on and rose from his chair. He went to Charlie's horse and lifted the blankets and stared at his brother's dead countenance. Buzzards or some other scavengers had worked on George Kerr's face, and it was hard to recognize him, even for men who had known him for years. Several of the men looked away from that gory visage, but not the Judge. He stared into that torn, tortured face for a long while, and then took several deep breaths before he looked a question at Charlie.

"Found him about two hours south of here," Charlie said.

"How'd he die?" the Judge asked.

"One of his arms is shattered. No other bullet wounds that I could see, but . . ." Charlie didn't finish what he was about to say—that there wasn't enough left of George Kerr to decipher much of anything about how he had died other than it had been a damned hard death.

The Judge's face was a sight to behold right then, the muscles and tendons beneath the skin and the clench of his jaw as tight as banjo strings. His voice quavered with hurt and anger. "Which way did they go?"

"Trail leads west into the mountains," Charlie said. "They're either headed for Davies Valley or going on to Jacumba Pass."

The Judge eyed the waning sun, already low down on the horizon. The men with him could tell he was calculating on what to do next. They had already lost the outlaws' trail once trying to run them down in the dark, and the odds of losing their sign altogether was going to get worse if they had made it to the mountains.

"What do you want to do, Judge?" Charlie asked after a while.

It took the Judge a moment to answer him. "How far is it to this Davies Valley?"

"Two, three hours, if we ride hard," Charlie said.

"Can you find it in the dark?"

"I can."

"Judge?" the county deputy said in a cautious voice. "Maybe we ought to wait here and set in on their trail in the morning. That's a bloody bunch we're after, and we're as apt to ride into an ambush in those mountains as we are to run them down."

The Judge pivoted in a surprisingly fast fashion for a man of his age and grabbed the deputy by the throat with one clawed hand. He rammed the taller, younger man back several steps until he pinned him to the adobe wall of the old station house. The deputy didn't fight him, and only choked and gasped for air.

The Judge kept hold of him and leaned in close. His voice was a raspy, quavering hiss. "Son, I wasn't always the man I am now. I've looked the Devil in the eye down many a cannon's bore, took broadsides and given them, grapeshot and ball, and listened to the dying screams of better men than you going down into the abyss never to return. I've had men tied to the mast and sentenced them to hang. Held the lash or knotted the rope myself more times than I care to remember. And never once have I batted an eye nor flinched, or lost so much as a single night's sleep for all of that. I was born the law and I was born a judge before you or anyone else ever called me such."

"Judge . . ." the deputy gasped. "I didn't mean anything by it."

"You know why I'm the Judge?" The Judge kept his chokehold on the deputy's throat, but relaxed his grip ever so slightly. "I'm the Judge because my will is greater than most men. Because I'm not afraid to decide how things are going to be. Do you understand me?"

The deputy gave a feeble nod of his head to show that he did, or that he simply wanted to be able to swallow again.

"Now, you shut your mouth and get on your horse, or you're going to see a side of me you won't like at all." The Judge gave the deputy a hard shove that sent him sprawling to the ground.

The Judge turned away and snatched up his rifle and strode across the sand toward the horses. Most of the posse could only stand as if locked in place and stare at him with a shocked expression on their faces. But one of them broke out of it quicker than the others and had the good sense to run for the wash to fetch the Judge's gray and bring it to him.

The Judge didn't once look behind him to see if they would follow him when he rode away. The deputy picked himself up off the ground in time to see Charlie Two Horses leading both their horses out of the wash.

"Come on," Charlie said as he handed the deputy his bridle reins.

"You're going with that crazy old fool?" the deputy asked.

Charlie got in the saddle and then squinted at him. "What was it Buck always said? Without the law there's nothing at all, or something like that."

"So?"

"The Judge might be crazy, but if he ain't the law, who is?"

"He's out of control."

"And you think those we're chasing aren't worse than the Judge? That's what you ought to keep asking yourself."

"You don't care where he drags us as long as you're getting your three dollars a day."

"Maybe, or maybe I understand posse work isn't always pretty. The law can work in mysterious ways, you know," Charlie said as he kicked his horse off after the Judge.

"The Lord works in mysterious ways, Charlie," the deputy said as he scrambled to get on his horse and catch up to the Paiute. "It's the Lord that works in mysterious ways, you hear me? Not the law, you half-breed heathen."

And then they followed the Judge toward Davies Valley. It was the Judge's intention to ride all the way to the southern end of it where it spilled into Mexico, no matter if they didn't know the way or if Charlie couldn't track in the dark, or even if the outlaws they pursued might be waiting to ambush them somewhere in that broken country ahead. The Judge didn't care about any of that. If he could get ahead of them he could be there waiting at the border.

CHAPTER THIRTY-SEVEN

Newt's long legs almost dragged the ground on either side of the mule when he rode it, but small or not, the little beast had surely saved his life. The mule's jigging walk ate up the miles before them, and the keg of water lashed to the packsaddle had enough left in it to fill Newt's canteen and the other two canteens he found on the pack frame.

He had stripped all the gear from the mule's back except for the packsaddle, hung the canteens and some other things from it along with a canvas sack containing a partial side of bacon wrapped in cheesecloth, and rigged the mule's halter rope into a set of reins. Thusly equipped and mounted, he set out to the west once more.

He had covered close to twenty-five more miles before sundown the day he found the mule. By then, two of his canteens were empty, and he debated whether to give the remaining water to the mule or to save it for himself.

All that he knew about the land over which he rode was that he was somewhere not far north of the border and the old emigrant trail that had taken him from Yuma to Los Angeles almost a year earlier when he had first come to California. The tracks of the outlaws he followed dipped toward the border then diverted suddenly to the west again. Twice he saw dust off to the south, but he ignored it and kept on the trail of the outlaws.

Not long after daylight the next morning he found where the outlaws had dug for water in the clump of mesquites at the bottom of an arroyo. Enough water had seeped back into the hole to more than meet his needs. He built a fire, ate the bacon, and used the cheesecloth it was wrapped in as a strain to pour the murky water through when filling his canteens. The little mule drank the rest of the water.

Not only were the Circle Dot horse's hoof prints to be found in the wash, but also mixed with the other tracks were a woman's footprints. Those tracks of a woman's shoes didn't belong to Poker Alice, and he guessed it might be George Kerr's daughter with them. It fit together with other things. Among the sign he had been following were the tracks of numerous mules. A mule's hooves were narrower in shape and easy to differentiate from a horse's hoof prints. The only mules that he could think of were those that had pulled George Kerr's wagons. Apparently, Mc-Cluskey and his men had robbed Kerr and had taken his daughter before they attacked Newt in the dunes.

He tried to determine how far ahead of him the outlaws were, but could come to no solid conclusion. He wasn't a good enough tracker to age the sign, and the only method left to him was to gauge how fast the water hole the outlaws had dug refilled itself after it was emptied. On that basis, he guessed the outlaws had left the wash sometime the afternoon or evening before.

After bathing his wounds and rewrapping the one in his side, he started off again. A few miles farther on he crossed the old Butterfield stagecoach road and emigrant trail where it turned northwest from below the border and headed into the mountains. He stopped in those wagon ruts and looked up and down them, knowing that either way would lead to water, but the outlaws' tracks kept going west.

And there were the tracks of other horsemen going up and down the trail. He considered what that might mean, but his head hurt too badly to give it the thought needed, and he stuck to the one thing he was sure of—the gang had gone west and that's where he needed to go.

At a little after midday he reached the first rocky outcroppings that marked the beginning of the mountains. He found where the outlaws had stopped again at the foot of a rocky outcropping rising up about a hundred feet over the desert. He deciphered from the tracks there that four other riders had joined the outlaws. Newt was pretty sure that one of those men was riding Remington's Thoroughbred, but what perplexed him most was that he found the tracks of another woman to go with those he thought belonged to Madeline Kerr. And he was sure that the second set of tracks belonged to Poker Alice. He had become well accustomed to the imprint made by her dainty little shoes.

He moved on again, winding his way through a disjointed chain of little mountains and rocky foothills that fronted the beginnings of the true mountains beyond them. He was not far into that broken country when the mule went lame.

He rode the limping mule for another mile before it could go no farther. He dismounted and examined the mule's right-front leg, grimacing at the sight of the bare bone exposed where the mule had gone down in the front end while climbing a rocky slope and struck that knee against something sharp. Already, the joint was swollen and the flies were picking at the edges of the raw wound.

He considered putting the mule out of its misery with his knife, but didn't have the heart to do so. Instead, he bathed the animal's wound with water he could little afford to spare, used the bacon sack to bandage it, and then stood and patted the mule on the neck.

"That's about all I can do for you. It ain't fair, but that's the way it goes sometimes," he said to the mule. "Appreciate the ride. You're a noisy little devil, but you're a fair traveler."

He slung the canteens over one shoulder and headed out on foot, his stride was the shuffling slow gait of a man about at the end of his rope. The mule hobbled after him for a short ways, but finally stopped. It brayed once, almost sadly, shaking its big floppy ears until a bit of burned grass stole its attention and it bent its head to nip off the tops of the plants.

Two hours later, with the afternoon sun burning at its hottest, Newt came into Davies Valley, where he found the skeleton of a dead horse. The bones looked to have been there for quite some time, but the age of anything was hard to determine in the desert. Strangely, the horse's skeleton was almost completely intact.

The deceased equine had been ridden somewhere up to the point of its death, for there was a saddle with its bones. Its rider had either survived the ordeal or died elsewhere, for there were no other remains.

There was a story there in those bones, of life and death and struggle and all that fell in between. No doubt it had been a hard death, and likely a lonely one. Newt had no reason to believe his own end, the same as much of his life, would be any different. No witnesses to how he died, whether bravely or whimpering at the end. When someone found his remains somewhere on that desert or elsewhere, what would it say of him and how he had died, much less lived? The marks a man made in his life should be more than fading footprints or a pile of bones. He should have friends to be remembered by, family, and things left behind that he had built or seen to fruition.

Yet, he had few friendships of any duration, for he was a man who never stayed in one place long. And what family he once had was either gone or scattered on the wind and lost to him. His father had fallen dead of a heart attack behind his plow when Newt was still a boy, and then a letter had come not so many years ago, after he had gone west, telling him that his mother, too, had passed on. He hadn't seen his siblings in all those years since he had left home, but supposed they were making it fine. They were all made of more solid stuff than he, sisters and brother alike, and not so full of wanderlust.

What would they think of him now, their brother who lived on the wild and seedy side and who had made nothing other than a reputation with his fists and a gun? It was likely that they wouldn't be surprised. He was the black sheep of the family, always wanting to test the confinement of anything that felt as if it might bind him, quick to anger when challenged, and stubborn when it came to his notions of what was right or wrong. Frustrated by his inability to put to words or thought the things that he felt, but good at things he could take hold of with his hands.

"Here you are taking off to see the elephant before you're even a man full grown, just like your father did when he walked to St. Louis and signed up with those fur men bound to trap beaver in the far western lands, and him little older than you are now," Mother Jones had said on that day she helped pack his traveling sack. "I saw that wildness in him when I met him the first time after he came back home, same as I see it in you. I loved him for it, but it worried me just the same.

"You're going to be a bull of a man, just like he was. Best I open the gate and let you out on the world, or you'll always be bellowing and walking the fence and come to hate me for shutting you in," she said. "Your pa loved all of you, but he never was the same after I gave him the choice to settle down or leave me be. This old farm suited a part of him, but that other restless part? Well, it was like putting a wild critter in a cage. He never strayed from me after we married, but I think in his dreams he wandered the wild country again. He tried to hide it, but I could see it in his eyes at times, the longing when he was standing at the window looking off in the distance. I won't do that to you.

"Be careful before you give your trust to anyone, but pull those close to you that you claim as kin," she had also said. "Stick to your raising and you'll never be ashamed of who you are. Be brave, son, as you always have been, for they say God hates a coward."

She had said all that and more. At times those words came back to him like they were only yesterday, along with the other old memories of home. And right then he could almost see her like he had the day he had stopped in the trail and looked back at her one last time. She sat there rocking that old chair of hers on the porch of the cabin his father had built for her, with a sad smile on her face and a knowing look in her eyes.

And then he shook away the memories, the fevered hallucinations or whatever they were, and licked his cracked lips and looked once more upon the horse bones. If anyone had been around to watch him, it might have seemed a strange thing when he ripped the jawbone loose from the skeleton's skull. In fact, it might have seemed the action of a crazy man. For by then his canteens were all empty and he looked more dead than alive, even if he was still on his feet. A sun-bleached jawbone with a few bits of dried flesh and hide still sticking to it wasn't something that should have fascinated a man in his condition, nor should he have found it of any use to help him survive. But he clenched it in his hand with a purpose.

Newt kicked the horse skeleton to pieces and moved on down the valley. Its north-to-south course was narrow, with the serrated summits of the low mountains and hills rising up to either side and the relatively flat bottom covered in quartz-laden gravel and rocks.

The salt sweat burned his eyes, and when he swiped at them his hand grated against the raw sunburn on one cheekbone. The blisters on his feet had broken and were bleeding, and he had a stone bruise where the thin sole of one of his boots had been punctured by something. The stiffness of the wound in his side and those bruised, blistered feet made each single step a challenge. He squinted down the valley, running as straight as a flatland plow furrow into Mexico.

He knew the chase had to end soon, because he wasn't going to make it much farther. In addition to his wounds, he could feel the effects of dehydration adding to his other issues, and the fatigue by itself felt like a load of rocks weighing him down. Wrath and willpower could take a man only so far.

But he had gained on those he followed. The anger burned hot within him again, and he kept going.

When he came to where the outlaws' tracks led him into the wide, sandy mouth of a side canyon, he paused there, thinking that he smelled smoke. His heart began to throb more heavily in his chest, and some of the fogginess left his mind. He clenched the jawbone more tightly in his fist and started up Pinto Canyon. That smoke couldn't have come from too far away. He would crawl if he had to.

CHAPTER THIRTY-EIGHT

Poker Alice sat on a rock with her back against the shaggy dead fronds of a palm tree's trunk with her bound wrists resting on her knees, as far away from the outlaws as they would let her be. The coming evening and the rock bluff behind her cast her in shadows, and she stole an occasional glance at the men around the campfire and made a point not to get caught looking at them. They had spent a night and the following day camped in the canyon, and she worried continually what such men might do to her with idle time on their hands. Accordingly, she was surprised and relieved that they had not laid a hand on her since the abuse she had taken back in the dunes, but she knew it was only a matter of time.

It had all happened so fast. One moment things were fine, and then Newt had been shot without warning. Everything in the next few minutes after that was confusion. She could barely remember jerking Newt's pistol from his holster and trying to get to her horse, only to see it running away. She had seen Mr. Smith wounded while fighting with one of their attackers, and then seen Mateo's body lying on the sand. She didn't have a clue what had happened to Pablo.

And then McCluskey had appeared in front of her out of nowhere. Her intention was to fight, but she had been too slow and had taken nothing but a beating for her troubles. Then McCluskey had finished off Newt.

It was likely that she was the only one who had survived the ordeal. She had to face up to that. She was alone.

Her trip across the desert valley with her captors had been horrible and almost as much of a blur as the initial attack had been. A part of her wanted to beg them to stop and let her get off her horse and simply curl up in a ball on the ground and cry, and she hated that weakness. It had taken her most of the day to fight down that feeling, and to look honestly at her situation for what it was.

She was long past any foolish hope that something might happen that would save her, some miracle would come along as if it all weren't real and nothing but some bad dream. There was reality to deal with, and that reality was so terrifying that it was almost more than she could bear. Rather than give in to the fear, she spent her time preparing herself for whatever was to come, reminding herself that she was strong and readying the will it was going to take to endure that trial.

Madeline Kerr sat on the ground nearby with her legs sprawled out in front of her and her soiled dress hiked above her knees. Her blond hair had come undone and hung in disarray over her face, partially covering whatever terror she felt in that moment. The girl had cried much of the way to the canyon, but now Alice heard not so much as a whimper out of her. She had either found her own strength or simply quit. Alice couldn't tell which it was, but she understood how the girl might have come to that point.

Alice smelled the bacon frying at the fire, and when the

big Swede brought the skillet to them for their share she snatched her piece while avoiding meeting his leering gaze. Madeline Kerr wouldn't look at him, either, and only stared at the ground when the skillet was held before her. Alice snatched the last two pieces of pork from the skillet before he could yank it away.

The Bull Swede slapped her across the face, knocking her to the ground beside Madeline, but he did not take the food back from her. Instead, he stood astraddle of her and grinned down at her. She pulled the fabric of her torn blouse back in place and held it there, feeling that leering grin crawling over her skin like greasy fingers.

"Now that isn't ladylike at all," he said. "This one needs to eat, too."

"I'll make sure she eats," Alice said.

"You do that," Bull said, and then snickered. "You two are going to need your strength."

"Bull," McCluskey called from the fire.

"You better leave us be or your boss isn't going to like it," she said.

"I could pour this hot grease right on you," he said, and made as if to tilt the cast-iron frying pan over her. "Burn you so bad that even those Yaquis Bendigo keeps talking about won't want you."

"Bull!" McCluskey's voice was louder and cracked sharply in the confines of the canyon.

"You better do like he says," Alice said as she looked him in the eyes.

Bull held the skillet over her for a long moment, breathing through his mouth. "They're over there right now deciding what to do with you. Zander says it's going to be one way and Bendigo says it's going to be the other. Maybe they will kill each other and I get both of you.

Either way, there is going to come a time when Zander isn't around to get in my way. Then I'm going to have a little fun."

"Bring them over here," Zander ordered.

He was standing now, and so was the one called Bendigo.

Bull stepped back and motioned her to get up. She did so slowly and backed away from him two steps once she was back on her feet. Madeline Kerr seemed oblivious to what was going on, but didn't resist when Alice took hold of her arm and pulled her to her feet. The poor girl stank horribly, and Alice wondered if she smelled just as bad.

Bull slung the bacon grease from the pan and motioned them to the fire. He followed close behind them, and she could still hear his breathing.

More wood had been thrown on the campfire, but some of the men were saddling horses. Alice noticed that one of the horses they readied was Remington's sorrel Thoroughbred that McCluskey had been riding since the fight in the dunes.

McCluskey went to the Thoroughbred and began stripping items off its saddle and adjusting his gear. She could tell he was lightening his load and preparing for another run.

"Bring her here," McCluskey said as another horse was led to him.

Alice tensed, but it was Madeline whom Bull shoved toward McCluskey. The slim Mexican with the big spurs, the one who never seemed to let his rifle out of his hands, helped McCluskey put Madeline up on the horse. The old outlaw, the one she had heard them call Henry, was already up in the saddle and took hold of her horse's bridle. The poor girl's chin was slumped down to her chest with her hair hanging over her face. She never once looked back at Alice.

"Are you sure you won't come with us?" McCluskey asked Bendigo.

The red-bearded outlaw shook his head. "You've got more guts than a slaughterhouse, Zander, but it ain't going to help you none. You try for that ransom and all it's going to do is get you killed. This old border don't suffer mistakes."

McCluskey looked to Bull. "What about you?"

Bull looked from the Kerr girl to Alice, and then seemed to make up his mind. "I'll stay with Bendigo."

McCluskey couldn't hide his surprise, and he looked at Alice and then back to him. "I see the new one has caught your fancy. Thought you liked them young."

"I think me and you fight if I stay with you," Bull said.

"Fight? If you were going to give it a go it would have been a long time ago," McCluskey answered.

"You push too much now."

"Bendigo told me you tried to get him to side with you and take both of the women," McCluskey said. "I ought to kill you for that."

Bull passed Bendigo a look, but Bendigo's face was expressionless.

McCluskey went to his Thoroughbred. "So long, boys."

"What do you think they're going to write about you in the papers after that judge hangs you?" Bendigo asked.

McCluskey smiled. "Why, Bendigo, they'll be saying what a good-looking, reckless devil I was standing on the gallows."

Alice was so intent on watching them that it took her a moment to realize that Bull had stepped closer to her.

"Maybe Bendigo doesn't make it to find Cut Face," he said barely above a whisper. "Or maybe I outbid that Yaqui or I don't let Bendigo sell you."

She had heard enough of their talk about selling her to some Indian to know that her time to escape was growing shorter. That they had not tied her or otherwise bound her was no surprise. Where could she go? That was going to be the question between now and wherever they were taking her. For she knew that once they had her down in Mexico in some Indian stronghold or hideout there would be no chance for her at all.

Bull had not gone far from her, and when she looked he was staring at her again. She went to the fire and stood with her back to him, chewing on a piece of bacon. He did not leave, and she could feel his eyes still on her. She knew that being sold to some renegade Indian wasn't the worst of her concerns right then.

She watched the other outlaws, studying each of their actions and their individual faces as if she could determine their thoughts and their intentions toward her. One of the Mexican outlaws rose from where he squatted by the fire and turned as if he had changed his mind and wanted to go with McCluskey or had to tend to some other chore. It was his movement that drew her eyes that way, and that was when she saw Newt Jones come striding through the evening dusk straight to the fire.

At first she thought she was seeing a ghost. He looked so horrible, like a man crawled from a grave. His clothes were filthy and tattered, and his face drawn and hollow. He was moving slowly when she first spotted him, but his step quickened when he saw the Mexican rise from the campfire.

She had no clue how he had gotten so close without any of them seeing him. Maybe it was because most of the outlaws were ganged around McCluskey to say their good-byes or to argue more. Newt held no gun to fight them with, but there was something else in one of his hands.

She was so caught up in watching Newt that she didn't see the other brown man shape slipping through the shadows on the opposite side of the fire.

CHAPTER THIRTY-NINE

The Mexican outlaw's mouth started to shape itself to form some kind of startled question or to call out in alarm when he stood and saw Newt coming for him. At the same time, his hand dropped for the butt of his pistol.

The jawbone struck the outlaw and he fell as if thunderstruck. Newt felt the impact of that blow all the way to his shoulder, and the savage thrill of it made him want to scream his fury.

The downed outlaw clutched him weakly around one leg with both arms, and he chopped down in a backhand stroke and broke the jawbone with a second lick on the man's head.

The rest of the gang stood in a cluster around four saddled horses. Madeline Kerr and an old man were already up in their saddles. They all seemed to recognize his presence in the same instant, and everything after happened very fast.

Another Mexican reached for a Winchester leaned against a rock nearby, and Newt closed the distance between them and drove the broken shard of bone into the man's throat and left it stuck there.

A gun blasted and Newt felt the hot lash of a bullet passing close by him. The old man up on the horse had his rifle held across his saddle swells and pointed his way. The horse lunged in fright while the other horses milled about it, causing the old man to hesitate before firing again. Newt charged into the bore of that rifle gritting his teeth in preparation to take a bullet. He hadn't gone two strides before another gun roared and the old man was knocked from his saddle.

Newt shifted his course and three running mules almost trampled him. He bounced off one of them and found a hatless man with a shaven head was standing ten feet in front of him clawing his pistol free of his holster. A naked brown body came flying out of nowhere and passed before Newt to tackle the outlaw, taking him to the ground. Newt barely had time for it to register that it was Mr. Smith who had come charging out of the dark.

A charge of buckshot splattered off a rock next to Newt and stung him with fragments. He swiped at his stinging face and spun to see who had shot at him. There was a red-bearded gringo in a Mexican hat tracking him with a double-barreled shotgun, but there was another gunshot and a bullet kicked up sand at the outlaw's feet and he jumped back and lost his aim. Newt had no clue who else was with Mr. Smith and fighting with him, for there was no time to stop and think. To stop moving meant you died.

He slid his sheath knife from his belt and ran straight for the red-bearded outlaw. Instead of firing his second barrel, the outlaw swung the shotgun with both hands at Newt's head. Newt ducked the blow and the two of them crashed together.

Newt hit the ground and then rolled to his feet with his knife leading the way. The outlaw had been staggered and had dropped the shotgun, but was still standing. He saw the knife in Newt's hand and went for the revolver on his hip. The snub-nosed British Bulldog was almost pointed at Newt's chest when Newt slid the blade of his knife down the inside of the outlaw's forearm. The knife was made of good steel and had a shaving edge. It bit deep into the outlaw's arm and then skidded across his collarbone on the follow-through.

The outlaw's pistol went off wide of his intended mark, and Newt felt the hot burn of black powder scalding his right shoulder. He lost his hold on his knife, and they crashed against each other again and grappled. The outlaw squatted and then lunged upward and headbutted him. Newt felt the skin on his forehead split under the impact as his head snapped back. He tried desperately to hang on and keep from going to the ground, and was barely aware that the powder burn had set his shirt on fire.

The redheaded outlaw was strong, and Newt lost his balance and was thrown aside. He was on one knee when the outlaw chopped a fist down into his wounded side and he groaned with the pain of that blow.

A flying knee missed his head. He caught that foot and threw his weight against the other leg, spilling the outlaw to the ground with him. There was little technique or method to either man's fighting after that. They simply grunted and strained and scrambled for some advantage, like two animals intent on destroying each other.

Somehow, Newt managed to get behind the outlaw. One of his hands was tangled in the outlaw's beard, twisting his neck and yanking his chin around. The fingers of his other hand dug at one of the outlaw's eyebrows, straining to reach down into the eye socket below it. Before he could gouge out that eye, the outlaw slung his head back against

Newt's face. Newt felt his lips split against his teeth and was knocked away.

His hand found the handle of his knife on the ground by accident and pure luck, and when he came to his feet again his opponent was also holding his own knife. It was a big blade. They faced each other panting and bleeding, not six feet between them, and both of them looking for an opening to drive their knives home.

Over the redhead's shoulder, Newt saw Mr. Smith and the bald outlaw fighting. The bald outlaw was screaming and cursing in Swedish like a madman while he fought to fend off the Mohave's war clubs. Those clubs moved in a blur, and Newt saw the bald outlaw go down again.

It was then that the redheaded outlaw lunged with his blade, and Newt cut wildly at him. Too late, he realized that the lunge was only a feint, and found himself overextended and off-balance. The outlaw's own knife drove forward and the point of it struck Newt squarely in the chest.

Instead of sinking to the hilt, the blade seemed to bounce off him, although he was knocked backward by the force behind the outlaw's thrust. He was still scrambling to regain his balance when the outlaw jumped and kicked him. He fell beside the fire and the outlaw was already standing over him by the time he made it back to his knees. He caught the man's plunging knife arm and stopped the blade just inches from where it would have pierced down into his neck. Newt used his other hand to stab his own knife into one of the outlaw's thighs. The outlaw tried to pull away, freeing the blade, but Newt held him by the arm and stabbed again. This time his steel found the man's belly right above his belt buckle. He plunged the blade in two more times. His knife hand was slick with blood and his muscles shook with exhaustion when the outlaw sank to his knees in front of him.

"You . . ." The outlaw's head began to wobble slightly. "You . . ."

Newt kept his knife where it was and watched him die. His own breath was coming in ragged gasps and the world swayed around him.

Then came the sound of running horses going down the canyon and then someone shouted at him. Poker Alice ran to him. It was she who was doing the shouting.

Mr. Smith loomed up behind her. Newt staggered to his feet and looked at the Mohave. The man was naked except for a breechcloth and a pair of sandals. Beyond him, the bald outlaw's lifeless body lay in a heap on the ground.

"I thought you were dead," Alice said to Newt, and then she looked at Mr. Smith. "I thought both of you were dead."

"Not hardly," Newt said.

Remington came running to them out of the dark. He was still wearing his funny helmet and clutching a rifle in both hands. "McCluskey and another one ran off with the Kerr girl."

Newt looked down the dark canyon to where he had last heard the sound of running horses. And then he looked back at Remington. "Was that you who shot the one on the horse off of me?"

Remington gave a grim nod.

"I guess you Yale fellows are good for something besides football and rowing boats," Newt said.

"You can buy me a beer when this is over," Remington said, and then pointed at the red-bearded outlaw's body on the ground. "I couldn't get a clean shot at that one with you two mixing it up. Thought you were a goner. Swore I saw him stick that knife right in your chest."

Newt lifted one hand and felt absentmindedly at his chest where the knife's point had cut a slit in his shirt. "Lucky, I guess. Why don't one of you go get us some horses? I need to catch my wind."

Mr. Smith and Remington left him and Alice standing by the fire. He caught her looking at the bodies lying around them.

"Don't look at them," he said.

She started to say something, but the words got hung up in her throat.

"You all right?" he asked, and put a steadying hand against her shoulder.

She bit her lower lip and looked him up and down. "You're asking me that? I don't guess you've had a chance to look at yourself in a mirror lately."

"Not many mirrors where I came from," he said. "And if you don't mind my saying it, I've seen you look better yourself."

She made as if to laugh, but her chin only trembled, instead. She wrapped both arms around her and turned her back to him. He knew that feeling. It was the feeling of not being quite sure you're alive or dead and of walking in that gray world between the two.

There came the sound of gunshots to the south, many gunshots. Both of them turned to look down the canyon, as if their eyes could pierce the gloom beyond the firelight.

"McCluskey and the others said there was a posse after them," she said. "George Kerr's brother, the Judge, is leading it."

"Where's the banker at?"

"They killed him."

Newt looked down the canyon again. The gunshots had stopped.

"If that's the case, I'd say McCluskey ran into that posse," he said.

"Help that girl if you can," she said. "She's scared and she's hurt, and she's got nobody. You can't imagine how that feels."

"Everybody gets scared."

"Maybe it's different for a woman. Maybe it's more the feeling of helplessness than the fear. I know you're hurting, Mr. Jones, but please go after her."

"You think I wasn't going to?"

"You want to get McCluskey for shooting you," she said. "I should have known that."

"Damn right I do."

He went and picked up the redhead's shotgun off the ground, and then began to move among the bodies, gathering other weapons. He found Remington's bolt-action rifle and his bandolier of spare magazines lying against a saddle back under the palm trees, and he pitched the weapon to the easterner when he and Mr. Smith returned to the fire, leading four horses. Newt was glad to see the Circle Dot horse was one of them.

Remington caught his rifle out of the air, and then the bandolier. "Are we going after her?"

Newt nodded at him, and then looked at Mr. Smith. "Are you coming along?"

It was the Mohave's turn to nod. Without a word, he began saddling horses.

"You look bad," Remington said to Newt. "Maybe you ought to sit down and rest. Let Mr. Smith and me go after her."

Newt turned back to Remington and grimaced as if every movement of his body took unusual effort or brought him pain. "I'd appreciate it if you would take care of Mrs.

Duffield. You take her to Yuma if we don't come back. It's not hard to find. Go east until you hit the road and then follow it."

"I'm going with you," Remington said.

Before they could argue over the matter, the sound of horses running up the canyon came to them.

"Do you think that's McCluskey coming back?" Remington asked.

"Could be," Newt answered. "You up for this?"

"I'm ready."

Newt looked to Alice. "You take our horses and go farther up the canyon and wait for us. If one of us doesn't come, you hide. That posse will be here before long. They'll take care of you."

"What do you want me to do?" Remington asked.

Newt pointed up the dark slope of the bulge of mountain looming over the canyon above them. "You and Mr. Smith get up there in the rocks. Don't shoot unless I do. You hear me?"

"I hear you," Remington answered.

"But if you have to shoot, you keep on shooting. You say there are only two of them, but there could be more. Either way, they'll be men that make their living with a gun. You keep your head down and you bang away until there's nothing left to shoot. Use every last one of those fancy magazines of yours if you have to."

"What about the girl?"

"That's why you don't shoot unless I do."

Mr. Smith was already climbing up the side of the canyon. Newt threw more wood on the campfire, and then more. It wasn't real firewood, only bits of brush and scrub mesquite that the outlaws had gathered, and wouldn't burn long. But it burned bright enough for the time being to light the floor of the canyon somewhat.

Newt went to where the saddled Circle Dot horse waited for him. He reached inside one of his saddlebags and found the spare pistol he had taken off the dead man back in the trading post at Agua Caliente. The Colt revolver wasn't a fit for his holster, so he shoved it behind his waistband. Then he stripped the leather belt full of shotgun cartridges from the redheaded outlaw and slung it over one shoulder.

He looked down at the redhead's body one last time. "Who was he?"

"They called him Bendigo," Alice answered. "Does it matter?"

He broke the shotgun open, loaded the empty chamber, and snapped it closed again. "He was a hard one, that's all. Take the horses."

She led the horses up the canyon, looking back at him until she was out of the light.

He stepped beyond the fire and didn't stop until he was standing on a smooth stretch of sandy ground exactly in the middle of the canyon floor. The sound of the running horses was closer by then, and he waited, plainly lit by the fire, for anyone to see.

Remington hadn't gone up in the rocks, yet, and stood watching Newt. "So, we're going to be up there. Where are you going to be when they come?"

"Right here. I'll be right here."

CHAPTER FORTY

Zander McCluskey pulled up his horse at the edge of the firelight. He kept Madeline Kerr's horse pulled close beside his own and between himself and Newt. Carlos stopped several yards behind him and a little off to one side with his Winchester ready.

Newt saw McCluskey take in the bodies of his gang lying scattered around the fire, and saw the worried way he tried to keep watch on the canyon sides out of the corners of his eyes, sensing a trap.

"You're supposed to be dead," McCluskey said.

"People been thinking that long as I can remember," Newt replied. "Let the girl go."

"Who have you got up there?" McCluskey asked, and jerked his head at the canyon wall above him.

"Let her go."

McCluskey gave a bitter chuckle. "I suppose you're going to tell me next that I let her go and you let me ride off."

"No, I'm going to kill you, one way or the other."

"This goes wrong, I'll cut her in half," McCluskey said.

McCluskey was riding Remington's Thoroughbred, and the nervous Kentucky gelding wouldn't stand still.

It fidgeted and moved enough that Newt was able to see that McCluskey held a pistol pressed against Madeline Kerr's side.

"You get out of the way and let us pass, or she gets it," McCluskey said.

"That won't help you any."

"I warn you, the vaquero behind me is more than a fair hand with that Winchester he's carrying. You so much as twitch with that shotgun and he's going to finish what I started back in the dunes, and the girl is going down with you. Now drop it and have whoever's with you come down here."

The Mexican behind McCluskey cocked his Winchester. The metallic clack of it was loud in the stillness of the canyon.

Newt stooped slowly and set the shotgun on the ground, and when he straightened up again he held both hands wide of his belt.

"Tell them to come down here," McCluskey said. "Now."

"Come on down," Newt called out.

There was no answer from the canyon sides.

"You do like I said. You hear me, tenderfoot?" Newt called again. "You do exactly like I told you."

A rock rolled loose and clattered on one side of the canyon, as if Mr. Smith or Remington were moving from their positions. That partially drew McCluskey's attention, and at the exact same moment, the Thoroughbred beneath him slung its head against the bridle bit and the hold of the reins and moved its feet enough to pull McCluskey's pistol from Madeline Kerr's side.

Newt's right hand dropped for the pistol at his waistband and came up spouting flame. His shot struck Mc-Cluskey and would have knocked him from his saddle if he hadn't fallen against the girl. The girl screamed, and the two horses mixed together. Newt couldn't take a second shot for fear of hitting her.

Carlos fired and shot Newt above his left knee and knocked him down. The outlaw vaquero worked the lever on his Winchester to chamber a fresh cartridge, ready for a final killing shot, but a gun bellowed on the side of the canyon above him. That shot missed the vaquero, but scared his horse enough to cause it to scramble sideways and crash into the thick mesquite brush beside him.

The rifle on the canyon wall boomed again, and then there were more shots coming fast. Bullets whipped through the brush around the Mexican or ricocheted off rocks. Carlos rolled his horse back over its hocks and spurred it off in a run, headed back down the canyon. His horse didn't run three strides before a bullet struck it and flipped it end over end. He went flying over its head, but somehow came up on his feet running and dove into the brush and rocks.

Newt was still down on the ground and saw none of that, but he propped himself up on one elbow, leveled his pistol, and waited for another shot at McCluskey. The two horses pulled apart, and McCluskey fought to hang on to the girl, causing them both to be dragged to the ground.

Carlos was now hidden in the dark on the opposite side of the canyon from where Remington and Mr. Smith had taken their positions. The vaquero's rifle blossomed orange flame, once and then again, two fast-paced shots only a breath apart. There was an answering shot from up on the mountain, and it sounded like the tenderfoot's .45-70. After that, both rifles roared and Newt got glimpses of their gun flashes.

He got his good leg under him and pushed himself up.

His wounded leg would take none of his weight, and he fought to keep upright. McCluskey stood at the same time, clutching Madeline Kerr in front of him. He held her around the throat with his left arm, using her as a shield. His revolver was cocked and the barrel of it pressed against her head.

The rifle fight between the outlaw vaquero and Remington continued behind him, and the gunshots reverberated loudly enough to feel them. And then those guns went quiet.

Newt leaned heavily on his good leg and felt the blood weighing down his pants leg on the other. His boot was already full of it.

McCluskey looked little better. Newt wasn't sure where his shot had hit the outlaw, but could tell by how hard he was breathing that he was hit hard.

"Your Mexican friend's out of it, and I've got two men up in those rocks coming down behind you," Newt said.

"Maybe, or maybe Carlos did for both of them," McCluskey answered. "I'll bet on my man in a rifle fight."

Newt wasn't sure how much longer he could stay on his feet. The pistol he held pointed at McCluskey was heavy in his hand.

"I should have killed you the first time I saw you back in the pass," McCluskey said.

"We're both shot to pieces," Newt said. "Let the girl go and let's finish this."

"Who the hell are you?" McCluskey asked.

"Nobody in particular."

"Carlos?" McCluskey called out. "Carlos?"

CHAPTER FORTY-ONE

Frederic Sackrider Remington, born of good English and French Basque stock, whose ancestors were some of the first to America and who had founded towns and hardware empires and helped the country win wars, staunchly Republican and of a family name well known and respected in the right circles, stared down his rifle barrel and waited for another rifle flash to tell him the outlaw vaquero's location. He, the failed student of the Yale School of Art, recently separated from his wife, and living on the last pennies of his inheritance and a loan from his mother, now found himself not in New York, but on a desert mountainside on a dark night in the middle of a gunfight, where a wrong move and a good shot by his opponent meant the loss of his life. He could not keep his hands from trembling, and never before had his nerves been shaken so. The fear and the adrenaline rush were both terrifying and exhilarating.

The outlaw he was faced off against was a very good shot, scarily so, as if some black magic guided his aim. Other than that, Remington had no clue how the man could shoot in the dark so accurately. Mr. Smith had advised him not to fire from one place too long, and to keep moving his position. Even doing so, the outlaw gunman had still managed to put two of his bullets very close to Remington. The side of his face was raw and stinging where one of those shots had spanged off the slope right beside him and splattered him with rock fragments.

He wished Mr. Smith was still with him, but the Mohave warrior had laid down his rifle, taken out his clubs, and vanished. The last Remington had seen of him he was slipping like a phantom down the side of the canyon. No doubt, he intended to sneak up on the outlaw and dispatch him hand to hand, but Remington expected him to get spotted and shot before he so much as made it across the canyon. But no shot came, and either Mr. Smith was exceptionally stealthy, or the Mexican was too busy moving positions again to notice he was being stalked.

Remington inched sideways a little to take better cover behind a slab of stone and rested his rifle's forearm across the top of it. He considered himself an adequate marksman, but the conditions were frustrating. He had long since given up trying to use the iron sights on his rifle, as it was too dark to see them at all. He simply tried to press his cheek to the stock the same way he would have if it weren't dark and to look down his barrel and point where he wanted to hit. He had fired two magazines at the outlaw and missed him with every shot, but he had at least been able to shoot the man's horse from under him in that fashion. It bothered him to have killed the poor, defenseless animal, as next to his Eva, he loved horses more than anything.

Since the Mexican had been dismounted, all Remington managed was to fire sound shots when he thought he heard the outlaw moving, or to shoot at his rifle flashes. But each time he shot he gave the outlaw a target to shoot back. His eyes scanned the black curtain on the far side of the canyon. He was so on edge waiting for the outlaw to reveal himself that he could barely sit still.

The gunshot came quicker than Remington expected. He felt the tug of the outlaw's bullet striking the top of his pith helmet even before his brain recognized the image of the short burp of flame erupting from the end of the outlaw's rifle barrel. That flash was straight across the canyon from him and at an equal height up the canyon wall. He moved his aim that way and fired two shots as fast as he could work the bolt on his rifle, and then he pointed and shot again and again. The rifle kicked hard against his shoulder each time, and by the end he was simply slinging lead in the general vicinity of where he thought the outlaw might be. Maybe, at the very least, he could distract the Mexican and give Mr. Smith a chance to close with him.

He pulled the trigger a last time, and his firing pin snapped on an empty chamber. He loaded another magazine from his bandolier, and worked his bolt. It came to him that he was breathing heavily and that his heart was thumping wildly. It took him far too long to remember that he should either move or get behind some cover, and he ducked behind the slab of rock and waited for return fire.

He waited that way for a few minutes, although it seemed like an eternity. During that time he picked his pith helmet up off the ground and ran a hand over it.. His fingers found the bullet hole in the front of it, and then the back where the bullet had exited. That bullet couldn't have missed taking off the top of his head by more than an inch, and his legs shook uncontrollably at the thought of how close he had come to dying.

The shakes eventually left him, and he took deep breaths to try and regain his composure. The more he thought about it, the more he was sure he had missed the outlaw again. He crawled on his hands and knees over the rocks, hugging behind what cover he could find. When he next peered over a hump of ground, he immediately ducked again for cover, expecting to be shot at. No shot came.

He rose again, rifle ready. Not far from where he thought the Mexican had been he thought he saw a moving shadow. It could have been his eyes playing tricks on him, but he saw it again. He pointed his rifle at it, and was debating on whether to shoot or not when there came a bloodcurdling cry from that direction. Although he had never heard such a sound before, he immediately recognized it for what it was. It was Mr. Smith's war cry. The canyon went quiet again.

And then he saw Mr. Smith's shadowed form standing on a ledge of rock above the brushy thicket on the canyon's floor. The weak moonlight barely lit him enough for Remington to make him out, and it took a moment for it to dawn on Remington that the Mohave was waving something to get his attention. It took another moment for him to recognize what it was being waved.

It was a big hat, a big Mexican hat.

CHAPTER FORTY-TWO

Mr. Smith's war cry of victory rang on the canyon walls, and both Newt and McCluskey could not help but hear it. And it was also plain what it meant.

"I'd say your man's out of it now," Newt said. "Let the girl go."

McCluskey chuckled bitterly. "You think this is the first time I've been in the pit?"

Newt shifted his pistol slightly as the girl sagged in McCluskey's hold and gave a weak moan. Instead of her eyes being drawn to McCluskey's pistol pressed against the side of her head, she stared straight at Newt. There was no terror in that gaze, only resignation and something else both pitiful and pleading.

McCluskey gave the girl a hard jerk of his arm to keep her on her feet. "I've lived in the pit my whole life. You want a try at me, well, here I am, you ugly son of a . . ."

Newt's entire world focused into one small frame centered on a Colt .45's front sight and the man beyond it, and through that narrowed, almost surrealistic lens he watched it happen as if it were another man pulling the trigger. The revolver in his fist roared just one time. He felt the buck of it in his fist and rode the recoil up and then back down.

His bullet struck McCluskey in the forehead, and the outlaw's whole body went limp and he crumpled backward to the ground, as if he were a marionette's puppet and all his strings were instantly cut.

"You talk too damned much," Newt said from behind the curl of powder smoke rising from the muzzle of his pistol.

The girl was left standing, still staring at Newt. She took a slow, hesitant step toward him, glanced at the gore splattered on her and then at the lifeless form of the outlaw at her feet. She made it only one other step before she, too, crumpled to the ground. Her sobs came quietly at first, and then louder.

Newt let his gun hand drop and stood there watching her. He was still standing there when Mr. Smith came up the canyon. For some reason, the Mohave was carrying a Mexican sombrero.

Mr. Smith gave only a cursory glance at McCluskey's body and the crying girl. He nodded at Newt. "Good fight."

Newt hadn't answered him by the time Remington came down from the rocks. He was hatless, and Newt thought he looked decidedly less ridiculous without that silly helmet on his head.

"We did it," Remington said.

Mr. Smith pitched the sombrero to the easterner. "You shoot good in the dark."

"You mean I got him?" Remington asked.

"You must have dreamed some power to shoot like that." Mr. Smith pantomimed holding up an imaginary rifle and looking down its sights, and then he poked himself in his aiming eye with his finger and threw back his head.

"First shot through the eye, and one more through the chest. I would like to hear of your dream."

Newt turned and made as if to hobble away, but fell to the ground before he made it halfway to the fire. The next thing he knew Remington was hovering over him.

"Don't try and move, Mr. Jones. You're very badly hurt," Remington said.

Hurt? Newt didn't hurt at all. In fact, he felt hardly anything. He tried to push the easterner out of his way, but his hands found nothing, even though the tenderfoot's face seemed only inches from his own. And then he suddenly lacked the energy or the will to do anything. He was floating, light as a feather on a dark cloud as soft and wispy as cotton balls, and it was a good place.

"Is he dead?" someone said from very far away.

That was the last thing he remembered before the peaceful nothing swallowed him whole.

CHAPTER FORTY-THREE

Poker Alice helped Remington cut away Newt's pants leg to reveal the wound in his leg. The bullet had hit him at the bottom of his thigh but hadn't passed all the way through that leg. There was a lot of blood, but the bleeding from the wound itself was slowed to an intermittent seep. They bathed it with hot water, plugged it with a piece of clean cloth, and bandaged it as best they could. There was no way to remove Newt's shirt without moving him and hurting him worse, so they cut it up the front.

Alice took a sharp inhale of breath. It wasn't the sight of the ugly bullet wound in Newt's side that he had taken in the fight at the dunes that caused Alice to gasp in surprise. No, it was something else altogether.

Both she and Remington had seen Bendigo stab Newt in the chest with his knife. Now, they both understood why the knife hadn't punctured him, for there was about Newt's neck a large golden crucifix on a heavy gold chain. Where Christ's body hung on that cross there was a nick in the gold, plainly where the point of Bendigo's knife had struck it. A bruise was already forming on Newt's chest behind that crucifix from the force of the outlaw's strike.

"Now where did he get that?" Remington muttered in a hushed tone.

Alice said nothing, too caught up by the sight of the crucifix to say anything. Without knowing why, she immediately recognized that the crucifix was very old. It was cast in a Gothic style and not only was it made of gold, but the cross itself was dotted with tiny rubies. Intricate, lacy filigree work ran along the edges of the cross, and each end of its four points were shaped into scalloped spades like spear points with a single green emerald set in each of them. The necklace chain was made of flat, heavy links.

"It's beautiful," she said.

"What have you got there?" the Judge asked, leaning over her shoulder.

He and his posse had arrived shortly after the shoot-out was over, and it had taken quite a bit of frantic talking to convince him that Mr. Smith and Freddy Remington weren't part of McCluskey's gang. Madeline Kerr wouldn't talk, and it was only Alice's appearance when she had come down with the horses that seemed to change his mind about hanging her companions on the spot, at least temporarily. She got the impression that in the Judge's mind the verdict was still out.

The last time she looked, the Judge had been sitting on a rock brooding beside Madeline Kerr on the far side of the fire from them while they tended to Newt's wounds. She hadn't heard his approach. Her instant reaction was to want to somehow hide the crucifix from him. She quickly folded half of Newt's shirt back over the crucifix, hoping he hadn't made out exactly what it was she was hiding.

"We were just admiring Mr. Jones's necklace," she said to the Judge.

"I saw that," the Judge replied, standing over them. "Quite a piece of jewelry."

She could tell by his expression that he had gotten a very good look at the crucifix before she covered it, or at least enough of a look to raise his curiosity. Several lies came to mind, but she stopped short of telling them. There was no way to pass off the crucifix as piece of personal jewelry. The crucifix was too large and gaudy even for a priest to wear. It was something only a bishop or a cardinal would wear, perhaps only a ceremonial piece at that, a church treasure.

"I recognize this man," the Judge said. "I sentenced him to thirty days for prizefighting. Jones, I believe."

"Yes, Newt Jones," she replied. "I did not realize he was a pugilist when I hired him."

"And what did you say you and this Jones and the other were doing out here before you were attacked by those outlaws?" The Judge shifted his gaze her way, and his tone was bland and meant to sound perfectly harmless.

She waited a moment to answer him. The difficulty with stretching the truth was keeping your story the same each time you had to tell it. "I told you, I hired Mr. Jones and Mr. Smith there to guide me to Yuma."

"A train would have been a far faster and better way for you to travel."

She gave him a practiced smile that was meant to suggest she had nothing but air for brains. She had found that approach worked on many men, the whole helpless, incapable-damsel bit.

"Oh, I know that now, but at the time I hoped to see a bit of the desert I have heard so much about. I have a few more weeks left before I have to be back in Philadelphia for the fall term at the ladies' academy where I teach, and it was Freddy who suggested we go cross-country and then catch the train at Yuma to take us home. He wanted to paint a few landscapes before he went back to New York. It sounded like such an adventure at the time, and I had no way of knowing that it could be so dangerous." She gave him that smile again and a bat of her eyes that she hoped she didn't overdo.

"Freddy?" The Judge nodded at Remington. "I take it you're her beau."

"Now you're being rude," she interjected before Remington could answer for himself. "But yes, if you must know, Freddy and I are engaged."

"I see," the Judge said.

Alice fought back the growing frustration and irritation she felt and tried not to show it. Newt was possibly dying and the Judge wanted to interrogate her one more time.

The Judge looked down at Jones lying on a blanket at his feet. "Will he live?"

"I'm afraid he is hurt quite badly. Perhaps if your men will build a litter of some sort we could get him to Yuma or some other place where there is a doctor."

"I'll see what I can do," the Judge said. "I'd like to talk to him if he comes to."

"He had been unconscious or in some weakened state of sleep since before you arrived."

"Well, you let me know if that changes. My brother was murdered, and I would like to hear what your guide might know about that."

She saw him look again at Newt's chest. The vague shape of the crucifix was faintly visible even through the bit of shirt covering it if you were looking for it.

The Judge went back to his rock and sat once more. He said something to his niece that Alice couldn't make out, and then gave orders to his men to find something to build a litter to carry Newt. The Judge said nothing else after that. He rested one hand on his niece's shoulder and stared into the fire.

One of the posse had brought Madeline a blanket, and she had draped it over her head and wrapped it around her. Her face was almost hidden in the darkness of that hood and she stared at the ground with her body gently rocking back and forth. She was a pitiful sight.

"Do you remember what Pablo said about the church treasures?" Remington asked in a hushed voice after look-ing to make sure the Judge or any of the rest of them were out of hearing range. "The ones that were supposed to be on the *Trinidad*?"

"How do you think I could have forgotten that? Of course I remember," she said.

"When would he have had time to find the ship?"

"Maybe he already had the crucifix. We didn't know how long Pablo had been hunting the treasure until we reached Indio. Remember, Mr. Jones already intended to go to the dunes before we read that captain's journal or looked at the map."

"That Indian back in Agua Caliente told him that the ship was to be found in the dunes."

"How do we know he and that Indian didn't know each other before?"

"I don't know." Remington shook his head in thought. "Do you think he could have found the crucifix after we split up?" Remington asked. "He was alone for two days on his way here. The odds of that seem too incredible to believe it to be the case, but I can't help but wonder."

She thought about what the Judge had said. "I'll be interested to hear what he has to say about what he's wearing around his neck, as no doubt you will be."

"If he lives."

They bathed the wound in Newt's side and wrapped his waist in a fresh bandage.

"I don't know what else we can do for him," Remington said. "He's lost a lot of blood, and there's still a bullet in his leg."

"How far is it to Yuma?" she asked. "Or is there someplace closer where we could find a doctor for him?"

He shrugged. "How should I know? I'll go talk with the Judge about it."

Remington got to his feet and left her. When he was gone she looked down at Newt again. His breathing was shallow and slow, but regular. She thought how fierce his face looked in the firelight, even in repose. It was a face that looked to have been carved with a chisel and a hammer instead of grown in a woman's womb.

She leaned closed to him and whispered. "Where did you get that crucifix, huh? Oh, you're going to tell me, I promise you that. You think I ever caught a man bluffing me? My cards are on the table and you've been called. Time to show your hand."

A couple of men from the Judge's posse were coming closer. She covered Newt with a blanket and rose and headed to find Mr. Smith. She passed by the Judge on her way, and it was while passing between him and the fire that she saw his saddle and other gear on the ground at his feet. Her stride faltered for a split second at the sight of Pablo's leather map tube tied to the back of the saddle.

Without meaning to, she looked at the Judge and found him staring back at her. His expression was unreadable, but something passed between them that left her cold in the brief instant that their eyes locked. As she walked away she was thinking that as soon as they reached Yuma, she wanted to get as far away from the Judge as possible.

CHAPTER FORTY-FOUR

The feather mattress Newt lay on felt so soft that he wanted to sink down into it and keep on sinking. His eyes opened, but the rest of his body was reluctant to awaken. The single lamp burning in the room was trimmed low, and he lay there without moving and tried to gather his wits.

He had only a vague idea of where he was, and his memories of how he had gotten there were only disjointed bits and pieces of lying flat on his back atop some improvised pole travois and being bounced and dragged along behind someone's horse. That journey had been one of fitful sleep and torturous pain, like a fevered nightmare. He would have made them stop and let him die, but his body failed him and he couldn't so much as lift a hand in his own defense.

And he remembered snatches of overheard conversation, and the words *Yuma* and *doctor* were prominent. He supposed the doctor was the one who had tortured him for what seemed like hours, the one who had dug the bullet from his leg. He felt ashamed about the way he had cursed and threatened the man, but wasn't sure if that had been real or simply the result of some fever sweat.

He was covered in a white sheet, and he pushed it back and saw that he was naked beneath it. There was a fresh bandage around his waist and one above his left knee. He flexed his toes and feet and gingerly drew up his good leg in order to push himself up against the iron headboard behind him. That attempt proved to be a bad idea. It was as if his whole body was one great bruise, and he decided to stay where he was for the time being.

He lifted one hand to gingerly feel the bullet wound on the side of his head in reaction to the headache he felt coming on again. His fingers brushed against another bandage there.

"You might want to pull those covers back over you," Poker Alice's voice sounded from somewhere across the room at the foot of his bed.

He grabbed for the sheet and yanked it back over himself too fast and caused a tearing sensation in his side. He gritted his teeth and closed his eyes.

When he opened his eyes again he lifted his head from the pillow high enough to make her out sitting in a chair in a shadowed corner beside the door. "Where am I?"

"The Colorado Hotel in Yuma."

"I've had some crazy dreams and I'm not sure what was real and what wasn't." His mouth and throat were so dry that his speech was crackly and weak. "How long have I been down?"

"We were two days getting you here, and then the doctor worked on you half the night. You've been sleeping ever since." She rose and went to the table beside his bed and poured him a cup of water and handed it to him.

He gulped down the water and handed the cup back to her. "I'm hungry."

She stood beside him, looking down at him with an odd look on her face. Her face was bruised and cut, but her hair was curled and bound fashionably high on her head. She was wearing a new dress and a little hat with a feather in it.

"Why are you looking at me like that?" he asked.

"The doctor said you had lost so much blood that he wasn't even sure you would survive the operation to remove the bullet from your leg." She turned her back on him. "One moment you're dying, and the next you're asking for food. You have the constitution of a horse."

"I feel like a ton of bricks was dropped on me," he said. "What about the others, the dude and Mr. Smith?"

"They're both fine. I believe Freddy has had enough adventure. He intends to purchase a train ticket and leave us before too long. Mr. Smith is . . . oh, you know, he's around somewhere."

She told him what had happened in the canyon after he had gone down, about the Judge and how he and his posse had brought them to Yuma along with Madeline Kerr and the recovered freight mules. She talked fast, and he had trouble paying attention.

"What will you do now that it's over?" he asked.

"Over? No, Mr. Jones, it's not over. At the bare minimum you and I need to have a talk."

"About what?"

"The ship. The treasure."

"We lost two good men, and the rest of us barely got out with our hides in one piece. Haven't you had enough? Even the dude has that much sense."

"I admit I might have underestimated you." She turned and strolled slowly away from his bed. "That's one lesson

I learned at the tables. Never underestimate the other players."

"This never was some kind of a game."

She stopped at a dresser beside the door, and opened the top drawer. From it she pulled something wrapped in a hand towel. She turned to him and unwrapped the object.

"How do you explain this?" She held up the crucifix so that he could see it.

"I found it."

"You found it? Was that before or after you came to George Kerr's camp that night?"

He fought to keep his eyes open. Even so little as talking tired him. "I found it after I walked out of the dunes."

"Where?"

"In the bottom of a wash."

"What else did you find?" She leaned against the dresser. Instead of looking at him she was looking at the crucifix, as if it entranced her. "And don't pretend you're asleep."

He opened his eyes, but gave her no answer.

"You found the ship."

"There was no ship."

"I don't believe you, but say you're telling the truth. At the very least you were very close. You and I both know this is one of the church treasures that Pablo told us about. What else could it be?"

"Maybe it is, or maybe it isn't."

"You thought you could keep the crucifix a secret, and then after we gave up, you could go back and look for the rest of the treasure."

"Is that what you would have done?" he asked.

She wrapped the crucifix with the towel again and put

it back in the drawer. "We all agreed to a partnership, but we never did get around to agreeing on how we would divide the treasure, did we? I told Mr. Smith to watch you if we found it. A man like you might be tempted to take it all for himself. It seems I was right."

Newt only stared at her through slitted, heavy eyelids.

"I'm not going anywhere," she said. "We're going to finish this talk, and then when you're well again we can go back to where you found the ship."

"I don't know if I could find my way back to that wash." Newt's speech was heavy and the words came too far apart.

She bent and picked something off the floor beside the chair where she had been sitting, and then came back to the bed. "Thought you might like to have this back. Call it a token of goodwill."

She hung the gun belt around one of the iron bedposts on the headboard. The double-loop holster held a Smith & Wesson revolver with blue turquoise crosses set in the walnut grips, his pistol.

His eyes closed again and he fell asleep. She did not wake him again. Instead, she took a seat in the chair beside the door with a blanket covering her. She leaned her head against the wall and stared at him for the better part of an hour, but eventually, she, too, drifted off.

CHAPTER FORTY-FIVE

Poker Alice was gone when Newt woke late the next morning, but the Judge was in her chair. He had been sitting behind his courtroom bench the last and only time they met, but Newt remembered him well.

"The doctor tells you me you are going to keep that leg," the Judge said. "I would have bet otherwise when I found you."

"What do you want?" Newt didn't try to hide his irritation at having to converse with the Judge the instant he woke up.

"I suppose I should thank you for what you did for my niece," the Judge said.

"That's not exactly thanking me."

The Judge took his hat off and laid it on one of his knees, and then he brushed back a stray strand of his long white hair and smoothed it down. "I did some checking up on you, Jones. Sent off a few telegraphs. Asked a few people I know."

"If you're going to keep talking, at least hand me that chamber pot," Newt said.

The Judge ignored his request. "Widowmaker, that's

what they call you, isn't it? It seems you have made a
name for yourself. As I understand it, you're the man that
tamed Shakespeare. They say you put down a riot single-
handedly."

Newt frowned at the Judge. His bladder was about to
bust, and he didn't relish trying to get out of the bed to
make it to the chamber pot. In fact, he wasn't even sure he
could stand. "Wasn't quite like that."

"No, I assumed as much," the Judge continued. "Never
met a man who was half his reputation. That Shakespeare
story makes you sound like some kind of hero, a real good
guy. But other people tell me you were nothing but a hired
thug for whatever mining company would pay you to crack
heads and to run men off their claims so the company
could gobble them up. Those that say that tell it that you're
a man who'll do anything for a price. That you're the one
who brought Javier Cortina's head back to Texas in a sack
just to collect the bounty on him."

"That's a damned lie." Newt squirmed and pushed his
back up against the headboard, and the pain of that sucked
the breath out of him so that he couldn't say anything else.

"The Cortina part, or the part about you being a thug?"
the Judge asked. "I think you're quibbling words."

"Did you come here just to pick a fight?" Newt asked.

"Maybe you're the hardcase you appear to be, or maybe
you're a man who keeps finding himself in bad circumstances. Let's leave that to the court of public opinion," the
Judge said. "But I learned one other interesting bit of information this very morning. One of the telegraphs I received tells me you got involved in a little stagecoach
holdup over in the Arizona Territory. It seems they would
like to talk to you about that matter."

"I was a shipment guard and had nothing to do with

that. I've already talked to the law about it, and they let me go."

"Seems they might have had a change of heart. Did you know there's a three-hundred-dollar reward for your capture?"

Newt took hold of his bad leg and managed to get it over the edge of the bed. He sat there and stared into the sunlight pouring through the window and summoned the willpower it was going to take to get up.

The Judge took a silver case out of his vest pocket and opened it. He took a thin cigar from it and then offered it to Newt. Newt didn't look his way, so he snapped the case closed and repocketed it. He took his time lighting the cigar, and he gave Newt a piercing look over the top of the match while he shook out the flame.

"Speaking of rewards. The prison warden and the governor put a price on the heads of Hileman and those other two escapees," the Judge said as he squinted through the tobacco smoke. "You've got six hundred dollars coming to you."

"Who's Hileman?"

"The one passing himself off as Zander McCluskey, the one you killed back in the canyon. He and Bendigo and the Swede broke out of the territorial prison here a while back."

"You didn't come here to talk about bounties or who's got a wanted notice put out on them. Say your piece," Newt said.

The Judge hooked one thumb in his watch pocket and tilted back his head and blew a smoke ring that floated to the ceiling. When he looked back at Newt he said, "I lost a brother and a son-in-law, both of them murdered. That's a bitter pill to swallow. I was of a mind to hang you for that when I found you in Pinto Canyon. Thought you were one of them, but my niece has recovered enough to talk coherently and to relay what happened after they left San Bernardino."

"Lucky me."

"Don't sass me, boy." The Judge's eyes narrowed and his voice became sharp and clipped. "You might not have been riding with Hileman, but I know you weren't simply out on the desert to nursemaid that woman and that artist on a sightseeing trip. Maddy tells me she overheard her kidnappers say you were looking for the lost ship."

"What of it?"

"Only liars tell lies. The question is, why are you lying?"

"I imagine my associates were trying to find a story you would believe. A man goes to talking about hanging folks and he shouldn't be surprised what people will say."

"What did you do with that crucifix?" the Judge asked. "Don't act like you don't know what I'm talking about. I saw it hanging around your neck."

Newt's bladder couldn't bear the strain any longer, and he hobbled across the room and took up the chamber pot atop the dresser beside the Judge. The Judge kept on talking, seemingly not bothered by a naked man standing beside him urinating.

"What did you find out there besides that crucifix?" the Judge asked.

"That old thing?"

"I told you not to play me the fool." The Judge ground his cigar ash out on the sole of one boot. "That's a rich piece of jewelry you have there. Real old. I might believe you stole it from some church, but word would have got out if something like that went missing."

"Where I got it is none of your business," Newt said.

The walk across the room had caused Newt's leg to ache badly, and the rest of his body didn't feel much better. He set the chamber pot on the dresser and went back to the bed and sat down. Even such a short time on his feet left him breathing heavily. He could feel something warm and wet on his thigh, and knew that he had likely caused his leg wound to start bleeding again.

"My business is what I make it," the Judge said.

"You've got the fever, don't you?" Newt asked. "Same as your brother and the marshal had it. You come up here talking about how you've lost your family and all of that, but what you're after is the ship."

"I think you found something," the Judge said. "You take me there, and we'll split anything we find right down the middle. Could be if you did that, I might forget about that warrant out for you over in the territory. I've got enough to tend to here, and let those Arizona boys handle their own business, huh?"

"I found that crucifix somewhere between Algodones and where you got your niece back. I was half out of my mind when I found it. That's a long damned walk, especially with half the stuffing knocked out of you. You expect me to be able to find my way back?"

"I say a man that can cross sixty miles of desert on foot with a bullet hole in him could."

"You've already had trackers out trying to back-trail me, haven't you?"

The Judge nodded. "I sent my Paiute before we even got to Yuma. He came back with nothing. Monsoon season is about on us. Thunderstorm wiped out the sign."

"Your Indian couldn't find where I went, but you think I can?" Newt asked. "I've had my fill of deserts, and don't care if I ever see one again. Last look I'm going to have is out of a train window when I get out of here."

The Judge put his hat back on and moved to the edge of his seat, but he paused there. "You think you can outwait me? Think you can go back to where you found that crucifix after things have had time to cool off? When you do, I'll know it. Doesn't matter how long you wait to make your try, but I'll be there. I've got men loyal to me scattered all up and down this border that I pay to keep me informed, and they'll pass the word."

The Judge rose and opened the door. "You think on it. I'd hate to have to telegraph that marshal in Phoenix and tell him I'm holding you here ready for extradition."

"You won't do that," Newt said.

"And why is that?"

"Because you're an old fool who believes in buried treasure, and I'm the only man you think can lead you to it."

"Boy, you don't know the kind of trouble I can bring down on you."

"Maybe you once were some kind of man, but I don't see anything now but an old windbag too full of himself that hides behind the law. Get the hell out of my room."

The Judge stiffened, and his hand started to push back one side of his coat.

"You pull that pistol. Go ahead, Judge."

For a brief instant, Newt thought the old man was going to go for the revolver he wore high on his hip beneath the coat. But then the Judge's gaze drifted to Newt's gun belt hanging on the bedpost. The holster was empty. The Judge whirled and went out the door, leaving it open behind him.

He was barely gone when Mr. Smith and Remington came into the room. The Mohave was wearing his suit again.

Remington looked out the door and down the hotel hallway at the Judge's back. "What did he want?"

Newt didn't answer, and pulled his Smith & Wesson revolver out from under his pillow and shoved it back in his holster on the bedpost.

Footfalls sounded outside the open door, as if someone was climbing a set of stairs. Remington flopped down in the chair beside the door and waved a dismissive hand at the sound behind him.

"It's just one of the waitresses down at the restaurant. I asked her to bring you some breakfast," he said. "Or maybe it's that newspaper reporter that wants to interview you."

Newt threw the tenderfoot a heated look. "Will someone please get me some damned clothes before the whole town comes trooping through here?"

Remington turned to Mr. Smith and smiled. "Well, I think he's on the mend. Got his usual pleasant demeanor back, I see."

CHAPTER FORTY-SIX

Newt and Mr. Smith sat in a pair of chairs on the hotel porch watching the street before them and listening to the sound of the arriving train. Newt had his bad leg propped up on a spare chair and his crutch laid across his lap. The crutch was really nothing more than a thick length of cottonwood limb that the Mohave had whittled into shape and then added a padded piece of leather at the top to rest under Newt's armpit.

It had taken two days for Newt to feel fit enough to come downstairs and sit on the porch, or to hobble about the hotel lobby. His convalescence had left him restless and cranky, and he and Mr. Smith sat there for an hour without either man speaking a single word.

Newt tugged at the throat on his new white shirt, pulling it away from where it was rubbing against a raw spot on his neck. The clothes Remington had retrieved for him from the nearest store fit him fine, but he never had felt comfortable in brand-new clothing, much preferring his garments properly "broken in."

The smoke off the train's engine was visible over the roof of the hardware store across the street from them.

Behind them, Remington came out the front door of the hotel. He was wearing a new suit and bowler hat and carrying a suitcase in one hand and his bolt-action rifle in the other hand.

Newt nodded his head at the rifle. "I doubt there are any banditos in New York for you to shoot."

Remington laughed.

"Didn't mean to hold you up. Best you go catch your train," Newt said.

Remington hesitated instead of leaving. "Tell me the truth. What did you find out there besides that crucifix?"

"You stick around and maybe I'll take you out sometime and show you."

"No, I believe I'll go."

"Newt pointed down at a newspaper lying on the porch beside his chair. "Papers say the government is sending General Miles after Geronimo this time. You going with him to draw your pictures of the Apache like you said?"

"I haven't heard back from my potential employers, so perhaps not. But no matter, I sent a telegram to my Eva, and surprisingly, she seems quite willing for us to talk and to see if we can patch our marriage back together."

"Good. Glad to hear it."

"If she will have me back I intend to take up studies at the Art Students League of New York to hone my work."

"You'll do well, I'm sure."

"You're not going to tell me, are you? No matter how often I prod you?"

"Tell you what?"

Remington smiled in a wistful way and then shrugged. "Maybe not knowing is best. I hope there's always buried treasure or lost mines waiting to be found. You know, things almost too big to believe in but there to search for.

Maybe you were after the treasure, but I've come to think a legend is sort of a treasure in its own right. No matter how long I live or where I'm at, there'll be times when I'll think on the lost ship. Sort of fun, you know."

"That's part of the fever," Newt said. "Some men hunt for riches, and some because they've got to know."

Remington leaned his rifle against the wall and sat his suitcase down. He produced two small packages wrapped in brown paper. He handed one of them to Newt.

"I hoped you won't mind, but I took the liberty of buying you a present in parting," Remington said.

Newt laid the package in his lap.

"And you, too, Mr. Smith." Remington handed the Mohave the second of the packages.

Mr. Smith unwrapped his, and gave an appreciative grunt. He held a small telescope in his hands.

"The man who sold it to me assured me of its quality and said it has the strongest magnification available for its size on the market," Remington said. "I had it engraved for you. Read the inscription."

Mr. Smith found the inscription on the brass tube of the spyglass and read aloud, "May you always be able to look back and see home."

Mr. Smith nodded gravely. "Among my people, a gift should always be answered with an equal gift. So I will give you a name, a Mohave name fit for a warrior."

Mr. Smith rose from his chair and leaned close and whispered something in Remington's ear.

"Say it again," Remington said.

Mr. Smith whispered again, and Remington nodded like he had it.

"Keep its power to yourself, and tell no other," Mr. Smith said when he sat back down.

Newt opened his present. It was a snub-nosed Webley British Bulldog revolver with ivory grips, the kind that some of the Southern Pacific Railroad men carried.

"That belonged to the redheaded outlaw you fought in Pinto Canyon. The one they called Bendigo. I understand he was quite the known villain in these parts, and that the Mexican guitar pickers in the cantinas here are already making up songs about how you vanquished him."

Newt noticed that the pistol's grip frame was engraved like Mr. Smith's spyglass. He could tell Remington was waiting for him to read the words, so he spoke them out loud, "To my friend, the Widowmaker. F.S. Remington."

"I figured a man like you could use a hideout gun. Never know when it might help you in a *pinch*, as you Tennessee mountain boys say," Remington said.

"Mighty kind of you, but I'm afraid I didn't get you anything."

"Oh, you have given me plenty. This trip by itself has given me no end of ideas for my art."

"I told you not to be drawing me anymore," Newt said.

Remington took up his rifle and suitcase and scampered down the porch steps laughing. He stopped and looked back at them and shook his head.

"You were right the first time I tried to sketch you, Mr. Jones," he said. "I'd paint you both and make you famous, but the folks back East want their legends a lot cleaner and more respectable."

"So long, pilgrim," Newt said. "You're not so bad for a Yale boy."

They watched the artist disappear around the corner of the hardware store, and then later listened to the train rolling out of the station. Newt turned to Mr. Smith when he was gone.

"What did that name you gave him mean?" he asked.

"If I told you it would lose its power for him," Mr. Smith replied with a straight face.

Newt noticed that there was a twinkle in the Mohave's eyes, despite his stoic response. "You know that boy is going to go back to New York and tell his new Indian name to everyone that will listen."

Mr. Smith's face broke into the hint of a smile.

"What's it mean?"

"I told him it meant 'Straight Shooter.'"

"What's it really mean?"

Mr. Smith smiled again and leaned back farther in his chair. "The closest I can come in English is 'He Who Is Always Lost.'"

Both of them laughed, and the laughing felt good.

Chapter Forty-seven

It was week later before Newt saw Poker Alice again. He was still using his crutch, but could get around without it if he didn't have to go too far or too fast. He and Mr. Smith went down to the livery where they were keeping their horses.

They passed by a saloon on their way there, and Newt went inside and left Mr. Smith waiting for him. When he came back out he was holding a small wooden box containing six brown bottles of beer.

"Would you carry this for me?" he asked.

Mr. Smith took the box, and Newt removed one beer and handed it to the Mohave, then opened one himself. The two of them walked on to the livery drinking beer, Newt hobbling on his crutch and the Mohave carrying the box.

Both their horses needed reshodding, and Mr. Smith held his horse for the blacksmith near the forge while hooves were trimmed and new horseshoes nailed in place. Newt sat in a chair in the open bay door of the shop with the Circle Dot horse standing over him. He was feeding the gelding beer when Poker Alice walked up.

She watched him uncork a bottle and hold it out for his horse. The brown gelding took the bottle by the neck with his front teeth and tipped it up with a sling of its head. The bottle was emptied quickly, and the horse dropped it and nudged the box beside Newt, wanting another.

"Giving spirits to a poor animal. Have you no shame?" Alice said in a mocking, playful voice.

Newt opened another bottle and gave it to the horse. "He doesn't ask for much, but he likes his beer. Can't give him more than three or four, or he gets unruly."

"Sounds like most men I've known."

"I hear you're winning big at the Turf Saloon," Newt said.

"I can't complain. The cards are treating me right," she answered.

Newt got up out of his chair. The Circle Dot horse nudged him with its muzzle and almost knocked him back down.

"The beer's all gone," Newt said to the horse, and then looked at her. "See what I mean? Maybe you're right. I might have the only horse in the world with a drinking problem."

"I can't imagine what other bad habits he must have picked up from you," she said.

"You ought to see him when he's on the whiskey."

She cocked her head and studied him for a moment. "You know, you ought to get yourself a new hat. That thing you're wearing is absolutely atrocious."

Newt took the black hat off his head and held it before him with a comical look, as if what she said shocked him. "This is a perfectly fine hat. Best hat I ever owned."

The black felt was faded and worn slick in places, and

marred with white salt stains. The brim and the crown both had been crushed more than once and would no longer hold their shape. There was a notch cut in the brim where O'Bannon's bullet had clipped it in the hotel at Indio.

"Maybe it once was a fine hat, but you really ought to buy a new one."

"This hat was given to me by a dear friend."

"Must not have been that good of a friend to let you wear that thing. You could always put your fancy hatband on whatever you buy."

"Wouldn't be the same."

"But maybe you wouldn't look like such a ruffian if you took a little more care with the way you dress."

"You'd have me wearing a suit like poor Mr. Smith there," he said. "No thanks."

She twirled the wrist purse she carried and was clenching her lower lip between her teeth. He could tell she was nervous about something.

"I came down here to see if you have had time to think about what I said to you that night in the hotel," she finally said.

"Is it the crucifix you want?" he asked, and stepped close to her, so close that he could smell the perfume she wore, and close enough she had to lean her head back and look up to see his face.

"I want to know where you found the ship!" Her voice raised loud enough that Mr. Smith and the blacksmith looked their way. She got control of herself, and her next words were quieter. "I want you to say that you'll take me with you when you go back."

"You know, there was a time when I thought about kissing you," he said.

"You flatter yourself."

"You're a pretty woman, there's no denying that. Got a way about you," he said as if he hadn't heard her. "Smart, but you're also a woman that's too used to working people for a win. Always putting on the act while you're trying to get the high card. Don't you get tired of that?"

"I don't know what you mean." A little of her usual cool left her, and she almost stammered the words.

"Here you are now, assuming I'm playing against you."

"You would come clean if I could trust you."

"Trust me or don't, that's your decision. I believe people always show their true colors before too long if you pay close enough attention. Some you can count on, some you can't."

"I think you've turned out to be nothing but the scoundrel they say you are. I entered an agreement with you in good faith, and now you're cutting me out because you want it all for yourself." She took a step back from him, and her face was turning red. "And you're crazy if you ever thought I would let you kiss me."

"Maybe so," he said. "What about your men standing down there by the depot and trying to act like they aren't with you? What are you paying them? That kind doesn't come cheap."

She took a deep breath and didn't look in the direction of the men he mentioned. There were two of them, and Newt knew the type—both tough gringos with pistols and a swagger to them. You could feel the violence oozing out of them, even from a distance. They were trying to appear nonchalant like they were only loafing about, but were unable to carry it off because they stuck out like wolves in a sheep herd.

"Mr. Smith informed me that he will no longer serve in my employ," she said. "Recent experiences have reinforced to me that a woman alone in this country had best buy a little insurance."

"It'll take a lot of poker winnings to make that payroll, or are you buying in to another game?" he asked.

"Take it for what you will. Let us simply say their job is to see to my interests."

"You send those men to try and strong-arm me, and I'll send them back to you in a pine box."

"Who's thinking the worst of who now?" she asked.

"Your turn," Mr. Smith called out from the shop. The blacksmith was finished with his horse and ready for Newt's.

Newt turned back to her. "I guess this is where we part company, then."

"I guess it is. Try and rethink your position on this matter, Mr. Jones. It would be for the best . . . for both of us."

"Call me stubborn."

"I've called you a lot of things. Right now I admit I hate you, but my temper sometimes gets the best of me. Give me a little time to cool off, and I'll be back to you simply annoying me."

She started to walk off, but turned back before she had taken more than a few steps. "One more thing, Mr. Jones. Did you come all the way to that canyon to save me, or was it only to have your revenge? And don't lie to me."

"A little of both, I guess."

"That's what I thought. Then I guess I should only be halfway grateful," she said. "That's not much of a debt compared to a treasure ship, now, is it?"

"Be careful who you bet on, Mrs. Duffield."

"You're telling me how to gamble?"

"People aren't poker chips."

She walked away without a reply. Her dress hem hissed on the dirt street, and the little purse twirled at the end of one hand in some strange timing with the sway of her hips and the bustle she wore.

Mr. Smith came up to stand beside Newt as he watched her walk away. The two men she had hired followed a few yards in her wake. They threw hard looks at Newt and the Mohave in passing, but said nothing.

"That one on the far side dressed like a cowboy is Bobby Dial," Newt said. "He's a Texas pistol-popper. I recognize him from when I was working at White Oaks over in New Mexico a few years ago. Some folks there were going to hang him for cattle rustling, but he got away. Last I heard he was riding for the Hashknife up around Holbrook."

"What about the other one?" Mr. Smith asked.

"Don't know him, but if he's running with Bobby he's a bad one."

Mr. Smith nodded. "She isn't the only one who waits to see what you do."

"That right?"

"The Judge rented a house down by the river."

"Any of his men still in town?"

"Only four of them. The rest went back north. He has been sending that Paiute, Charlie Two Horses, to the desert. Charlie is gone a few days, and then he comes back. And then he is gone again."

"And you know all this how?"

"I watch. It is what I do. A warrior must know his enemies."

"The Judge and Mrs. Duffield think I've found the ship and that I intend to go back after it."

Mr. Smith didn't seem bothered by that, for the expression on his face was bland. As usual, it was impossible to tell what the big Mohave was thinking. "You might like to know that I saw her having lunch with the Judge yesterday."

Newt watched Poker Alice and her gunmen disappear around a corner, and then he pointed at where she had been. "How'd you ever go to working for her?"

The Mohave gave one of his usual grunts that could mean a variety of things. "It was after I had left the ship."

"You were on a ship?"

"That is a story for another time," Mr. Smith said. "I went to visit my people but I was arrested at Needles. A white man had been found dead on the road, and it was believed that an Indian had murdered him."

"And there you were, the only Indian handy."

Mr. Smith nodded. "Bad timing on my part, you might say. They were at one of the saloons drinking and working themselves up to hang me, but Mrs. Duffield was gambling there and somehow convinced them to let me go."

"She bought you out of jail?"

"She never said how, but they let me go."

"And you went to work for her?"

"She bought me this suit. She liked it that I had manners and that I knew how to make tea the way the English like it."

"And now you reckon your debt's paid?"

"For more almost two years I have traveled with her."

"You put up with her longer than I could have."

"You think you know her, but you do not. She does not like to lose."

The two of them took their horses back to the livery and then went to the hotel. They went around to the back door. The hotel proprietor did not allow Indians in his establishment and was already chagrined about Mr. Smith sitting on his porch with Newt most mornings and disturbing his clientele.

Newt's injured leg was fatigued and bothered him some, and he made slow work of the stairs leading up to the second floor. Mr. Smith already had his room door open and went inside by the time Newt reached the landing.

Newt hobbled down the hallway, and when he got to his doorway he leaned a shoulder against the doorjamb. "I tell you, this hole in my leg's better, but it's still got me gimping like . . ."

He stopped short, for Pablo was standing by his bed. The Mexican liveryman had a pistol pointing at him. Mr. Smith stood backed against the window.

"Come in and shut the door," Pablo said.

Newt did as he was told. "Thought you were dead."

"No, as you can see, I got away." Pablo stepped to the far side of the room where he could keep watch on both Newt and Mr. Smith. "You take that pistol out of your holster very carefully, no? Throw it on the bed."

Newt eased his pistol out and tossed it on the mattress.

"And you, Señor Smith," Pablo said, "Do not make a move for those clubs of yours. I have no wish to kill you."

Newt nodded at the Colt revolver Pablo held cocked and pointed in their direction. "Thought you didn't have any use for one of those."

"How is it you say?" Pablo used his free hand to show

a little space between his thumb and forefinger. "A little white lie?"

Newt backed against the window beside Mr. Smith. "What's this all about?"

"All about? I think you know," Pablo said. "Where is the crucifix you found?"

"How did you know about that?" Newt asked.

"You cannot keep such a thing a secret. Where is it?"

"I put it in the bank for safekeeping."

"How would you like a hole in your other leg?"

"And here I thought you were a nice fellow."

"That crucifix does not belong to you."

"I suppose this is where you tell me it belongs to you."

"No, it is a holy thing that once belonged to Santos Ignatius himself, and was brought to the New World as his gift to the order."

"And it's worth quite a lot," Newt said. "You left out that part."

"You think I would sell such a thing? I am not a mercenary like you. I am no heathen bandito who would sell my soul for gold."

"You're holding two men at gunpoint. That kind of makes you a hypocrite, if you ask me."

"Give me the crucifix so that we don't have trouble," Pablo said.

"Who are you?"

"I run a livery," Pablo said. "And occasionally I hunt for the lost ship. I think that is enough for you to know."

"Who are you working for? The Jesuits, or is it the Dominicans or somebody else? Was Mateo one of you?"

Pablo gave a sly smile. "Ah, you are too smart for your own good. Let us say that there are those in the Church who have sought to find the lost ship for a long time. I am but a humble servant to those whose holiness I can never aspire to. Mateo was the same. He came up from Guaymas to help me when he heard that Señor McCluskey had found the ship. And that is more than I should tell you."

"It's in the closet. Reach above the inside of the door and you'll find it stuck behind the trim," Newt said.

Pablo didn't attempt to hide his surprise, expecting an argument. He turned and started to go to the closet, but stopped. "You think to trick me. Why don't you get it?"

Pablo backed into a corner where he could see both men and the closet at the same time. Newt went to the closet and reached one arm inside it and upward. When he turned around he held the crucifix out to Pablo.

"I did not think you would give it up so easily," Pablo said.

"Never intended to keep it. Like you said, that ought to be in some church," Newt answered.

"That is hard to believe, a man like you."

"What is it the priests say? Have a little faith?"

Pablo hung the crucifix's necklace around his neck and tucked it inside his shirtfront. "I do not suppose you will tell me where you found it?"

"You best leave now before my friend here decides he's going to make you eat that pistol. He's not as patient as I am."

"I was instructed to kill both of you after I found out what you know, but we journeyed together, broke bread. That is not a thing easy to forget, is it? I will tell them some story how you got away," Pablo said. "But I would advise you not to go back to where you found the crucifix. There are those who are always watching."

Pablo opened the door and took a quick look down the hallway to make sure there was nobody there. He looked back at them. "Do not try to follow me."

"Adios," Newt said. "If we ever meet again I wouldn't advise pointing a pistol at me. I'm sort of touchy about that kind of thing. Never could get the knack of that forgiving and forgetting."

"Vaya con Dios, hombres." Pablo gave a tip of his sombrero's brim and disappeared out the door.

When he was gone, Newt went to the bed and retrieved his pistol and holstered it. Then he went to the closet and reached up inside it the same way he had when he got the crucifix. This time, he pulled out the British Bulldog pistol Remington had given him.

Mr. Smith saw the pistol and grunted at the sight of it. "You could have gotten that instead of the crucifix. I do not understand."

"I guess I could have shot old Pablo, true enough, but he seemed a decent enough sort," Newt said.

"He is your enemy. He stole from you."

"I think he was telling the truth."

"Then you truly weren't going to keep the crucifix to sell it? You are a strange man."

"That's something, you calling me that." Newt sat down on the bed and waited with the Bulldog .44 pointed at the door.

"You think he will come back?" Mr. Smith asked.

"I'll just sit here for a bit in case he changes his mind about us," Newt said.

Pablo did not return, and after some time Newt tucked the snub-nosed revolver behind his waistband and pulled the rest of his belongings out of the closet.

Mr. Smith watched him packing his saddlebags and

making sure his bedroll was rolled tight. "Are you going somewhere?"

. "I've had about enough of this town. Thought I'd slip out of here as soon as it gets dark. Want to come along?"

"Where will you go?"

"Oh, just a little ride back toward Pinto Canyon," Newt said. "Got some unfinished business there. Something's bothering me that I need to attend to."

"They will follow you," Mr. Smith said.

"Who?"

"All of them."

"Let 'em come."

CHAPTER FORTY-EIGHT

It was 108 degrees in the afternoon and not so much as a hint of a breeze could be found on the desert when Newt and Mr. Smith rode into the scattered, broken chain of the Jacumba Mountains east of Davies Valley. They picked their way through the rock-pile ridges, winding and turning to find the best way for their horses. They stopped often at high points, scanning the terrain around them as if they searched for something.

"You are sure this is the way you came?" Mr. Smith asked. It was hot enough to cause even him to take off his suit coat and hang it over his saddle horn.

"This looks right. We're close," Newt replied.

They rode for another hour, turning south and down-slope onto a flat that suddenly appeared before them. There, some of the cobbled stone gave way, and the slopes around the little hollow had provided enough soil washed down over the centuries to allow some grass to grow.

Out on that flat, belly-deep in a patch of buckskin-colored grass, stood the little red dun mule. It raised its head and looked at them, and then stretched out its neck and let out a long, bawling bray.

"There he is," Newt said.

They dropped off the ridge they had stopped on and crossed a shallow wash. In the bottom of that wash there was a slab of flat stone that had been eroded and scooped out in the middle over time by flash floods, leaving a shin-deep basin. That basin was half-full of water from some recent thunderstorm, and they could see hoof scars on the stone around it where the mule's shod hooves had scarred it.

In another hundred yards they reached the mule. Newt dismounted and stood before the flop-eared beast. "Nice little spot you've found for yourself."

The mule gave him a bored look while it ground a mouthful of grass between its jaws. The bacon-sack bandage Newt had put in place was gone, but the mule's knee looked surprisingly good given how bad it had looked the last time he had seen it. The swelling was almost totally gone, and the wound was dry and scabbed over. He knelt and took hold of the knee joint with both hands, but could feel no heat that might mean inflammation or infection.

"Tough little booger, aren't you? I figured the coyotes would be picking your bones by now."

Newt retrieved a halter and a lead rope from his saddle. He led the mule around for a while to determine its soundness, seeing no sign of a limp. He got back on the Circle Dot horse and led the mule back the way they had come.

Again, Newt seemed to have a certain point in mind. An hour before dark they came onto a narrow trail that led through a rock-choked pass between two bluffs. Some little ways before the pass they came to the mule's packsaddle lying atop a couch-sized rock.

Newt dismounted again and went to the packsaddle.

"We are being watched," Mr. Smith said from behind him.

"Saw that," Newt said. "Somebody on top of that mountain behind us is glassing us. Saw the sun hitting his lenses."

Neither man looked in the direction of the flash of light they had seen on the mountaintop. Newt led the mule close to the rock, positioning it between himself and whoever was watching them. He put the pad and packsaddle on the mule's back and cinched it in place.

Finished, Newt flexed his bad leg a couple of times to try and stretch some of the stiffness out of it, and then he got back on his horse. They rode into the pass, where he stopped again.

"Let's make camp for the night," Newt said. "My bad leg is talking to me some."

They tied the horses and the mule to a picket line stretched between two big boulders. They built no fire, for it was still too hot and there was no firewood to be had. Both men sat in the shade and watched the way they had come. They could see for at least two hundred yards down their back trail.

"You want them to come?" Mr. Smith asked.

"What do you do if there's a big old boy giving you dirty looks and you know there's no way you aren't going to have to fight him?" Newt asked.

"I attack."

"Exactly. Gonna happen anyway, so you just walk over there and knock that big old boy in the mouth. Get it over with."

"There they come," Mr. Smith said.

Newt looked and saw a line of horsemen winding their way through the rocks down the mountain where they had seen the flash of sunlight on a pair of binoculars or some kind of spyglass. Newt counted eight riders.

Mr. Smith's saddle was beside him on the ground, and he shucked his Whitney-Kennedy rifle out of the rifle boot. He rose and went and stood behind a boulder at the foot of the rockslide. He rested the rifle across the top of the boulder and waited.

Newt had lost his own rifle during the fight in Pinto Canyon, but he broke open his Smith & Wesson revolver and checked the loads and then reholstered it. He took the British Bulldog from his saddlebags, checked it, too, and then shoved it behind his waistband.

He walked a few steps toward the other side of the narrow pass, putting some space between him and Mr. Smith. The riders coming their way were only one hundred yards out and coming on at a trot.

He took off his hat and ran a hand inside it to wipe the sweat from the sweatband. He gave the hat a frown, thinking that maybe Poker Alice had been right. It was looking pretty ragged, and it was long past time to buy a new one.

The riders stopped not ten yards from him, scattered out in a line, side by side. He wasn't shocked to see Poker Alice with them. She sat her horse beside the Judge in the middle of the line.

"Hello, Mrs. Duffield," Newt said, still holding his hat and looking down at it instead of them. "I see you've made some new friends."

It was the Judge who answered him. "I think it's time you showed us where you found the ship."

"You know?" Newt said like he hadn't heard the Judge. "It's come to me that a man ought to be buried in a new hat."

"We know what you're doing out here," the Judge said. "We've been following you since you left Yuma, and I think you knew that. That's why you've been leading us on a goose chase all over these mountains."

"No, I just came to get that mule," Newt said.

Poker Alice scoffed. "You came to get a mule? *Please.*"

Newt put his hat back on his head and cast a glance at the red dun mule standing at the picket line. "That mule is the only reason I'm still alive. Hadn't been for finding him I wouldn't have made it across the valley. He lamed up and I had to leave him. Bothered me ever since."

"You came all this way for a ten-dollar mule?" the Judge asked, and then snickered. Several of the men to either side of him laughed, too.

"You ain't me," Newt said.

"You're a long ways from anywhere, Jones. The only way you ride away from this is on my say-so," the Judge said. "So, let me tell you how this is going to be."

"No, let me tell you," Newt said. "Come morning, I'm going to take that mule and I'm going to ride north. Don't care if I ever see this sorry country again."

"Newt," Alice's voice was almost pleading, "do what he says. It doesn't have to be this way."

"Stand down, Jones!" the Judge said.

Newt locked eyes with Alice. "I tried to tell you, but you wouldn't listen."

"You can't win," she answered.

"Born loser, that's what the Judge here said when he sentenced me to thirty days in the calaboose," Newt said.

"This ain't right, Judge," the one to the Judge's left wearing a county deputy's badge said. "Ain't right at all."

"You do like I tell you if you want Buck's job," the Judge said.

"Maybe we ought to rethink this," another man said.

"Do you want a cut of the treasure, or not?" the Judge

asked the four men on his left. "Don't act like you didn't know how this was going to be."

It was Newt's turn to laugh. "Has the Judge been filling your heads full of stories about that ship? How he was going to make you all rich men?"

"Shut up," the Judge snapped.

Newt waved a hand around his campsite. "You see any treasure? Me and my friend here are on our way to Los Angeles. If we knew where the ship was, how come we're here in the mountains?"

"Let me handle this," the man beside Alice said. He was the one dressed like a cowboy that had been with her in Yuma.

Newt's hard gaze shifted to him. "Is that you, Bobby Dial? Been a while. Thought you were up at Pleasant Valley pestering sheepherders. You always were a two-bit badman."

Dial's gun hand rested on his thigh, with his horse turned slightly so that his gun was handy to bring up in line with Newt. He had a mean face, and Newt's words had drawn it tight as a fiddle string.

"You cut a wide swath, Widowmaker. Big man, they say. Tougher'n hell and twice as mean," Dial said. "Me, I figure it's all nothing but talk and chicken feathers."

"The lady's right, Jones," the Judge said. "We've got you outnumbered and outgunned."

"You go ahead and call the tune, Judge, but you do and you're a dead man," Newt said. "First I'm going to shoot Bobby Dial there, because he's supposed to be some shakes with a six-gun. And then I'm going to shoot you. I promise you that. No matter what, I'm going to get you before I go down."

None of them moved and none of them said anything to that.

"Figure my Mohave friend over there will take one or two more of you. Tight little notch like this, it's going to be hard to miss. Real bloody. Might not be a one of us that rides out of here the same way we came in, and it's a damned hot day to take a bullet."

"Nothing but talk and chicken feathers," Dial repeated. His gun hand had inched a little higher up his thigh and closer to his pistol. "Just say the word, Lady. Me and Kirby will trim him down to size a little bit. Have him singing for you like a choirgirl."

"Quiet, you fool," the Judge said to the gunman. There was more than a hint of hesitation in the Judge's voice, as if he was just then coming to realize the precipice they all stood upon.

Newt glanced at Alice's other gunman sitting his horse beside Dial. He was a big man, like Newt, though heavier, wearing a bowler hat and a pair of bird's head–gripped revolvers in double shoulder holsters over his striped shirt.

Newt looked at Dial again. "Chicken feathers, huh? You going to pull that pistol, Bobby, or are you going to just sit there and squawk?"

"You're crazy!" Alice said, already backing her horse away.

Bobby Dial didn't wait for her to get in the clear. His hand went for the Colt on his hip. Newt's own hand moved, and then there was the roar of a gun.

Newt's bullet struck Dial right through the watch pocket on his vest before the Texas gunman's pistol was half out of his leather. Dial gave a groan, reeled back slightly, and then made another try for his pistol. Newt's second shot took him dead center in the breastbone, and he toppled from his horse and landed on the ground.

Surprisingly, Dial's partner made no move for his own guns.

Newt swung his pistol toward the Judge, but neither the Judge nor any of the others were doing anything, either. Some had hands on their guns, but none of them made a move to go farther than that. Out of the corner of one eye, Newt saw Mr. Smith standing up behind the rock with his rifle shouldered and ready.

There came upon all of them a deathly quiet moment, a standoff of silence and raw adrenaline. Newt could feel his own nerves twitching and firing like a bolt of lightning was running through him, and he knew those faced off against him were no less on edge. It appeared like they all had realized that what he had said was true, that every man's number was thrown in the hat when the shooting started. But no matter, it was still touch and go. So much as a single cough or the creak of a saddle could set the whole thing off, like a lit fuse slowly burning.

"Easy, boys," Newt said, and his own voice sounded far off and strange to him. "This here's between me and the Judge. I don't care what he told you. Nothing here but a mule. Nothing worth dying over."

The Judge's hand was on the nickel-plated revolver he wore at a cross-draw on his left hip. His face was livid with some mix of rage and fear. "I'll give a hundred extra dollars to the man who puts this son of a bitch in the ground!"

Newt lowered his pistol until it hung alongside his leg and pointed at the ground. "Why don't you do it yourself, Judge? I'm right here."

"I said, take him!" the Judge shouted.

None of the men with the Judge reacted. They remained where they were, hands still on their gun butts and gunstocks, but coming to their own decisions. Newt sensed a

narrow window of opportunity available to him before
they made up their minds.

He shoved his Smith & Wesson back in his holster.
"Here's your chance. You're a big man in these parts, but
how are you when you don't have someone to hide behind?"

The Judge's mouth was moving, but no sound came out,
such was his anger.

Newt took a step forward, and his voice was calm and
quiet. "Go ahead, skin that hogleg. I won't even pull on you,
'cause I don't think you've got the guts to do it on your own."

The Judge glanced at his men, but none of them so
much at looked at him. The Paiute tracker on the Judge's
right, Charlie Two Horses, lowered his rifle to his saddle
swells and side-passed his horse a few steps to put some
space between him and the Judge. The others beside him
began to back away.

"You sorry, backstabbing half-breed," the Judge threw
at the Paiute.

Newt kept coming closer to the Judge, walking slow.
"I'm going to show these men the kind of coward you are."

"Shoot him!" the Judge said.

Newt's voice came louder than before. "Come on, tinhorn."

The Judge yanked his nickel-plated Remington Army
from his holster, but by then, Newt was already right
alongside his horse. The pistol came out and started down
toward Newt, but he caught the Judge's wrist with both
hands and yanked him from the saddle.

The Judge landed hard, but scrambled to his feet cursing. His pistol had been taken away from him, but he
pulled an ivory-handled push dagger from his vest and
lunged at Newt.

Newt backhanded the Judge across the mouth. Not as

hard as he could, but hard enough to put the older, smaller man down again.

"Come on, show some fight," Newt said.

The Judge pushed up on his hands and knees, and Newt stomped down on his knife hand. He kicked the Judge in the seat of his pants and sent him sprawling.

"Damn you!" the Judge cried.

"Don't you get up," Newt said. "You crawl."

"Help me," the Judge begged his men.

"Nobody's going to help you. Crawl, damn you!" Newt said.

The Judge managed to get to his feet, but Newt tripped him. The old man started crawling on his belly, trying frantically to get away.

"Take him and go," Newt said.

One of the hired men took hold of the Judge's horse and led it to him. The Judge got up. His white hair hung wildly over his face and he was bleeding from the corner of his mouth. He wouldn't look at Newt; he wouldn't look at any of the other men. Nobody said a word as he climbed on his horse.

"Take Dial with you. He had nerve and deserves a burying, not left for the buzzards," Newt said.

Some of the men dismounted and began loading Dial's body on his horse belly-down over his saddle and tying him in place. Dial's partner, the second of Alice's hired men, remained on his horse, looking at Newt.

"You looking to take up where Dial left off?" Newt asked.

"Bobby never was as good with a Colt as he thought he was," the man said. "He called the play and he came up short. Happens in this business."

"He was getting paid, same as you."

"The lady and I are going to have to renegotiate if she wants your hide."

"Glad to hear you're bowing out."

"Oh, I'm not bowing out. You just aren't included in my rate, and I don't shoot for pleasure. No profit in it, and too much risk. And besides, there's that big Indian over there pointing a rifle at me."

"If she offers, you ought to think on it some before you agree," Newt said.

"Only thing I would have to think on about you is how much I'd charge. And frankly, you shouldn't be so on the prod. I promise you I'm way better than Bobby ever thought about being, and truth is, right now you look all tuckered out."

Newt stood a little straighter and winced with the pain of his wounds. "Me, hell, I'm in my prime."

The big man laughed. "She hired us for protection, and to make sure she didn't get cut out of this little treasure hunt you all have got going. So far, I saw more treasure in a Yuma whorehouse than I've seen out here."

"Folks been looking for that lost ship since before you and I were born," Newt said. "Reckon I was just as big a fool to go looking for it myself. See what it got me?"

"I suppose you'd take it personal if I asked to look through your things just so the lady can feel at ease," the man said.

"You go ahead. You won't find anything."

The man studied him for a bit, and then shook his head. "No, I think you're telling the truth. You know Bobby has a brother, don't you? He's likely to come looking for you when he finds out."

Newt nodded. "Always that way. It's bad history that usually gets men like us, ain't it?"

The other man nodded.

"Don't believe I know you," Newt said.

"Kirby Cutter."

"Ah, heard of you. They say you're good."

"Good enough so far."

"You still working for the mining companies?"

"Depends on when you ask me, but not now or I wouldn't be out here in the middle of this mess," Cutter said. "How do you know me?"

"I was the one who held old Joe Smith's claim up on Buckskin Creek when your boss tried to take it. He should've hired better men."

"I was gone on other business and missed that one, or you might think different," Cutter said. "What say you have your Indian put away his rifle? Grant me a little professional courtesy, if you will."

"Mr. Smith, blow him out of his saddle if I can't take him." Newt's mouth formed a grim smile. "How's that, Cutter?"

Cutter was starting to get mad, but he kept it in check. "Maybe we'll meet again."

"Not if I can help it."

The Judge's men rode away in single file, leading the horse with the dead man behind them. The Judge followed several yards in the rear.

Cutter gathered his bridle reins and nodded at Newt. "Fixing to ride up to Colorado, Willow Creek way. Man's got a job for me, and I could use a few more guns."

"Believe I'll pass," Newt said.

"Probably for the best. I'm coming to think you and I might not get along," Cutter said.

"I'm sort of difficult that way."

"You ready to ride?" Cutter said to Poker Alice.

She sat her horse beyond Cutter, and did not make a

move to go. She looked shaken, but she took a deep breath and composed herself.

Her gaze fell on Newt. "Is it all right if I stay with you? I'd like you to take me back to Yuma."

"You made your bet and you lost," Newt said.

"We all end up losers sometimes."

"There's a man dead because of you, and it could have been worse."

"I'm sorry."

"No, you're not."

One corner of her mouth curled in a sad half smile. "You got me there. I'm a high-stakes player. That's what I do."

"I'm sure you're paying Cutter here enough to take you back to Yuma or San Bernardino, or wherever." Newt moved his attention to Cutter. "You look after her, and if I hear she didn't make it back I'll come hunting you."

"Never seen a man who works so hard to make enemies," Cutter said. "But she's safe with me."

Both men looked over at Mr. Smith. The Mohave still had his rifle rested across the big rock and pointed at them.

"Is he going to let us ride out of here?" Cutter asked.

"You'd have to ask him, but I think you'll be fine," Newt said.

Cutter turned his horse and headed out after the Judge's men.

Poker Alice still didn't go. She waited until Cutter was out of earshot before she spoke. "I'm beat and I know it, but tell me one thing. Did you find it?"

"I found the crucifix and some old cannon. The ship, if there was a ship, is long since gone. Didn't see a single bit of its timbers or any such thing. Either the wood wasted away or was carried off."

"But you could go back and look for the other things. The chest of pearls. The other church treasures. You could be a rich man."

"I'm not going back. If you want to go have a look, you start in those dunes where we were and go southwest. There's a deep gully running down from that big dry lake bed we came past. You walk the bottom of that gully and maybe you'll find something, maybe not."

She shook her head. "No, I'm done. Like you said, I bet wrong. Time to cut my losses and move on."

"Take care."

She still didn't go, staring at Newt intently with a funny look on her face. "You know, I wonder if I should have let you kiss me. You're not my usual type, but you're the least boring man I've ever met. Makes me wonder. Look me up in San Francisco if you're going that way. I'll buy you and your horse a beer."

She turned her horse and trotted it after Cutter.

Mr. Smith came out from behind his rock when all of them were out of sight. "Do you think they will come back?"

"Might not be a bad idea to change camping spots," Newt said.

"I think she will not go back to Yuma," Mr. Smith said. "Not until she goes and looks for where you found the crucifix."

"Probably so."

"She would have made you a good woman," Mr. Smith said. "A man should have a woman to give him strong sons."

Either Newt didn't hear the Mohave, or he simply ignored him. He limped over to the mule and started putting the packsaddle back in place.

"You're limping again," Mr. Smith said.

"Maybe I'm getting too old for this."

When he was through with the mule, he saddled the Circle Dot horse while the Mohave saddled his own mount. They rode through the notch and up the side of a ridge where the trail led over it.

Mr. Smith looked behind them at their back trail, searching for signs of pursuit. "Will you go and look for the ship again?"

"Had all the treasure hunting I can stand," Newt said.

He stopped and pulled on the mule's lead rope until the mule came up beside him. He drew his knife and leaned down and cut a few crude whipstitches made from yucca fibers that sewed a tear closed in the edge of the saddle pad beneath the packsaddle. Reaching inside the outer canvas shell and into the wool felt between, he pulled out a little leather bag with a drawstring at the top. The leather was dry-rotted and brittle.

Sheathing the knife, he loosened the drawstring and poured something into one of his palms and held what was there out for Mr. Smith to see. There were several black pearls in Newt's hand, a part of what was still in the sack.

CHAPTER FORTY-NINE

The Judge stopped his horse on the side of the mountain and turned back to look down the trail to the notch in the rocks where they had left the Widowmaker. The others rode on, not noticing he wasn't coming along behind them.

It was a long ways across the flat and back to the notch, but the Judge could still make out the Widowmaker and the Mohave preparing to break camp. He shucked his Marlin rifle from his saddle scabbard.

He guessed the range to be at least three hundred yards, and adjusted the tang peep sight on the rifle to the proper elevation. It was too far for him to shoot offhand accurately, and he dismounted and turned his horse sideways so that he could rest the rifle across his saddle.

He cocked the hammer and found the Widowmaker in his sights. He pressed the set trigger to lighten the main trigger and let out half a breath while he watched the rise and fall of his front sight in time with the beat of his heart. When that front sight stilled he placed the pad of his forefinger on the trigger and prepared to squeeze.

Somebody jerked the rifle out of his hands before he could fire. He whirled on his assailant, and saw Charlie

Two Horses and the county deputy above him. The other men waited uphill, watching.

"Give me my rifle back," the Judge said. "Tell me to crawl, will he? I'm the law. The law!"

"The Widowmaker was right," the deputy said. "You're nothing but a tinhorn."

"You say that about me?" The Judge was so frantic that he sprayed spittle from his lips. "You're through in San Bernardino! Through!"

The deputy worked the rifle's lever and jacked the cartridges out on the ground, one by one. When he was finished, he hurled the rifle down the mountain. It clattered on the rocks and went out of sight.

"I don't want Buck's job anymore," the deputy said. "Not if it means I answer to you."

Charlie Two Horses nodded his agreement.

"What are you nodding about, you filthy half-breed?" the Judge asked.

"Reckon we're all just ready to get back home," Charlie said. "I've got some new colts that need riding, and my woman will be missing me."

"I'll not pay you a red cent. You'll never track for the county again."

"I can live with that." Charlie Two Horses rode his horse up toward the others on the top of the mountain.

"Cowards, every one of you," the Judge said.

The deputy rode away, too.

"Nobody crosses me. Nobody," the Judge said to the deputy's back.

It took the Judge some time to get a boot in the stirrup and to get up on his big gray horse, and by that time his posse had already disappeared over the top of the mountain.

The trail was narrow and littered with rocks. It was

barely a trail for a man on foot, much less a horse. In spite of that, the Judge's anger was so great that he lashed his horse across the hip with his braided riding quirt. The gray gelding was a strong sprinter, and squatted its hindquarters and bolted up the trail. Sparks flew where its shod hooves struck the rocks. The horse leapt over the larger rocks where it could, and ducked and twisted through others, with the Judge still lashing it across the hip.

"You wait for me!" he shouted after the men who had left him.

He was about to whip the gray gelding again when it stumbled and then fell. It rolled over once over the top of the Judge. The Judge screamed as his bones cracked.

When the horse came up again, it broke downhill, running again. The Judge's right boot was hung up in the stirrup, and he was dragged behind the horse. His body bounced and flopped limply and helplessly, and he cried out for help.

The men of the posse heard his screams and came back to the top of the mountain barely in time to see the runaway gray horse make it out onto the flat. They watched the event with grim faces, and then one by one they turned and disappeared over the crest of the mountain again, leaving what they had seen behind them.

The Judge's foot came free of the stirrup down on the flat. The gray horse kept running, and the Judge was left lying on his back, broken and torn.

He blinked his eyes and stared up at the sky. He tried to move, but the pain was more than he could bear and his legs would seem to work. He continued to lie that way through sundown, and then on through the night.

Come daylight, he thought to get up, for he knew to remain lying there was to die. He could walk to Campo, or maybe back to Yuma. Water was scarce, but not impossible to find on the desert. If all else failed, surely he could make it to one of the old stage stations on the Butterfield Road where there was water to be had. Yes, make it to the road. Travelers were bound to come along and give him aid.

But he could not get up. So he lay there, staring at the sky. The heat came early, and it was barely two hours into the morning before the dull pain on the skin of his face told him that he was burning. He licked his cracked lips, and when he raised his hands to his face he felt the blisters break and tear open.

Something moved high above him. He shaded his eyes with his hand and saw four black dots up there, moving across the sun in some odd dance. He blinked and found his focus again, and saw that the dots were buzzards gliding and circling above him. He cried then, and the tears seeped out of the corners of his eyes, down the sides of his face, and were lost in the sand.

The buzzards kept circling for the next hour, lower and lower. As always, they were patient. It was only a matter of waiting a little longer.

The Judge talked to himself for a time, and he threatened the buzzards in a voice so dry and weak it was barely a whisper. The buzzards came anyway, and his was a slow death. The desert didn't notice or care.

CHAPTER FIFTY

"You found the chest of pearls," Mr. Smith said.

"It was a small chest." Newt made a showing with his hands that indicated the dimensions of a tiny box. "Not hardly the fortune Pablo claimed it to be, but I imagine they'll bring plenty."

"Are they worth so much?"

"I don't know, but half of them are yours."

"I don't want them."

"A man could do a lot with that kind of stake. I've been working a plan around in my head. I'll need more money, but these pearls are a start. I reckon all any man needs is a start."

"My people believe that many of the things of tribes are impure and will poison you," Mr. Smith said. "That which you found has been buried for a long time. Maybe there is a reason for that. Maybe it was not meant to be found."

"Are you talking about a curse?" Newt asked.

"It does not matter. My needs are simple. I have no wishes for a white man's riches."

"A man can live his own way if he's got enough money."

"Do you not live your own way now?"

Newt had no answer for that question, although he

thought about it until sundown when they made camp. And he thought about it well into the night while he listened to the coyotes yip and howl and couldn't sleep. He never had liked coyotes.

They turned north the next morning toward Warner's Ranch, and rode all through the next day without talking. Finally, when the day was about over and the sun was sinking, Newt glanced at Mr. Smith.

"Been thinking about going to Montana," he said.

"Is it far? I have never been to Montana," Mr. Smith asked.

"Far enough. You're welcome to ride along. Man up at Willow Creek in Colorado sent me a telegraph a few weeks back. He's got a little job he wants done. Got him a silver find there that he wants to keep on the quiet while he goes back to San Francisco to raise some money. Needs some men to babysit it over the winter till he gets back. Could be a tough one. That's why I haven't answered him, yet. But he's offering top money."

"This Willow Creek you mention, is it the same place where that man, Cutter, said he was going?"

Newt looked at him and grinned. "It is."

"I will go with you," Mr. Smith said with his eyes locked on the trail ahead.

"You sure didn't think on it long."

Mr. Smith grunted and his neck and big shoulders moved in a shrug. "I think you are a man who will find a good death. I will ride with you and see if that is true."

They rode on, taking pleasure in the silence while the setting sun cast them in shadows. Big men on good horses, violent men with their own strange codes of honor, loners and outcasts, as much by their own choosing as the will of the world, but now a tribe of two.

HISTORICAL NOTES

Webley British Bulldog—Colt, Smith & Wesson, and Remington pistols hold a monopoly when it comes to the short guns portrayed in most western novels and Hollywood movies. However, in late 1873, a smaller-framed double-action, big-bore revolver with a stubby two-and-a-half-inch barrel came onto the American market and was an immediate hit. Made by the English gun manufacturer P. Webley & Son, the British Bulldog was to become one of the most popular revolvers in the Old West.

Originally chambered for the .442 Webley, and then the .450 Adams and .455 cartridges, the compact self-cocker filled a need on two fronts for American buyers in the aftermath of the Civil War. There were great numbers of citizens going west to seek their fortunes, and a large part of them were looking to arm themselves as matter of self-defense. Even on the wild and wooly frontier, many towns and cities had laws against the open carrying of firearms, and a concealable weapon that would fit in a pocket or a purse was of great benefit to get around those laws and to ensure one stayed well heeled. The big American firearms companies had long produced pocket pistols, but those offerings were chambered in more anemic calibers, lacking knockdown power in a gunfight. The Bulldog, with its full-grown, harder-hitting cartridge and compact design, exactly fit the bill. What's more, for those on a tighter budget, a Bulldog could be purchased far cheaper than the cost of a Colt, Remington, or Smith & Wesson revolver.

Webley's Bulldog design was soon so successful that it wasn't long before other firearms manufacturers were making their own versions of "Bulldogs." Numerous American and Belgian copies hit the market. Some of those Bulldog knockoffs could be bought for as little as $3.50 during the early 1880s, whereas a Colt Single Action Army cost $30–$35. Webley trademarked the British Bulldog name in 1878, but its competitors devised plenty of ways to keep a bulldog in the name of their models. The American Bulldog, Boston Bulldog, Western Bulldog, and other stampings were found on the imitators' pistols, pushing the limits of trademark infringement while trying to cash in on the popularity and name recognition of the original pistol. In time, people simply referred to these types of revolvers as Bulldogs, regardless of what company made them, and regardless of slight variations in style and a wide variety of new cartridges being offered.

As evidence of the Bulldog's place in Old West lore, General George Armstrong Custer was carrying a pair of Webley Bulldogs when he died at the Battle of the Little Bighorn. John Tunstall, the murdered Englishman whom Billy the Kid worked for during the Lincoln County War, recorded in his diary, "I never went anywhere without my Bull-dog." After Bob Dalton was killed during the Dalton Gang's attempted robbery of two banks simultaneously in Coffeyville, Kansas, a Bulldog revolver was found in his vest pocket.

Frederic Sackrider Remington—Remington was an illustrator, painter, sculptor, and writer. To many, Remington is quite possibly the greatest western artist who ever lived, with Charlie Russell being his only competition. His art focused on action and romanticism and a sometimes nostalgic look at the rapidly passing frontier and those who lived it.

More important for the sake of this novel, in 1884–85, he and his new wife, Eva, became temporarily separated. She went back to New York, while he stayed in Kansas and spent his time with his art, and possibly too much time in the saloon he and a partner owned. During 1885, he roamed over the Southwest, returning to New York later in the year to win back his wife. Having returned home, he began studies at the Art Students League of New York to hone his technique, and eventually, in 1886, one of his illustrations was the cover for an issue of *Harper's Weekly*, his first big break. He was only twenty-five. His later drawings and illustrations would be published in forty-one different periodicals. He served as an artist-correspondent during General Nelson Miles's campaign into Mexico where Geronimo was captured, and later as a war correspondent for the *New York Journal* in Cuba during the Spanish-American War where he drew images of American soldiers and Teddy Roosevelt's Rough Riders. His bronze sculpture of a cowboy riding a rearing bucking horse is probably the most iconic small western bronze ever cast. His paintings have been exhibited in the finest galleries and sold all over the world. He died in 1909 at the age of forty-eight due to complications after having his appendix removed.

But it is that period while he was still out West and his estranged wife was in New York that gave me the idea to have this young, heartbroken, and adventurous artist land in California and join up with the Widowmaker. Remington was forever an outdoorsy and adventuresome man who loved boxing and horses and camping, and he roamed over the Southwest during much of 1885. However fictional his character and his actions may be in the novel, I have tried to portray his general background accurately in the course of my tale, as well as to portray him in a manner that I feel might be authentic and in keeping with what I have read about him. I think he who did so much to tell the story of the Old West might have enjoyed becoming one of the cast himself.

Poker Alice—Alice Ivers was born in Devonshire, England, and became one of the better-known female professional gamblers in the Old West, if not the most famous. The daughter of a schoolmaster, her family immigrated to Virginia when she was a young girl. After attending a boarding school for young ladies, Alice's family moved to Leadville, Colorado, during the silver rush there. It was where she met and married her first husband, Frank Duffield, a mining engineer who also liked to gamble. She often went along and watched him play, eventually sitting at the table herself. After he was killed in an explosion she took up gambling as her profession. She was widely known as a high-stakes poker player and faro dealer in the mining towns and boom camps over a wide swath of country. Her beauty, wit, and sense of style made her hard to forget.

Having married three times and outlived all her husbands, she wound up running a gambling den and brothel near Sturgis, South Dakota. Now an elderly woman with lots of hard living behind her, she gave up her fashionable New York dresses and began to clothe herself like a man. She could still be found at the gambling table chomping on a cigar, winning money from the boys, and packing a .38 revolver. And she was no stranger to a gunfight, once wounding one man with that .38 in an altercation, and at another time taking on two drunken soldiers with nothing but a .22 rifle, resulting in both soldiers being wounded, one of them mortally so. Before her passing in 1930 she claimed to have won more than $250,000 at the gaming tables in her career and without having ever cheated. She also reportedly said, "At my age I suppose I should be knitting. But I would rather play poker with five or six 'experts' than eat."

If Poker Alice ever had a Mohave bodyguard that tidbit has been lost to history, but it might have been a good story if that were true.

The Lost Ship of the Desert—The legend of a ship lost on the Colorado desert somewhere between Dos Palmas and the head of the Gulf of California lives on today, and treasure seekers still go out in search of it, usually somewhere in the Imperial Valley and the area around the Salton Sink, now the Salton Sea after the Colorado River flooded the old dry lake bed in 1891 and 1905. While I may have attributed the ship to Capitan Ulloa's expedition, ask one of those modern treasure seekers their personal theories on where that ship might lie or how the ship came to be there, and you will get a multitude of varied theories. Everything from one or the other Spanish expeditions, to Viking longships and lost steamboats. In 1870 there were rumors and newspaper articles stating that a party of Americans had found the bones of a ship sticking out of the sand. A man named Charley Clusker caused quite a stir in San Bernardino when he claimed some knowledge of the ship and voiced his intentions to go in search of it. The local newspaper, the *San Bernardino Guardian*, reported on his claims. Due to the stir caused by the newspapers and word of mouth, a few citizens chipped in to aid Clusker in returning to find the ship, and an expedition was formed. In fact, Clusker led at least four exploring expeditions in 1870–71, the second one being funded in part by the *Guardian* and all with the same results. Clusker claimed to have found the ship during his second expedition, but could not return to it again on his subsequent forays into the desert. Treasure hunters since then have had no better luck. If the lost ship ever existed, then it's still out there waiting.

Pinto Canyon—The mouth of the canyon is there, right on the border between Mexico and the United States, exactly as I have portrayed it in this story. Numerous ancient Native American petroglyphs can be found marked on rocks at points within the canyon. Curiously, one of those petroglyphs is of a sailing ship with a square sail rigging and rowing oars sticking out of its hull, much like the Spanish caravels Captain Ulloa supposedly used to sail up the Gulf of California.

Keep reading for a special excerpt of
GUNPOWDER EXPRESS,
a Widowmaker Jones Western by Brett Cogburn.

TIME TO MEET THE WIDOWMAKER

Vulture City is home to a prosperous gold mine and
every badman in the Arizona Territory knows it. Nearly
every stagecoach attempting to deliver the gold to the
railroad at Maricopa has been ambushed on the trail—
a trail known as the Gunpowder Express for the
bullet-riddled bodies along the way.

With gold piling up and a lack of volunteers to transport
it, the mine manager hires Newt "Widowmaker" Jones to
ride shotgun on the next stage. Foolhardy and desperate
for money, Newt joins three other guards—and a
passenger, Jenny Silks, a stubborn firebrand with her
own stake in seeing the delivery through. But waiting on
the Gunpowder Express is Irish Jack O'Harrigan and his
band of outlaws. There's not a soul alive he wouldn't
think twice about putting six feet under. But he's never
traded lead with the man known as the Widowmaker.

Look for GUNPOWDER EXPRESS on sale now.

CHAPTER ONE

The punch was the kind of blow that comes out of nowhere, and the kind you're never really set and ready to take. It was the kind that'll knock you flat like a Texas tornado; the kind that can make tough people slobber and crawl, and the weak ones won't get ever get back up.

The big man, as ugly and scarred as he was tall, took that punch square and true on his jaw. He felt the sharp bite of knuckles crash into the marrow of his bones and the hard thud of the ground rising up to meet him. The dust rose up and floated around him as wispy and ephemeral as the dull roar of the crowd cheering and screaming for his demise. Truly, he couldn't have told you where he was in that instant, or even so much as his name. But the pain was real, and it was something to lay hand to.

Slowly, his senses returned until he was aware of other things outside the throbbing of his skull. He tasted the dirt in his mouth mixing with the blood, and the grit of sand scraping under his eyelids. He rolled onto his back and stared up at the face of the referee floating in the furnace sky above him and waving his hands to signal the end of the round.

The big man got one hand under him and then the other, followed by his knees, and pushed his belly up from the ground. The ropes that marked off the fight ring came into focus, at first a blur, and then one, two of those ropes with the screaming crowd behind them cheering and slopping beer down the fronts of their sweat-stained shirts. None of those things came to the big man in clear, individual thoughts, but rather as a wave of impressions, a blur of sights and sounds. He was sure of none of those impressions, and only one thing, one instinct, screamed for attention above it all. He had to get up or they would ring the bell. The bell meant you were done; the bell meant you lost. You had to beat the bell. You had to toe the mark.

The crowd went silent, if only for a brief instant, when he got a leg up under him and wobbled to his feet. But their shock quickly turned to anger over the audacity of the man to take what most couldn't, to fight back against the narrative of his demise. They heckled him while he nodded drunkenly at the referee and raised his fists to show that he was ready to fight again. Somebody flung an empty beer bottle at him, but it went wide of his head and sailed into the crowd on the opposite side of the ring from whence it had come. He didn't even notice the flying bottle and kept shuffling his feet to keep his balance, lest he fall again. All the while, he was listening for the sound of the bell. He was half-afraid it might have sounded without his hearing it.

But the bell had not rung, and he was still in the fight. In a determined, weaving march, he made his way back to his corner, turned, and propped his shoulder blades against the corner post and draped an arm over the top rope to either side of him. His whole body sagged, and only his hollow eyes seemed alive when he stared across the ring at the man who had knocked him down.

And then there came a slight quirk at one corner of his mouth and the parting of his lips to reveal a slit of bloody, clenched teeth. Slow to form, this expression, like the breaking apart of an old scab or wound. Maybe it was only a muscle spasm on the face of a man as punch-drunk as they came, or simply a grimace of pain. Regardless, to the crowd, it looked like a defiant snarl.

The big man pawed at his forehead with one hand and slung the sweat from it to the sand at his feet. He blinked once, twice, at the fighter across the ring from him, as if he was still having a hard time focusing his vision. He blinked a third time, and then that quirk formed at the corner of his mouth again, every bit as wolfish as it had been the first time it cracked his face.

The devilish name and the reputation of the man passed through the crowd like a slow whisper riding the tobacco smoke hovering over them, blown from one to another like an accusation until more than one of them voiced his name as if it explained what they were seeing. Most of them had bet good, hard-earned money against him, yet, there he stood with that snarling expression and glaring back at them and the whole damned world in general. He should have stayed down; he should have been out cold no matter how damned mean he was supposed to be.

Should have. It dawned on some in the crowd then that the damned fool wasn't snarling at all, and that realization made them all the madder. He was trying to grin like the whole thing was funny. Who grinned at a time like that? Poor bastard was out on his feet. That had to be it. One more round and he would go down for good and get what he deserved.

They wouldn't have understood his expression even if they had been sober, or even if they had known him better. He was an unusual man in any place or time, and they wouldn't have understood even if he had the words to explain it to them, which he didn't.

But the crowd had guessed one thing right. The odd contortion at the corner of his mouth was truly a grin, or at least the closest his battered face could come to such an expresion at the moment. And to his way of thinking, he had plenty of reason to grin. Yes, he was punch-drunk and hurt and hanging on by a thread, but there was still the chance to walk across that ring and draw back and knock the living hell out of the bastard who had downed him. That mattered a lot to him. However, what mattered most, and the real reason he grinned, was simply because he was back on his feet and not a one of them had gotten to ring that bell and take him out of the fight. Not yet.

And then he heard someone in the crowd speak his name, and then another—that old name that was none of his choosing but that he wore like another of his scars.

"Widowmaker . . . Widowmaker . . . Widowmaker," the whisper went.

CHAPTER TWO

There were some who said Vulture City got its name because the prospector that founded it spotted some buzzards hovering over the site, a simple enough and slightly romantic tale. While it was true that even such humble and homely creatures gliding high overhead on a thermal wind would have added some romance and color to an otherwise drab place, it was also true that the story of its naming was undoubtedly nothing more than a folktale. Or, in other words, a load of horse pucky to those cynical sorts with enough common sense to realize certain facts.

For starters, such a place held little interest for even a single buzzard. Yes, there was often death—a thing one would think would attract such avian scavengers—but even the promise of a ready meal wasn't enough to tempt the city's namesake birds. Vulture City was simply too damned hot and miserable for anyone, even buzzards, to live there given any other choice.

Secondly, it was really no city at all, except in name, but rather a ramshackle sprawl of construction scattered on a brushy, gravel flat amidst the litter of rocks, cacti, and cast-off junk at the foot of an eroded, red ridge rising up out of the desert. Some might say it was unremarkable, and others less kind could have reasonably claimed it was ugly. Thirsty men usually pointed out that Vulture City had three saloons, a thing worthy of overlooking the place's other faults.

Three saloons or not, there was no denying Vulture City's builders apparently gave little thought or effort toward aesthetic appeal and pleasant architecture. Every bit of man-made habitation seemed to exist only for practical purpose, mainly that it would grant the occupants some modicum of shade when the worst of the afternoon heat bore down on the camp. The buildings were a mismatch of framed lumber, sheet iron, stacked stone, or poorly plastered adobe bricks. None were built exactly the same and were similar only in the uniform coating of dust they shared.

If substance counted for anything, the commissary was the only building that held promise at first glance. Although it was built of dull brown and burnt red native stone stacked in a most common way and coated in more than its share of common dust, it was at least tall—two stories tall—and all that imposing height and those tons of rock were meant one day to hold the offices, assay room, and the treasure vault for the Central Arizona Mining Company. That ownership and any mention of treasure should have made it at least an iconic tower of optimism and civilization in such a frontier hamlet, no matter how plain and ordinary its rectangle design, but sadly, it was still under construction and only three-quarters complete. Its walls had been slower to take shape than they would have been in an ordinary place. Three months of work so far, to be exact, because the piles of sunbaked stone and mining rubble gathered around it and meant to add to its structure would unfortunately blister your hands any time except at night or in the earliest hours of the morning. As it was, for a newcomer, it was hard to tell if the commissary was a new building under construction or an ancient rock tomb whose walls were slowly crumbling down over the centuries.

Beyond the commissary and slightly uphill stood an eighty-stamp mill, usually pounding away incessantly with a mind-numbing racket at the gold ore its crews fed it, but ominously silent for the afternoon. And beyond that, slightly more upslope and rising above everything, stood the massive hoist and headframe of the Vulture Mine. The hard-rock shaft burrowing deep into the earth beneath it and the vein of high-grade ore it promised were the only reasons that such a place came to be at all in that expanse of desolate nothingness. And the shiny tin water pipeline snaking out of camp to the east toward the Hassayampa River ten miles away was the only means by which Vulture City survived long enough for anyone to dig their hearts away for gold or to take a break from the grueling monotony long enough to get drunk and watch a Saturday-afternoon boxing match.

And such a boxing match was currently under way.

The promise of getting to see two men pummel each other wasn't to be missed, considering how much Vulture City's citizens admired a good fight. And no usual fight, this one, but a genuine, imported professional pugilist had come to the mining camp, a thing as rare as it promised to be bloody. Bloody was good.

The peeled cedar posts that had been used to build the crude boxing ring glared under the desert sun like old ivory tusks, and the two large strands of grass rope strung through holes bored in those wooden supports sagged under the oppressive afternoon heat as much as they did because of the press of the crowd of cheering miners they held back. A single, massive ironwood tree stood on one side of the ring, and the furnace breeze periodically gusting through its grotesquely twisted and gnarled limbs cast dappled shadows across both the spectators and the two shirtless and sweating combatants doing their best to punch each other into bloody oblivion inside the ropes. The sounds of those two fighters' bare fists smacking flesh and their grunts of exertion filled in the brief moments when the crowd of spectators paused to catch their breath, mop their brows, or to purchase another mug of lukewarm beer.

Some five hundred hardy souls called Vulture City their home, most of them working for the Central Arizona Mining Company, and the rest consisted of those trying to make a living off those miners, honestly or otherwise. Add another score or so of itinerant types passing through on their way to hell or some other similar place more promising and pleasant than Vulture City, and you had a sizable population, especially considering that neither God nor nature probably ever intended a single human soul to reside there for so much as a minute. And it seemed as if every one of that population had turned out to watch the fight.

All but two.

A man and a woman stood at the completed end of the commissary building in the narrow shade it cast. From their vantage point they had a good view of the fight, and although only thirty yards away, their position behind the crowd let them go unnoticed.

The man was middle-aged and indistinct of look from almost any other adult male of the camp, from the thatch of grizzled, gray hair sprouting out from under the slouching brim of his hat, to the sweat-stained white shirt pinned to his torso with a pair of suspenders, and to the faded canvas pants and lace-up work boots scuffed so badly that they looked as if an entire pack of coyotes had gnawed on them. He puffed thoughtfully on a curve-stemmed pipe, eyes squinted slightly in thoughtful repose.

The woman beside him, on the other hand, would have caused most of the camp to do a double take at the sight of her had they looked away from the fight long enough to notice she had come outside, and not only because she resided in a place in short supply of females. In truth, there were things about her so unusual that she would have drawn stares no matter where she stood, in backwater Vulture City or anywhere else.

It was hard to tell whether she was young or old, for next to nothing of her was revealed, but the way she dressed was unique, to say the least, and lent her an air of mystery that she might or might not deserve. She wore a long-sleeved, red cotton dress, despite the afternoon heat, and where the ends of those sleeves should have revealed the flesh of her hands a pair of tight, kid leather gloves covered them. Where a bit of ankle perhaps might have shown at the bottom of her dress when the furnace breeze lifted it, there were only the high tops of her riding boots with a dainty pair of silver-overlaid California spurs strapped to them. A broad, flat-brimmed felt hat of Spanish style sat atop her head, and a black lace veil was secured around the crown of it. That veil entirely covered her face and shoulders to the extent that her features were hidden to the world.

The shade cast by the commissary was slowly retreating toward the foot of its stone wall, and for a brief instant the sun caught a few scattered strands of pale blond hair beneath the edge of her veil. She moved quickly back into the shadows, as if that brief touch of the sun might melt her, and as if she were as out of place beneath the burning sky as was hair the color of snow in the desert.

The man with the smoking pipe noticed her retreat into the shade, but remained where he was, now half cast in sunlight. He gave a brief, scornful glance at the sky as if it were an old enemy that he could do nothing about.

"It's a hot one today, sure enough," he said more to himself than to her, like a man long used to spending time alone with his thoughts will do.

She did not reply, instead, continuing to watch the fight playing out down the hill from them.

Inside the roped-off boxing ring, the two fighters shuffled their feet and circled each other, their movements lifting dust from the raked sand. One of them was a red-headed man, half a foot taller than anyone in camp. He wore a pair of black tights with a green sash tied around his waist and a pair of high-topped, lace-up boxing shoes on his feet.

The man with the pipe muttered, "The damned fools put up a collection and ordered that boxing getup for him. Had it sent here all the way from San Francisco."

"Hmm," was all the woman gave in reply.

"Guess we couldn't have our local champ looking like any old country bumpkin, could we?" the man with the pipe continued.

Instead of answering him, the woman shifted her gaze to the other fighter squared off against the redhead.

He was a big man himself, although not so profession-ally attired for a bout of pugilism. He was stripped to the waist like his counterpart, but instead of tights he wore only ragged work pants, and his feet were encased in, of all things, a pair of Indian moccasins. Well over six feet at a guess, still tall, but a couple of inches shorter than the redheaded giant he faced.

She studied him closer to see what it was that had given her the initial impression that he was larger than he was. He was an abnormally big-jointed and big-boned man, true, and all angles and jutting jaw. Maybe that was it. And the muscles and tendon cords stretched over that outsized frame were visible even from a distance, as if every bit of spare fluid and finish had been sucked out of him. His waistband was bunched in wads and cinched tight over his gaunt belly with a piece of rope that served as a belt, as if the pants were two sizes too big for him or as if he hadn't eaten regularly in a long, long time.

Truly, he should have seemed almost a sad, comical figure standing in that ring in his ratty, oversized pants and Indian moccasins, and with the shaggy mop of his black hair hanging lank and sweat damp over his brow as if he hadn't had a haircut in months. And to add to that impression was the still, almost bored expression on his face, as if it didn't matter that the mining crowd was cheering for the redhead to cave his head in. Just a raggedy man too far from where he had come from and too far from his last good luck. But still, there was something about him. Maybe it was the scars.

To say that the big man's face was scarred was putting it nicely. Maybe he had been handsome once, and maybe he still was if you liked them rugged, but it was hard for her to look away from the scars. In between the broad swath of his forehead and the jut of his blunt chin, the bridge of his nose was knotted and bent, obviously having been broken more than once. And his eyebrows were so scarred that one of them was all but hairless, and similar scars marked his cheekbones and the rest of his face. All like a roadmap of pain, and story symbols of a life of battles painted on him for all to see.

While she was contemplating such things, the redhead swung a wide, awkward fist that clipped the scar-faced man on the jaw. Even with no more than she knew about boxing, she could see that the redhead had little skill for such things. But skill or not, he was powerful. And that slow, ponderous fist he threw had enough power in it to knock his opponent down, even though it had only grazed him. The scar-faced man lay in the dust while the referee called for the end of the round and made sure the redhead went back to his corner.

"I thought he was supposed to be a professional," she said to the man with the pipe. "*Professional*, you said."

"I didn't use that word," the man answered. "I said he was tough, or at least that's the rumor."

"Well, his reputation isn't doing him much good."

The man beside her nodded, but didn't seem especially bothered by what they had seen. "They say he brought Cortina's head back to Texas in a sack."

Her voice was quiet like she was short of the air required to speak in a normal tone, breathless and slightly husky, as if the afternoon heat had sucked the oxygen from her lungs. "A tramp boxer who cuts off heads in his spare time? Not exactly inspiring, and a poor recommendation for employment if I ever heard one, if that's really even him."

"Oh, it's him, all right. I'm certain of that. Same one that tamed that mob in Shakespeare a few years back, and the one that got back that Redding boy from the Apaches last fall. Read it in the newspaper and I heard it from an army officer I ran across in Tucson," the man said. "And there's another rumor going round that he spent the winter in Mexico hunting after another kid he lost down there while he was after the Redding boy."

"You know how people like to talk."

"Maybe."

"How did he end up here?"

The man took another thoughtful puff on his pipe and shrugged before he answered. "Rode in about two weeks ago wearing rags and riding a horse about as starved as he was. Said he'd been in Mexico and lost his traveling stake. Wanted a job."

"Is that why you believe that story about him going back to Mexico after the other kid? Because he said he had been in Mexico?"

"No, I didn't even know who he really was until somebody who had seen him box up in Silver City recognized him and came and told me. But that story fits with what I saw. He came from the south, and unless I miss my guess, he'd ridden a far piece on nothing but guts and bad water." The gray-haired man pulled his pipe from his mouth and used it to gesture at the scar-faced man in the ring. "Notice what kind of Injun moccasins he's wearing?"

"They're Apache, I presume."

He put the pipe back in his mouth and nodded while he drew on it. "You always were a smart girl."

"What else?"

He shrugged. "Shows up to work every day. Doesn't complain. Doesn't say much at all, for that matter. Best man with a double-jack I've got unless it's Ten Mule there. That redheaded devil can swing a sledgehammer, I promise you, but that man yonder isn't far behind him."

"That's not much to go on."

"Any man that will pester an Apache has got plenty of

guts, and he got Cortina. Cortina was good with a gun. Real good."

"Still . . ." She put a gloved pointer finger to where her mouth would have been if not for the veil, as if rethinking what she had been about to say and shushing herself.

"Who else could I hire?" he asked. "There aren't many around here that might handle the job and fewer that wouldn't laugh at us if we asked them. There was a man over at the store yesterday claiming he saw Irish Jack and two of his gang on the road between here and White Tank."

The mention of that name caused the woman to turn her head and look at him, and she took a deeper breath before she spoke again. "You said we need at least four men."

He nodded. "Six or eight would be better."

"I don't think you're going to find six or eight, and neither do you. So, let's say four guns." She gave an inclination of her veiled face toward the boxing ring and the scar-faced man only then getting up off the ground. "Say that's one. Who else have you got in mind?"

"The Dutchman will come."

"Waltz? You trust him more than I do."

"He's tough, knows the trail, and if he says he'll go, he'll go."

"Who else?"

"The Stutter brothers."

She nodded again, as if she, too, had thought of them but didn't like it. "I'd trust them farther than I would the Dutchman, but they aren't exactly the brightest stars in the sky."

"Maybe not, but they've both got good rifles and they've offered to let us use the company coach."

"I still don't like it," she said.

"You forget that this isn't your run. It's mine." The man squinted at her through his pipe smoke.

Her reply came no louder than any of those that came before, but her voice was stronger. "I've got as much riding on it as you do. Don't you forget that."

They stood in silence once more, watching the fight. By then, the scar-faced man in the moccasins had gotten himself back up and to his corner.

"Got to give that to him. Not many can take a lick from Ten Mule and get back up." The man beside her jabbed a thumb in the direction of the boxers, and the corner of the man's mouth curled in an ironic smirk around the stem of his pipe.

"Widowmaker," she said. "That's what they call him, isn't it? The Widowmaker?"

"That's what they call him."

She turned as if to go, not toward the boxing ring below them, but the opposite way. She had taken several steps before she called over her shoulder, "It will take more than a name to get that gold to the railroad."

"Are you saying we ought to try and hire him?"

"If Ten Mule doesn't kill him first," she said without looking back.

Connect with U s

Visit us online at
KensingtonBooks.com
to read more from your favorite authors, see books
by series, view reading group guides, and more.

Join us on social media

for sneak peeks, chances to win books and prize packs,
and to share your thoughts with other readers.

facebook.com/kensingtonpublishing
twitter.com/kensingtonbooks

Tell us what you think!

To share your thoughts, submit a review,
or sign up for our eNewsletters, please visit:
KensingtonBooks.com/TellUs.